In Shadows

"Before you start reading *In Shadows,* lock all the doors
and turn on all the lights. Its suspense moves like a bullet
train and whispers your darkest fears."
—Dennis Burges, author of *Graves Gate*

The Darkening

"McGrew's creative, addictive novel is one part Rapture
drama, one part Lovecraftian horror story and one part
blood-soaked chase. . . . 'Mysterious' is a good word to
describe this book, which reveals its secrets slowly and in
small increments. But McGrew keeps the pacing brisk and
eschews overly florid prose, making this a thrilling one-sit
read, right down to its explosive, delightfully hokey finale."
—*Publishers Weekly*

"There are many great horror novelists writing today,
including King, Koontz, and Barker, but Chandler McGrew
proves with *The Darkening* he is their equal. The
protagonists don't want to be world saviors but when push
comes to shove they find the courage to try."
—Harriet Klausner

"*The Darkening* is a treat for fans of horror, action,
theology and mythology, as well as those readers who just
like a good book in which they can quickly get lost . . . a
trip into realms some feared would never be explored
again." —TheBestReviews.com

"As the lights go out in this tension-packed tale you'll make sure yours stay on as you read long into the night!"
—cyber-times.com

Night Terror

"McGrew ratchets up the tension and plays on the primal fears that cause most adults to lose sleep. . . . Intersperses the action and suspense with moments of assured portrayals of character . . . It will be interesting to see what area McGrew will tackle in his next novel but based on his first two books, he is an author to watch, and read." —*Denver Post*

"Unsettling . . . an engaging read . . . Fans of Kay Hooper and Linda Howard will readily dig into this fantastic tale." —*Publishers Weekly*

"Chandler McGrew's *Night Terror* is a skillful tale, well-paced and intricately constructed—a good read." —Chelsea Quinn Yarbro

"*Night Terror* sweeps the reader along at an unrelenting pace. . . . This is a read-it-in-one-sitting book that will have you awake long past midnight, looking at the shadows outside your window." —*Romantic Times*

"Chandler McGrew has written a masterful work of psychological suspense. . . . *Night Terror* is a fascinating reading experience." —*I Love a Mystery Newsletter*

"This story is a spine-tingling blend of mystery, thriller, and a bit of the paranormal, where a surprise lurks around every corner. The characters are ordinary people dealing with their own private pain, as well as the extraordinary circumstances in which they find themselves." —*Old Book Barn Gazette*

"If you thought *Cold Heart* was a good book by Chandler McGrew, *Night Terror* will have you sleeping with the lights on! . . . Suspense at its best, there are so many plot twists and turns." —BookReviewCafé.com

"A taut thriller . . . Fast paced with plausible characters, *Night Terror* is a top-flight story and bonafide 'page-turner'!" —*Aromos* (CA) *Tri-County News*

Cold Heart
"The best opening ten pages I've read this year. . . . This suspense mystery reads like a good martini tastes: ice cold." —*Contra Costa Times*

"This first-time author has crafted a tale that compels the reader to turn page after page. This book has incredible tension and suspense." —*Mystery News*

"An engrossing reading experience." —*Midwest Book Review*

"A fast-moving tale of suspense and bloody mayhem." —*Lewiston* (ME) *Sun Journal*

"This is a very well-constructed, action-packed novel . . . a tense and satisfying read." —*I Love a Mystery Newsletter*

"What an unbelievable read! I'm telling you, McGrew could very well be the next Dean Koontz. He's that good. That's why we had to pick his book *Cold Heart* as the number 1 read!" —BookReviewCafé.com, Best Author, 2002

"Chandler McGrew has written one hell of a suspense thriller. . . . His suspenseful narrative voice is perfection, and he keeps us on the edge of our seats with a bang of an ending!" —ScreamTV.net

ALSO BY CHANDLER MCGREW

The Darkening

Night Terror

Cold Heart

IN SHADOWS

CHANDLER McGREW

A Dell Book

IN SHADOWS
A Dell Book

Published by
Bantam Dell
A Division of Random House, Inc.
New York, New York

This is a work of fiction. Names, characters, places, and incidents either
are the product of the author's imagination or are used fictitiously. Any
resemblance to actual persons, living or dead, events, or locales is entirely
coincidental.

Dell is a registered trademark of Random House, Inc., and the colophon
is a trademark of Random House, Inc.

ISBN 0-7394-5980-5

Printed in the United States of America

For Amanda
Light of my life

Many people contributed to the creation of this book, and I would especially like to thank all the deafblind and their families who were without fail responsive and helpful, asking only that they be treated fairly and with compassion. Until I began my research I was regrettably unaware of their silent, dark, but surprisingly multifaceted world. I would certainly never have expected to receive a series of very funny deafblind jokes from a gentleman who e-mailed them to me from his braille-equipped laptop. Heartfelt thanks. As always I appreciated the help of Dr. Kevin Finley for his medical expertise. Finally, of course, I have to give credit to my faithful agent, Irene Kraas, without whose efforts you might not be reading this. To my editor, Caitlin Alexander, whose patience is legend. And to my wife, Rene, soul mate and friend.

*Without a dream to light your way,
the world is a very dark place.*

—Marion Zimmer Bradley

IN
SHADOWS

Sometimes its countenance is death
I've smelled decay upon its breath.
Just as night defeats the day
In shadows fierce the demons play
While aloft for those who cannot see
The dragon hums a memory.

—*"Thunderstorm" by Cooder Reese*
From Dead Reckonings

Tuesday

IERCE MORIN LIVED IN A WORLD of touch and taste, and strange, wonderful odors that wafted through the darkness of his days and nights. Deaf and blind, and smaller than most thirteen-year-olds, most of his exercise consisted of exploring either the house or the yard, or joining his mother on her weekend errands to Arcos.

Still, he was wirier and stronger than people expected. His fingers were calloused from hours of reading braille and working with the maze of electronic parts and tools he kept neatly organized in plastic bins over the wide folding table that took up one wall of his bedroom. His mother had grown as weary as he had of trying to explain to people how he could repair radios and televisions that he could neither see nor hear.

So the boy spent his days in quiet anonymity, fiddling with transistors and transducers, with solid-state circuits that no one could fix. No one but him. Even Pastor Ernie was curious just *how* he repaired them. But the best explanation Pierce could give—spelling it out into Ernie's palm since it was too complicated for American Sign Language, and Ernie wasn't that *good* with the signs, anyway—was that he could *see* what was broken inside and how the parts were supposed to fit together.

But that morning he wasn't in his seat at the worktable. Instead he sat on a straight-backed chair beside the open window, resting his fingers on the sill, feeling the warmth of the sun on them, smelling the new-mown grass in the backyard, the rich loamy aroma of the creek down below, phasing out the leftover house odors of cereal, and coffee, and his mother's shampoo and perfume. Feeling the hairs on his arms tingling as the faintest of breezes stirred the air, he wondered what strange sense of gloom kept him so still. He felt like a rabbit huddling beneath a bush, but he had no idea what danger approached, only that it was coming and he needed to be ready.

Suddenly it seemed as though a cloud had passed the sun, chilling his cheeks, and yet the warmth of the light still lingered on his hands. Twisting his head to one side, as if searching for some errant sound with his deaf ears, he tried to understand what was happening.

Something was terribly wrong.

But not wrong in the way an open door in the night was wrong. It was more like the world he knew had somehow broken. Some part of the universe had turned dangerous and deadly. Shivering, he clutched his shoulders.

He stood slowly, sliding his fingers up to find the top of the window sash and slamming it shut, tripping the latch and wishing that the thin curtains he jerked across it were more than just for show. If sunlight could get through them to warm him in bed, then whatever was coming might be able to look right through them, too. What good were curtains like that, anyway?

Suddenly he knew that the indefinable something was right on the other side of the glass. He could sense it peering inside, studying him through the gauzy curtains as though he were some kind of specimen. He knew scientists did that to small animals, like bugs, and Pierce had always wondered if the bugs minded. Now he knew. If the bugs were anything at all like him, they experienced the unreasoning terror of *knowing* they were in the grip of something so powerful they had absolutely no defense against it.

Against his will he was drawn nearer to the window, parting the curtain again with shaking hands, bending until he was so close that he could feel the coolness of the glass radiating toward his nose even as the refracted sunlight still heated his skin. There really was *something* on the other side of the pane, inches away from his face. He knew it in the same way he knew when an electronic circuit was broken. He sensed thoughts as though he were reading someone else's mind, only it was wasn't a *mind* that made any kind of sense to him. He was filled to bursting with a maelstrom of emotions, and without thinking he lashed out with his fist, shattering the window, the vibration shooting through his arm.

He stood frozen, the jagged edge of the glass pressed against the soft underside of his wrist, as the presence on the other side of the window slowly eked away. It was as though his abrupt release of anger had driven it out of the yard, but he sensed that it had left for some other, unknown, reason.

He felt lightly around the broken pane with the fingers of his other hand, slowly and carefully drawing his fist back out of the shards. Testing with his fingers he discovered that, miraculously, he had not cut himself.

Not even a nick.

JAKE CROWLEY SQUINTED THROUGH THE RAIN rattling against his parked sedan. Storm-tossed Galveston Bay was little more than a roiling, brown illusion through the sheeting windshield, and the late-afternoon sky barely contained enough light to allow him to read the letter in his hands.

Uncle Albert was murdered, Jake, and we need to talk. I don't know if you're ever going to answer my calls, but won't you come home to at least pay your respects? I love you, Jake. I miss you.

He folded the crumpled letter, slipped it carefully back into the envelope, and returned it to the glove box.

Jake sighed. He'd driven all the way from Houston through the downpour to meet a man who refused to show his face anywhere near the city, and Jake could understand why. If Reever gave up the information Jake needed, two of the biggest crime lords in Houston might be making license plates for years to come. If, that was, they could be prosecuted successfully through the corrupt and politicized legal system that had taken hold in recent years.

Distant tympanies of thunder rattled the air, and now Jake could barely make out the rolling gray surf through the curtain of glassy droplets. His cell phone buzzed, and he snapped it open, expecting to hear Cramer, his partner, who was home sick with the flu. He'd bust Jake's chops for being stupid enough to hold a meeting like this alone.

"Yeah," said Jake.

"'Yeah'? You don't speak to me three times in fourteen years, and 'yeah' is what I get?"

"Pam?" His cousin's voice filled him with dread and pain. In his mind's eye, she still stood waving at him from the airport window, but incongruously it was his mother's voice—from an even more distant past—that echoed through his thoughts.

Run away, Jake. Run away.

"Glad you remembered," said Pam.

"Look, I don't have time right now. How did you get this number?"

"A desk sergeant gave it to me. I guess I was pretty persuasive. How come it doesn't work on you?"

Jake shook his head. "Honestly, Pam, this is a really bad time."

The wind picked up, the storm roaring in straight off the water. Marble-size raindrops threatened to burst through the windshield. Why the hell had Reever insisted on meeting here in this seawall parking lot? Jake didn't like it that the place he'd supposed would be very *public* ended up being all too secluded because of the storm. But even Reever couldn't have known the weather was going to be this bad.

"Jake, Uncle Albert was beaten to death. It was bad. Real bad."

A muscle spasmed in Jake's belly, and his fingers tightened on the phone. Albert was another old, long-buried memory.

"Jake? You there?"

"Yeah." His voice sounded shaky. Hell, it *felt* shaky.

The only thing visible now was the veneer of water cascading across the glass, and Jake found himself wondering how so much fluid could be diverted down into that little cavity concealing the windshield wipers without making its way into the engine compartment.

"Jake, you're not saying anything."

"What do you want me to say, Pam?"

"Nothing, I guess. I'm sorry I called."

"I'll call you back. I'm meeting someone, and it's kind of important."

He glanced around and noticed that the windows were just as useless as the windshield. It occurred to him that if this was more than just a rainstorm—if a tornado or water spout were heading in his direction—he would have no way of knowing it was coming, and nowhere to run.

"Sure, Jake. I'll be waiting for your call." The click of the receiver on the other end was like a slap in the face.

Jake slipped the phone into the pocket of his sports coat. He and Pam had been raised like brother and sister. Hearing her voice after so long . . . a swirling cauldron of emotions gurgled within him. The bile of shame, and fear, churned in his throat, and he knew that if he couldn't stifle it, it would remind him of Mandi. He could hear Cramer's husky voice chiding him, his partner's deep drawl heavy with Cajun weirdness.

Watch yo ass, not de bitch on de street. Man, you better keep you ducks in a row or you gonna end up on a slab.

The giant black man could just as easily slip into slick white jive with an inflection tighter than a frog's behind. He formed his persona to fit the situation. But the Cajun was real enough. Cramer's grandmother, his memere, had been raised in the deep bayous of Louisiana, and *she* didn't speak anything but patois-twisted English.

The trouble was that Reever was no street tough. He was a trigger man for the Houston mob who had become disenchanted after his brother had taken a fall for one of the higher-ups and gotten stiffed. Usually the organization was smarter than that. Either you took care of your own when they did you a favor or you got rid of them. Apparently they'd made a mistake this time, and Jake planned to capitalize on it.

But where was Reever? The beachfront parking lot had been empty when Jake arrived. He'd driven slowly around the area, circling a couple of blocks of old Victorian homes. But no one was sitting in any of the cars parked on the street. No one stared at him from the dripping front porches. Reever was probably pulled over on the highway now, waiting out a storm this strong. Jake could have gone ahead and carried on the conversation with Pam if he'd had the nerve.

A memory of Albert flashed through his mind, heavy flannel shirt across thin shoulders, the old man's gray beard flecked with sawdust. Albert was equipment- and land-poor like most small loggers, and he had already been getting too old for the business when Jake had left Maine fourteen years earlier. He was a lifelong bachelor who always smelled of pipe tobacco, axle grease, and pine pitch. And Jake loved him like a father.

The dampness was seeping into Jake's pores. Even though it was still in the seventies outside, he started the car and turned on the heater. Over the thrum of the engine and the pounding of the rain, he heard another car behind him. He flipped on his lights and stomped the brake pedal several times, and a set of headlights answered, the car itself just a ghost through the downpour.

Reever parked the sedan so close to Jake's driver's side door that Jake wondered for an instant if he was being corralled. He instinctively rested his hand on the gearshift, then slipped it to the Glock in his shoulder holster. The familiar feel of the weapon stirred up mixed emotions, and Jake let his hand slide slowly away. There was no sign of anyone else in the car, and as he watched, Reever jumped out and ran around to drop into the front seat with Jake, already soaked in the seconds it took him to get there.

"Fuckin' like the fuckin' flood out there!" said Reever, shaking his greasy black hair.

"How come you didn't park on the other side?" said Jake, eyeing him closely.

Reever shrugged, water dripping off his wide forehead. "Couldn't see! I told you it's like a fucking Noah flood out there, you jerk."

"Nice to see you, too."

"Yeah. Fuckin' right. How's the ball and chain and the kids?"

Reever's grin reminded Jake of one he'd seen on a burn victim in the morgue, skin peeling away from widely spaced yellow teeth, and he had the uncomfortable feeling that something grotesque was growing inside Reever's mouth.

"They're fine."

Reever knew perfectly well that Jake was unattached. Jake wondered if he used similar banter on people he was about to off. He didn't believe the guy would be stupid enough to try to murder a cop in such a public place. But that was the trouble with Reever. He was unpredictable.

"What have you got for me?" asked Jake, keeping his eyes on Reever's hands.

"I took a big chance coming here."

"Me, too. So cut the crap. Do we have a deal or not?"

"How you gonna protect me?"

"Come on, you know the skit. If what you have is solid enough for convictions, then I'll go to bat for you with the Houston DA, and you'll probably go into witness protection. New name, whole new identity."

Jake had no way of knowing if the DA would go for anything of the sort, and he was sure Reever was street-savvy enough to know that. They were both kidding themselves and each other, Jake because he wanted the bust so badly, Reever because he wanted the cash.

"And a lot of money," said Reever, grinning.

"I don't know what you mean by a lot. I'm not Bill Gates."

Reever's laugh sounded like the screech of a head-on collision. "Shit! You're not even my cleaning lady! If I thought *you* were going to pay me I'd still be in my hotel room in San Antone getting blown by that blond whore. If your bosses want to put the Torrios away, then they'll come up with the money."

"How much?"

Reever laughed again. "We'll talk once I go into protection."

"That'll be a little late for negotiation on your end. And maybe way too late for me to get the info I need."

Reever shook his head, and Jake noticed something in his eyes, like an errant thought tightening the laugh lines at the corners, but then it was gone.

"That'll be plenty of time," said Reever. "I got a lot to tell. You can buy it word by fuckin' word. Ain't that the way they pay magazine writers?"

"I guess."

Jake glanced out his window as a microburst of pebble-like rain struck the glass. He hated the other car blocking his view. But he turned his attention quickly back to Reever.

"Nervous?" said Reever, laughing. "Big-city pig like you? What you got to be afraid of?"

"Double-crossing a cop is not a good thing."

Reever frowned. "You threatening me?"

"Should I be?"

Reever shook his head. "You got no cause to jack with me. We're each other's insurance. I don't play straight with you, you got nothing, zip, nada. You don't play straight with me, I'm dead."

"You got that right."

But there was still something bothersome in the way Reever held his head, in the way his finger kept sliding back and forth on his thigh just a millimeter, as though squeezing a nonexistent trigger. Jake had had a lot of hunches over the years, and Cramer had drilled it into his head to listen to them.

A bad hunch don't cost you much. Maybe somebody will laugh at you. Being laughed at alive is a hell of a lot better than being laughed at dead. It's bad mojo ignoring hunches.

There it was again. Reever *almost* turned toward his window. What was he looking for? *Who* was he waiting for? Jake gave the car some gas, listening to the engine race, resting his hand casually on the gearshift lever again.

On your gun, insisted Cramer's voice. But Jake ignored it. Cramer was always giving Jake a hard time for not being quick enough on the draw.

"So talk," he said, playing the game. "Give me something to prove you're not full of shit."

"The Torrios are in with the Zinos."

Jake frowned. That was news, if it was true. The Zinos were big in Vegas and LA. What the hell would they be doing in Houston? "You mean the Zinos are here?"

"Here, there, everywhere." Reever chuckled. "Where ain't they?"

"The Torrios wouldn't share with the Zinos. They have no reason to."

Reever shrugged. "Pot's big enough, you don't mind sharing."

"There's no pot big enough for Jimmy and José Torrio to share. This sounds like a crock."

"Banks," said Reever.

"Now I know you're full of shit," said Jake, relaxing a little. Maybe that's all this was, Reever bullshitting, playing him, seeing if he knew enough to even deal with. "Neither of the Torrios is stupid enough to rob banks."

"I didn't say they were going to rob them," said Reever. "They're going to *buy* them. Then they can do what they want with the money. The Torrios have the local connections with crooked bankers. The Zinos have the laundered money in mutual funds to do the transactions clean."

Reever wasn't a Harvard economist, but Jake got the picture. The Torrios' group was muscle. The Zinos had finesse. They were used to dealing in figures where the zeros strung out right to the horizon. The Zinos probably had plenty of people on their payroll who *had* graduated from Harvard. If they and the Torrios got together and ended up owning controlling interests in Houston banks, installing their own people inside, who knew what kind of billion-dollar mischief they could concoct?

Jake heard the loud roar of a powerful engine and splashing water behind the car. A dark sedan skidded sideways, almost striking the rear bumper, blocking him in. A hazy pair of figures leaped from the car, and Jake glanced over just as Reever was reaching under his coat.

"You son of a bitch!" spat Jake, backhanding Reever hard, crushing his nose.

Reever's head snapped back and then forward, and Jake backhanded him again. He jerked the gearshift down into drive and floored the car. The sedan crashed into the low concrete retaining wall just as a shotgun blast sent shards of glass ricocheting around the interior. Jake ducked, jerking the lever into reverse, and floored the car again, ramming the sedan. He jerked his pistol out of the shoulder holster just as the man with the shotgun prepared to pump off another round.

"Not me!" screamed Reever, coming to and finding himself staring through what had been the windshield right into the barrel of the shotgun.

The guy blew Reever's head off, and Jake shot the gunman twice in the chest, causing the second shooter to drop down out of sight. But there was no way Jake could make a getaway in the car now. His sedan was wedged in the pocket between the seawall, Reever's car, and the attackers' sedan like a bad parallel parking job. But at least he'd opened a little space on the driver's side.

He whipped open his door and rolled onto the pavement in time to see a set of shoes approaching the other side of the sedan. So he scrambled toward the back bumper. As he crabbed alongside the open rear door of the attackers' sedan, he was surprised to find himself face to face with José Torrio. The door started to slam shut, but Jake jerked it open and snatched Torrio's coattail to stop him from exiting the car on the other side. He jammed his pistol into the small of José's back and shouted at the top of his lungs.

"Drop your weapon. I have your boss!"

The steady thrumming of rain on the roof of the car drowned out any answer and also kept him from seeing where his attacker was positioned.

"You're fucked, man," spat Torrio as Jake released his jacket and wrapped his free arm around the man's throat, dragging him out into the rain where they both crouched between the cars.

"If you don't drop your weapon I'm going to shoot this asshole!" shouted Jake.

"You aren't shooting anybody," said a husky voice behind him.

Huge hands grasped his shoulders, dragging both Jake and José to their feet. Jake's fingers clawed across José's throat, latching onto a thin chain that snapped in his hand as José twisted away. Jake felt a pistol barrel pressing into his side, and he knew that in a split second a bullet was going to follow. Without thinking he spun, snapping the man's pistol aside even as he shoved his own gun into the man's gut. He pulled the trigger, and the man went down.

Whirling, he found himself face to face with Torrio again, but this time José had a hideaway gun in his hand. Jake lurched to one side as the pistol fired near his face. He jerked the trigger of his own pistol again, and a neat hole appeared on José's forehead. A bullet whined across the top of the sedan, and Jake spotted another gunman leaning out of the window of a car barreling into the parking lot. He dropped to the ground and scuttled back to the front of his car, crawling along the narrow space between the bumper and the concrete embankment. As a pistol barked again he grabbed the top of the low wall and vaulted over. He hit the sand running. Almost instantly he spotted another set of headlights paralleling the beach, and he knew instinctively that it was yet another batch of Torrio goons trying to cut him off. Either José *really* thought he was dangerous, or he had intended the killing to make a showing for all his boys.

He shoved José's chain into his pants pocket and dug his cell phone out of his jacket, punching the autodial for the Houston police. When the dispatcher answered, Jake told him in three-word sentences where he was and what was happening. If nothing else they might be able to triangulate the phone and find his body. But with any luck sirens would sound any minute, and that would drive the shooters off. At the moment, he couldn't do anything but race along the surf through rain as thick as a wool curtain, trying to put distance between himself and the killers on foot.

Reever had known something was up. But then the guy with the shotgun took point-blank aim and blew his head off. So maybe Reever *was* playing both ends against the middle and got caught, or maybe the Torrios or the Zinos just wanted to kill two birds with one stone.

Jake's shoes were saturated with water and sand, and he kicked them off. The beach felt cold beneath his bare feet, even as sweat mixed with the rain. There was a flash of light ahead as a car slipped into a hidden drive and headed straight toward the shore to cut him off.

It would take a minute or two for the dispatcher in Houston to get hold of the Galveston police, then another few minutes at least for them to respond. In two minutes he could be dead. The car turned in his direction, and he could hear the engine grumbling as the tires dug into the sand. Maybe the assholes would get stuck.

But the headlights bounced and whipped from side to side as the big sedan roared ahead, and Jake turned to stumble headlong into the pounding surf. The piss-warm water slowed his advance, and chest-high breakers lifted his feet off the sand and drove him back. He glanced over his shoulder. The car was close now.

He dove.

The current was strong but not overpowering, and he swam beneath the waves for all he was worth. He broke the surface on his back, gasping—the pistol cradled on his stomach—praying the car had driven on past. But it had pulled right up to the waterline. He felt a splash beside him even as he heard the dull pounding of a shotgun. He aimed for the lighted interior of the car—he could barely make out anything else through the deluge—and pulled the trigger again and again. He didn't expect to hit anything, but at least the fucking goons would have to keep their heads down.

As he fired he continued back-kicking into the surf, and every time he disappeared over another breaker he paddled to one side or the other so that when the next wave took him he didn't pop up like the same old target in a shooting gallery. If he could make it to deeper water, he'd be safe until the cops arrived. But where were the sirens?

As he squinted through the darkness, rain, and waves, still kicking and paddling wildly, a shadow moved across the beach, as though a cloud even darker than the solid overcast above had swept between the shore and the sun. Another wave caught him, and a stinging sensation lightninged up the right side of his chest, paralyzing him for an instant. The pistol dropped away into the water, and Jake heard the delayed crack of the shot that had hit him. Horror-stricken, he felt himself rising upward, spread-eagled, flopping like a landed fish. Blood spread across his sodden jacket. Twisting to face the beach, he could only watch as gun barrels flashed repeatedly, and he held his breath, waiting for the shot that would kill him.

But through the haze of the saltwater and rain it appeared as though the guns were firing *up and down* the beach. Had the cops finally arrived? Had he missed the sirens? Surely they wouldn't have come without them.

Then, abruptly, the firing ceased. Jake counted off one minute. Two. He was hesitant to swim back toward shore, but with only one good arm he was afraid of being dragged out by the tide. Finally he heard the wail of sirens, but it seemed like hours before he spotted a cruiser's high beams barreling down the beach with lights flashing overhead.

When he reached water shallow enough to stand in, he staggered through the waves toward the cops who were approaching the sedan with drawn pistols. One of the patrol-men saw him and blinded Jake with his flashlight.

"Detective Crowley!" shouted Jake, fumbling for his shield.

The cop signaled Jake in with the flashlight. But it wasn't until he got a closer look at Jake's badge that the officer re-laxed. In the glow of the headlights the cop's red hair shone like neon. But then all of Jake's senses seemed heightened. By that time a second cruiser had pulled up alongside the sedan, and all the cops were flashing their lights up and down the beach. A flurry of footprints muddled the sand. Jake peered at the tide pools around the car and noticed that they were more blood than saltwater.

"Where are they?" he asked a burly officer with a black mustache and a beet-red complexion.

The man shrugged. "Two down in front of the car. One more down the beach. All shot to hell." He glanced at Jake's shoulder. "You hit?"

Jake gingerly pulled aside his jacket. From the hole in his shirt it looked like he should have a bullet in his right lung. But he felt okay except for the damned stinging. Feeling was working its way back into his arm and fingers at least. The cop eased Jake back against the sedan and ripped open his shirt.

"Lucky sonofabitch," said the mustachioed cop, whistling through his teeth.

The hole was low because he'd been lying on his back in the surf. But the bullet had only torn some skin as it bounced over his ribs, skittering off his collarbone, now exposed like one of the white shells on this beach.

"Come on," said the redheaded officer as the other police-man left to join the other cops near the shooters' sedan. "Hop in my car. I'll get you to the hospital."

Jake shook his head. "I want to see the men that were shooting at me."

"You need stitches."

"I'm not going to bleed to death," said Jake.

The cop finally shrugged. "Want to tell me what happened?"

When Jake had finished recapping the attack, the cop just stared at him. "You didn't kill these guys down here with any handgun," he said.

"They're all dead?" said Jake, shaken. He recalled the shots going *down* the beach. Who had they been shooting at if not him or the arriving police?

"They're dead, all right."

Jake staggered around to the front of the cruiser where the other officers held their flashlights on the corpses.

Jake had seen plenty of bodies before. Auto accidents, murder victims, suicides. Harris County wasn't LA, but Texans didn't like being outdone by Californians. They had their own host of serial killers, bar fighters, and road ragers. And of course shoot-'em-ups were as traditional as rodeos. But these guys looked like they'd been in the St. Valentine's Day Massacre. Their bodies were riddled with bullet holes and shotgun wounds.

The redheaded cop ambled close enough to question Jake with his eyes.

"What I told you was what I saw," Jake croaked, swallowing a giant lump in his throat.

"How long ago did the shooting stop?"

"Maybe four, five minutes."

"Nobody else with you or on the beach but Torrio's men?"

"No one I saw," said Jake.

Lights and sirens were coming from both ends of the beach now. Jake started to say that the cars were going to destroy any footprints or tire tracks, but the rain was already accomplishing that.

"Okay, then," said the cop, coaxing Jake toward his car. "There's no sense *us* standing here getting pummeled."

Jake slid into the passenger side of the cruiser, and the officer dropped into the driver's seat, flipping on the heat.

"There's bandages in the console. You want me to put something on that wound?"

Jake shook his head, ripping open one of the packs of cotton gauze. He smeared the cloth with an antiseptic and pressed it against the gash, grimacing not so much in pain but at the awful sensation of some alien substance oozing *into* his flesh.

The radio crackled. "Looks like we got another one washing up."

Jake nodded into the wall of rain. "Let's go."

The car dug into the sand, then slid and slithered along the beach to a second dark sedan bogged down near the surf. The cop was out first, trotting toward the headlights of the other cruisers. Jake followed slowly, ignoring the pain that was beginning to radiate from his ribs.

One body lay on the sand, and two uniformed officers were up to their waists in the breakers dragging another corpse toward the beach.

Jake felt a sinking sensation in the pit of his stomach.

"You okay?" said the redheaded cop. "You're looking pretty pale."

"I'm all right," insisted Jake.

But he wasn't and he knew it. For fourteen years he had miraculously managed to avoid violence in a job where gunfire was an accepted hazard. Now, in a matter of a few moments, he had slaughtered three men in the parking lot, and Reever and at least four others were dead as well.

He nudged his way past the cops to stare at what was left of the corpse on the beach. It looked as though the man had tried to eat one of the shotguns. Jake turned quickly away, striding out into the surf toward the oncoming cops and their grisly baggage.

One of them managed a macabre grin, lifting the last body out of the water by its arm. Again, there were bullet holes everywhere. "This all of 'em?"

Jake frowned, shrugging. "I don't know how many were in the cars."

The cop nodded, pointing down the beach. "There's another puddle of blood there, bigger than the one by the car. Who the hell killed these guys?"

"I don't know," said Jake.

He shivered from the rain and wind and shock. Slipping his hands into his pants pockets, his fingers wrapped around the chain he'd ripped from José Torrio's throat, and he lifted it to his face. A beveled stone the color of fresh blood was attached to the chain with a gold jeweler's mount. Jake stared at it, wondering what impulse had caused him to safeguard the bauble through the murderous events of the past few minutes.

"You must have a real guardian angel," said the cop, grinning sarcastically. He jerked on the corpse's arm again, and it came away from the torso. The cop whistled under his breath as his partner caught hold of the corpse's lapel and continued dragging the body toward the beach. "You ever seen anybody get fucked up this bad?"

"What's that?" whispered Jake.

"I asked if you'd ever seen anybody this fucked up."

"Not in a long time."

He shoved the necklace into the pocket of his jacket and turned away, heading back toward the beach.

Run away, Jake. Run away.

THE STORM BLEW OVER BEFORE DARK, leaving the smell of ozone in the air and brilliant stars dangling from a sheet of black crepe. It had taken the rest of the day and half the night before both the Galveston and Houston Police were done questioning Jake. Both departments wondered just what the hell he thought he was doing meeting with Reever alone, and how eight men ended up dead, four shot so many times they looked like sieves. Jake had no reasonable answer—which bothered him as much as it did anyone else. But what bothered him worse was the explosion of violence itself. He couldn't get the thought out of his head that he was somehow responsible for it.

If he had planned the meeting better, at a more public location, then José wouldn't have dared try the hit. If he had informed Cramer beforehand, his partner would never have okayed the meeting. If . . .

By three in the morning he was well into his third double Scotch when he heard the lock clicking on the front door. A bottle of pain pills rested unopened on the glass-topped table beside him, and the liquor hadn't yet dulled his senses, not nearly as much as he wanted it to. He could see the brightly lit interior of his apartment reflected in the liquor bottle so he didn't turn, just glanced at the Glock, resting in a box beside the liquor.

"Hello, Cramer," he said, as his partner sauntered out onto the balcony.

Jake could have bounced a baseball off Cramer's frown as the man dropped into the other lawn chair like a giant cannonball. His face looked as though it had been carved out of black granite, then shot head-on with a bowlful of dry Grape-Nuts, and he was so dark people said the whites of his eyes blinded them. A tough, streetwise cop, he bore not one but three bullet scars from separate encounters with what he called "percolators." Jake expected to hear some homespun Cajun platitudes, but tonight Cramer was in plain-speak mode.

"Nice," said Cramer, staring at the bottle and the painkillers. "I could have been one of the Torrios for all you knew, and you'd be too messed up to do anything but smile while I blew your stupid head off."

Jake shook his head. "I'm sticking to Scotch. And to my knowledge none of the Torrios' men has a key."

"New piece?" said Cramer, nudging the pistol with a finger the size of a hand-rolled cigar.

"Backup gun."

"Goddamn it, Jake! That meeting was about the stupidest fucking stunt you've pulled since I've known you."

Jake shrugged. "You still look a little peaked."

"I'll give you *peaked,* you sonofabitch. If you don't want to be partners just say so."

"I never said I didn't want to be partners. You're the only friend I've got," admitted Jake, discovering that it was hard to mouth the words.

Cramer hesitated. "Then act like it. What the hell were you doing down there alone?"

Jake shook his head. "You were sick. I didn't start feeling hinky about the meeting until after Reever was in the car."

"After it was too fucking late, you mean."

"Yeah. Well, I didn't think Reever'd feel quite so chatty around you."

Cramer huffed. "Because he charged me with police brutality?"

"Twice."

Cramer shrugged. "I'm okay, by the way. Thanks for asking. I been puking my guts out all day long, I have to *run* to shit, and my head feels like I got the fucking Budweiser Clydesdales line dancing in there."

"Memere can't fix you up?" asked Jake, grinning.

"Don't go ragging on Memere. People laugh at her cures, but they still pay out the nose for her *paket kongos* and *pot'et*."

Jake had only seen one *pot'et*—a strange white china pot filled with hair and nail clippings and a banana leaf wrapping leaking the burned and powdered remains of something Jake hadn't wanted to know about. It rested in a place of honor in Memere's living room. But Cramer had forced a *paket kongo* on him the first month they'd met.

"It don't mean nothing," Cramer had assured him, as Jake gingerly took the onion-shaped contraption—constructed of bright red cloth and what he guessed were chicken feathers—and placed it on a bookshelf, where Cramer had insisted it remain. "If it don't work, fine. If it does, fine. What do you lose?"

Jake glanced in the bottle's reflection. The *paket* was still on the shelf.

"You should have stayed in bed," he said, staring into Cramer's bleary eyes.

"And miss sitting up drinking with you in the middle of the night?" said Cramer, wiping the mouth of the bottle with his sleeve and taking a long drag. "Why don't you answer your fucking phone?"

"Didn't feel like talking," said Jake, recalling the message he'd found on his answering machine from Pam. She must have called his apartment before reaching his cell phone. "Jake, I wish you'd come home. Please call." She'd recited her number and hung up.

"I talked to Doc Miller," said Cramer.

Jake's eyebrows rose. Miller was the best pathologist in Houston. But Galveston had their own medical examiner. "Why Miller?"

"They called him down to look at the bodies."

"He can't have found out much so fast."

"Enough."

"What?"

"He said he couldn't be sure just yet, but it *looked* like at least some of the wounds were self-inflicted. And the boys on the beach found most of the hardware those guys were carrying. They emptied their weapons. Probably at each other."

Jake frowned, waiting.

"He also said they weren't just shot. There were multiple contusions, abrasions, broken bones. They were run through a blender. You want to tell me your side of the story?"

Jake told him. When Cramer blinked twice he knew his friend didn't believe everything he was hearing.

"That's the way it happened," insisted Jake.

Cramer's eyes narrowed, but he just nodded, and they sat in silence for a while. When Cramer finally spoke again his normally raspy voice was soft as a whisper.

"Sometimes questions are better left unanswered."

Jake chuckled mirthlessly. "You are such a closet philosopher."

"That's not to say that this is one of them. The department will eventually want to just forget the whole thing if you stick to your guns and they can't close the case—not like they give a rat's ass about a bunch of dead Torrio boys. But our friends in the media are going to be on you like stink on shit."

Jake frowned, nodding. "I have nothing to tell them."

"They won't believe that."

"Do you?"

Cramer leaned way back—making the chair groan ominously—and took another long swig from the bottle before resting it on the table again. He stared up at the black bowl of sky and frowned. "I have to believe what you tell me, I guess."

"Thank you."

"You wouldn't lie to me."

Jake tried to meet his eye but couldn't.

"Don't end up like me, Jake."

"What the hell does that mean?"

"I've been watching you for years. You're a good cop. Hell, you may be a great cop."

"Bullshit."

Cramer never gave out compliments. The statement sounded more like a deathbed confession, and it gave Jake the creeps.

"It's not bullshit, and don't interrupt me. You care about people. Maybe too much. And you get hunches that are downright spooky, even for me. But I've watched you in a lot of tight situations. You think too long before you get rough or go for your gun, like you want to make doubly or triply sure before reacting. I've never once seen you bust a cap, and you know damned well there have been situations that called for it."

"I didn't hesitate out there today," said Jake miserably. "And I'd never let you down."

"No. At least I'm still in one piece, and I never got shot because of you. But you scare me sometimes, Jake. I worry that I'm gonna get killed because you're not up to pulling the trigger when you really need to."

"Do *you* want another partner?"

Cramer sighed. "Did I say that? I'm forty-two, and I look fifty. Sometimes I feel sixty, and I probably won't live to see it with you or without you, because I'll keep doing this until I'm too damned old, too goddamned slow. But I won't die because I was worried about hurting someone."

"What about your *paket kongo*?" said Jake, smirking.

"The spirits don't help the stupid," said Cramer. "And doing what we do past our time is stupid. Happens to cops all the time. We lose our edge and then *Gede* comes to pass us on. He don't care much whether we think it's time or not."

"Max Hartley's sixty-one, and he's one of the best detectives on the force."

Cramer nodded. "Max has enough seniority to take only the cases he knows he can clear, the ones that won't cost him any grief or blood. I can't do that. Now shut the fuck up."

Suddenly Cramer wasn't talking like an old, eccentric uncle anymore. His voice was harsh again, and Jake heard real pain in it.

"I've never wanted to be anything but a big-city detective," said Cramer, leaning even farther back in his chair and kicking his feet up on the balcony's rail. "It's the only thing in the world I'm good at. I tried having a wife. It didn't work out." He glanced at Jake. "I never mentioned her because there was nothing to tell. I had the job, and it meant more than the marriage. I think a good writer would say that I was a two-dimensional character. You're not. You just want to be."

"What exactly are you rattling on about?"

"You're carrying a lot of baggage, and you need to fix it or forget it. In this business you make way too many enemies to be thinking about your past all the time or twitching when you should be shooting."

"I never had any enemies that made me really nervous until the Torrios," said Jake, stretching the truth to the breaking point.

"At the very least you're going to get yourself killed. And I don't want to watch it happen. I'm your friend, Jake. I don't want to see you die."

"Have I ever unloaded on you?"

Cramer shook his head. "That's just it, you don't *have* a past. So that tells me you have a *lot* of past. Eight people are dead on that beach, and apparently—instead of shooting you—half of them just decided to kill each other. The way I see it, you got a golden opportunity here. That *graze* you got on your shoulder and the investigation into the shooting will buy you a few days off if you want to take them instead of sitting behind a desk. You can spend the time putting whatever's behind you behind you and turning yourself into a cardboard character like me, in which case you'll make one hell of detective. Or you can find out what the hell is wrong with you and maybe figure out you don't *want* to be a cop after all."

"That's the stupidest shit I've ever heard. I worked my ass off to get where I am."

Cramer nodded. "I know you did. But were you working toward something or away from something?"

Jake felt as though Cramer had opened up a drawer filled with his most private thoughts. The only thing he hadn't discovered was the box in the back, under the socks, the one labeled

DO NOT OPEN. INSANITY INSIDE.

"Can we cut to the chase here? I'd like to go to bed now."

"I read all the reports, and I spoke to every officer on the scene today. Every cop that was on that call thinks you know more than you're saying."

"I was in the fucking water! I couldn't see a thing. Just what is it I'm supposed to know?"

Cramer shrugged. "I've got to be honest with you. You're stretching your credibility with me, too. I'll buy that *you* didn't kill all those people. Hell, I don't think anyone, including the medical examiner, would have any idea how you *could* have. But someone did, and you need to tell me who, and how . . . and why."

"It happened like I said."

"You have to admit that's kind of hard to fathom. You claim you were in the water maybe five minutes max, and at least some of those guys were shooting at you most of that time."

"I told the cops that they started shooting up and down the beach."

"At each other."

"I didn't know that."

"Why would they do that?"

"Cramer, I know it sounds unbelievable. Maybe there was a mutiny in Torrio's organization. Maybe some of them were Zino's boys. But the story I told you, the story I told the Galveston boys, is gospel."

Cramer sighed loudly. "But you definitely killed José Torrio?"

"Yeah."

"Well, Jimmy isn't going to be pleased. The brothers are very tight. Or they were."

"I'm aware of that."

"It might be a good idea to take that vacation just to let things cool off."

For a while silence reigned. Jake poured himself another dollop of liquor, but it tasted raw and unsavory. When

Cramer finally spoke again his voice sounded hollow, airy and distant, and the pain in it was undeniably heartfelt.

"You going back to take care of business at home or not?"

"What's that supposed to mean?" said Jake.

Starlight reflected off the whites of Cramer's eyes.

"You ought to answer your messages. Then people wouldn't bother your sick partner. I think Sergeant McCallister would give out the pope's number if a woman with a sweet-sounding voice asked for it."

"Pam called you? What did she say?"

Cramer shrugged. "She takes after you. She didn't volunteer a lot. But it's amazing what you can wheedle out of someone in the space of a conversation if you listen good. How come you never told me your father killed your mother?"

Jake sighed. "That came up in a conversation about my uncle's death?"

"When I said baggage I didn't mean *baggage*. That's why you left Maine?"

Jake nodded. That was as good an excuse as any.

"I'm really tired," he said at last.

"Don't you want to call your cousin?"

Jake tried to stare Cramer down. When that didn't work he looked at his watch. "It's five in the morning there."

"Call her later," said Cramer.

"All right. Now go home. You look like shit."

"Thanks," said Cramer, rising. "You don't look half bad yourself."

"Lock the goddamn door, and leave your key with me."

Cramer chuckled, sliding the glass door to the balcony shut behind him.

CRAMER PARKED HIS FORD SEDAN beside a rusted Volvo station wagon. Two of the streetlights were out, and the parking lot of Memere's apartment building was filled with sinister shadows. But several windows were ablaze with light, and he knew from experience that those belonged to the meth-heads. This part of town had been okay when Memere had first moved in twenty years earlier. Now it was shady and dangerous, and Cramer hated that there was so little that he could do about it. Busting people like the Torrios might cut down on wholesale drugs in the city, but it wouldn't touch the real pool of vice that never ran dry. Sometimes he felt like Hercules shoveling out the Augean stables. He slammed the car door loud enough to rustle a couple of curtains, knowing that the assholes were well aware he was a cop.

He checked the Glock under his arm, but he wasn't expecting trouble. Most of the neighbors were as afraid of Memere as they were of him. He smiled, imagining strung-out dopers with God only knew what kind of armaments, terrified of an eighty-year-old woman who didn't weigh ninety pounds soaking wet.

His footsteps echoed on the metal landing as he strolled to Memere's door, peering across the flickering lights of the kidney-shaped pool at a couple of wired-up kids smoking pot. They turned in his direction, then went back to toking. He flipped through his key ring, found the master, and opened the dead bolt and then the door lock without knocking. The smell of peppermint incense blasted his nostrils, and he had to sniffle to keep from gagging. Memere was always trying something new.

A cedar post—the *poto mitan,* the cosmic axis of Memere's temple that connected heaven and earth—reached all the way to the ceiling from the center of the living room rug. Several tall candles burned in saucers on the floor, and there was an intricate design laid out in cornmeal on a broad piece of canvas. A *veve,* this one the symbol for Cramer's guardian, the machete-wielding Ogou. From the back bedroom he could hear a rattle, and he stepped carefully around the candles.

Memere wore a traditional, stark, white cotton shift, her gray hair pulled back tight against her skull. She leaned over one of the tiny alcoves filled with candles, tiny cups of rum and sweets, and small idols of each of the most important Voudou spirits. In her hand she held the *ason,* the sacred rattle. She was speaking to each of the spirits in low whispers, shaking the *ason,* and nodding to herself. But Cramer knew she was aware of his presence.

Finally she straightened and walked over to him, hugging him tightly. Her head rested just above his belly button, but her withered arms were surprisingly strong. When she leaned back to look into his eyes he knew she was seeing straight into his soul. Drawing him out of the room and into the kitchen where a pot of tea was brewing, she poured both of them a cup and laced each with a healthy dollop of rum.

"You come by so early to see me wake the spirits up?" she asked, sipping across toothless gums, her dark face glowing with warmth.

Cramer shrugged. "I saw the light."

"You know I leave candles burning all the time. You come because of dat boy."

Cramer knew *dat boy* was Jake.

"Why do you say that?"

"I tink Jake in a world of hurt. I tink you know dat."

"He's got a lot of baggage. I know *dat.*"

"I don't know baggage. I know trouble. Ogou say you stick wid dat boy, you got trouble, too. You gonna do dat?"

Cramer sighed. "I don't know. I don't think he wants me to stick with him. He's been closed up tighter than a drum since the day I met him. But now something's happened."

"Men get kilt on de beach."

He frowned. "How did you know that?"

She laughed. "It on de news! You tink Ogou come tell me dat? Why for I need spirits to tell me what's on CNN?"

"Something funny happened out there, but he won't talk about it. Jake almost got killed. And I got a call from his cousin in Maine. His uncle was murdered."

She nodded thoughtfully. "I tell you, dat boy got big trouble you maybe don't want no part of. Maybe you do. You got to decide."

"How do I decide?"

"Is he worth it?"

"Worth what?"

"Dyin' for."

Cramer felt a chill rise between his shoulder blades. "You think maybe that's what's gonna happen?"

"I tink dat boy got a ton a misfortune comin' for him.

Maybe he be okay. Maybe not. He kill José Torrio, right? People around dat boy gonna be swimmin' in shit, I tell you dat."

"That's what you're worried about, the Torrios?"

Memere made a face that said maybe so, maybe no. "The Torrios are bad juju. They mix up the spirit nations, like stirring a pot of soup wid a dirty toilet brush." She shook her head, and a strand of gray hair seemed to slice one dark eye. "But dat boy got de baggage, all right. The Torrios are just icing on a cake made outta cow patty. You got to decide."

"But you haven't told me *how* to decide."

She smiled, slapping him on the shoulder. "You gonna know when you know. Some t'ings worth dying for. Some t'ings ain't."

"I'd die for you," he said softly.

She leaned to hug him again. "I know dat."

"I gotta go," said Cramer, chugging the tea, even the heat of the liquor failing to thaw the ice that had settled in his bones.

"Ogou watch over you. I see to dat. But you got to watch out for you self. You got a problem always wid you."

"I'm just too darned easy," said Cramer, smiling.

"You just too darned easy for de spirits. You a soft touch for dem. Always has been. You got to harden up and not let dem in so quick. It not funny, boy. One day something gonna get in and der gonna be hell to pay gettin' it out."

"You used to tell me that I was going to be a great *Houngon* one day."

"And maybe so you could be. But to be a priest you got to know how to keep the spirits in they place. You stay mixed up with Jake, no telling what trouble you two get into. You be careful."

"You just make sure you lock this door behind me."

This time Memere smirked. "Anybody break in here, dey be sorry, I promise you dat."

Thursday

JAKE SAT STARING ACROSS THE TARMAC at the sunrise, waiting for the rest of the passengers to board the jet. But the commotion all around was as inconsequential to him as the bubbling of an air compressor on an aquarium. He had spent most of the previous day arguing with himself over whether or not to return Pam's calls. Then she'd called again, and now her voice kept hammering in his head.

"Please come, Jake. Pay your last respects. You owe him that."

He could hear her husband in the background, counseling her to take it easy. Pam had married Ernie Peyton, a Protestant minister, after Jake left. He assumed the man Pam wed had to be something special. Probably a man he'd like a lot.

"I'm sorry, Jake," said Pam. "I know you never wanted to hear from me again or to see this valley. But Albert loved you like a son."

Jake felt a stabbing sensation around his heart. "I never said I didn't want to see you again, Pam. I had to get away from Crowley. That's all. I'm sorry."

"From Mandi, too?"

The stab became an ax. He started to say *yes, Mandi most of all.* But his voice wouldn't wrap around the sentence, his lungs wouldn't exhale her name.

"Please come home, Jake. Even if it's just for a visit."

He heard the hurt in her voice, the sense of betrayal, just as he'd heard it fourteen years earlier when he'd climbed on another plane, running from who he was. Only he couldn't take it now, not again.

"All right, Pam," he said quietly. "I'll come."

Cramer's voice knocked the wind out of his thoughts. "You're taking up two seats, asshole." He waved his ticket in Jake's face, pointing at the aisle seat. "That's mine."

"What are you doing here?" asked Jake, shifting, dull pain radiating from beneath the bandage on his shoulder.

"Taking a vacation. I always wanted to see Maine."

"No, you didn't. You hate the country. You hate any place that doesn't have a shopping mall. How did you know what flight I'd be on?"

Cramer flipped his shield in Jake's face. "I keep trying to tell you, I'm a detective."

"You don't need to do this. I'm just taking a little time off."

Cramer shrugged. "Believe it or not, the chief actually likes you. When I told him you were taking a trip he agreed that it might be a good idea for me to cash in some of my vacation time and go with you. It seems like Jimmy Torrio has suddenly disappeared."

"You spoke to the chief?"

To Jake that was a little like speaking to God.

"You were on the news, dumbass."

Being on the news and getting noticed by the chief were not good things.

"What do you mean Jimmy Torrio *disappeared*?"

"Nowhere to be found. That's kind of curious seeing as how his brother just died. He and José were close. So tell me about your lovely hometown."

Jake sighed, fastening his seatbelt. "Crowley isn't really a town. It's a valley. There's nothing there but a few scattered homes tucked away in the woods. The kind of place where no one locks their doors at night. You're gonna love it."

"The valley was named after your great-great-grand-father?"

"Jacob Crowley," said Jake, giving Cramer the eye.

But Cramer merely tapped the pocket holding his badge again. "And *you're* the king!"

"More like the prodigal son."

"Are they going to barbecue a fatted calf for your return?"

"I doubt if anyone except Pam even remembers me. Did you contact anyone else in Maine besides her?"

Cramer squinted, glancing past Jake out the window. "Some local yokel in Arcos named Milche."

"He isn't a yokel," said Jake. "Virgil Milche is the county sheriff, and he's a damned good police officer. It was because of him I decided to become a cop myself."

"Really? Well, he was curious why you didn't show for the funeral and why you were coming now."

"*When* did you talk to him?"

"Right after Pam called."

"Why didn't you tell me?"

"Like you were talking. How come you couldn't make it to the funeral, but you're going back now?"

"Pam called again."

"And?"

"I guess she's taking it pretty hard."

"She and your uncle were close?"

"Not as close as he and I were. Look, I'm going to Crowley to pay my last respects and to settle Pam's nerves. She's high-strung."

"And maybe to investigate your uncle's murder?"

Jake sighed.

"What makes you think you can find out anything this great cop friend of yours hasn't?" asked Cramer.

Jake closed his eyes and leaned his head back against the seat. "Have a nice flight."

The engines revved up, and he turned toward the window. The tarmac became a gray river as the plane rumbled inexorably down it into the thunderous roar of some great cataract just ahead.

ITH THE ARRIVAL OF THE SUN, Memere rose slowly to her feet, blanking out the pain that scorched her knees, elbows, and hips. Rheumatoid arthritis, the doctor called it. She laughed to herself, thinking of the bottle of pills he'd given her, still sitting unopened in her medicine cabinet. Passing quickly into the second bedroom she'd converted to a shrine for the spirits, she nodded to each of the alcoves filled with objects the *Iwas*—the spirits—attached themselves to. In front of each was a fresh offering. *Iwas* could be very naughty, even dangerous, if not treated with the proper amount of respect.

The smell of honey hung in the air, and Memere twisted her nose. This variety of incense stick was too *woosy* for her taste, not nearly as satisfying as the peppermint. She'd remember not to be using it again. She made one last bow to the altars and headed into the kitchen, where she prepared a fresh *paket kongo* for her ails. That and a good long spirit bath would fix her up better than any doctor medicine. Or fix her up as well as an eighty-year-old Voudou priestess—a *Houngon*—could expect. She shook the new *paket kongo* to make sure Loko Atizou and Ayizan, the patron saints of *Houngon*—and the spirits this *paket* had been created to appease—were really awake. Sometimes the *Iwas* were just like Cramer as a kid, only pretending to wake up.

Sixty years before, at Memere's initiation as a *Houngon* in the swamps outside of Baton Rouge, she had been presented with the traditional seven *paket kongos*. But of course all *pakets* only held their power for seven years. Even so, those originals held a place of honor atop the dresser in her bedroom. Now she touched each knee ritually with the silk onion of the fresh *paket,* then each elbow, finally each hip, sighing as she called out to Loko Atizou and Ayizan and felt relief flowing slowly through her old bones. The bath would make her even better. She rested the *paket* back on the kitchen counter, glancing back toward the altar room to make sure she hadn't forgotten any of the many rituals required daily. The *Iwas* should be pleased with her for now.

She ambled off to the bathroom, turned the tub faucet on very hot, and tossed in a handful of jasmine flowers, then a drop of orgeat syrup and some crushed almonds, drops of water from a spring in Florida, more drops of Holy Water from a mostly friendly but sometimes snotty priest up the block, and, finally, a dollop of flat champagne. Memere packaged the same contents in Ziploc bags for sale to her clients—many of whom were big shots around town and came to her because they knew she would respect their privacy—but for her own consumption she preferred to use only the freshest ingredients.

Like the rest of the house, the bathroom walls were covered with framed religious icons and hand-painted images of Voudou spirits. An ornate idol that looked like a minia-

ture termite mound capped with a Barbie doll head sat beside the bottle of mouthwash. She nodded to it in passing,
mumbling a prayer to Danbala, one of the spirits of the
Rada. The spirits were divided into two nations—*Rada*,
cool, and *Petwa*, hot and impetuous—not good or evil, a
concept that meant nothing to the spirits. Danbala was the
snake spirit, who could be equally hot or cold depending
upon the situation, but like all snakes he was best catered
to and watched carefully, and he could be a very good ally
in time of need.

She let her white cotton shift fall to the floor, shaking her
head and chuckling to herself as she stared at her wrinkled
black frame. Every year she looked more and more like one
of the prunes she was forced to consume to keep from getting all bound up like a rock.

You are what you eat.

She chuckled even louder.

Finally she slipped gratefully into the tub, straining to
turn off the water before leaning back and immersing herself in the scalding liquid. The heat and the special ingredients of the spirit bath finished the work of the *paket kongo*.
She could feel her muscles relaxing, ancient joints loosen-
ing as she dragged in long, deep breaths of the healing,
jasmine-scented steam. The bath was as good for the soul as
it was for the body. She felt herself drifting into that soft
place where her worries eased, and she could think more
clearly.

Cramer had been a handful since his mother—her daugh-
ter Angelina—had left him in Memere's care. But that girl
had been a lot more than a handful. She was a slut woman
from the time she bled, and Memere had been unable to control her no matter what offering she made to the spirits. A
woman alone shouldn't have to raise a kid, but she had been
forced to do it twice in her life. At least Cramer had turned

out better than his mother. Still, he'd wanted to go off running after wild chances from the time he was old enough to walk. It had taken a lot of years to settle him down and convince him to take life one day at a time and to pay attention when the spirits spoke to him. Now he was heading way up north on a fool's errand, and she didn't like it. She didn't like it one bit. Jake Crowley was going to get him into a lot of trouble. A lot.

She'd met Jake several times, and deep down she liked him. Cramer liked him, too, probably a lot more than he should, because Jake Crowley had some serious spirit problems. Both the nations, the *Rada* and the hotter, more impetuous *Petwa,* stirred up like hornets whenever Jake came around. That didn't make Jake a bad man. It just meant the spirits were tuned to him, but for some reason *he* wasn't tuned to them. She'd just as soon Cramer had nothing to do with that boy. But that was not to be, and so she tried to protect both of them. She prayed to the pantheon for them every night, and she had insisted that Cramer force Jake to take her most powerful *paket kongo* to keep the *Iwas* as pacified as they could be in his presence. But she knew that wasn't going to be enough in the end. Jake had a peculiar destiny waiting out there somewhere, and she was afraid that Cramer had already been dragged into it.

A noise from the other room startled her, and she stiffened, listening to the faint lapping of the water across her flat, pendulous breasts. It was true that most of her drug-boy neighbors gave her plenty of space, respectful of an old *Houngon* who some of them probably suspected wasn't beyond using the powers of a *Bokor,* a dark priest. But she also knew that some of those same drug-boys were so hopped up that they might not be afraid of anything.

But whatever the sound had been, it did not repeat itself,

and she sank back against the tub. Sometimes she'd fall asleep like this, dream of her days as a Voudou queen back on the bayous, before Angelina was born, when she spent her nights dancing to the sound of the drums, surrounded by the heady smell of swamp water and the taste of rum, and red beans and rice. When she spent her days in the arms of Jean Coupe, the man who ran away and left her with a full belly and an empty cookie jar when he found out he was going to be a father.

It wasn't the thought of Jean that opened her eyes, though. It was another sound from the living room, stealthy, like a click beetle snapping its shell.

She climbed slowly out of the water, testing her joints, glad the bath and *paket* had done their work. She felt little fear at the thought of an intruder. The spirits would be more agitated than she was, and woe to the *sac-de-papier* who disturbed one of their altars.

But she dried herself hurriedly and wrapped a frayed terry-cloth robe about her before opening the door. The smell of a Houston morning struck her, even stronger than the honey smoke of her incense. The aroma was a mixture of gasoline and carbon dioxide, oak, pine, magnolia, and something Memere could only describe as the odor of dirty money. She knew instantly that her front door was open. As she strode into the living room it slammed closed behind a man as big as her grandson but pale as the shroud on a corpse. A Mexican of much smaller build was in the altar room, bending over the statue of Ogou. A third man surprised her by speaking from directly behind her, and she whirled to face him.

"My name is Jimmy Torrio," he said, with a gleaming smile that reminded her of a toothpaste commercial. He had short, curly black hair, a razor-sharp nose, and bony cheekbones, and she found the combination—along with his dark, cunning eyes—disturbing. But she supposed some women would like his slick manner. He had the aura of the very rich, and he smelled of the same dirty money as the morning air. "I really don't want to cause you any trouble, Memere. I just need some information."

"You get out of my house!" she spat, blood racing to her face.

"That's not going to happen, old woman. I need to find your grandson, and unfortunately my contacts in the police department aren't cooperating this week. Now, where is he?"

"I tell you nothing. You come in here like you own this place, you and your drug-boys. You get youselves in deep trouble, Mister High-and-Mighty Jimmy Torrio, I tell you that right now."

Torrio laughed, and the sound hardened the faces of his men. Memere glanced at each of them in turn and saw nothing but deep-rooted evil.

"I have nothing against you, old woman," said Torrio, shaking his head. "But you are going to tell me what I want to know. Talk now, and we'll walk out of here without hurting you."

"I tell you one more time for your own good. Leave now while you okay."

Torrio's eyes narrowed, and she could sense the spirits stirring around her. Then he backhanded her so hard she blacked out. She came to in the arms of the pale white giant, and Torrio hit her again. This time she remained conscious, but the pain was fierce. She spat blood onto the carpet, and she knew that would disturb the *Iwas*. The smell and taste of blood always aroused them. The blood of a *Houngon* would excite them doubly.

"Where is your grandson?"

"Why you want him?"

"That's not information you need. Now tell me, or Paco over there will start tearing this little nuthouse apart."

Torrio waved at the Mexican in the altar room. The man lashed out with a sweeping hand. Glass crashed and pottery shattered as Agwe's altar was desecrated. Memere started to scream, but Torrio slapped her again.

"Tell me!" he shouted.

Paco kicked at another altar like a man stamping out a fire. Memere could feel the ire of the nations rising. There was no telling what they'd do. Sometimes they could be fierce for almost no reason. Other times they reacted not at all to the worst insults. But she hoped this time their vengeance would be stern.

She closed her eyes and called on Ogou, Cramer's protective spirit and her own. Of all the spirits, Ogou was the most unpredictable, but he could also be one of the most dangerous. After offering him her grateful service in the future, and stroking his male ego by envisioning him in all his warrior glory, she asked for added protection for Cramer and herself.

"I don't want to kill you," said Torrio. "I never killed anyone's grandmother before. But you're going to tell me what I need to know."

She cringed. "He gone out of town."

"I know that. Where out of town?"

"What for you want my boy?"

Torrio's laugh was something Memere thought no one should have to endure for long. It sounded to her as if gas were escaping the lips of a day-old corpse. "I don't want your boy, old woman. I want his friend. But your boy will lead me to him."

Memere nodded. Jake's *baggage* was falling on them after all. This Jimmy Torrio was no spirit. But he worked his own evil in the spirits' employ, whether he knew it or not.

"So? Are you gonna tell me what I need to know?"

She shook her head, and he backhanded her again, not quite so hard this time.

"If I tell you, it not good for you," she mumbled through swollen lips.

Torrio smirked at the *poto mitan*. "I'm very, very afraid. Now where did they go?"

She shrugged. "You go there, maybe you die."

"Tell me!"

She wiped blood away with her sleeve. "Place called Crowley. Like Jake. In Maine."

"Where in Crowley?"

"That all I know."

Torrio studied her with hard eyes, and she met them with her own. Finally he nodded and waved at his two gunmen. Paco scurried out of the altar room, like maybe he was being followed, and Memere smiled despite her aching jaw. The big, white, fish-looking man opened the door and stepped out onto the landing, but Torrio stopped on the threshold, turning to the Mexican. "You stay and watch her until we get back."

"Me?" said Paco, looking around as though the icons on the walls might come crawling out of their frames at any minute.

"What's the matter, Paco?" asked Torrio. "You scared of *spirits*?"

Paco shook his head. "This place just gives me the creeps, boss. Why not make Jules stay?"

Torrio laughed again, but his eyes narrowed as he glanced from man to man. Finally the big white monster shrugged, and Paco breathed a sigh of relief.

"All right," said Torrio, shaking his head. "Come on. You might come in handy at that."

As Paco hurried out to join Jimmy, Jules stepped back

into the apartment and closed the door without another word. He and Memere studied each other like a pair of boxers sizing up their opponents.

"You like snakes?" she asked, hissing the word through her gums, and grinning.

CRAMER LEANED PAST JAKE to stare out the window at the blanket of green below. Casco Bay rolled deep and blue off to the other side of the plane. But it was the vast swath of forest that fascinated him.

"I've never seen that many trees in my life."

"Wishing you hadn't come?"

Cramer shrugged. "Just want to know what I'm up against. The whole state must be loaded with dangerous animals."

Jake laughed. "The biggest predator out there is the black bear. They're few and far between anymore, and they don't attack men except in self-defense."

"Right. That's why you hear all those stories about bear attacks."

"Why are you so afraid of the forest?"

"Never been in one."

"Never?"

Cramer shook his head. "Memere didn't have a lot of money for tours of the National Parks. I know you're supposed to be able to frighten off bears with whistles or pepper spray. Think I'd rather trust my pistol."

"Do you know what spoor is?"

Cramer nodded. "Animal poop."

"Black bear spoor is filled with berries and nuts, okay?"

"So?"

"Grizzly spoor is filled with pistols and containers of pepper spray."

"Very funny."

"There aren't any grizzlies within a thousand miles of Crowley."

"My luck, there will be when we get there. What about wolves and coyotes and mountain lions?"

"No wolves. Coyotes don't attack people, and if there are any mountain lions I never heard of them."

"Bobcats, lynx, wolverines?"

"How come you know so many predators?"

"Been doing research for the trip."

"Any bobcat, lynx, or wolverine that's stupid enough to attack a man your size I wish the best of luck."

"You're saying the woods are perfectly safe, then?"

"No. I'm saying you're not going to get attacked by a predator. You can fall in the river and drown. You can get lost and die from exposure. And before you start, there are no poisonous snakes in Maine."

"You're absolutely sure."

"Absolutely."

"I'll take your word."

"That'll be a first."

Their landing and debarkation was uneventful, despite two old ladies who seemed to be much more interested in staring at Cramer than in getting out of the airport. Jake spotted Pam through the glass separating the secure space from the waiting area. Her wavy auburn hair hung to the shoulders of a blue cotton dress, and there were new lines on her forehead. A frown darkened her face as she crossed her thin arms, watching him passed through the turnstile. He stood nervously in front of her, searching for an opening that seemed impossible to find.

Despite the years, his cousin's eyes were the same deep blue he remembered staring into on those long-ago summer nights when they sat up late on the porch and discussed their futures. Pam was going to be a movie star back then—at least that was *one* of her ambitions—and he was going to work with Virgil in the sheriff's department. Neither of them ended up where they'd thought they would, and he wondered if she was any happier with her final destination than he was. In the end he just sighed loudly, opening his arms wide.

She fell into them, burying her head in his shoulder. He winced, and she glanced up.

"Got a scratch there. It's kind of sore."

She stared at the bump of the bandage under his shirt. "A scratch?"

He shrugged, still holding her. "I missed you."

"You didn't act like it," she said, easing out of his arms. "Who's your friend?"

He introduced Cramer, and Cramer told them he'd take care of their bags.

Pam nodded. "Thanks. You can meet us out front. I have an old yellow Jeep."

She led Jake down the stairs and across the street to the parking garage.

"All these years," she mused, shaking her head.

"I'm sorry, Pam."

"You say that like you mean it. But why, Jake? You never told me why."

"It was just best for everyone that I went."

"Why in the world would you think that?"

Jake didn't answer. They got in the Jeep and drove around to the baggage claim area.

"Is there any new information about Albert's killing?" asked Jake.

"How much do you know?"

Jake shrugged. "Cramer managed to get a deputy to fax him a report of the investigation. But it's a week old."

"He was attacked in his house. Beaten to death. It was . . . Virgil said it was brutal."

Jake stared out the window at people bustling by. The old man had never even looked at anyone crosswise in his life.

"Why was it so important I come home?"

She sighed, focusing on the steering wheel. "I just needed you, Jake. Is that too hard to understand? We're family."

"Sorry."

"Did you *ever* think about coming back?"

Should he tell her just how many times he'd thought of it? That some nights he sat up until dawn thinking of it?

"Some."

She nodded, swallowing a lump in her throat.

"Pam," he said. "You have to believe me when I say I couldn't come back. Not to stay, I mean. I'm not sure it was even a good idea coming back now."

"Didn't you miss Mandi at all?" she whispered.

How could he tell her that Mandi hadn't left his thoughts in fourteen years? That the few women he had touched in that time had never satisfied, had never been Mandi, that every one of them had finally realized that they were competing with a phantom that he couldn't even bring himself to name, let alone exorcise?

He sighed again, staring out the window as Cramer exited the terminal towing two large suitcases.

"We'll talk later," said Pam, as Jake escaped to help with the luggage.

BLUE JAY SKITTERED THROUGH THE TREES as Cramer wandered down Pam's long gravel drive. Only moments before he had been eavesdropping, hoping to find out more about what there was between Jake and Pam—maybe why Jake had run out to begin with—but neither of them wanted to talk about it while he was in the house. So he'd slipped out of the kitchen while they were still arguing about the church social she wanted them to attend that night.

The sun moved behind a cloud, and Cramer stopped in midstride, surprised by how suddenly the forest changed. The trees wrapped around the winding drive and hovering overhead reminded him of a narrow alleyway, triggering an old warning buzzer in the back of his head. And it was so damned hard to focus. A man's eyes were constantly trying to rest at different depths in the woods. It was dizzying.

A twig snapped somewhere to his left, and he spun in that direction.

"Hello?" he yelled, recalling Jake's reassurances about predators.

The forest seemed to soak up his voice, but he thought he heard an answer, like a whisper, or maybe the lightest verse of a song on the wind. Just enough to tease his imagination.

"Who's there?" he shouted.

He looked up and down the narrow lane as the sun struggled vainly to escape from behind the clouds. There wasn't a breath of a breeze.

He glanced at the weeds, bracken, and pine needles, and then at his shoes. Bad enough they were getting dirty from the driveway. But just then he could have sworn he heard the *voice* yet again, light as a feather, still not quite discernible.

Against his better judgement he stepped off the road and between twin spruce trees, joined at the roots. To his right the slippery terrain sloped toward the valley road somewhere below, while ahead the ground rolled away around the curve of the mountain. In places the trees were sparse. In others timber, brush, and early-growth conifers barred his view.

"Who's out there?" he called again, traipsing deeper into the woods. "Show yourself!"

The sound—fluttering in and out like an annoying insect—slipped around the hill, and he considered turning back. Jake had told him how easy it was to get lost in the forest, but he was only twenty yards from the drive and could surely find his way back to the house.

His street shoes skidded down the side of a steep gully, slicing through the thin frosting of pine needles. By the time he reached the bottom he was cloaked in shadow. He glanced slowly up and down the length of the narrow, overgrown cleft and realized that if there were man-eating beasts in the woods, this was where they would hold their feasts. But the most dangerous animal he encountered was some sort of giant beetle that scurried across his sock and then away beneath a rotting log.

By the time he clambered up the far side of the gully, his hands were covered with scratches and his forearms itched. He wiped sweat from the back of his neck with his handkerchief. Rocks or brush had sliced thin gashes in his shoes, and when he glanced at his sports coat he noticed brown brambles covering his sleeves and matching chinos. He tried pulling the burrs out, but he'd no sooner remove one than another would appear out of nowhere, stuck to some other part of his anatomy.

"Fuck it."

He turned slowly in a full circle, experiencing again the awful sensation of not being able to focus amid all the trees and bracken. But the murmuring sound was even clearer and now seemed to have a fixed direction. He ignored the brambles, slapping and shoving his way through a thick stand of pines, finally stumbling into a small dell. The sun burst through the clouds like a battering ram, cascading golden light across the tall grass.

"Looks like a park," he muttered in surprise, searching for the source of the whispering.

Suddenly the eerie sound stopped, the air in the clearing went deathly still, and he instantly recognized the jittery sensation in his arms and hands. He'd experienced the same feeling just before a man with a gun had stepped out of a doorway and pumped a bullet into his chest. He squinted, trying to put form to the shadows that clustered beneath the wall of trees. But separating anything of substance from the surrounding gloom was like trying to spot one fish in a school.

"Ogou, now the time to watch this boy," he muttered, crossing himself.

He strode into the center of the dell, snatching his pistol from its holster and targeting what appeared to be a very large man crouching amid a clump of small firs. "Who are you? Come out where I can see you."

But the shadow didn't move. After a couple of long, deep breaths, he crept nearer, steadying his two-handed grip on the pistol. The closer he got the more imposing the shape of the man appeared, until it seemed impossibly large.

"I don't want to hurt you!" he said, feeling silly. "Identify yourself."

Hesitating at the tree line, both he and the forest held their breath. Sweat burned his eyes, as he took one tentative step beneath the canopy of trees, then another. As he approached the dark form it began to reveal itself as a branch here, a clump of gnarled limbs and brush there. He glanced right and left, but there was no giant, no lurking killer or violent wacko. No bear. He backed into the clearing and stared into the trees again.

What the hell was going on? The sound had been real. He'd swear to it. And he didn't think any *animal* had been making it. But he just wasn't forest savvy enough to say for certain.

He searched for the way back out—more frightened than he wanted to admit when he didn't instantly recognize his path in. But finally he spotted the edge of the gully through the trees. All the way down and then back out of the ravine he kept one eye over his shoulder. As he dusted himself off on the far side he could hear the eerie whispering starting again.

He turned, but there was only thin yellow sunlight and sharp black shadows delineating the trees.

THE DAY WAS ALREADY SURRENDERING to evening by midafternoon, white tufts of clouds thickening to gray, the air so heavy it clung to the walls of the house. By six o'clock the darkness outside seemed impenetrable. It was the kind of weather that bred its own sense of gloom. Mandi fought to break through the depression that gripped her by getting ready for the fellowship meeting at the church, but Pierce was running behind schedule as usual.

"Hurry up, honey," she called, out of habit.

She often spoke to Pierce, even though he heard not a word.

Her son spat toothpaste into the bathroom sink, wiping his face unhurriedly with a towel. She tapped his chest, and he buttoned his shirt, and when she wrapped the tie around his neck he completed the knot himself. When he was finished she took his hand and used the American Sign Language that was faster than simply finger spelling each letter into his palm. *We're going to be late.*

He signed back into her palm. *Makes us seem important.*

She laughed, kissing his cheek. *You are important.*

She handed him his cane, waiting patiently as he made his way down the walk to the car, letting him find it. But she made sure he buckled up before she started the Subaru station wagon. As they drove, Pierce leaned back against the seat, tapping his fingers lightly on the armrest, where she knew he could feel every vibration of the engine and the road.

Mandi always volunteered to help out at church affairs. That was why she and Pierce had to be there early tonight, to get ready for the small group of staunch parishioners. Every Sunday morning she and Pierce sat in the front pew next to Pam, and Mandi would sign the service into Pierce's palm. When he was younger he had missed a great deal because he kept stopping her to ask questions, but as he grew older Pierce became quite a Bible scholar.

Mandi was torn between wishing that the state had more money to fund better schools and equipment for kids like Pierce and being happy that he was homeschooled. What he had lost in socialization with children his age, she thought he had gained in the time to learn to deal with his disability free from the hazing of other kids. She knew she was often overprotective, but Pierce seldom complained unless she got into what he considered his personal territory. The government *had* at least been good about supplying her with teaching aids and books on how to work with the deafblind. And when Pierce was a toddler, a nice old woman from Portland had driven up almost every day for three years to help Mandi *reach* him. It had been a major breakthrough when Pierce suddenly realized that he could communicate. Little things at first.

Hungry.

Hurt.

Sad.

That had been another hurdle, communication of an abstract thought. But Pierce learned quickly, faster than anyone the woman had ever worked with. Mandi was pretty sure he was a genius. He could focus on one subject to the exclusion of all others, often for days, and you only had to tell Pierce something once for him to remember it.

He intuitively understood that there was a larger world around him that reached far beyond the limits of the darkness and silence encompassing his body. When he was younger Mandi had spent every free moment with him, patiently finding ways to explain things like sky, and telephone, and television. By the time Pierce was four he could read braille, and he spent almost as much time asking Mandi for explanations as he did reading. Now Ernie was trying to get donations to buy Pierce a used laptop with a braille display. Mandi hadn't told the boy yet because she didn't want him to get his hopes up. But Ernie was determined.

Pierce was remarkable in many ways, not least of which was his uncanny knack for fixing things. Things he shouldn't have been able to understand, let alone repair. Mandi had first discovered this skill when he was only six. She'd been trying to explain to him that he couldn't have toast for breakfast because the toaster was on the fritz. When she came back into the kitchen she discovered burnt crumbs all over the counter, and Pierce screwing the appliance back together with a butter knife. Miraculously, when she stuck a piece of bread into it, it worked even better than before. After that, Pierce began to fix other things. A radio that got nothing but static, a vacuum that kept burning up belts. Dr. Burton said it was a savant talent, but Mandi had done some research and discovered that most people with those had very low IQs. Pierce was far too intelligent to be called an idiot savant.

Mandi parked as close to the front doors of the church as

she could. The tall wooden steeple had a definite lean so that
the bell seemed ready to leap out the side opening. But the
building had been standing for over one hundred years, and
the steeple hadn't fallen down yet. As they walked down the
aisle toward the tiny kitchen in back Pierce tapped his cane
across her shins to get her attention, and she stopped. His
brow was furrowed, and his brown eyes seemed to be
searching the pews. She stared at him, imagining that he
could see, that he was as normal as any other boy. It was a
daydream that haunted her often. One that she would live
with until the day she died.

She reached down and took his hand. *What is it?*

I'm listening, he signed back, continuing his search.

Listening? she signed, frowning.

Pierce frowned, too. *It's here somewhere.*

What?

The thing in the valley. Now it's here. I can hear it.

There's nothing here, honey. Honest. Nothing but us.

But Pierce shook his head, unconvinced.

She stared up at the two stained-glass windows, one of
Jesus, one of Mary. Pierce had never heard a single sound,
just as he had never seen light or shadow or color, and no
one had ever tried to teach him to talk. The doctors had told
Mandi that a limited form of speech was possible, but there
was no state money for the training, and she couldn't afford
a therapist. She felt guilty about that, as any parent would,
but what could she do?

She bowed her head and said a prayer that whatever was
happening was God's will, and she told God that she would
deal with it no matter what. But she sure would appreciate it
if He would take care of her boy, since in her opinion Pierce
had already had more than enough bad things dumped on
his plate. She patted his shoulder reassuringly, guiding him
toward the kitchen door.

She found him a folding chair in the corner of the kitchen and brought him the braille Bible Ernie kept in the church for him. Then she began digging out serving dishes, wiping them clean and setting them onto the table out front. She plugged in the big coffee urn and filled it, then ripped open packages of paper plates and plastic knives, forks, and spoons. As she worked she began to sing.

"Amazing grace, how sweet the sound . . ." As she checked the coffee and began to load a tray, a strong male voice chimed in from the front of the building. She smiled, continuing on through the end of the chorus.

"Coffee ready?" asked Ernie, poking his head through the door and reaching over to ruffle Pierce's hair. Pierce grabbed his hand, testing both sides with the tips of his fingers.

Hi, Ern! he signed.

Ernie ruffled the boy's hair again in reply.

"Mandi," said Ernie. "There's a couple of people here Pam said you ought to say hi to."

Mandi rested the tray she was holding on the counter and followed Ernie out into the church proper. She nodded at Pam—who hurried away to greet people arriving at the front of the church—and leaned around Ernie to meet the two men behind him.

"Jake!" she said, startled as he stepped out of the big black man's shadow.

"Hi, Mandi," said Jake, glancing away from her toward Pam, who smiled wickedly as she flounced away up the aisle. "This is my friend, Cramer. Cramer, this is Mandi Rousseau."

"Morin," said Mandi, frowning.

"Sorry," said Jake. "Pam said . . . I thought."

"I haven't changed it since the divorce. I heard you were coming home. How have you been?"

"The same," said Jake, flustered. "Yourself?"

"Not quite the same," she said. "Let me show you."

She led Pierce out into the church, introducing him by way of long, slow handshakes to Cramer and Jake. Pierce studied each of their faces with questing fingers, taking an especially long time with Jake. Jake couldn't take his eyes off of the boy.

"He can't see or hear at all?" Cramer asked Mandi.

"Pierce is one of the rare kids born deafblind. He's never heard or seen *anything*."

"*Mon* poor *petit ami*," muttered Cramer.

Mandi stared at Jake. "I often wondered how you were, Jake."

"I've kept a low profile."

She nodded. "Not a phone call or card."

Jake flushed. "I'm sorry."

He glanced at Cramer, but Cramer pretended to be paying a great deal of attention to some muffins on the table.

"I got over it," said Mandi. "I just always wondered if you were going to let me know what the real story was, why you ran out like that. Are you back for good?"

"Just visiting."

People began filtering in through the double doors down the aisle. Mandi glanced at Pierce, but he was sniffing the air and twisting his head from side to side. He probably knew as well as she did who was in the church and who was missing.

"What do you think of Crowley?" she asked Cramer.

"Exciting."

"Well, that's a description I never expected to hear."

Jake smiled. "Cramer got lost in the woods today."

"Are you serious?"

"I thought I heard something, and I went to investigate," said Cramer. "Cop instinct."

"You're a cop, too?"

"Jake's partner."

Mandi nodded. "What was it you heard?"

"I thought perhaps someone was lost," said Cramer.

"He thought maybe it was a grizzly bear," said Jake, smirking.

"We don't have grizzly bears," said Mandi.

"So I've been told," said Cramer.

"You didn't get a good look at it?"

"It kept to the shadows."

"Probably just a trick of the light."

Cramer nodded. "The light was making funny noises."

"What kind of noises?"

Cramer frowned. "I couldn't put my finger on where it was coming from, but it sounded like someone whispering or singing to me."

Mandi nodded noncommitally, then turned back to Pierce.

"He's a fine-looking boy," said Jake.

She nodded. "The apple of my eye."

"Where are you living now?"

"The old Miller cottage, between Albert's place and the highway."

She stared into Jake's eyes, sensing the old attraction like a storm building inside her. She knew that all he had to do was open his arms, and she would fall into them like a fool, and she prayed that he did nothing of the sort. Instead she searched for the heat of anger that had sustained her for the past fourteen years. But this close, it was difficult to kindle much more than a flickering warmth.

Pierce took Cramer's finger, showing him how to finger spell by "writing" each letter of the alphabet on his palm, and Jake watched the two of them.

"Must be hard, raising him alone," he said.

She shrugged. "I wouldn't have it any other way," she

said, discovering that that sounded harsher than she had intended. "You do what you have to do."

Jake nodded.

But she wasn't letting him off that easily.

"Why'd you run out, Jake?" she whispered. "Was it another woman?"

His face fell. "Don't ever think that. Not ever."

"Then what? Tell me."

He glanced around the church. People were heading their way, and Mandi could tell that Cramer *really* wanted to hear their conversation although he was pretending to pay attention to Pierce.

"Can we talk later?" pleaded Jake.

"Sure, Jake," she said. "We've always got later."

Pam walked up to them with an old woman on her arm. Barbara Stearn wore a red dress that Mandi thought might have been expensive in the early eighties. Her heels were so high she wobbled when she walked, and a string of fake pearls that would have choked a sperm whale dangled around her throat.

"Jake Crowley!" she said, stroking back bottle-blond hair. "I thought you were dead."

"No, Barbara," said Jake, extending his hand. "I'm alive and well. How are you?"

"Getting crotchety, that's how. Are you moving back into the family home?"

Jake gave Pam a long-suffering look. "I don't think so."

"Too many bad memories?"

"I have a life out West."

"Do you now? Doing what?"

"I'm a police detective in Houston."

"How thrilling. You must tell me all about it sometime." She patted Jake on the cheek as though he were a ten-year-old and grabbed Cramer's bicep in passing. "And by all means, bring your friend!"

She flittered away toward the food table. They all watched her go as though she were a strange sea creature crawling along the shore. Even Pierce wrinkled his nose at her perfume.

Mandi laughed first. "*Getting* crotchety? And by all means, bring your friend!" she said, giving Cramer another squeeze and leaning close to keep her voice down. "Barbara claims she made films back in the fifties, but no one seems to have ever seen one."

"What were you guys talking about, earlier?" asked Pam, slipping between them and giving Mandi a reproachful grin. "You looked thicker than thieves."

"Old times," said Jake, frowning.

"Whispered voices," said Mandi quickly, smiling at Cramer. "Cramer heard them in the woods."

But Pam didn't echo Mandi's smile.

"It's a weird coincidence, I guess," continued Mandi, "but a few minutes ago Pierce told me that he heard something, too."

"Pierce?" said Pam.

Mandi shrugged. "When we entered the church Pierce said he was *listening* to something. He's been acting weird for a couple of days. He says he's heard something at his window. I don't know what's going on with him . . . Maybe it's the Crowley curse. Remember how your mother used to tell us bogeyman stories about the valley?"

Jake was silent.

"Curses are like baggage," muttered Cramer, staring at his partner.

Jake frowned and turned away.

JAKE SPOTTED ERNIE TALKING TO VIRGIL MILCHE near the front of the church, and he and Cramer made their way through the crowd. Jake could tell Ernie was alarmed as he waved his arms, calling for people's attention.

"Sheriff Milche has an announcement!"

Virgil took a deep breath, glancing at Jake and nodding. "Ladies and gentlemen, there's no easy way to put this, and I hate to have to bring it up here, but we've had another homicide."

Murmurs filled the air. Cramer bumped Jake's arm, and Jake noticed an evil grin on his partner's face.

"I knew this was gonna be a good trip," Cramer whispered.

"We've got a positive ID," said Virgil, glancing around at the crowd. "Girl was a runaway from North Carolina, and we think she was probably hitchhiking. I don't believe my going into the details right now is necessary. We just need to know if any of you here saw anyone hanging around the old school bus stop on the highway recently. No? Well, she was wearing jeans and a tie-dye shirt."

Mandi gasped.

"You saw her?" Jake asked, as Virgil stepped alongside.

She nodded. "It must have been her. Work was slow, and my boss let me out early. I came up here to the church before going home, thinking I'd get a jump on preparations for tonight. When I pulled out on the road again I spotted her, coming from somewhere up near the old Crowley house."

"When was that, Mandi?" asked Virgil.

She frowned. "Yesterday. Around three maybe."

"See where she went?"

"No. I started to ask her if she wanted a ride. But . . . I don't know . . . we waved and she seemed okay . . . and I wanted to get home to Pierce. Maybe if I'd picked her up, offered her a place to stay—"

Virg shook his head. "You can kill yourself with maybes, Mandi. There's just no way of knowing. Don't beat yourself up over it. Are you sure about the time?"

She nodded. "Pretty close."

Virgil was silent for a moment.

"Well," he said at last, "if anyone thinks of anything, you all know where to contact me. Something that seems trivial to you might make all the difference."

He patted Mandi on the shoulder, turning to Jake. "You picked a heck of a week to come home. Sorry about your uncle Albert. You staying?"

"Just visiting. My partner and I needed a break," said Jake, introducing Cramer.

"Big-city law enforcement getting you down?" said Virgil, giving Jake the once-over.

"Why do you say that?"

"I'm a cop."

Jake laughed, but his face clouded when Virgil nudged him out of the crowd.

"I want you to take a look at something, Jake," said Virgil, slipping a Polaroid photo out of his jacket.

Jake stared at what appeared to be two crystal candlesticks resting atop a canvas pack. The sticks were cut into a swirling diamond pattern, larger at the top than the base. They looked ungainly, possibly unstable, and terribly familiar.

"The girl had these on her?" he asked, shaken.

Virgil nodded. "I thought I recognized them. They're the ones from the mantel in your parents' house, aren't they?"

Jake nodded. "Unless there's another pair like that in town."

"Not likely."

"All right, then. Tell me more."

"You're on vacation."

"Apparently she broke into *my* house."

"Nothing more to tell, yet. She was beaten up pretty good, but it didn't look like it was bad enough to kill her. Don't know if she was raped yet, although I expect so. I'm waiting for the medical examiner's report."

He looked at Jake as though waiting for him to add something.

"Anything new on Albert's murder?" Jake asked.

"No. But whoever did it is crazier than a mule on whiskey sodas. It wasn't pretty, Jake. Way I figure, it had to be strangers. Nobody around here is that crazy. It wasn't a robbery gone bad. Not a damned thing was taken that we could see. Seems like some loony just ended up at the wrong place at the wrong time. I hate to admit it, but you know how it is. More than likely the case will never get solved without some real luck."

Jake frowned. "You want some assistance?"

Virgil eyed him as though weighing the idea.

"No," he said at last. "You got no jurisdiction here. And you made it pretty clear years ago you didn't want any part of the sheriff's department. Besides, Albert was family."

Jake shrugged. "Cramer and I might be helpful."

Virgil nodded. "You might at that. And you might muddy up my chain of evidence and let the guilty parties slip through the court system. You know what defense lawyers are like."

"We've both had training you haven't," said Jake. "And you could be wrong. Two murders in Crowley in a month? Both beatings? Don't you think they just might be related?"

A couple of Ernie's congregation had casually edged close enough to listen in, but Virgil shooed them off with his eyes. "The two murders probably *aren't* related. The girl's killing could be just a rape gone bad."

"Albert's body was found upright against the kitchen table. What was the crime scene like for the girl?"

Virgil frowned. "How do you know that, Jake?"

Jake shrugged. "Cramer got hold of the report." When Virgil gave Cramer a surprised look, Jake smiled. "He's resourceful."

"Well, *she* was lying facedown. Fully clothed. Blue jeans, T-shirt, hiking boots. It was almost like the killer didn't want her to look at him."

"That happens," said Jake. "A disorganized killer might feel remorse. He'll dress the victim or cover her. Sometimes it's a signature, other times it's just something the guy feels like doing. But Albert was sitting up."

"So no signature there," said Virgil.

"They were both beaten," said Jake.

"Yeah." Virgil grimaced. "But the girl was nothing like Albert. In fact it looked like she might have done a lot of the damage to herself, running through the woods."

"It would be odd for a second victim to be less brutalized than the first, though," mused Cramer. "Usually a killer *progresses.*"

Virgil studied both Jake and Cramer. "I'm heading for the autopsy from here," he said, frowning. "My boys will be going door to door in the valley and up and down the highway again tomorrow. If anyone saw anything, we'll hear about it."

"Good luck," said Jake as Virgil headed out the door. "Nice seeing you again."

Virgil didn't look back.

Cramer glanced at Jake. "What's going on?"

Jake frowned. "What do you mean?"

"Why the bad feelings between you and the sheriff?"

Jake shrugged.

Cramer shook his head, glancing back at the crowd. "Guess I'm supposed to find out the old-fashioned way, eh?"

"Pierce wasn't born with a limp," said Pam, handing Jake a cup of punch and a sandwich.

"What happened?"

"Mandi thinks Rich did it, but that Pierce's afraid to tell. But Rich claims he's innocent and Claude, Rich's cousin, swears that Rich was with him at the time. So there were never any charges."

"Rich and Mandi had already split?"

"They separated when Pierce was only three. But Rich kept . . . going back. Until Mandi finally got a restraining order."

"Where's Rich now?"

"He lives up along the old Burnout road in a trailer with your second cousin Carly."

"Carly and Rich?"

"Carly comes from the really rotten side of the Crowley family, that's for sure."

"That's not a Christian attitude, is it?" said Jake, smiling.

"A slut's a slut," said Pam, shaking her head and looking quickly around the church. "I'm sorry. I shouldn't have said that. You know, you look at Mandi just the way you did fourteen years ago. It breaks my heart to see the two of you so close and yet apart."

Jake stared into his punch, but there was no escape in the paper cup. "Mandi and I just didn't work out."

"You mean because you had to get out of the valley."

He nodded.

"You know, Jake, family and friends are to *share* troubles, not to hide them from."

"What about protecting family and friends?"

She shrugged. "Sometimes we don't want to be protected."

"Mandi and I were a long time ago."

"I guess old girlfriends are trouble," said Pam, eyeing him.

"You're trouble," said Jake.

Pierce pretended to pay attention to Pastor Ernie as he spelled out silly questions.

How's things been going?

Good.

What you been reading?

Lord of the Rings.

But Pierce was preoccupied with the vibration of the crowd walking, the movement of the air around him, and more than that by the feeling that the *presence* he had sensed in front of his window was close by. Finally Ernie let him go, and Pierce sniffed the air.

Many people he recognized by their smell. Occasionally

someone would place their hand on his shoulder, and he'd grip it. Others he'd pull toward him until he could run his fingers over their face. Then he'd smile, take their hand under his, and slowly spell out their names in their palms by way of greeting. His mother must have noticed that something was still wrong because she tried to divert him by taking his hand and signing for other people as they came up to say hi. But he didn't want to be distracted. He shook her hand hard to accent his need.

I don't know what's happening, honey, she signed back. *Maybe we should see the doctor.*

Pierce shrugged. Dr. Burton was okay, but what was she going to know about something he was *hearing* inside his head? Because that was what it was, not hearing like other people did it. He knew that. He imagined it might be the way they would *remember* a sound. But he didn't have any memories of sounds. Not until now.

Cramer heard something weird, too, she spelled. *Out in the woods today.*

Pierce's head popped up. Anyone who didn't know him might have thought he was searching the crowd. *Really?*

He said he did.

Probably just wanted to make me feel better, spelled Pierce, shaking his head.

He told me before I told him about you.

Pierce paused. *It felt really bad.*

Bad how?

Like sometimes when I have nightmares.

She squeezed his arm, then signed slowly. *Nothing bad's here. And nothing bad's going to happen to you. Not ever again.*

He nodded, really wanting to believe her. She had always taken care of him, protected him—except that once, and that wasn't her fault—and she never lied to him. Never. But this

time he knew she was stretching things just a little. Something was really bothering her.

What are you afraid of, then? he signed.

Her grip tightened almost imperceptibly, and he sensed
the minute hesitation before she replied.

Someone else was killed.

Here?

No. Down by the highway. A teenage girl.

Pierce nodded slowly.

*It doesn't have anything to do with what you've been . . .
hearing,* signed Mandi. *You don't believe that, do you?*

This time it was his turn to hesitate.

I don't know.

She slipped her hand out from under his, and he sensed
her moving away. His end of the building felt suddenly
empty. The crowd had milled away. He could still detect
aftershave, deodorant, tuna fish salad, coffee, and other
odors that lingered even though their original owners had
wafted away. But when his mother told him to stay in one
place, Pierce stayed. He'd learned that lesson the hard way.

When he was a toddler he had always had the entire bottom floor of their house to be independent in, but he was not
allowed upstairs. By the time he was five he'd explored
every inch of the first level and even the yard outside in
minute detail, and then—one day while his mother was at
work and the baby-sitter was sleeping soundly on the back
porch—he'd climbed the mountainous stairs. He'd rum-
maged inch by inch through his mother's sleeping loft, fingering the soft wool blanket on the bed, sniffing every bottle
of perfume and nail polish. Every drawer was inspected,
every item of clothing, every piece of liner paper. He discovered two windows whose existence he had suspected due to
drafts through the house, finding his way to them by the
smell of pine on the breeze and the warmth of the sun.

Finally, growing bored and hungry, he had wound his way back to the stairs, careful to approach along the wall, his fingers playing across it like spider feet, his toes tapping rhythmically ahead. When he reached the first step he started to squat and slide down on his butt. Suddenly powerful fingers gripped his shoulders, lifting him off the floor. He flailed for balance but found nothing solid with his hands or his feet, and then he was flung like a piece of wadded wastepaper into the air. For the merest instant he was afraid he'd been thrown into some even deeper darkness, where there was nothing to touch and nothing to smell or taste, forever.

His hand shot through the banister at the same instant his shoulder struck a step. He felt a sickening crunch as his arm was ripped out of its socket, and then pain flared all over his body as he continued head over heels down the stairs. Finally there was a dull thud and then merciful oblivion. When he came to he was in an unfamiliar bed, but his hand was clutched tightly in his mother's, and she was signing forcefully to him that nothing like that would ever happen to him again. Every time she removed her signing hand and then replaced it, he sensed the dampness of tears on her fingertips.

It had taken months of painful rehabilitation for him to relearn to walk.

Now he waited patiently in a brightly lit corner of the church surrounded by utter silence and darkness, sensing that—for all his mother's reassurances—the world outside was growing darker still. And there was nothing at all that she could do about it.

ERNIE WALKED MANDI and Pierce to their car.

"Thanks again," he said, patting her on the shoulder as she slipped behind the wheel.

She looked out toward the dark woods. "You know I'm always happy to help."

Ernie frowned. "Why don't you and Pierce come and stay with Pam and me for a while?"

She considered the offer for a moment. "No. You've got company already. We'll be all right."

"Maybe you two shouldn't be alone right now."

"We'll be fine," said Mandi. "I'll keep the doors locked. And I'll call if I get nervous."

He lightly touched her arm. "All right. You do that, then. But drive careful. If you change your mind you just hop back in the car and head on up, any time, day or night."

"Thanks, Ernie," she said, rolling up her window as he backed away and waved.

She pulled down the long drive, following Barbara's ancient Buick. Why anyone would live in the north woods and own a dinosaur like that, Mandi couldn't understand. Her own Subaru was eight years old, but at least it had four-wheel drive. As the old lady pulled away up the valley, Mandi turned toward home.

But she couldn't help but think about the young hitch-hiker. What if she had stopped to pick the girl up or offered her a place to stay for the night? She would probably be alive right now instead of lying on a cold morgue table. She was someone's little girl. . . .

But Mandi knew there was only so much room in her heart for guilt. And for eight years—ever since Pierce's accident—it had been overflowing. She had made the choice between offering assistance to a stranger and rushing home to take care of Pierce. She would always make the same decision.

Without the other car ahead to help light the way the forest loomed ominously all around. She glanced at Pierce, but he was facing out the window.

Just then a large buck shot out of the trees, almost colliding with her grille. She slammed on the brakes, reaching for Pierce at the same time. The tires slung gravel, and the woods seemed suddenly closer. Pierce grasped her hand, questioning her with his fingers, but she ignored him, bending to peer through the windshield as they coasted down the road.

She pulled over to catch her breath, Pierce still signing feverishly into her hand. She signed back, trying not to shake, but she knew he would read her anxiety.

What happened? he asked.

We almost hit a deer.

Wow.

She squinted, trying to see into the dark forest. Why had the animal burst out of the woods like that? She thought of

Cramer's grizzly bear and smiled. But the buck was definitely running from *something*.

Is it gone? signed Pierce.

Yes.

Too bad.

Too bad we didn't hit it?

We could have had barbecued deer.

She shoved his shoulder, and he grinned.

They rest of the ride home was uneventful, but as Mandi climbed out of the car she continued watching the woods, barely managing to shrug off her anxiety while she waited for Pierce to make his way up the ramp into the house. She flicked on the kitchen lights as he headed for the bathroom. Pouring herself a glass of milk from the fridge, she stared out the window into the night. As she sipped the milk she sensed Jake slipping back into her mind.

She couldn't help but compare what she had shared with Jake with the life she had had with Rich. The two were like opposite poles of a magnet. Jake had always been so gentle, sweet, and loving, while Rich wanted her for only one thing. Being so close to Jake tonight had been wonderful and painful at the same time. Regardless of what she had said to him, she had known in her heart all along that whatever had driven him from the valley, it hadn't been another woman. And tonight in his eyes she'd seen the same old hurt she knew was there in her own. What terrible wedge had driven them apart? She'd been over their last night together so many times that she wondered if she even remembered it correctly any longer. There was just no reason for him to suddenly wake up and insist that he was leaving. But that was what had happened.

The toilet flushed, and the bathroom door rattled as Pierce headed for his bedroom. She heard him digging for his pajamas, and she strolled over to the bedroom door. He was standing beside the bed in his briefs, neatly folding each item of clothing before setting it on the bedside table. Then he slipped on his pjs and tucked himself in. She waited until he'd signed his prayers, then took his hands.

Nothing bad's here, she signed. *And nothing bad's going to happen to you. Not ever again.*

He nodded slowly.

Good night, she signed, holding one hand against her cheek.

Love you, he signed back, smiling.

You, too.

She left the door open a crack and flipped off the light.

As she climbed the stairs she noticed that the moon had disappeared behind the clouds, making the night dark as pitch, and the window was covered with a thin mist.

Pierce could still feel the residual touch of his mother's fingers in his palms.

Nothing bad's here. And nothing bad's going to happen to you. Not ever again.

But as much as he knew that she loved him and would die to protect him, he wasn't sure what she could do. He lay stiffly beneath the covers, sensing the dark presence on the other side of his window.

But instead of just quivering in fear, he let his mind roam, trying to understand what it was that stared through the window, and what it wanted. Once again he discovered tangled almost-thoughts that made no sense, and then something beyond *thoughts,* almost like something he *could* understand.

Suddenly he experienced the all-too-familiar and terrible feeling of being alone in some darkness where there were no smells, no vibrations, no tastes, just a horrible empty void. And then into that emptiness came the same presence that hovered outside his window. He could feel it reaching out for him, testing him in some way that he couldn't quite understand. It wanted something from him, and he knew that it would kill to get it. But he didn't know what it was that the thing needed. And he knew that there was no way his mother or anyone else could protect him.

It was up to him to protect them.

And suddenly he felt very small and alone.

Friday

AFTER BREAKFAST, Pam asked what he and Cramer had planned, and Jake shrugged.

"Why not run into Arcos and say hello to Mandi? Her office is right downtown."

Jake shook his head. "I don't think that's a good idea."

"She missed you, Jake."

He hadn't gotten that feeling last night. More than likely she hated his guts and just covered it real well. It was probably better that way.

"You just gonna hide out here all the time?"

"I'm not hiding just because I don't want to pester an old girlfriend."

"I thought you two were a little more than that."

Jake frowned, but she was right. He and Mandi had been a lot more than just boyfriend and girlfriend. He wasn't sure what to call it, but soul mates had always sounded too feeble to explain what they'd shared.

"What did I say that finally caused you to cave and come back?" Pam asked, surprising Jake by bringing up the subject in front of Cramer. And Cramer seemed to be enjoying the conversation *far* too much this time to let something like simple etiquette force him to leave.

"Respect for Albert," he muttered.

"I can appreciate that," she said, letting him know with her eyes that she knew there was more to it than that. "I really am glad you came."

"You aren't acting like it."

"How do you want me to act?" she asked, setting a pan in the drainer.

"I don't know why I said that. I'm sorry."

"Are you gonna visit his grave?"

"I guess I should. Is he in the family cemetery?"

"Close to your mother," she said quietly.

Jake stared at Cramer.

"I'll warm up the car," said Cramer, rising at last.

Jake watched him go, wondering again why he'd come. It seemed incredibly unlikely that Jimmy Torrio would be stupid enough to follow them to Maine. But he sensed that Cramer felt somehow as though he'd let Jake down on the beach, even though the whole thing was Jake's fault. Cramer was like that, although he'd never admit it.

"That's what family does," said Pam.

"You reading my thoughts?"

"I don't have to. I could see it in your face. You were wondering why he took care of you."

She really could read him. She'd always been able to. Only his deepest, darkest thoughts were hidden from her. And sometimes he feared that she might be able to read them, as well.

"I tried to get you to come back to work out the thing that's inside you, Jake," she whispered. "So that we could all help you work it out. If you want to leave again after that, then fine."

"What if it's not something that can be worked out?" he asked, fighting to keep his voice steady. "What if it's not that easy?"

She squeezed his arm before giving him a nudge toward the front door. "I never said it was going to be easy. Nothing worth doing ever is."

The family cemetery clung to the slope of the largest of the mountains that rimmed the valley like worn dragon's teeth. Jake stood with one hand resting on his mother's simple stone, looking across at Albert's grave, still too fresh for a monument. The smell of earth and flowers hung in the air, interwoven with the clean scent of the surrounding pines. As Jake surveyed the valley rolling away beneath them he felt empty, as though he were standing in the center of some infinite black space with another even more powerful vacuum inside of him. For almost a decade and a half he had hidden from his family and friends for their own good, or so he thought. Fourteen years of living like a hermit, of not hearing familiar voices, of not touching a single one of his family. Incongruously, he had discovered a modicum of peace in a very dangerous and potentially violent profession. But at least in Houston he had believed that he had distanced himself far enough that *he* would not be the cause of danger to those he loved.

And now he'd never see Albert again. Had he made the right choice? His mind wandered to Mandi, and he blinked back a tear. He'd given up so much.

"Albert taught me how to use a chain saw and how to drive a bulldozer," he mused.

"Nice talents to have. How about table manners?" Cramer said.

Jake smiled. "Albert wasn't much on those. He taught me how to be a man."

"And the sheriff fit in, how?"

Jake shrugged. "Virgil came around pretty often after . . . after my mom was killed. I think he felt sorry for me as much as Albert did. He got to taking me on patrol with him sometimes when it was slow. I hung around the jail in Arcos, and I learned a lot from him, like how to keep quiet."

"Dat one I don' know," said Cramer.

"I'm aware of that."

"Stop me anytime. How was your mother killed?"

Jake started toward the car, but Cramer paced him easily with his longer stride. Jake jerked open the door of the rented Camry, glaring at Cramer as the big man walked slowly around to take the driver's seat.

"She was beaten," said Jake at last. "But the ME said cause of death was heart failure."

"Your father ever attack her before that?"

"He never touched her."

Cramer shook his head. "So what set him off?"

"I don't want to talk about it," said Jake, closing the subject.

By the time they got off the mountain, Jake was certain Cramer was going to get them killed. Instead of watching the dirt lane that was little more than two tire ruts, he kept peering out through the trees, more than once edging perilously close to a ravine or gully. When Jake finally spotted the valley road ahead he breathed a sigh of relief, and Cramer gave him a funny look.

"Son, I could have driven for Nascar if I'd wanted the fame and fortune," said Cramer.

"You couldn't have done it anywhere with trees."

"It's true I'm not your frontier type. Want to start investigating now?"

"We're not supposed to interfere."

Cramer waited.

"If Virgil catches us at it, he'll be really pissed," said Jake.

"What else are we doing here? You didn't fly two thousand miles to stand over a grave. And you don't seem to be any good at family reunions."

Jake was still trying to figure that out himself. He had climbed on the plane almost by instinct. But since returning to the valley his subsconscious had been ominously silent. He stared at the gravel intersection realizing that only one direction might lead to answers. But were they answers he was prepared to face?

"Take a right and then the first driveway," he said quietly.

"I'm guessing your uncle's place?"

Jake nodded. When they reached the driveway he pointed to the side of the road. "Stop at the mailbox."

He slipped his fingers underneath the box, removing a key with a magnet attached.

Cramer wound the car up the drive and parked in between Albert's weathered old trailer and a large, tin-sided shed. Yellow police tape formed an X across the trailer's front door. Jake peeled it away. Cramer looked at him but only shrugged and followed him inside.

The place still had the familiar salty, urine odor of death, and the carpet and walls were streaked with brown bloodstains. But to Jake the air reeked of Albert's sweat and the Old Spice he used to cover it up, of the garlic and Tabasco with which he saturated his food, and lastly the pipe smoke that followed the old man everywhere. Jake's throat tightened as he stared at the worn sofa where he had often sat playing checkers or just jawing with the old man. An easy chair lay on its back in the corner, and several ripped-up magazines rested on the floor along with scattered newspapers.

Over the years Jake had placed everyone in the valley inside a time warp where they never aged or changed. Discovering that one of the people closest to him had been murdered was stunning. That Albert had been savagely beaten to death was totally unnerving. Staring at the bloodstains, he could picture the carnage that had taken place. Albert was small and old, but he was feisty. He would have tried to put up a fight.

"Probably not much to learn here," said Cramer. "The scene is old, Jake. The local cops and medical examiner have been all over it."

"I know . . . but this just doesn't make sense."

"No," agreed Cramer. "Crazed killers out for blood and cheap thrills leave clues."

"Right."

The outline of a lower leg lay permanently dyed into the worn green carpet beside the overturned recliner. Blood spattered the low plasticized ceiling, and brown scabs trickled down the window. From the trail, the violence appeared to have started near the sofa. Jake surmised that Albert had been sitting there when he realized what was about to happen.

Cramer walked past Jake into the small kitchen, opening and closing drawers and cupboard doors. There had to be *something* Virgil had missed.

Jake lifted Albert's tattered chair back to its feet beneath a dusty, freestanding reading lamp. Gray light filtered in through the windows, but it was so weak that it seemed to soak away into the carpet, and the humidity intensified the musty smell of old blood. Jake ran his fingers along the walls. The killer must have battered Albert like a madman to create the carnage the bloodstains revealed. And the sight of it was far too familiar.

"One thing bothers me," mused Cramer, after he and Jake had inspected the rest of the trailer.

Jake stared at him.

"Where's his guns? Did the killer take them? The report claimed nothing was missing."

Jake shook his head. "Albert didn't like guns. He wasn't a hunter."

"A logger in a backwoods hole-in-the-wall like this who was an antigun nut?"

"He wasn't a nut. He just didn't like them. His father killed himself. Albert would never talk about it."

"His father would be your grandfather?"

"On my mother's side. Albert was my mother and Aunt Claire's brother."

Cramer closed the front door behind them. Jake tried replacing the tape, but it wouldn't stick, and finally he just let it fall.

As he started down the rickety stairs he glanced toward the empty shed where Albert usually kept his bulldozer. His eye was drawn to a frazzled sheet of newspaper clinging to the wall of the tin building, quivering in the breeze above the stacked firewood. It was almost certainly just a bit of trash pasted there by the wind. Virgil or one of his men would have been over the shed already. But the familiar tingling of one of Jake's hunches drew him toward the scrap. He slipped across the gravel drive to the side of the shed and stood on a couple of fallen logs to reach the paper. But before he could pull it from the splinter it was snagged on, Cramer caught his wrist.

"Don't," said Cramer, staring at the paper and shaking his head.

"You don't think . . ." said Jake, eyes glued to the scrap.

"I don't *know*," mumbled Cramer.

On one corner of the torn page, the toe of a shoe sole was clearly visible in a brown stain that looked like blood. In the center of the sole was an equally legible eight-pointed star.

There had been bloody shoe prints on the trailer's carpet, of course. But they were all so smudged that it would have been impossible for the cops to tell what size they were, let alone what kind of shoe.

Jake shook his head, unwilling to believe they'd found something so easily that Virgil had missed. Cramer read his mind.

"Look at it," said Cramer, nodding toward the sheet flapping in the breeze. "If it was windy the day Albert was killed it could have been blown anywhere."

"And then it just floated up here and got caught?" said Jake, frowning in disbelief.

Cramer shrugged. "Stranger things have happened. Sometimes the *Iwas* are watching out for you."

"Try telling that to a judge."

"First we have to find out who did the killing. Then we can worry about a judge."

Cramer gently wedged a piece of firewood against the paper to hold it in place.

"Call your buddy the sheriff."

IRGIL WASN'T PARTICULARLY HAPPY that Jake and Cramer had found evidence he had missed, or that they had been messing around a sealed crime scene. And since Jake had a familial connection to the case they all knew that anything he discovered could be construed as tainted by a good defense attorney, anyway.

"I didn't have anything to go on until you found that print," Virgil finally admitted, as the three of them sat in his cruiser. "But that doesn't change the fact that you shouldn't have crossed that tape, and both of you know that. I also got a report about *you* from Houston. You aren't planning on dragging your problem with these Torrios here, are you?"

Jake frowned. "Cramer and I *can* help."

Virgil eyed Jake as though weighing the idea again.

"No," he said at last. "You made it pretty clear you didn't want any part of local law enforcement a long time ago."

Jake reddened. "So? What are you gonna do now?"

Virgil sighed, resting both hands on the steering wheel and staring out into the drizzle that had just started. "I have no suspects other than the usual town reprobates. But they all have alibis, and even if they didn't, Albert's killing was out of their league. Hell, that kind of brutality should be out of anybody's league. My boys have been to every house in the valley and along the highway. We had dogs all over Albert's land. They didn't find anything to track. How they missed that newspaper, I'll never know. There were no fibers in the carpet or on any of the furniture, and all the blood in the house was Albert's. But that doesn't mean I'm giving up. The paper will go to the crime labs in Augusta. If they can't find anything for us it will be sent to the FBI. Now, you stay out of it."

"Good luck," said Jake as he climbed out of the cruiser. "Nice seeing you again."

Virgil shook his head.

Cramer nudged Jake as they walked back to their car. "He's just mad because you're back one day and you find evidence he couldn't."

Jake shook his head. "It's a lot more than that."

Cramer nodded. "Baggage," he muttered.

They watched as Virgil's cruiser disappeared down the drive, and for a while longer they sat there in silence, both lost in thought.

A S CRAMER PULLED OUT OF ALBERT'S DRIVEWAY a bright red sports car nearly took off their bumper. Jake caught a glimpse of a youthful face—barely high enough to see through the steering wheel—before the car banked away around the corner in a squeal of rubber and a roar of exhaust.

"At last," said Cramer, gunning the car out onto the valley road. "Some excitement!"

"We're not traffic cops," said Jake, tightening his seat belt and pressing the soles of his feet down into the carpet as though *he* had the brakes.

"Yeehaa!" shouted Cramer as the Camry lifted up on two wheels in the turn.

"*I* rented this car," Jake reminded him.

Cramer showed him a wicked, toothy grin before turning his eyes back to the winding road. "Sucks to be you, *mon ami.*"

They almost caught the little guy when he slowed at the valley's mouth to make the turn onto the highway. But then the Mustang shifted gears, and it was all Cramer could to do keep it in sight. The driver of the car must have spotted the state trooper ahead even before Jake did, because he whipped off the highway and onto another farm road, and when Cramer and Jake made the turn Jake hung out the window, flagging his shield at the cop, who nodded and flipped on his lights.

"This is a bad road to speed on," muttered Jake.

Cramer glanced at him, then back to the road. "Something I should know?"

"Something I hope *he* knows," said Jake, nodding toward the disappearing car ahead. "There's all kinds of drop-offs around here, and not many of them have guardrails."

As Jake spoke Cramer burst over a low hill just in time to see the sports car fail to negotiate the next curve. That one *did* have a rail, but it didn't slow the Mustang much, and Jake knew the road well enough to be certain the kid wasn't going to survive the crash.

On the rim of the overlook Cramer ground the Camry to a halt, and Jake ran to the torn guardrail. He could hear the roar of raging water before he got there. Still shaken from the chase, he watched what was left of the car sink beneath the white water in the stream below. The boy's body lay draped over a granite outcrop, forty feet down. Sirens heralded the approach of more than one police cruiser, and Jake noticed that the second car belonged to Virgil. Tires slashed gravel, car doors slammed, but they were faraway sounds that couldn't touch Jake. When Cramer slapped him on the back he barely felt it.

"Nice vacation," said Cramer, glancing up into the thin drizzle.

Jake waved toward the ravine. "A boy's dead down there."

"Car booster. I keep telling you, Caucasians are all criminals. You people just got no values."

A deputy started looping a rope around the rail, preparing to rappel down over the lip of the road. Jake watched, feigning interest.

The deputy's partner checked out both their IDs, nodding to Virgil as he approached the scene.

"Tourists?" the cop asked Jake.

"Family reunion," said Cramer.

The cop stared at him and Jake glared. The black population in Maine was only slightly higher than the number of carrier pigeons.

"What happened?" asked Virgil, trotting up to them.

"The kid blasted by us on the valley road at about a hundred miles an hour," said Jake. "We couldn't catch him."

The deputy glanced over his shoulder at the taut rope where the other cop had disappeared. Virgil nodded for him to go help, and he passed his clipboard to the sheriff.

"Anything else?" asked Virgil, turning back to Jake.

"Not much," said Jake. "The boy was so small I couldn't see the top of his head through the rear window."

"Fill this out, then," said Virgil, handing Jake the clipboard so he could write in his own statement. "Didn't take long for you two to find more trouble."

He shook his head as he walked away to join his deputies.

"You look tired," said Cramer, giving Jake the once-over.

"I'm tired of people dying," said Jake, shielding the clipboard under his arm.

"Neat vacation, huh?" said Cramer.

"Want to go back to Pam's?"

"Nah. I'm going to rent another car, drive out to the coast, and kill myself."

ANDI HAD REPAIRED THE BROKEN PANE by duct-taping cardboard where the glass had been. Pierce sat quietly beneath it, enjoying the smell of wet grass through the open window and the feel of misting rain on his hands.

But suddenly he experienced a sensation that didn't seem to be coming from his nose or his tongue or his skin but actually entering his head somehow, like a vibration that wandered eerily up and down in pitch, somewhere inside his skull. He felt as though he were being sucked right out of his bedroom and blasted somewhere else. He could feel his feet still resting on the floor, but he could also feel the vibration of what he knew instantly was an automobile as it raced through the gears. And there was something else happening, as well. Strange explosions inside his skull like . . . shapes . . . only he sensed them as *patterns* rather than felt them. Weird, undulating, ever-changing . . . differences . . . variated *things* rather than the blank wall of darkness he was accustomed to. Then suddenly the vibration ceased and instead he had an awful feeling of falling. But throughout the entire experience there was fear, as well. A weird and not quitc definable terror that had nothing to do with the eeriness of the encounter or the imagined fall. And for the life of him he could not quite grasp whether it was *he* who was afraid or some other.

He gasped, clenching every muscle in his body, finally letting out a sigh that seemed to last forever, as though his life were slowly exhaling from between his lips.

With his arms still resting shakily on the windowsill, he closed his eyes and concentrated, trying desperately to hold onto the horrible sensation, to understand it. Closing his eyes had no physical effect on Pierce. It just always seemed to help him think.

He kicked off his shoes, and let his socked feet rest on the hardwood floor.

Nothing was moving in the house. His mom was at work, and he was alone.

He ran his wet fingers along his face, tracing the skin up his jawbone to his earlobe. The strange contact had appeared out of nowhere, and then just as abruptly it had been cut off, like flipping the switch on his mother's electric razor.

Buzz.

No buzz.

But he did understand a *little* of what had happened, and the possibility filled him with both wonder and dread. His mother had explained the idea to him. Sound. For only a scalpel moment, for just that sharpest of times, Pierce knew that he had *heard.*

And just maybe, oh, just maybe . . . he had *seen.*

More than anything else in the world, Pierce had always wanted to see and hear. There was only one other wish he could imagine that he would have traded for either if God had suddenly chosen to come down and say *Pierce, you've been a great kid. What would you like for me to do for you today?* But he had never thought that he was any more likely to gain his sight and hearing than he was a real father. Until this moment.

But *what* had he heard? *What* had he seen?

And what had he *felt?*

The terror had gripped him in monster talons, and he knew that it was a fear so deep-rooted it could only come from the knowledge that death was very, very near. And then it had all stopped just like the razor.

Someone was dead.

Wonder, awe, and fear bubbled up so fiercely in his chest he was convinced he could hear *them.* The last thing in the world he wanted to hear or see was people dying. If that was the only channel he was going to get, he thought he could live without it. Would God do something like that? Was it some kind of test, like he'd given to Job?

Pierce's fingers slipped along the soaked windowsill, scratching at the flaking paint.

I don't want to know that people are dying, Lord. Especially not if there's nothing I can do about it. Please don't ask me to know about that.

But in his heart he knew that something like that was happening to him, because he still sensed danger. Not immediate. Not a vibration in the house. No evil odor drifting through his bedroom. Something tantalizing but even more hateful and horrifying in its faint faraway feeling. The thing that had come to watch him was out there somewhere. On the move.

He leaned closer to the open window, and anyone who passed across the backyard would have been certain he was staring up at the mountains. His nostrils flared with each soft inhalation. The sense that something was broken in the valley came over him again, and he knew that whatever it was it was getting worse. And even without eyes or ears, Pierce knew better than anyone that a real storm was blowing in high overhead.

But other than the constant dripping on his hands, the day below was still as death.

JULES WATCHED THE OLD WOMAN as she waddled around the apartment, tossing some kind of clear liquid here, pouring shots of rum into tiny porcelain bowls in front of strange conglomerations of glass and grass and feathers and beads and God knew what all else. He'd heard of places like this, but he'd never expected to be living in one. Unlike Paco, Jules didn't have a superstitious bone in his massive body. But he had to admit that the crazy old bitch made him nervous.

He'd developed the knack of sleeping with one eye open during his days in the pen, and last night he'd gotten up several times, but she was always right where he'd left her, sitting against a thick pile of pillows in her bed. Not once—although he crept to the door silent as any mouse—had she been asleep. She was always wide-eyed, staring at him blankly like a corpse. The first time he'd seen her like that he thought maybe she *was* a corpse. But when he waved a hand in front of her face she blinked at him with those same dead eyes, and ice had slid down his spine.

He watched her now like a rabbit observing a circling hawk. When the phone rang he jerked, knocking over the cold coffee on the counter beside him. Memere stared at him innocently, then glanced at the phone.

"Answer it," he said. "But make it good. Unless you want more of what you got from Jimmy."

Memere placed the receiver on her shoulder. *"Oui?"* she said.

She frowned, holding the phone at arm's length, as though it had a bad odor. "It's for you," she said.

"Yeah?" said Jules, cradling the phone against his neck but not taking his eyes off of Memere. "Oh, boss! Yeah, no problem. She's not going anywhere. You and Paco find the bastards?"

He saw the old woman's ears prick up, but he didn't give a shit. Let her listen. Time for her to get a little nervous.

"You mean you didn't take off till this morning?"

The voice in his ear grew strident.

"How long are you gonna be stuck in D.C.?"

He nodded as the voice on the other end became downright threatening. When Jimmy was irritated it was best to just try to carry on a normal conversation with him as though he weren't calling you a stupid sack of shit.

"I'll take care of it, boss. You don't have to worry. But the old bitch is a little weird. Yeah. Paco was right about that." He listened and laughed. But after he stared at Memere for a moment his voice became more somber. "I don't know if she's putting a spell on me or not . . . No. I was just kidding. I'm okay. I can handle her."

He nodded again and hung up the phone.

"Spells!" cackled Memere. She took a tiny sip from the bottle of rum, then poured some into a cup and disappeared into the altar room again.

Jules followed.

She'd cleaned up all the glass, but one of the dolls had a shattered face, and its base had been crudely pasted back together with clear silicone. The cups Paco had broken had all been replaced, and if any of the feather and cloth contraptions had been wrecked Jules didn't think he'd have been able to tell. The whole fucking assortment was just too over the top for him to figure out.

The old bitch leaned over one of the little altars, lighting a candle and pouring more of the rum. The spirits seemed to be a bunch of drunks. She muttered to herself and peeked over her shoulder at Jules, and her dark eyes and toothy grin sent his creep factor up a couple of notches each time she did. He shook his shoulders and cursed under his breath. No way the old slut was getting to him with a bunch of hoodoo.

"You boss having trouble now, hey?" she said.

Jules shook his head, startled. "No trouble."

"No? Why for he in D.C. and not up to Maine by now?"

"The plane had a problem. They had to divert."

She smiled knowingly. "He gwine have a lot more trouble than you t'ink."

"Bullshit," said Jules. "You telling me you caused the plane to break down?"

Memere shrugged. "I don't cause nuttin'. *Iwas* be causin' whatever they likin'."

"What the fuck are *Iwas*?"

"Spirits!" said Memere, swirling her hands around in the air as though catching some of the invisible deities with her nimble fingers.

Jules sighed loudly. "You're just a crazy old bitch. Nobody can fuck with a jumbo jet, and your mumbo jumbo sure as hell can't do it."

"You don' believe?"

"Do I sound like I believe?"

Memere cocked her head and studied him. "You sure *look* like you believe."

In exasperation he ripped one of the ugly fucking pictures off the wall, ready to hurl it to the floor. Memere stood calmly, waiting. When she shook her head he tensed, wanting to hear the glass shatter, to see the cheap wood frame crumble, to enjoy the fear on her face. But he knew she'd look just as she did now. Like a crazy old woman.

"You didn't do anything!" he said, tossing the picture onto the carpet but not hard enough to break the glass.

"I tole you dat," she said, smirking.

Saturday

JAKE SAT ON PAM'S FRONT PORCH sipping coffee and staring out into the gray half-light. The drizzle draping the valley all night had turned to a steady rain. Tree limbs sagged and dripped, and the incessant, low-level thrumming was as irritating as a fingernail tapping at the back of his neck. He could feel the bloodred stone he'd ripped from José Torrio's throat nestled in his pants pocket. He knew the bauble should have been turned in as evidence. But as far as he was concerned the Torrio situation had gotten personal when José tried to kill him, and for some reason the stone was more than a reminder of the deadly night on the bay. Whenever he touched it he felt a strange tingling along his skin, as though the jewel were electrified. And he couldn't get the idea out of his head that he'd had the same feeling before.

He hadn't slept at all. At first he kept reliving the kid's

death. He went over and over the car chase, trying to find some way he could have saved the boy. Then images of Albert's mangled corpse began to plague him. By dawn he had begun envisioning the old man sitting up on the autopsy table, the Y incision gaping, his face reproachful.

But for what? What was *he* supposed to do?

Something. Anything.

The shoe print was more confusing than enlightening because it pointed to a reasonable explanation for Albert's death. But a nasty little voice kept telling him that all the violence that had happened was related. That the craziness on the beach was old demons coming back to haunt him, no matter how he tried to deny it. But even if there was a connection between Albert's death and the men on the beach, between his mother's murder over twenty years before and the hitchhiker's death, between all of that and a kid who stole a car, what was he supposed to do about it? A feeling of dread cloaked him the way the rain cloaked the valley.

The screen door slammed, and Pam dropped into the chair beside him. When her arm slipped through his he turned toward her, and she smiled. Her touch brought back good memories, ones he wanted to hold on to. He wished that they could be the *only* memories.

"It's good to have you back," she said.

"It's good to be back."

"Really?"

He nodded. "Good and bad. It's kind of hard to explain everything I'm feeling. How was Albert the last few years?"

"He always defended your leaving," she said, scrunching her face. "He said you did what you had to do."

The ache in Jake's heart sank a little deeper.

"Jake, your mother's death was years ago. You were barely ten, and what you saw . . . what you experienced . . . is it any wonder your memories would be all screwed up?

You're a cop. You must know what can happen to a kid's mind in a situation like that. You don't believe that whoever left that shoe print also murdered your mother two decades ago, do you?"

"I don't know," said Jake, shaking his head. "Cramer told you what happened on the beach in Galveston?"

She nodded. "Surely you don't think *that* had anything to do with your family. There must be a reasonable explanation."

"I keep searching for one."

They sat in silence for a long time, before Pam spoke again.

"Virgil called. The kid in the car . . . It was Dary Murphy."

"Not Karen and Bert—"

She nodded. "Their son."

Karen and Bert Murphy lived just up the road. Jake had graduated with Bert. Played football and baseball with him.

"Jesus," he muttered.

She squeezed him tighter. "Virgil said they both took it hard. He ran into Ernie and Ernie went to see them. I'm going to call around and let everyone know so they can help out."

He nodded.

"Cramer seems like a real nice guy," she said, after a moment.

"The best."

"You never had a lot of friends. Even when you were little you were pretty self-contained. But the people who loved you knew you were worth loving."

That pushed the ache to its limits. Jake closed his eyes, fighting back tears, but one slipped down his cheek anyway.

"It's gonna be all right, Jake Crowley," promised Pam, hugging him. "You're home now. And it's gonna be all right."

He wanted to believe that. With all his heart he wanted to believe it. But in the back of his head he heard his mother.

Run away, Jake. Run away.

When the screen door creaked again Jake opened his eyes. Cramer waited until Pam disappeared inside before dropping into the empty chair.

"Nice rainy morning," said Cramer, staring pensively into his cup, stirring the hot brew with his finger.

Jake smiled. "No chicory, right?"

Cramer shrugged. "Wouldn't expect Yankees to understand anything about coffee. You know, I'm still trying to reason a few things out."

Jake nodded, waiting.

"You didn't leave a good-looking woman like Mandi because of a killing that happened when you were a kid. And it wasn't another woman. So it had to be something bad, real bad."

"We Crowleys are cursed," said Jake, grimacing. "Sooner or later someone will tell you all about it."

"Why not you?"

Jake stared into the rain, the old ache suddenly crashing down on him full force. "I loved Mandi," he blurted, shaking his head. "I loved her so much."

"You still do," said Cramer quietly.

"Yeah," he admitted, at last.

"So, if you're not here to rekindle that old flame, and your buddy Virgil is on the case and such a great cop, then why *are* we here? You've paid your respects."

"I guess I came back to see if there really *could* be any link between my mother's death and Albert's murder. Are you satisfied?"

Cramer shrugged. "Not until you tell me how the hell there could be."

Jake sighed. "Because the style of the killings were so much alike."

"Twenty-some-odd years ago a woman gets beaten to

death here, and you think *that* ties them together? You're a better cop than that. Don't bullshit your partner. What is it you're afraid of? What is this Crowley curse?"

"I've been told all my life that it's a myth," said Jake, shaking his head. "I tried to tell myself that. Whether it is or not, I thought that I'd finally escaped it."

"Okay, then, we'll treat it as a myth for now. In that case there's a real, live killer around here. You ready to go back to work?"

"Virgil told us not to."

"And you think I listen to county sheriffs? Didn't seem to bother you at Albert's."

Jake shrugged. "If the chief finds out we're butting into someone else's case up here it'll be our asses."

Cramer stared around at the dull green foliage surrounding the house. "The chief don't scare me."

Jake smirked. "What exactly *does* scare you?"

"Baggage," said Cramer, standing and striding out into the rain.

IERCE PLACED THE CLOTHES HE'D CHOSEN for the day on his dresser and turned to take his mother's hand when she tapped him on the shoulder.

What do you want for breakfast? Mandi signed into his palm.

You home?

Saturday!

Pierce smiled and asked for pancakes.

By the time the first batch of silver dollars were stacked on a platter, Pierce was sitting at the table. Mandi placed a glass of milk near his hand, waited until he found it, and filled his plate with pancakes. He dug in heartily, barely catching the syrup off his chin with a napkin.

"You've got an appetite this morning," she said, smiling.

Even with the defects nature and man had given him, even though he remained small for his thirteen years, he was still perfect in her eyes. But she wondered for the millionth time if there wasn't more she could do for him. Maybe she *had* been wrong to shelter him so closely. He had no friends his own age. He had been forced to grow up in the company of adults. But he never seemed to mind.

She sipped her coffee, glancing out the window into the woods. What depressing weather. If the steady rain kept up, the grass would be over their heads before she could mow it again. She needed something to keep her busy. When she and Pierce had finished their breakfast she tapped his hand, and he offered her his palm again.

Your plans? she signed.

Tinkering. What's up?

I'm going to clean house. Then later I thought we'd drive to Arcos for ice cream.

Pierce smiled and nodded vigorously.

All right, signed Mandi. *Keep yourself occupied for a while.*

Pierce deposited his plate and glass in the sink and turned on the water, but Mandi signed to him.

It's all right. I'll do them.

As he pattered away down the hall she washed the dishes in silence. It was always silent in the house.

She shook her head and laughed at herself. It wasn't any quieter now than it had ever been. If Rich was here right now he'd be cleaning one of his guns or passed out drunk. Rich had never been a husband. He'd been a boarder with a hard-on. What in the world had she been thinking?

She'd been thinking that her son needed a father, and she'd panicked. That was what. Hindsight was twenty-twenty. At least she'd gotten rid of Rich. But she should have gotten the restraining order *before* Pierce got hurt.

Not that it would have helped.

She dried the dishes, put them away, and wiped the table and stove clean. Then she slipped into Pierce's room and stripped his bed while he sat at his work table, his fingers tickling a small circuit board. She straightened his braille magazines, dusted his dresser, and then brought the vacuum from the hall closet. When she turned on the machine Pierce sensed the vibration and turned for just a moment, then went back to work.

She vacuumed the bedroom, then the kitchen, the living room, and the downstairs bath. Then she dragged the heavy canister up into her sleeping loft. Resting the machine against the wall, she turned and looked down the stairs at the wide gray spot on the tired old beige carpet, just as she had a million times in the past, and just as she had each time, she felt the heat surging in her chest.

Ernie had repaired the broken spindle on the rail. Now she had to count them in order to remember which one had dislocated Pierce's shoulder. But the bloodstain was still there at the foot of the stairs. She had knelt for hours, scrubbing until her fingers were raw and tears soaked the carpet along with the soapy water. She'd refused to replace the rug—knowing Pierce couldn't see it—as a reminder to herself that she was her son's only protection. Sometimes she wished that Rich would come back one last time, that she could somehow induce him to stand on the landing, right where she was standing, so she could slip up behind him and give him a good push. Pierce seemed able to forgive, or at least forget.

She never could.

She plugged in the vacuum and went at the floor hard, banging the powerhead against the wall and the old iron bedstead. Finally, when the heat in her breast became unbearable, when she pictured herself standing over Rich's broken corpse, she dropped to her knees beside the bed and flipped off the vacuum. Steepling her fingers, she bowed her head and prayed.

"Dear God, dear sweet Jesus. Please forgive me . . ."

BARBARA STEARN—that was her stage name, her real name was Ethel Mundy, and practically everyone in Crowley knew it—checked her coif in the full-length mirror beside her bed one last time and adjusted her silk blouse. The single strand of pearls she wore this morning was real, but the diamond brooch was as false as her teeth. Her corgi, Oswald, lay like another fat throw pillow on the bed.

"Mama will be back soon, dear," she said, stroking the dog's head before kissing its wet snout. "I have to run some errands. You'll be good, won't you, Sweetums?"

The dog gave her a bored look, and she kissed him again. When she glanced out across her side porch where the lawn sloped down to the creek, thick rain blanketed the air and rivulets of water streamed through the grass, disappearing into the trees. Nasty weather. Not like Hollywood.

The thought of California still saddened her. Her career had been real enough, regardless of what the local hicks wanted to believe. She'd been a star. Well, not a big star, but she was in the movies right enough. And she'd married a producer. She only wished that Stephan had been a little more successful and not so attracted to Las Vegas showgirls and the stock market. When he suffered his fatal heart attack he'd left her barely enough money to fix up her mother's old house and pay the bills. At least she'd never had to work nine to five like the hoi polloi.

She checked her makeup one more time and patted Oswald again, but when she reached the front hall a noise stopped her. The sound was faint, like a radio left on in some other room, but she hardly ever listened to the radio. The music for the past fifty years had been atrocious. The sound seemed to come from behind her, vague and indefinable yet mesmerizing, like the murmuring of a stream. It wafted through the semidarkened library—an old bedroom she had lined with unfinished pine bookcases overflowing with paperback romance novels.

She followed the sound through the library—across a frayed Persian rug that covered most of the hardwood floor—and into the passageway leading to the storage shed. As she entered the near-total gloom, the murmuring took on the darker tone of an overzealous undertaker whispering beside a deathbed. The hairs on the back of her neck stood on end, but she couldn't turn away now. The noise seemed to be slipping under and through the rotten barnwood door that opened into the shed.

It occurred to her then that old Albert had lived alone just like her. Lord knew what the valley was coming to. She rested her shaking hand on the rusted doorknob and wondered if she shouldn't just grab Oswald, climb in the car, and go get the sheriff.

But she wasn't going to be chased out of her own home. Certainly not by a bunch of whispering. It was probably just wind under the eaves.

She twisted the knob and jerked the door aside. The shed

smelled of dust and gasoline. One dirty window let in a minimum of light. Ancient beams were visible through the cracks between the rotten pine floorboards. A rusting rototiller sat dejectedly in the far corner gathering cobwebs, along with an assortment of rakes, hoes, and a lawn mower with one cockeyed wheel. The sound was louder here, audible over the rain pounding on the tin roof, but it certainly wasn't coming from inside.

Barbara didn't trust the old pine floorboards at all. They creaked as she tiptoed toward the far wall, placing her feet where she could see rusty nailheads so that her weight would be directly over the beams below. But when she reached the door, she realized she'd made a mistake. The latch on the outside was bolted. Of course it was. The Murphy boy didn't traipse through the house when he came to mow her lawn.

The murmuring seemed to be coming from just the other side of the door. She placed her head directly against the wood, and the sound reverberated in her ears. She slipped over to the window, rubbing hard at the grit on the glass in the paint-encrusted, six-paneled frame, and peered out into the rain. Something dark and hulking seemed to waft along the edge of the looming forest. She leaned closer to the window, but the sound and the light shifted, and the shadow disappeared. Water pouring off the roof splattered on the sill. She'd have to go back to her bedroom window to see if she could spot the thing in the woods again.

She spun on her heel, took two quick steps, and her leg snapped through a floorboard. Reaching to catch herself, she slammed her hand against the floor, twisting her wrist. Her other hand punched through another floorboard. Her head struck something solid, and she blacked out.

When she came to, her nose ached, and she tasted blood as she breathed noisily through her mouth. She could raise her arms, but they were swollen and terribly painful below the elbow, and she could barely move her fingers. Her legs seemed to be trapped in the floor by jagged splinters of wood. She couldn't feel anything beneath her feet, and she tried to remember what was underneath the shed. Was it a basement down there, or just an old crawl space?

Neither possibility made her particularly happy. If she was suspended over a basement it might be a long way down to the floor, and if it was a dirt crawl space no telling what kinds of creatures were creeping around her legs right now.

The thought that she had surely ruined her stockings bothered her, but she couldn't dwell on it. She had to find a way out. But every time she moved, the floor gave a little more, making terrible noises, as though the beams supporting the boards were ready to crack, as well. She tried wiggling her trapped legs, but when she felt splinters stinging muscle she stopped.

No one but Pam or Ernie ever visited, and if she didn't show up for church tomorrow her absence probably wouldn't be noticed because she was an on-again, off-again Christian anyway. She got no mail other than catalogs, and when they piled up the postmistress would more than likely just assume she'd gone out of town for a few days. By the time anyone got around to checking, she'd be a withered mummy.

She tried kicking again. Pain shot up her thigh and seized her torso, and she gasped for breath. She felt a warm trickling down around her toes, and she wondered how long it took to bleed to death.

ANDI SLIPPED HER RAINCOAT out of the hall closet and carried Pierce's to his room. She was surprised to find him waiting quietly, facing the door. She took his hand.

Ready to go for ice cream?

He nodded distractedly.

Hearing something again?

He shook his head.

What's up then?

Pierce shrugged.

Mandi frowned, studying his face. Pierce was never uncommunicative. Inside his silent, dark world he was always eager to make contact. He seemed all right, just preoccupied.

Let's go, she signed. But he wouldn't release her hand.

Jake is nice, he spelled.

Yes.

He's scared.

Did he tell you that?

She couldn't think of any reason Jake would frighten Pierce with a revelation like that.

The boy shook his head. *I just know.*

What would he be afraid of?

I think he's afraid of what's here.

Mandi had to withdraw her hand for a second. But she still couldn't read his face. When she took his hand again hers was steady once more.

Nothing's here but us, she signed.

Not in our house. There's something in the valley.

Like what?

Pierce turned toward the window and frowned.

He squeezed her hand as though he wanted her to think about every word. *I get scared when you're gone.*

Why didn't you tell me? she signed, feeling the familiar weight of guilt tugging at her heart. When Pierce had turned twelve he'd announced that he was way too old for a babysitter, and Mandi had very reluctantly agreed. She'd had a hard time coming up with the money to begin with, and a good sitter had always been difficult to find. Even so, the transition had been tough for her, knowing Pierce was home alone and unprotected. Very tough. She thought about him all day for weeks, hurrying home during lunch, hugging him when she got there, checking and rechecking the locks. Now she knew her instincts had been right.

I can feel it sometimes, at my window.

Everyone has that feeling. It's just your imagination.

I think it wants something.

She sighed. *What does it want?*

I don't know. I can't figure it out.

That Pierce was special went without saying. His talent for fixing things he couldn't see bordered on the supernatural. That he might sense something she couldn't stretched her credulity, but not to the point of breaking. She had heard enough old wives' tales attributing Jake's mother's death not to Jake's father but to the Crowley curse, and she was sure after Albert's murder people's tongues were wagging again. But *she* didn't believe in any curse, and she didn't want Pierce believing in some unseen presence in the valley, either.

Nothing will ever hurt you as long as I'm around, she promised him again, praying she'd always be able to fulfill her pledge.

CRAMER DROVE UP THE MUDDY DRIVE to Pam and Ernie's neighbors' home, and Jake sighed as he stared at the walk leading to the front porch.

Cramer gave him a questioning look.

"Let's start somewhere else," said Jake.

"Where else?"

"Anywhere," said Jake. "Bert's an old friend. His wife, Karen, is a cousin."

"Like there's anyone around here who isn't. Seemed like everybody at the get-together Thursday night was either a cousin or someone you dumped."

Jake frowned. "It's a small valley."

"Small ain't the half of it. This place is *petit petit*. Look, I don't like having to disturb the Murphys, either, but if we're going to investigate, then let's investigate. We have to talk to everyone in the valley sooner or later, and they're the closest."

"Mister Business," said Jake. "*You* tell them it was us chasing their kid."

"I'm hoping it won't come up. There's no reason the cops had to tell them anyone else was chasing the boy."

Jake knocked on the door as water trickled down the back of his neck. The rain was heavier now, penny-sized drops pattering down from a dark but still-silent sky. Karen Murphy answered the door in her bathrobe. Her face was puffy and red, and her dark-rimmed eyes looked like two burnt holes in a blanket. She had a cigarette in her hand, and the smell of stale tobacco assailed Jake. She stared at the two of them for a moment as though she couldn't quite focus.

"Jake!" she said finally, her voice worn and raspy. "Come on in. You guys are getting soaked."

She herded them over to a wide sofa that had seen better days, adjusting the floor vent so warm air would blow in their direction. Jake introduced Cramer.

"Bert's in the bedroom, lying down. I'll get him," said Karen.

As they watched her amble away down the hall Jake noticed how much her shoulders sagged, and he suddenly wished that Bert would refuse to come out and meet them. But then Bert stumbled into the room, and it was obvious he didn't recognize Jake. Bert had always been thin and short of stature, but the weight of Dary's death seemed to have compressed him even more. He looked as though one more blow might make him disappear altogether.

Jake took his hand and shook it gently. "It's me, Bert. Jake Crowley."

To Jake's amazement, Bert fell into his arms and jerked him close, slapping his back. "Jake! Jeez, I'm so glad to see you."

Jake tried to introduce Cramer, but Bert dragged Jake down onto the sofa, still hugging him like a long-lost brother.

"I can't believe you came back, Jake. I missed you."

"I missed you, too, Bert." Jake gave Karen a look, but she shrugged. No salvation there.

"We didn't know what to do," said Bert. "I mean . . . you know . . . After the deputies came and told us about Dary. We have to go to the funeral home this afternoon and pick out a casket . . ."

Without warning he buried his head in Jake's shirt again and began to sob.

"I know, Bert. I'm sorry."

"They say he stole a car. Dary would never do anything like that."

Jake bit his lip.

"He was so afraid the last couple of days," whispered Karen.

"What was he afraid of?" asked Jake, a sense of doom worming its way between his shoulder blades.

"He kept saying there was something bad here that was going to get us," said Karen, sitting on the edge of a coffee table that was more cigarette burns than veneer. "Bert told him it was just the bogeyman."

"I didn't mean to make fun of him," said Bert, sniffling. "I just didn't want him to be a sissy."

"He wasn't a sissy. He was a fine boy," Karen said between tight lips, as tears rolled down her cheeks. "The funeral is day after tomorrow."

Cramer shook his head. Karen and Bert didn't know anything beyond their own grief.

"I don't know how to say how sorry I am," said Jake, taking Karen's hand.

She nodded. "We know it was you that followed him," she said.

"Cramer and I tried to stop him," muttered Jake, feeling trapped and guilty.

"Was he going real fast?" said Bert.

"We couldn't get around him to head him off."

"Was he running from you?" asked Karen, her eyes boring into Jake like wet lasers.

Jake had no answer. The silence burned.

"He was running from the thing he was afraid of," said Bert, shaking his head. "Mark told the deputy that when Dary jumped in his car he looked like a frightened rabbit."

"Mark?" said Cramer. "You know the owner of the car?"

Bert glanced at Cramer. "Sure. Mark Robbins. Jake knows him. He was there when they brought up Dary and the car. I guess the police called him."

"I didn't realize it was Mark's car," said Jake.

"So you were at home when it happened?" said Cramer.

Bert nodded.

"Were either of you out and about the day Albert was killed?" asked Jake.

"No," said Bert, glancing at Karen. "I've been laid off from the mill, and we haven't been anywhere in a couple of weeks. Why do you ask?"

Jake shook his head. "I just wondered if you had any ideas about Uncle Albert's killing."

Bert seemed to take a minute to wrap his mind around the concept of something other than his boy's death. "No . . . One of Virgil's deputies came by to ask questions. But like I say, we haven't been out of the house. It's terrible about Albert. I'm really sorry for your loss, too, Jake."

"We won't bother you any longer, then," said Jake, nodding and rising.

Bert rose with him, taking Jake's hand in a firm grip. "I know you were trying to do what was right, Jake."

All Jake could do was nod.

But Cramer wasn't done. "What do you think Dary was running from?"

"He was acting real funny the last few days," said Karen,

her voice quavering. "Up till then Dary'd never been afraid of anything. He used to ride his bike up and down the valley. He hiked as far as the old swimming hole by himself. But Bert made him promise never to go in without one of us."

Jake frowned. "Up by my parents' old house?"

Karen nodded. "That's what I mean. Most small boys would have been afraid of that old empty place. You know how it is. The kids around here think it's haunted. But not Dary. Or at least not until the last couple of days."

"What changed?" asked Cramer.

Bert shrugged. "He started having bad dreams. Only he couldn't seem to recall what they were about, just something *bad* was all he'd say. He seemed preoccupied during the day, staring off into the distance a lot. Said he could hear whispering. I thought maybe he was coming down with something, but Karen said he was just daydreaming."

"That's what I thought," said Karen defensively. "Then yesterday while he and Bert were working in the garden, Dary wandered off into the woods."

"I didn't worry at first," said Bert, beginning to sob again. "I thought maybe it was a good thing. If he was out in the woods, then maybe the fear was going away."

"Is Mark home, do you know?" asked Jake.

Bert shook his head. "I wanted to talk to him . . . But I guess he was just getting ready to head back to the coast when Dary . . . the deputy told us Mark caught a ride. He works on a fishing boat out of Gloucester now."

"Thank you for your help," said Jake, nudging Cramer toward the door.

They shook hands all around. Then Jake and Cramer hurried back to the car.

"The hitchhiker and the boy were both up by your old family home," mused Cramer.

"So?" said Jake irritably.

Cramer shrugged. The rain pounded even harder against the windshield, and he shook his head.

"Storms follow you around these days," he said. "And there seems to be a hell of a lot of whispering going on in this valley. Did you by any chance hear people whispering out on the beach?"

"No."

"Did you hear them the night your mother was murdered?"

Jake turned up the road, gripping the wheel between white knuckles.

"Did you?"

"Yes."

Cramer nodded, leaning back and giving Jake another of his evil grins. "The plot thickens."

J IMMY TORRIO WATCHED the New England landscape slide by through the downpour. He was equally at home in a million-dollar boardroom or a Guatemalan jungle. But the rolling hills and big dairy farms of rural Massachusetts felt alien to him. Even the cows huddled together beneath the storm seemed wrong. Instead of the sleek red Herefords or creamy-gray Brahmas with their humped backs that he might see wandering through the oil wells on the outskirts of Houston, there were fat, low-slung, bony-hipped dairy cattle and some kind of black, alien breed with perfect white belts around their midsections that looked as though they'd been painted on by a bunch of college kids pledging a fraternity.

He tried to clear his mind by focusing on his prey. He'd had it in for both Jake and Cramer before Jake murdered his only brother. It had been no secret that the two of them had been investigating him and José for months. And getting rid of one of the nosy cops and the double-dealing hit man at the same time had seemed to Jimmy to be nothing short of an act of genius. Only it hadn't turned out that way. Reever was dead, all right. But somehow Jake Crowley had taken out six of their best men *and* José. And that made things not only business but personal.

The driver of the old Crown Victoria, a man named Smitty, smiled at Jimmy, and Jimmy smiled back, glancing at Paco lolling in the backseat half asleep. Paco snapped to a sitting attention. He knew he was still on Jimmy's shit list. Ever since he'd been sent to Crowley to dig up dirt on Jake, things had gone downhill as far as Jimmy was concerned. Bringing the dunce along had seemed like a good idea back in Houston. At least Paco knew the lay of the land. But he had the ability to irritate Jimmy just by opening his mouth.

The original plan had been for Paco to threaten Jake's uncle, and then Jimmy would let Jake know that *he* knew where Jake's family lived. But the old man had ended up dead, and the fuckhead swore he hadn't had anything to do with the killing. So Jimmy had been forced to move on to plan B. Only plan B had cost José his life. Now Jimmy was formulating plan C as he went along. But he knew that regardless of what he had told the old woman, it was going to entail both Cramer and Jake dying.

"Nice of you to pick us up," said Jimmy, smiling at the driver again.

Smitty nodded, brushing back a lock of wavy black hair. Jimmy figured him for thirty but he might have been younger. The few wrinkles could have been caused by heredity or stress instead of age.

"I told you, it's no problem. I needed to go to Boston next week anyway to meet some potential clients. This way I go early and get that out of the way. And you can never rack up too many points on the other side, eh?"

Jimmy nodded. "Nothing like good karma."

"You got that right. I do need to stop at the next gas station and phone my wife, though." He glanced at the cell phone stuck in the console between them and shook his head. "Figures it would be on the blink at a time like this."

"No way I can talk you into giving us a ride on up to Maine?"

Smitty frowned. He was one of those people who really had trouble saying no, but it was clear that Jimmy was approaching the limits of his hospitality.

"I can't, fellas. Sorry. You can catch a train or bus in Boston."

Jimmy shrugged. "I had to ask. The way our luck's been running both the train and the bus will be out of service."

He gave Smitty one his best grins, and Smitty responded with another of his own, clearly mollified. Jimmy loved that word. Mollified. He was good at mollifying people.

"Tell you what," he said, "I'm up for a big lunch, how about you?"

"Well . . . we're almost there," said Smitty.

"Come on," said Jimmy. "It's on us. Pull over at the next exit, and we'll find a really nice restaurant."

"I am getting hungry," agreed Smitty. "And I hate to pass up a free meal."

The exit turned out to be more of a rest area than a real village. McDonald's competed with Burger King directly across the street, and four gas stations lined the road. But a half mile up the straightaway a sign flashed, and Jimmy pointed at it.

"That might be the best we can do after all," he said.

Smitty shrugged, squinting. "*Way Out Steak House.* I wonder if that's way out in the middle of nowhere or way out of our price league."

"Don't worry about our league," said Jimmy.

"You never told me exactly what it was you did for a living."

"A little of everything. I'm a businessman, but I own several enterprises."

"You need any management seminars, call me. I can book you the best in the business."

"I'm afraid there's not much your consultants could teach me," said Jimmy, looking at the worn upholstery next to his leg, "but I'll take it under consideration."

"You got my card," said Smitty, pulling into the restaurant lot.

The building was long and low slung with faded clapboard siding milled so that the bottom of each board still held rough bark. A wide shaded porch ran the length of the building, shielding the large, dusty windows from another approaching thunderstorm. Smitty parked between a car and a pickup near the front door.

"They probably have a pay phone," he said, nodding to himself.

Jimmy glanced at Paco, who leaped out of the car as though scalded and ran up the front steps. Smitty looked at Jimmy, and Jimmy shrugged.

"Weak bladder," he said.

As Smitty started to follow, Jimmy caught his eye again. "Aren't you going to lock it?"

"Here?" said Smitty, glancing around the lot that held only four other cars.

"You never know."

Smitty turned around, digging for the keys as Jimmy moved around the car beside him. He glanced over his shoulder when Jimmy approached.

"I got it," he said, fumbling the key into the door and turning it to lock the car.

Jimmy nodded, waving toward the restaurant entrance and following Smitty inside. The place smelled of french fries and hamburger, but the couple in the first booth were both eating thick steaks.

"How about there?" said Jimmy, pointing toward a table in the back.

"That looks fine. I'm just gonna find a phone."

"Let's get seated first so Paco can find us."

Smitty frowned but followed Jimmy. A waitress wove through the empty tables, giving them a look that said she wished they'd sat a little closer to her other customers.

"Do you have a pay phone?" asked Smitty.

She gave him a funny look, pointing toward the rest-rooms, and he disappeared.

Jimmy glanced at his watch as the waitress poured three waters. The acid in his stomach was starting to churn. He and José had never been all that close, but, even so, he hadn't allowed himself time to mourn. Grieving was not the Torrio way, anyway. Revenge was in their blood and had been instilled in both brothers from the cradle. When Jimmy was only eight his own father had slit a man's throat in front of his eyes for stealing from the family. Don't cross a Torrio wasn't a motto with Jimmy. It was genetic code. Cramer and Jake Crowley were going to pay dearly for ever messing with his business. For murdering José, Jake Crowley was going to pay doubly dearly.

Smitty stared at the receiver in his hand. The metal cord dangling near his knees had been jerked right out of the phone. You wouldn't think in a small place like this that kind of vandalism would be common, but for all his naive optimism Smitty had come to see the growing sense of desperation in the world. It was something he chose to combat a little at a time, with random acts of kindness, such as picking up two stranded strangers and going out of his way to help them reach their destination. Still, the violation of private property ruined his appetite, and the fact that he could not get in touch with his wife bothered him even more.

He'd never gone so long without phoning Molly before, and he knew she'd worry. This was her first pregnancy, and even with her mom living two doors down, she was still a bundle of nerves. If there was any way at all he could have stayed home with her he would have, but he had to earn a living, and with the increasing availability of Internet training it was becoming harder every day to sell small companies on live seminars. He turned away from the phone but decided to wash his hands before lunch. Entering the restroom, he was struck by the smell of urine. There must be a drain plugged up, and he wondered if this was even a decent restaurant after all.

He splashed water on his hands and pumped soap into them, then lathered his face, as well. He leaned down with his eyes closed and slapped more water on, rubbing the suds away, shaking his hands under the cold flow, reaching blindly for the towel dispenser. A hand caught his wrist, and he jerked. All he could see through soapy eyes was a blurry figure.

"Hey!" he said.

He heard the sound of the towel dispenser ratcheting, and a paper napkin was slapped into his palm as his wrist was released. As he wiped the suds out of his eyes he saw Paco grinning at him.

"Thought you needed help," said Paco.

"Th-thanks," said Smitty.

"Sorry. Did I make you nervous?"

Smitty noticed that—like Jimmy—Paco tended to crowd a man's personal space. He could smell not only Paco's minty aftershave but a touch of feral body odor, as well. And the squinty brown eyes and thin lips made him even more nervous.

"No," he lied. "You just surprised me."

Paco nodded, straightening and peering in the mirror to brush back his wavy black hair.

"Okay," he said, taking Smitty's elbow. "Let's get something to eat."

ANDI RACED BACK THROUGH the pouring rain to the car, carrying two soft-serve vanilla cones. She kicked twice on the door, and Pierce leaned over to open it for her. She made a squishing noise as she dropped into her seat.

"Here you go," she said, slipping the cone into Pierce's waiting hand. He licked greedily as one long drop formed, running down his chin.

"Damn," she said.

She patted his knee to let him know she'd be right back. Then she raced back inside and returned with a pile of paper napkins, only to find that it was too late. Pierce's T-shirt was splotched with ice cream, and he was obliviously crunching the cone. He chomped his way down until the only thing left to do was lick his palms. He had to have an ice cream headache the size of Manhattan. She dampened a napkin and handed it to him, but there was no way to clean up all the mess.

She took his hand and signed. *You jump in the tub when we get home.*

She made certain his seat belt was tight—even though he frowned at her—and still licking her own cone, she backed out and headed home. By the time she'd finished her ice cream she'd dripped some on her pants, as well.

"Guess we'll both need hot baths," she muttered, watching the wipers splash across the windshield.

She drove slowly down Route 26, following the river that had already spilled out of its banks in several places. The Androscoggin was one of those muddy waterways that had been domesticated by a hundred mills over the centuries, but never really tamed. Crowley Creek fed into it, as did a thousand other tributaries, and the river meandered through a hundred villages and towns on its way to the sea. In most places it wasn't deep enough to be navigable except by canoe, but in a flood it could roar across farms and fields like a river four times its size.

Like almost every township in Maine, Crowley had its share of flood zones, but Mandi and Pierce lived on higher ground. At least it was high enough that the house had never been inundated since she'd lived in it. But if the Androscoggin flooded—like it had the year before—the junction of the valley road and Route 26 would be closed, and they'd be trapped.

As she approached the intersection, she couldn't help but glance at the police tape in the trees where the girl's body had been discovered. How could two horrible murders happen in such a peaceful place in such a short time? How could they happen anywhere? In the seat beside her Pierce rode blissfully along, unaware of the scene of horror they were passing.

The gravel in her driveway was turning to muck, and she had to put the Subaru into four-wheel drive to avoid sliding off into the trees. By the time she and Pierce negotiated the ramp into the house they were both soaked to the skin, and he was shivering. She signed for him to strip down while she ran him a hot bath. Then she toweled herself off and donned her bathrobe. She turned off the water and let Pierce know it was ready. He wouldn't take off his briefs if he knew she was in the room, so she headed for the kitchen to make herself a cup of tea.

Inexorably her thoughts were drawn back to Jake, and she bit her lip as the old hurt welled up again. It had felt so good and so bad at the same time to see him with Pierce. She loved Jake as much now as she ever had, and she knew that she always would. But he was carrying around a bunch of hidden demons that she didn't know how to deal with, and she didn't want to expose Pierce to that. He'd suffered enough in his life.

It was probably best not to see Jake anymore while he was here.

BARBARA'S LEGS BURNED LIKE FIRE where they hung down through the busted floor, and an equally impressive heat radiated around her hip. She stared at Oswald, sitting on his chunky haunches in the dark hallway.

"Are you stupid? Or don't you give a shit?" she hissed.

Oswald gave no sign that he understood the question or that he cared to answer.

"Help me!" she shouted.

The dog rose, spun on its heels, and pattered away into the gloom.

"Fucking mutt!"

When she got out of this predicament she was going to trade the little shit in for a poodle. Only getting out didn't look to be happening. Her energy level had drained to almost nothing, and she had stopped struggling when she realized that no matter what she did, movement only made things worse. But if she didn't do something soon, she was going to die.

At least the damned whispering had stopped.

"Come back here, you ratshit dog!" she shouted.

Calm down. Oswald isn't Lassie.

Right. Bring me the crescent wrench, Oswald. No. That's the monkey wrench. The crescent wrench. Good boy.

"Well, I have to get out somehow," she muttered, smirking at the image in spite of her predicament.

The last time she'd moved, the beam beneath her had creaked so loudly she'd frozen in place. It was an ominous sound, half crack, half rotten crunch, and the floor supporting her was so spongy it bounced around like a wooden trampoline.

I'll bet I could fall right through.

Right. And what if it's twenty feet down?

Don't be silly. It's a crawl space. The dirt floor is probably an inch from my toes.

And if it's not?

If it's not I'm going to die here, anyway.

She took a deep breath and kicked, ignoring the stabbing pains that struck her in both thighs. Her feet touched nothing but air, and the cracking noise grew louder as the floor swayed rhythmically up and down. The whole room danced to the beat of the straining beams. The dim gray light filtering through the rain and dust created silver ghosts that swirled before her eyes.

"Screw it," she muttered, shifting her weight and rocking even harder.

She was jumping up and down now, the pain in her thighs flashing up her hips into her back. The floor gave one last rise, and then it felt as though she dropped lightly through a ripped sheet, the beams and floorboards cracking and groaning, lowering her gently to the dirt below. The beams fell away to either side, and she wobbled to her feet. She leaned back against a tilted section of floor, studying her legs. Her hose looked like scarred battle flags, and they were blood-soaked to boot. Her skirt was ripped in numerous places, and one of her shoes was buried somewhere under the debris. Splinters as long as her fingers protruded from her thighs, and she jerked at them, wincing as she withdrew each one, although the real pain in her legs now was the blood returning.

The cellar was deeper than she had imagined. But the wooden crater formed by the busted floor wouldn't allow her to explore it even had she cared to. She glanced up, measuring her chances of making the climb. Other than tiny gaps between the rotten floorboards there was nothing for a handhold, and even if there had been stainless steel handles for her to hang onto, she couldn't imagine that she had the strength to make the climb back out.

Oswald yipped and peeked over the lip of the floor. She managed a smile for him.

"Come back with the crescent wrench?" she asked.

He took a tentative step forward, but hastily withdrew his foot when it slipped on the sharp incline.

"Stay back," said Barbara, waving at him.

He whimpered as though he might disobey.

"What? Are you getting guts in your old age, or are you just hungry?"

He whimpered again, glancing nervously back toward the corridor, and for the first time Barbara noticed that the whispers had returned.

CRAMER STARED AHEAD INTO THE DOWNPOUR. "Memere would tell you there really *are* monsters. Sounds to me like you know that. The boy was running from something when he stole the car."

"Kids get spooked. And it wasn't a monster that killed Albert. You saw that shoe print."

"Which doesn't prove the man who was wearing that shoe did anything but step in some blood and then leave a track on an old newspaper."

"Come on. That's a little thin."

"Just saying."

Jake caught Cramer's eye. "What did you see in the woods?"

Cramer took a minute answering. "I told you, I couldn't get a good look at it because of the shadows."

"Then maybe it was just shadows."

"You don't say that like you really believe it," said Cramer, studying Jake closely. "You said your father never struck your mother before that night."

"That's right."

"What did *you* see on the beach?"

"What's the beach got to do with anything?" said Jake quickly.

"You tell me. I'm just trying to add things up. You don't want to talk to Pam. You get pissed at me for bringing Mandi up. You spend fourteen years away from this place. Then eight men get killed under . . . strange circumstances, and all of a sudden you're on a plane."

Jake sighed. "It was dark and stormy. Torrio's men were trying to kill me. *I* was killing people. It was crazy. I can't tell you what happened while I was in the water."

"So you didn't see anything strange at all?"

"Maybe . . . just a shadow."

Cramer nodded. "And the night your mother was killed?"

"I was ten years old."

"But you said you heard whispers."

"Maybe."

The wipers slapped noisily. Alongside the road water streamed from the balsam limbs.

"This is Barbara's drive," said Jake, sounding relieved.

"The crazy old lady that wants to hump my brains out?" said Cramer.

"Yeah," said Jake.

Cramer frowned. "Why don't we skip Barbara?"

"Why? You scared of a little old lady? You didn't want to skip the Murphys."

"I've met hookers with less hormones," said Cramer.

Barbara's home had a blue metal roof, fading gray stain on the clapboard siding, and blue trim. There were lace curtains in the windows.

"Lovely place. Probably has cats," muttered Cramer.

"Goldfish," said Jake.

"Lynx more likely."

"What do you have against lynx?"

"I don't like the way it's spelled," said Cramer, shielding his head under both hands as he climbed out of the car. They raced up onto the front porch.

Jake rang the bell and peered through the window at a fat little dog dancing in the foyer and barking up a storm.

"Feisty little mongrel," said Cramer. "They're the ones that will bite the shit out of your ankles."

"Nobody home," said Jake, ringing the bell again.

"Duh," said Cramer.

"You are definitely getting me down. You want to go back to Pam's?"

"No. I'm having way too much fun."

"I can always tell when you're enjoying yourself."

"How's that?"

"Your sense of humor improves."

"No kidding. Come on. We got places to be."

"You think that mutt is acting weird?" asked Jake.

The dog was running around in circles and yelping, and running around didn't look to be an everyday activity for the fat mutt. Jake stared at the dog, waiting for it to calm down, but it gave no sign of slowing. After a couple of minutes he began to wonder if the dog wasn't going to give itself a heart attack.

He knocked on the door this time and shouted. "Barbara? Is anybody home?" He shrugged at Cramer. "Check the garage."

"Sure," muttered Cramer, heading down the steps into the rain. "I jus' paddle de pirogue over dere."

Jake paced the length of the front porch, peeking in every window. The dog followed him from the foyer to the dining room, never stopping its whirling dervish imitation or its high-pitched yaps.

Cramer stomped back up onto the porch, shaking off like a wet hound. "Her old clunker's in the garage."

"That's what I was afraid of," said Jake. "Want to break in?"

"With that guard dog?" said Cramer.

"Look for an open window," said Jake.

Cramer turned, stepped back to the front door, and opened it. The dog ran into the foyer and stood like a statue, waiting.

"*You* told me no one locks their doors around here," said Cramer.

"I forgot," said Jake, sticking his head in the door and shouting for Barbara again as Cramer slipped past him into the house.

Jake followed. The place smelled of lavender, and disinfectant, and maybe garlic. Jake wrinkled his nose, and Cramer laughed. As they followed the dog down the hall, Jake stopped at an antique side table, staring at the gilded oil lamp atop it. He ran his fingers along the ornate base, staring at the bas-relief floral shapes.

"What?" said Cramer.

Jake shook his head. "There was a lamp just like this in our house. Outside my parents' room."

"You think the old lady stole it?"

Jake shrugged. "The house has been sitting up there empty a long time."

"Maybe Pam gave it to her."

"Maybe."

"What was that?" said Cramer.

"I didn't hear anything."

"I thought I heard somebody whispering," said Cramer.

Jake listened to the rain on the roof. There *did* seem to be another sound beneath that one. An undercurrent. A hissing. But as they entered the house the sound seemed to die away.

The dog gave them a haughty look and took off into the next room. Cramer and Jake followed, hurrying through the cluttered parlor. Jake pointed as the dog's tail disappeared into the dark passageway ahead. When they emerged in a small shed, Cramer immediately sidestepped, grabbing Jake before he could fall head over heels into the hole.

The old woman lay facedown on the sloping floorboards below. Jake noticed a bald spot on the top of her head, and he wondered if Barbara was aware of it.

Cramer sighed. "We have to get down there."

"How the hell are you gonna do that?" asked Jake, surveying the wreckage. Barbara's plummet to the lower level had turned the shed floor into a funnel. There was barely enough room on the planking and joists along the perimeter for the dog to work its way around to the far side. The mutt stared down at the old woman as though trying to decide whether to make the leap to the dirt below.

"Slide down, I guess," said Cramer.

"You'll break your neck."

"You see another way?"

Jake reluctantly shook his head. Cramer bared his teeth and locked viselike fingers on a bare stud. Then he eased himself into the hole. When his feet were halfway down he released his grip and crashed to the bottom.

"Careful," said Jake, grimacing as Cramer caught a jagged-looking splinter in his hand.

"Right," said Cramer, tugging the sliver out with his teeth, spitting it into the dirt. As he reached for Barbara's shoulder, she rolled over as though she were a mummy that had suddenly been revived. Cramer jerked.

"Come to save me?" she asked weakly.

"Something like that," said Cramer. "Did you break anything?"

She glared at him. "My floor." She stretched, and a wide grimace twisted her face. "Maybe my shoulder."

"Nothing else hurt? No neck injuries?"

"I don't think so."

"You should lie still until the paramedics get here."

"Like hell," she said, rising shakily to her feet. "I'm not having those morons tracking mud all over my house and trying to give me CPR. Now get me out of here."

Cramer steadied her as she wobbled like a porcelain doll in his hands. When she reached up to wrap her arms around his neck and smiled, Cramer looked to Jake for help, but Jake was busy stifling a grin of his own.

"You're so strong," said Barbara.

"Yes, ma'am."

"I think if I hold onto the wall here, I can reach down and give you a hand," said Jake.

"Okay," said Cramer uncertainly. "Come on in."

Jake slipped his fingers around the doorjamb. Then he slid carefully down toward Cramer. Cramer placed one hand under Barbara's arm and reached for Jake with the other. It took two lunges for them to connect. For just an instant the outcome seemed in doubt as Jake's shoes lost their grip on the slope, but Cramer had enough momentum to gain the top. Jake leaned back and pulled them toward the door.

The three of them huddled on the lip of the hole for a moment, catching their breath. Oswald pattered his way around to greet each of them with a yap and a sniff at their feet.

"We ought to get her to the hospital," said Jake.

"Took a genius to figure that out," said Barbara, slipping out of Cramer's embrace and dusting herself off. But she made a face when she bent to straighten what was left of her skirt, and her eyes glazed when she stood back up. Cramer caught her by the shoulders.

"I heard voices," she whispered. "I came in here to find out who it was."

"Voices?" said Cramer and Jake at the same time.

"I thought I heard whispers. Then this old floor just gave out on me. Damn near killed me."

"No one whispering around here now," said Cramer, a little too jovially. "Let's *fais-do-do* into the house, and everybody can lick their wounds."

He strode into the dark passageway with his arm wrapped around Barbara's waist, Jake taking up the rear. As the gloom surrounded Jake he was suddenly certain he was being watched. Goose bumps crawled up the back of his neck, and cold sweat broke out on both palms.

Their passage seemed to take forever. The sense of being watched became one of being *probed*, as though some unseen presence were testing him in some way, searching through his brain like invisible fingers flipping through a Rolodex. By the time they exited the narrow corridor into the little book-lined parlor, Jake was ready to scream. He shifted past Barbara, edging to one side of the door, staring back down the long tube of darkness.

"What's up?" whispered Cramer, sliding in beside Jake, instinctively keeping his bulk out of the line of the open doorway.

Jake shook his head. "Just a hunch."

"I like your hunches. What's the matter?"

"I felt like something was in there with us."

Cramer leaned around Jake to peer down the hallway. "No room for anybody else in there."

"I guess it was nothing."

"Want to check it out?"

More sweat broke out on Jake's palms. "No," he said, nibbling his lip. "It was just nerves."

Cramer frowned. "We ought to get the old lady to the doctor, then."

"Right," said Jake.

But as they led Barbara down off the front porch and eased her into the backseat of the car, Jake could have sworn he heard the vaguest of whispers. He glanced at Cramer, who was staring into the woods.

"Ready?" said Jake.

Cramer started the car and jerked it into gear without comment. But all the way down the drive Jake had the nasty feeling they were still being watched.

CAN'T BELIEVE IT," said Smitty, shaking his head as he wove between two trucks flying down the interstate. "The phone at the restaurant was totally vandalized. What kind of people would do something like that?"

Jimmy shook his head, too. "Criminals. Lowlifes. We'll find you a phone, don't you worry."

"I should have stopped in Providence," said Smitty, craning his neck to stare up into the bean-size drops of rain. The day was thick and gray, the clouds barely holding back the flood that hung threateningly over their heads. "She worries."

"How many months?" asked Jimmy.

"Five. But she's really big already, and this is our first. I should stay home, but how am I going to support us if I don't get out and press the actual flesh? She kind of understands. And she kind of doesn't."

"Five months isn't bad," said Jimmy. "She's got plenty of time."

"You got kids?"

Jimmy laughed. "Not that I know of. But I got lots of cousins. And they're pregnant all the time."

Smitty sighed. "I'm sure you're right. But like I say, it's our first. I really should be there with her. At least in the same town, I guess."

"A man's gotta do what a man's gotta do," muttered Paco.

"You sound like you're really scrambling for money," said Jimmy.

Smitty laughed. "Who isn't?"

"Me," said Jimmy.

Smitty gave him a questioning look. "Your companies do really well, then?"

Jimmy nodded. "Extremely."

Smitty sighed. "Most of the companies we deal with are struggling. I guess I shouldn't complain. That's what pays my bills. But I'm glad someone's making it in today's economy."

"What economy?" said Jimmy, laughing.

"You got that right," said Smitty.

"So, how about I *pay* you a lot of money to drive us to Maine?"

Smitty frowned. "How much money?"

"How much you want?"

"No, seriously."

"I am serious."

Smitty computed. "A thousand dollars."

"Are you for real?"

"Seven-fifty?"

"Five thousand."

Smitty choked and Jimmy slapped him on the back.

"One condition," said Jimmy.

"What?" asked Smitty suspiciously.

"No phone calls until we split up. And I'd appreciate it if you didn't tell anyone else you'd seen us."

"I knew it," said Smitty. "This is something illegal, isn't it?"

"No."

"It has to be."

"Only mildly," Jimmy said.

"How mildly?"

"You won't be involved, and no one is getting hurt, and there are no drugs. How's that?"

Smitty made a face. "So what kind of crime is it that no one get's hurt, and doesn't involve drugs? I really don't want to be a part of this, guys. I'm sorry."

"Hey!" said Jimmy, holding up both hands. "I'm telling the truth. But there's no hard feelings."

Smitty took a long time considering. When he spoke his voice was resolute.

"I don't want to be involved in this, whatever *this* is. I'm sorry. I made a mistake picking you guys up."

Jimmy spread both hands. "You can drop us off when we stop for gas again, and you'll have seen the last of us. I really would appreciate it if you wouldn't mention you'd seen us, though. All right? I mean, have I done you any harm?"

"You aren't like escaped criminals or something, are you?"

Jimmy laughed again, fingering the lapel on his suit. "Does this speak to you of escaped criminal? I don't think so."

Smitty shook his head, jumping a little when a bolt of lightning flashed across the sky followed quickly by thunder. "Corporate crime. That's what you're talking about, right?"

"Right," said Jimmy. "No one gets hurt."

"What about the investors, the little guys?"

"Well," admitted Jimmy. "I guess you're right. Someone always gets hurt a little."

"When you're little already it doesn't take much to hurt you pretty bad."

"Sounds like you're talking from experience."

"I lost some retirement to a company that folded. The accountant had been embezzling."

"That's too bad. Guess you could really use that five thousand."

"Not that bad," said Smitty, taking the next exit.

A sudden gust of wind pummeled the car as Smitty spotted the lights of a gas station ahead and whipped into the lot. "I have to, fellas. This just isn't my kinda deal. I'm sorry."

Jimmy shrugged, waving toward the side of the building. "No hard feelings. But I need to go to the bathroom, and I'm sure Paco does, too."

Smitty nodded, pulling up to the white metal doors. Rain poured down the white stucco sides of the station, glistening.

"You're probably going to have to go inside to get a key, anyway," he said.

"That's all right," said Jimmy, shoving a pistol barrel up under Smitty's arm and pulling the trigger twice. "I don't have to go anymore."

Paco raced around to the driver's side while Jimmy slipped out of the car and into the backseat. Paco shouldered Smitty's corpse over against the passenger side door.

"Why didn't we just rent another car?" he asked nervously.

Jimmy frowned. "We already *had* this one."

He didn't like having to explain himself, especially when he wasn't sure why he'd just murdered Smitty. It had been an impulse, and Jimmy didn't often act on those. Perhaps it was as simple as him transferring some of his hatred for Jake Crowley and his partner to Smitty. Whatever. They had a car now. They didn't need another.

"What now, boss?" said Paco.

"We're here. Fill her up."

Paco pulled the car under the roofed pump island, as

Jimmy leaned across the seat and adjusted Smitty to look as though he were sleeping. When the tank was full Paco hurried inside to pay cash, then slipped behind the wheel again, easing back out into the storm and heading for the highway.

"Now let's quit fucking around and get to Crowley," said Jimmy.

"How come you spent all that time telling him we were some kind of corporate criminals, boss? All that stuff about no one getting hurt. Why bother making up a bullshit story? Why all the talking?"

"I wasn't talking," said Jimmy, shaking his head and sinking back into the seat. "I was mollifying."

JULES SLAMMED THE RECEIVER of the phone back into the cradle so hard he had to check to make sure he hadn't shattered it. The message kept telling him the boss was out of his cell phone carrier area. Jules really needed to know how things were going. But mostly he wanted to have the boss tell him that the job was finished, and now the old woman was expendable. Because she was seriously creeping him out.

She didn't seem to have anything in her wardrobe but clothes made out of sheets, and she padded around the apartment on rubber flip-flops that sounded like a giant frog smacking its lips. She always seemed to be watching him, and constantly muttering in that indecipherable Cajun bullshit. When he shouted at her to stop, she just laughed.

Now she was mixing up some kind of evil-looking concoction in the kitchen, smashing it together in a stone pot and nodding to herself like some old witch, which was exactly what Jules thought she was. She tossed in herbs from crockery beneath the cupboards and juices stored in murky green bottles in the fridge and kept mashing with the stone pestle, grinning to herself and muttering.

"What the hell is that?" he finally blurted. "What are you doing?"

She shrugged, leaning the pot so he could see the nasty-looking green goop. "Making de guacamole. You want some?"

He squinted. It might have been guacamole. Or it might be some kind of poisonous paste. He shook his head, and she shrugged again.

"Can't get you boss?" she said, nodding toward the phone.

"He's busy."

She laughed. "Gonna be heap busy. You bet."

"You are so full of shit, old woman. You don't scare me."

"Scare you? Big fella like yourself? Howso little old woman like me gonna scare man like you?"

"You better believe it."

"You like snakes?"

"What?"

She nodded toward the living room carpet. Jules glanced over his shoulder and froze. The biggest rattlesnake he'd ever seen was winding its way toward him. His breath froze in his lungs, his stomach tightened like a giant rubber band, and his mouth went dry all in that instant. With a quivering hand he reached under his left arm and tried to pull his pistol out of its holster. But it seemed to be stuck. He whispered a curse as the snake wove slowly around the post in the center of the room, never taking its gleaming eyes off Jules. Finally the snap broke free, and he jerked the gun out, trying to get a bead on the snake.

"You gonna shoot dat in here? Make one hell of a noise. Probably sure de cops come."

He glanced at the old woman, wanting to slap the grin away. Instead he shoved the gun into her face. "Do something!"

Her smile never broke. "Sure. I do something. Big man like you can't do something. No."

She walked casually around the counter and right up to the snake, who eyed her curiously but didn't show any sign of striking. She reached out and, crooning in that damned Cajun lingo again, gently stroked the wide back of the scaly head as though the poisonous reptile were a house cat. Then she took it by the throat, and as it wrapped sinuously around her arm she disappeared into the other room. When she returned the snake was gone.

"Don't let that thing out again if you know what's good for you," said Jules.

Memere dipped a chip in the bowl and stared at the guacamole on the end for a long moment. "Snakes get de bad rap on account of de Bible. But serpents be de guardians of good. Dey see ever' t'ing wit dem eyes. I'm gonna set a snake on you boss," she said thoughtfully. "Gonna set a serpent against him dat don' know how to stop."

Sweat broke out on Jules's forehead, and he wiped it away with his sleeve. "You fucked with the wrong man, you old bitch. You and that grandson of yours. Jimmy Torrio is nobody to screw with. When Jimmy's done with Jake Crowley and that boy of yours, I'm personally gonna blow your brains out."

"Why for you wait, then, hunh?" teased Memere, smacking another chip between toothless gums.

"Your time's coming," said Jules, shoving the pistol back into his holster.

WHEN MANDI HEARD PIERCE splashing around in the tub she rushed to the door. He was halfway out of the bath, climbing the tile wall, slapping the shower curtain aside. His face was deathly pale when she grabbed him by the shoulders. He tried to shove her away, and she shook him. But even as his body went limp his fingers raced beneath her palms.

It's here!

There's nothing here but us.

Pierce nodded violently, his chin beating against his chest like a drumstick.

She signed into his palm. *There's nothing here!*

He scratched along the wall, jerking a towel from the rod and wrapping himself in it. His face was a mask of fear, embarrassment, and hurt. Mandi stared at him with a sinking heart. He knew she didn't believe him, and she was the only one he had to trust.

"There's nothing here," she whispered. "Nothing."

When he finally calmed a little she eased him onto the

edge of the tub and dried him off. Then she handed him his robe, and he let her put his slippers on his feet.

"There's nothing here," she muttered again, staring around the bright, windowless bathroom. But Pierce seemed so sure, so terrified. She hugged him, and he hugged back hard. She stroked his face, and he shrugged.

Finally she took his hand and signed. *I'm right here. Always. Nothing is going to hurt you again. I won't let it.*

He pulled her close, and she stroked his back, feeling the familiar burn growing within her, her hatred of Rich welling in her throat. She placed Pierce's hand on the door, and he took over from there, finding his way down the hall and into his room without bumping into the wall once.

Nothing but door. That was what Pierce said when he made it through one of them without touching the jamb. She finally managed to settle in the living room with a paperback she'd been trying to finish for weeks. But every time she looked down at the words on the page they blurred and twisted, and she finally realized that she'd been reading the same sentence over and over.

Albert's home lay a hundred yards through the trees beyond her window. On the other side of the house it was probably three times that far through the woods to the highway. To the spot where the girl had been murdered. She was still staring out into the storm when a distant streak of lightning lit the sky, and she wondered if she'd allowed her stupid pride to place Pierce in danger. Since Rich had left she hadn't wanted a gun in the house, and even if she had one, she wasn't sure she'd be able to use it on a human being.

She glanced at the phone and then out at the car.

Not yet. She wasn't ready to freak out yet.

But what if a stranger knocked on the door right now? What would she do? The thought of something terrible happening to her, and Pierce being alone and helpless in the house, not knowing . . .

What was stopping her from snatching Pierce and climbing in the car? Was it Jake?

She had to admit that was part of it. Maybe a big part. The last thing she wanted was for him to think she couldn't take care of herself or her son.

But her fear was beginning to overcome her pride.

Pierce lightly traced his fingertips across the rough cardboard covering the window. It was damp and cool, and now and then he could feel the wind brush it. An almost imperceptible vibration ran through the floor and then was gone, and he assumed it had just thundered.

But the sense of dark presence that had assaulted him in the bathroom was still out there, as well. Breathing slowly, opening himself to the night outside, he could sense it moving. It seemed almost as if it were lost. Or hunting for something.

Or someone.

The thought sent a quiver up his spine.

He didn't know how he could stop it if it returned. But he had to. Because his mother would never even know that it was here until it was too late. The most he could think of to do was keep a watch on it, try to tell when it was coming nearer. Maybe, just maybe he could get his mom to run away. Maybe they could get in the car and go.

Only he knew she'd never believe him until it was too late. A tear of frustration trickled down his cheek, and he wiped it away on his pajama sleeve.

He wished he wasn't deaf and blind. Wished he wasn't crippled.

He wished he had a father who was big and strong and brave.

JAKE WONDERED WHERE THE DAY HAD GONE. It seemed as though he and Cramer had hardly gotten started, and already the storm made late afternoon seem like early evening. The infrequent lightning bursts only accentuated the growing darkness. As he rounded the bend in Pam's driveway he had to pull around Virgil's cruiser in order to park beside Ernie's truck. He held Barbara's elbow as Cramer assisted her up onto the porch. When Pam opened the front door Oswald raced through her legs and began exploring the house. Pam guided the old woman to a chair in the living room, and Virgil rose from the sofa to shake hands all around.

"What happened?" asked Virgil, staring at the bandages on the old woman's arms, legs, and forehead.

"She had an accident at her house," said Jake. "Cramer and I took her to the hospital. But she wouldn't stay."

"How are you?" Virgil asked Barbara.

"How do I look?" she groused.

Virgil gave her a forced smile, then turned back to Jake. "What were you doing up at Barb's place?"

Jake shrugged.

"Pam tells me you're *helping* me out," said Virgil pointedly.

"Cramer and I went for a drive."

"Don't get involved."

"I think I am involved."

Virgil frowned thoughtfully. "Because of Albert? Or because of what happened years ago?"

Jake hesitated. "Maybe both."

"Jake," said Virgil. "I told you way back then that what you *thought* you heard and saw . . . I thought you got over all that. Is it starting to come back?"

"I'm not crazy."

"I didn't say you were crazy. I just don't want you taking off on a tangent here and going and frightening a lot of people."

"I'm not going off on any tangent."

"Then let me do my job."

"I'm not stopping you."

"If either of you get in my way I'll charge you with obstructing an investigation. I don't want to do that."

"Is that what you stopped by for, to warn Cramer and me off again?"

"Pam," said Virgil, "don't you think Barb would be more comfortable in her own room?"

Pam nodded. "There's a small back room down the hall."

"A back room?" said Barbara, raising her eyebrows.

"I'm afraid it's all we have right now since Jake and Cramer are using the spare bedrooms."

"It's just that Oswald and I don't like to be cramped. Of course I don't want to be a bother."

"Maybe you'd rather I put the roll-away in the living room," said Pam.

"A roll-away?"

Cramer cleared his throat. "I don't mind a roll-away." He stared at Jake, but Jake just smiled. "I'll bunk in with Jake."

Jake glared at him.

"Are you sure?" said Pam.

"No problem," said Cramer. "I was starting to get too comfortable."

"Good," said Barbara, turning to Cramer. "Would you show Oswald where the bedroom is so he can get acclimated?"

Cramer looked as though he were about to explode. "Sure," he said, striding between them like Moses parting the Red Sea. "Come along, Oswald," he said, waving his hand majestically at the dog, who trailed along disdainfully.

"Where's Ernie?" Jake asked Mandi.

She frowned. "In the woods, hunting for moose poops."

"What?" said Jake.

"I thought you knew," said Pam, laughing. "We take the poops, dry them, lacquer them, and add gold or silver jewelry. Ernie sells them to a bunch of tourist shops. They go like hotcakes."

"You're in the backwoods again now, son," said Virgil, chuckling at Jake's look of disbelief. "I can't believe he went out on a day like today, though."

Pam shook her head. "I told him not to. But you know Ernie. It doesn't matter if the Deluge comes. He's still gonna do what Ernie does. He should be home any minute."

Virgil nodded. "Good thing he's got God on his side. What really happened to Barb, Jake?"

"She fell through the floor of her shed," said Jake. "Dr. Burton says she has a minute fracture on her collarbone and some pulled muscles. Other than that and a lot of splinters she survived remarkably well, considering the fall and her age."

He gave the sheriff an abridged version of what had taken place—including the fact that Barbara had thought she heard whispering voices.

"Something evil has come into my home," announced Barbara.

Jake frowned. "Doc Burton gave her some pretty good pain pills. Barb, you really shouldn't be up."

"Pam," said Virgil. "Why don't you go ahead and show Barbara her room?"

"All right, Virg," said Pam, giving him a look but chatting with Barbara as she nudged the old woman down the hall.

"It was probably just the wind, Jake," said Virgil.

"Cramer and I heard it, too."

"Did you see anything?"

Jake shook his head.

"Jake, your mother's death was over twenty years ago. You yourself found the footprint at Albert's. No curse caused that. And your father . . ."

Jake's eyes told Virgil he'd gone far enough.

"I know what you told me, Jake. So as far as I'm concerned the case is closed. He's dead, either way. That part of your life is over. Let it lie."

"I wish I could."

"Just leave it alone. Let me investigate Albert's and the girl's killings, and I promise to keep you updated."

"We're good detectives, Virg," said Jake.

Virgil sighed. "So? Other than your interesting day at Barb's place, did you boys find out anything new today?"

"Virg, our asking a few questions isn't impinging on your authority. Lighten up."

"Well, I don't think anyone's going to be doing any more investigating in Crowley for a few days, anyway. The river's rising, and if it keeps raining the way it has been the crossing will be closed any time now. You guys just hunker down and try staying out of trouble for a while."

"Right," said Jake, walking him to the door.

Lightning burst through the sky over the mountains and thunder rumbled down the valley.

"Leave it alone, Jake," said Virgil, as he hurried down the steps and ran to the cruiser.

RICH MORIN PULLED THE HOOD UP on a raincoat that was more duct tape than plastic and headed across the lawn—which was more mud than grass—toward the woodshed.

It was fucking ridiculous having to light a fire in early June, but dampness invaded the old trailer through a million invisible openings, chilling the house. And Carly had sat on her butt on the sofa and whined until he couldn't take it anymore. Sometimes he wanted to pick her up by her ratty blond hair and sling her around like a keychain, but she'd been right for a change. He was cold, too. He just didn't want to admit it.

So he stumbled down the rotting wooden steps into the yard. Slimy mud stuck to his boots, and he kicked his way through a puddle to clean them. Like that would do a fucking lot of good. He had to go back the same way.

Good. Track it all over the goddamned living room carpet. Give her something to do besides her fucking nails.

Bitch must have the prettiest nails on any wide-assed whore this side of Vegas.

Thinking of Carly's fat butt reminded him of Mandi's cute little ass, and he rubbed his crotch. But that bit of fluff had been closed to him for years. The last time he'd had any of it he'd had to wrestle her to the ground, and she'd sworn she'd have him arrested if he came around again. For almost eight years now—he'd had it in the back of his mind that one day he was going to do her again, restraining order or no. In fact, the more he thought about it, the more the idea of taking a drive down to see the bitch sounded like a good idea.

He trotted under the roof of the woodshed and tossed his hood back. Water ran from his greasy black hair down the nape of his neck as he stared back toward the trailer, but it was barely visible. Rain struck the ground so hard the drops seemed to be bouncing. It sounded as though he were inside a giant spigot.

He ambled to the far end of the shed, peeking around the corner, but he couldn't see any farther in that direction than he could back toward the house. With the rain coming down the way it was, the creek could overflow any minute, and the trailer had been washed out once before. Even if it didn't get high enough to actually swamp the house, there'd still be broken limbs and shit everywhere, not to mention mud and muck to clean up.

He lifted a couple of small pieces of split wood from the top of the pile and started searching for a larger one to make a good armload. A rustling noise caught his attention, but when the sound didn't return he started picking through the top of the pile again. Then another rustling sounded. What the fuck was that, a rat? He set the first two pieces of wood on the pile and stood back, up against the rain.

Where're you at, you little fuck?

Squatting, hands on his knees, he peered in between the

spaces in the stacked wood. It was then that another noise caught his attention. He turned slowly, but it seemed to come from all directions at once. It sounded like someone whispering.

He stood up again and closed his eyes. The sound seemed closer when he did that, almost as if a woman was talking sexy to him, breathing right into his face. He opened his eyes and sucked in his breath. He could imagine her warm breath, smell the musky odor of her body, hear her husky voice murmuring in his ear.

But there was nothing in front of him but the rain.

"Too many fucking beers last night," he muttered.

But he knew he'd heard the sound once before. And the memory sent a chill up his spine. He'd been up at the old Crowley house at the head of the valley snitching some furniture. Carly had told him the place was still full of stuff even though none of the Crowleys had lived there since Jake was a kid. Rich hadn't believed her at first. What kind of idiots would leave furniture and appliances and stuff in a house no one used? But she'd been right. He'd loaded a couple of dining room chairs on the back of his truck and was going back in for more when the same weird whispering noise came out of nowhere.

That day had been cloudy and cool, and at first he'd thought he was just hearing the wind through the trees. But the more he listened the more the sound seemed to be circling the house. Like a warning. He forgot the rest of the furniture and headed for the truck, racing back down the valley road like a scorched cat. And he'd never gotten up the nerve to go back. He told Carly he didn't like stealing. She'd looked at him like he had two heads and just stuck the chairs beside the kitchen table. He'd slapped the shit out her for good measure.

He leaned against the stacked cordwood. His fingers

roved over the splintery ends as the murmuring filled his ears, drowning out the rain until it seemed as though the sound was right under the canopy of the shed with him. Suddenly the noise took on a painful bass tone, and Rich covered his ears. He stared through the rain toward the trailer, considering a quick dash, but the sound was hypnotic, weakening his knees.

As the volume kicked up another decibel, he broke out of his trance. He ran four steps out into the downpour, then stopped as though he'd hit a brick wall. The sound surrounded him like a giant hand, crushing him, pressing so hard on his chest he could barely breathe. The pounding noise seemed to want to get *into* him. He could feel it beating down inside his ears, trying to pump itself into his gasping mouth, up his dilated nostrils. It was as though something was inspecting him, poking and prodding. He lurched toward the house, but he wasn't sure he was going in the right direction anymore.

The rain was a slick wall, pummeling the mud around his feet in counterpoint to the heavy bass beat. Suddenly he became aware of something slinking around *inside* the wet gray sheets. Something huge. It moved like a cross between a giant snake and a cat, almost as if it was a part of the falling water, and Rich made no mistake about its intentions. He'd been a hunter all his life. The thing was stalking him.

"Get back!" he screamed.

He could barely hear his own voice over the roar of the rain and the crazy, airy sounds that were as loud as thunder. He waved both hands in front of him, warding off the half-seen thing as it circled closer. It seemed to be all water, and darkness, and snippets of even blacker shadows.

"Stay away!" he screamed at the top of his lungs.

He caught a glimpse of the trailer as he spun, and he backed in that direction. But just as he was about to make a break for the house the giant shadow cut him off again, and his heart stopped. He tensed, sensing the attack, trying to decide if the thing had any vital points that he could kick or poke, but he couldn't even tell for sure if it had a head.

He remained frozen for what seemed an eternity, the rain drenching him to the bone, the sound tattooing his eardrums so he was sure he'd never get it out of his head. Then the shadow started circling again. Closer. Close enough that Rich could make out the shape of something that might be a head after all.

Was it a bear? No. More like a dog. Only not like a dog. Almost like a snake.

As the thing moved from the space between Rich and the trailer, he found his feet again and ran like he hadn't run since his senior year in high school. He stumbled up the stoop, nearly ripping the cheap metal door off its hinges as he lurched into the living room and slammed the door behind him.

Carly stared at him from the couch, the nail brush still dripping onto the middle finger of her left hand. "What the fuck is the matter with you?"

Rich could barely catch his breath. He was afraid he was going to have a heart attack.

"You didn't bring in any goddamned wood," said Carly, continuing her nail painting.

"There's something . . . something out there," sputtered Rich, ripping his shotgun from the pegs over the door. He checked the chamber, then clicked off the safety. "Didn't you hear anything?"

Carly slowed but didn't stop her manicure. "Hear what?"

"I don't know," said Rich, pulling aside the ratty drapes on the window. The dust on the sill was thick enough to write his name in, and he frowned. "Something big. Real big."

"A bear?"

He whirled on her, and she stiffened.

"Did I say it was a fucking bear?" he shouted.

"What is it then?" she said in her best childlike voice.

"I don't know," he said, softening a little. "Go back to your finger fucking."

She made a face but did as she was told.

Rich paced the length of the trailer, checking each window carefully, pulling aside the curtains with a shaky hand. He was afraid each time he moved a drape or lifted a blind that the dark shadow would be right on the other side, with giant snake eyes.

Waiting.

JAKE SAT AT THE KITCHEN TABLE, sipping coffee, listening to the rain and watching Pam pretend to do dishes. But she kept looking toward the window that viewed the driveway. It wasn't yet six-thirty, and yet the last of the feeble daylight was already gone. And Ernie was still out in the woods somewhere.

The rain was a pounding gray wall that reminded him uncomfortably of the scene at Galveston Bay, and he had a queasy sensation and nasty tickling between his shoulder blades. But he shook it off, smiling reassuringly at Pam.

"I tell him not to go out in weather like this," she said. "But will he listen?"

"Ernie's fine," said Jake, wondering how much he believed that. "He's probably just stuck in the mud."

"I swear sometimes I don't know what he's thinking."

She hugged her elbows, and he could see tears forming at the corners of her eyes.

"There's nothing out there to be afraid of," insisted Jake. But he knew that *she* knew he was lying.

"I've never forgotten what you told me about the night your mother died," she said. "The Lord knows I've tried. And I've never told anyone. Not even Ernie."

"I imagined it," he insisted.

"That's what I always thought. But Cramer saw something in the woods. Barbara heard something. Why did you leave? If you really don't believe any of it's real, then why did you run away?"

"Sit down. If Ernie doesn't show up in the next few minutes we'll call Virgil and organize a search. What are you cooking?"

She glanced at the pots on the stove and leaped to her feet. "I forgot! There's bread and a pot pie in the oven." She jerked the oven door open, but the pie was fine. So she turned the burners under the pots and pans to low and returned to the table.

"I know he's okay," she said, speaking more to herself than to Jake. But she didn't sound that sure.

"No Ernie?" asked Cramer, sticking his head in the door. Jake shook his head and Cramer frowned.

Pam stared at the darkness through the window as though some answer were about to spring out at her. Cramer eyed her with a helpless expression on his face.

"All right, then," said Jake, rising. "Cramer, why don't you fix plates for us while I make the call."

He could tell Cramer was grateful to have something to do. Jake dialed 911, identified himself, and asked to be put through to Sheriff Milche. Luckily Virgil was in the office.

"What's up?" asked Virgil. "Don't tell me you two renegades solved the case."

"Afraid not," said Jake. "Ernie still hasn't come home from traipsing through the woods."

"I swear sometimes that boy makes me wonder if preachers have a lick of sense. Pam pretty worried?"

"She thinks he should have been home a long time ago."

"Okay. I'm on my way, but all my men are out patrolling the roads. They're washing out all over."

"Thanks, Virg. Cramer and I will be ready when you get here."

"No sweat. Hope you got raincoats and high-water boots."

Jake hung up the phone. Pam stared at him expectantly. Cramer already had three plates full of food waiting on the table, and Jake dug in, knowing he might be starving before he had a chance to eat again. But Pam wasn't going to be put off.

"Is he on his way?" she said, ignoring her dinner.

"Be here in a few minutes," said Jake between bites. He noticed that Cramer was wolfing down his meal, too. But Jake figured that was more to keep himself out of the conversation than from hunger.

"Has Ernie got any rain gear Cramer and I can use?" asked Jake.

"What?"

"Rain gear. Cramer and I didn't bring any."

"I'll see. He should have at least a couple of old sets. But I don't know how good they'll be."

"This is too much of a coincidence," muttered Cramer as Pam disappeared.

"Don't add up two and two and get seven," said Jake, thinking exactly the same thing. If anything had happened to Ernie . . . He didn't want to think about what that would do to Pam. What it would do to his own sense of guilt.

Cramer nodded toward the window. "Ain't looking forward to traipsing through those trees again. Especially in this storm."

"You don't have to go. Maybe it would be better if you stayed with Pam."

"Like she isn't going."

"That would be stupid. What if Ernie shows up? We wouldn't even know it."

"I realize that. Do you think she's going to listen?"

"I'll make her listen."

When Pam returned with two very worn raincoats and a couple of pairs of rubber boots she was wearing a coat of her own. Cramer just stared at Jake.

"What?" said Pam, handing Cramer one of the yellow slickers.

"You need to wait here," said Jake, pulling on a raincoat.

"Not on your life."

"You can call the station if Ernie shows up. *When* Ernie shows up," said Jake quickly. "And they'll let us know."

She shook her head. "You know as well as I do that most of the time radios don't even work in this valley. And I'm not going to just sit here any longer while Ernie's out there in the woods somewhere."

"Pam, you need to stay with Barbara. Anyway, you won't be any help out there, and you can be here. We don't need you getting lost so we have one more person to worry about. Besides, what happens if Ernie gets home and you aren't here? Then he'll start worrying about *you*. Listen to me."

They locked eyes, and for just a moment Jake was convinced there was no way he was going to win the argument. But finally her face softened, and the strength drained from her. She walked into the living room and stood in front of the window, staring out into the downpour as Jake and Cramer struggled into Ernie's old rain gear. Cramer looked like a gorilla in a child's outfit. Black forearms stuck out of the yellow jacket, and his rain pants barely covered his shins.

Jake slipped behind Pam and rested his hands on her shoulders.

"We'll find him," he said.

"Promise?"

"I promise."

She placed a hand over his without turning and squeezed.

"You all right?" Jake asked, as Cramer stomped around still trying to get the boots on his feet.

"Damned things are biting like crabs."

"Better than going without."

"Maybe."

Virgil's cruiser pulled up, and Jake hugged Pam before he and Cramer ran out to meet the sheriff. In spite of the situation, Virgil couldn't help but laugh at Cramer as he tried to weasel his way into the car in the tight-fitting suit.

"Can you send anyone to stay with Pam?" asked Jake, climbing into the front seat.

"I got no one to send. Everyone's on road duty with the storm."

"Where we going first?" asked Cramer.

Virgil glanced in the rearview mirror. "You guys don't have any idea where Ernie went today?"

Jake shook his head. "Pam said he was going to try up the old Burnout trail behind Rich Morin's place. But if he didn't find anything there he was liable to go wherever the urge struck him."

"He ought to know better," said Virgil.

"Why don't you have a four-wheel drive?" asked Cramer, as the car wormed its way up the slimy road.

Virgil eyed him in the rearview again. "I put them all out on patrol today. With this rain half the highways are washing out, and it's all the road crews and my boys can do to find the flooded spots and barricade 'em. Besides, I didn't expect I was going to be doing any back-country driving until you fellows called. We'll be all right. Betsy here has had her share of off-road excitement. If Ernie's on the old Burnout trail we ought to come up on his truck pretty quick. That's a start. If his truck isn't there then we have problems, and we probably won't find him until morning."

"If then," muttered Cramer.

Both Jake and Virgil gave him a dirty look.

"Here's Rich's drive," said Virgil, turning in. "Past his house it turns into the trail."

"How long has Rich been living here?" asked Jake.

Virgil shrugged. "Since he and Mandi were separated. Around the time Pierce . . . You know."

"Yeah," said Jake, staring at the trailer as they drove past. "What's your opinion on that?"

Virgil sighed loud enough to be heard over the *slish*ing of the tires and the rain pounding on the roof. "I try not to have an opinion. Rich is innocent until proven guilty, and his cousin swears he was with Rich at the time. Pierce couldn't give us much to go on. So what could I do?"

"Pierce is blind and deaf," said Jake.

"That's right," said Virgil, frowning. "And now he limps, too."

"Yeah . . ."

"I thought you and Mandi were a real item all those years," mused Virgil. "King and queen of the prom. And all through your days at the academy everyone was just figuring you were going to pop the question any time."

"It was better for everybody this way."

"She cried her eyes out after you left."

"How come you know so much about Jake's love life?" asked Cramer.

"Mandi's my niece," said Virgil, frowning into the rearview. He glanced at Jake again, and it was Jake who turned away first. "I didn't care for the way you ran out or what you did to Mandi, Jake. But I always figured you had your reasons. She and Rich married right off, it's true, and that was a big mistake. But I know it took her a long time to get over you, and I'm not sure she has yet."

The car was silent until Cramer spoke again. "So what's the origin of this Crowley curse?"

Jake snorted and turned to face his window.

"According to legend the original Jacob Crowley stirred up something in this valley," said Virgil, smirking. "Some say it was an Indian spirit. I've heard some nuts claiming it was aliens. But the gist of the story is that it's supposed to be the same thing that's caused Crowley men to go off their rockers ever since. But some say there is no Crowley curse, just a monster in the valley, and some say the opposite."

Cramer shook his head. "Is it or ain't it?"

"You'll have to ask Jake," said Virgil, staring straight ahead through the windshield.

"According to the story only the direct descendants, the male line, go crazy. That's the myth," muttered Jake.

"You," said Cramer.

"Yeah."

"So what's that got to do with whispers and shadows?"

Jake shook his head. "I don't know."

But there was a time when he had *thought* he'd known, had thought he really did understand the curse. The answer seemed simple enough. Crowley men really did go crazy. And everything he remembered was all in his fevered imagination, or worse . . . things he himself had done.

Only then Albert had been murdered. And eight men ended up dead on a beach. Four of whom he couldn't possibly have killed.

"Shit!" said Virgil, spinning the wheel and slamming the brakes just in time to stop the cruiser from hitting a deadfall pine. The tree blocked the road like a two-ton gate.

"What the hell caused that?" said Cramer.

"Gust of wind," said Virgil. "Or more likely the rain washed away some of its support."

"Guess we have to hike," said Jake.

Virgil peered through the gloom. "I don't want to park like this. If we're a while in the woods, it may mud up enough so's I can't get turned around again."

He spun the wheel and backed the car into a small grassy space between two tall birch trees. Then they all climbed out into the rain. Virgil handed Jake and Cramer flashlights from the trunk, and they trudged up to the fallen tree. Deep into the woods they could see the torn and twisted roots grasping skyward. Virgil shone his light across the trunk and up the trail, then turned back to Jake and Cramer.

"I was hoping maybe Ernie's truck was stuck on the far side of the tree," said Virgil.

"You are an optimist," said Jake, scrabbling his way through the branches and sliding over to the uphill side. He reached back and took Virgil's flashlight before helping him across.

"Come on, Cramer!" he shouted.

Cramer had trouble negotiating the twisted limbs because of his skintight rain gear, but he finally skittered across. Virgil was already disappearing into the night ahead, and Cramer and Jake slogged through the mud to catch up.

"How far does this road go?" asked Cramer, huffing alongside Jake.

"Miles," said Jake. "It's an old logging trail. The area up ahead burned out when I was a kid. Big forest fire. You won't see trees as big as the one back there up in the burn, but I'm sure it's all grown back now."

"Miles," muttered Cramer.

"Yeah," said Jake. "But the good news is, because it hasn't been logged in years there are no branch trails off this one. If Ernie's truck's on it we're going to run into it."

"It's not Ernie's truck I'm worried about running into," muttered Cramer.

*A*RE YOU SURE A CAR WENT PAST?" said Rich. He stared out the window, clutching the shotgun in a death grip across his chest.

Carly watched him the way a rabbit watches a fox. "I saw the lights."

"Who the hell would be driving up that old road in this?"

"How would I know? If you weren't roaming the back of the house like an itchy hound dog maybe you'd have seen 'em, too."

"You shut up. You don't have a fucking clue what's going on."

"Why don't you explain it to me?"

"You don't believe me, that's fine, woman. But there's something out there. The same thing I ran into up at the old Crowley place."

"You never told me you ran into anything up there."

He glared at her. "You remember when I come back though, right?"

"Yeah," she whispered, cowering. "I remember. And you saw the same thing outside the trailer here?"

"I saw it and I heard it."

"Whispering to you."

"Yeah. Something like that. And it's bigger than a fucking bear."

"Well, if there's something all that bad out there, maybe you ought to call the cops."

"Fuck the cops," said Rich. He stumbled to the fridge and snagged another beer, snapping the top with one hand, leaving the other hand glued to the gun. He took care of the brew in one long guzzle, tossing the can into the sink.

"Bet there's a reward out for that thing," mused Carly.

"What?"

She shrugged. "Bet there is."

"Why would there be a fucking reward?"

"It sounds dangerous."

"It by God is dangerous."

"Then I'll bet there's a bounty on it."

"Somebody else can claim it. You didn't see that goddamned thing."

"Just saying."

"Shut up."

He grabbed another beer from the fridge and plopped down into his recliner, resting the cold can on the pistol grip of the shotgun and staring at the blank TV screen. He'd made Carly turn it off so he could hear better. The only sound in the trailer now was the hammering of rain on the sheet-metal roof.

Maybe there was a bounty on the damned thing. But then, even if there wasn't a bounty, there might be some kind of money in killing the thing. He'd seen the stories of those guys out west who'd shot the Sasquatch. The *Enquirer* would pay big bucks for a dead monster.

He swigged the beer slower this time, savoring it, taking it in three gulps instead of one. Then he tossed the can back over his shoulder without looking, satisfied by the metallic clink as it bounced around in the sink. He ignored Carly's frown.

Might just get my ass killed going after that thing.

But the more he thought about it, the more his fear seemed groundless. The thing hadn't attacked him when it had the chance. Was it going to come after him when he had a shotgun full of buckshot? He tried to picture the thing again. It was big. Damn big. Bigger than any bear. But hell, buckshot at close range would drop an elephant.

He staggered into the kitchen for another beer and stood sipping it, staring out the window into the darkness.

"Get me my rain gear and my flashlight," he shouted without turning.

"Get 'em yourself."

"Get 'em!" he screamed, kicking over a chair.

Behind him he heard the patter of feet.

DO YOU REALLY THINK HE'S UP THIS FAR?" asked Cramer. Jake stared at the muddy tire tracks that told him *someone* was up ahead.

He, Virgil, and Cramer were all catching their breaths, huddled beneath a mass of spruce boughs, but the rain still got through. Jake was soaked to the skin by water that meandered around his neck, down his back, and puddled in the back of his shorts. And the deluge caused the darkness to close in around them claustrophobically.

Virgil frowned. "There's only one set of tire tracks in. Someone came up here. Can't believe it would be anyone else but Ernie on a day like today. Can you?"

"No," said Jake, glancing at Cramer.

Cramer shrugged. "Nothing like a brisk walk after dinner."

"All right, then," said Virgil, heading up the trail again.

The mud was a dangerous slurry, and deep rivulets ran down the tire ruts. The rain panned a dull staccato on the million pine needles overhead and echoed on the sodden ground below.

"I've never seen it pour like this in Maine!" Jake shouted.

"Not very damned often. Trouble is it's been a hell of a rainy spring, and the ground is soaked through. Nowhere left for this rain to go."

"You know where you are?"

"Yeah. I'm halfway up a mountainside, in the dark, in a rainstorm, with two city slickers."

"Thanks," said Jake.

"You probably remember more of this road than I do. I know it wanders all the way down to the mouth of the valley. It dead-ends down by the river, doesn't it?"

"Yeah. But I have no idea how far we are from there."

"Quite a ways, I suspect."

"So we could have quite a walk yet."

"You petering out?"

"No. Just belaboring the obvious."

But as luck would have it, Ernie was right around the next bend. And when they spotted him—even more wet and tired and bedraggled than they were—he let out a shout as though they were a special task force sent out by AAA. He glad-handed the three of them, slapping Jake on the back and nearly driving him into the mud.

"Man! Am I happy to see you guys! I thought I was going to be up here all night! I am stuck! Stuck with a capital S!"

He was all of that. And it looked as though he had done everything short of using explosives to get himself out. His old Chevy truck—buried up to the axles—rested in a low spot in the trail, and the area around it was swiftly turning into a pond. Jake figured he must have tried to take the dip at a run because the mud splattered over the top of the hood was so thick that even the heavy rain had not succeeded in washing it away. Branches and sticks were piled around the tires and the sides of the truck as though the vehicle had nested for the season.

"Tried to get some traction," explained Ernie.

"We're never getting you out of there without a tow truck!" shouted Virgil.

Ernie nodded expectantly. "Where are you guys parked?"

They all laughed at once.

"About three miles back down the hill," said Jake.

Ernie glanced at him as though trying to understand the joke.

"There's a big deadfall down at the bottom of the trail," said Virgil.

"You hiked up all this way looking for me?"

"Pam's worried sick," said Jake.

"I was afraid she would be. Sorry I brought you out in this."

"Just enjoying the great outdoors," said Cramer, frowning.

"Come on," said Virgil, leading the way. "Fun's fun, but it looks like it's going to be a long night for me as it is."

RICH ALMOST RAN HEAD-ON into the tree blocking the trail, and as he skidded to a stop his rear end clipped the front bumper of Virgil's cruiser, hidden back in the woods. He stared at the deadfall in front and the empty police car behind, and tried to figure out what was going on, wondering if someone else really had seen the thing.

Maybe the stupid bitch was right. Maybe there was a bounty on the son of a bitch, and the cops weren't telling anyone. That would be about par for the course.

He grabbed the shotgun and his flashlight and climbed out into the rain. If the cops were after it, then maybe they'd spook it back his way. He clambered over the fallen tree and took a minute adjusting the shotgun under his arm so he could get a better grip on the light. Frothy water ran down the road. In another hour or two his front yard was gonna be completely flooded, and he briefly considered leaving the hunt for another day. But if the cops killed the thing, he was out whatever money was on it. The best thing to do would be to follow the trail for a spell and then hole up. If the cops came back down the mountain driving it in front of them, he could blast the hell out of it and claim the money for himself.

Screw the cops.

He hiked up a quarter mile to the first bend and searched for a likely spot where he could see up and down the narrow lane. Finally he settled on the exposed roots of a big spruce, pulling the alders and brush back around himself. The trunk of the tree was rough and oddly shaped against his back, and he couldn't get comfortable no matter how he twisted and turned. But it was better that way. He didn't want to be falling asleep.

But the longer he sat there, the more his alcohol-induced confidence dwindled, the darker the surrounding forest seemed, the more strange and horrid became his memory of the encounter with the shadowy creature in the yard. He fingered the shotgun nervously. Was the safety on now, or was she ready to fire?

Finally he broke down and flicked on the flashlight long enough to ascertain that the safety was indeed on. He flipped it off, and turned off the light.

Blind again. Smooth move, Ex-Lax.

He remembered childhood stories of the Crowley curse. How it wasn't just crazy Crowleys but a monster that had been raised from the dead by old Jacob Crowley himself. How he kept it in a hole in the ground behind the house. How kids had disappeared up there. Never kids that anyone knew . . . Over the years Rich had outgrown the story, laughing when anyone brought it up. But he knew that a lot of people laughed out the sides of their faces. And now he knew why, because whatever the hell he'd seen in his yard, it wasn't an old wives' tale.

The rain took on a wavelike rhythm, stronger, then lighter, then stronger again. A million tiny rat feet playing through the pine needles. But even as he imagined a horde of vermin surrounding him he was squinting, listening, searching the woods nervously.

Because he could have sworn that he heard the whispers again.

BY THE TIME THEY NEARED THE START OF THE TRAIL, Jake was not only waterlogged but covered with mud. Their flashlights reflected off the wall of water ahead of them as though it really were solid, yet they passed through it like ghosts.

"Your car's going to look like hell after we get out of it," shouted Jake.

Virgil kept his head down—rain pouring off the brim of his hat—plodding alongside. They looked like a mismatched team of worn-out plow mules headed for the barn. "That's what deputies are for."

"You hear something?" asked Ernie, catching up.

"Stop," said Cramer, holding out his hand.

Everyone froze. Jake's hackles rose, and goose bumps played along his arms when he heard the telltale sound of the eerie whisper all around him.

"What's that?" said Ernie.

"Where's it coming from?" asked Virgil.

"I think it's louder down the trail," said Jake, squinting into the rain.

"Careful," said Virgil quietly. Jake noticed that he had unsnapped the strap on his holster.

The four of them advanced down the hill more mindful of where they placed their feet, their eyes and ears peeled. When they approached a sharp bend Virgil nodded, and Cramer did, too. The sound was louder, but it seemed to come and go, like wisps of breeze.

"Watch out," said Jake, waving at the others to slow down even more.

"It's moving," said Ernie, turning slowly in the middle of the road.

Even though the sound echoed all around them, when Jake listened carefully it still seemed just a little stronger down the trail, in the direction they were hiking. Suddenly it felt as though the branches overhead were reaching down for them. Jake could tell that Cramer felt it, too. Virgil flicked his light back and forth, nervously studying the trees. The only one who didn't seem all that alarmed was Ernie. He smiled, searching the rain with his flashlight for the elusive sounds.

This is going to happen fast, thought Jake.

Cramer drew his gun at the same time as Virgil. Jake shielded his eyes from the rain, trying to see through the trees.

ICH HAD THE SHIVERS, and they weren't just from being wet and chilled. Before, sitting in his warm pickup, he'd managed to convince himself that he could take care of whatever it was that was running around in the woods. But now—as the weird whisper sounds slipped around him again, like sharks circling bloody prey—he didn't want to be sitting here on his ass against this tree.

He drew back the bolt and fingered the shell in the chamber.

A man could blow a hole through an oak tree with this gun. But you have to hit the fucking thing first. What if it's fast?

What he'd seen of the thing had looked big enough to kill a bull, but it hadn't moved all that quick. But then neither did rattlesnakes. Until they struck.

Suddenly he saw the faintest glint of light through the rain and night. Was that headlights?

The lights got a little clearer. Not headlights. There were

too many of them, and they seemed to shine all over the fucking place, down, up, all around.

Flashlights.

As he stared into the night a darkness crept between him and the light and began to swell, as though a bear were slowly rising up onto its hind legs. His hands shook so hard the stock of the gun rattled against the tree beside him, but he managed to shove himself up the rough trunk to a near-standing position, lifting the gun to his shoulder. His breathing was ragged, and his knees felt like jelly. The darkness kept expanding, and inside that darkness, for the first time, he saw eyes.

His mind couldn't process the darkness, the deluge, the strange sounds, the fear, and the sudden explosion of light and sound caused by the shotgun. His fevered brain needed to relinquish control of some nonessential systems.

He dropped a load in his shorts.

But he still managed to chamber another round into the gun and fire again.

And again, and again.

Until the darkness had him. Until it was deep inside his brain, and terror was as real and hard as a hammer driving him back into madness. Until there was only one escape.

SHOTGUN BLASTS SUNDERED THE CURTAIN OF RAIN, the roar thundering at them through the trees. Cramer fired first, then Virgil's pistol burped along with him. Finally Jake drew his pistol, but he couldn't find a target, and he was afraid of hitting Cramer or Virgil. Above the roar of the guns, the strange whisper noise was now as loud as thunder itself. Screams of pain erupted as the trail became a cacophonous, muddy, swirling madhouse of darkness, sound, and flashing lights.

When the gunfire finally ceased the screams and whispers died away, replaced by low moans from behind Jake. Ernie was down in the mud, his face white as a sheet. His pant leg was soaked with blood, and he was gasping for air.

"Calm down, Ernie. I'm here. You're going to be all right," shouted Jake, not certain at all if that was true.

"My leg."

"You're gonna be all right."

"Hurts p-p-pretty bad," stammered Ernie.

Virgil and Cramer advanced toward the woods where the

shots had come from, each taking a side of the trail in the direction of the original muzzle flashes.

Jake jerked off his belt and used it as a tourniquet, tightening it around Ernie's upper thigh. When he glanced back down the road, both Cramer and Virgil were gone. But he could see their lights through the trees. He noticed that—except for the rain—the woods were silent again.

"Hurts," gasped Ernie again, doubling up.

Jake grabbed him by the shoulders, dragging him out of the runoff and up into some high grass, checking his face for pallor, keeping him talking. "It's not far to Virgil's cruiser. We'll have you to the hospital in no time."

"Who shot me?"

"I don't know," said Jake. "Cramer! Virgil! You hear me?" he shouted.

Silence.

"Cramer!"

"Yeah! We hear you. How's Ernie?"

"Stable. He took a load of shot in the leg. We need to get him out of here."

"Sounds like that thing is gone. You better come here first. We found Rich."

Jake glanced down at Ernie.

Ernie grimaced, but nodded. "Don't take all night, huh?"

"Right back."

Jake trotted toward the lights. Cramer and Virgil were holding their flashlights low, aimed at their feet. Their faces, lit from below, looked skeletal and eerie.

All around them the branches and bracken and forest floor were twisted and torn, as though heavy equipment had ripped its way through. But even in the half-light and the rain, Jake could see that the tree was slathered with knuckle-size globules of bloody flesh. Beside the big spruce lay a man's corpse, shotgun still gripped tightly in one hand. The man's head was half blown away, and Jake knew instantly that none of their pistols had done that.

Cramer shone his light around, and Jake could see more blood dripping from a thousand pine needles.

"What do you make of this, Jake?" asked Virgil.

Jake shook his head, staring at the shotgun resting close to the body. "Looks like he killed himself."

"Why would he do that?"

"I have no idea. Must have gone off his rocker."

Cramer glared at him but said nothing.

"Are you sure that's Rich?" asked Jake, pointing at the corpse.

"Yeah," said Virgil, showing Jake a sodden leather wallet. "Unless someone planted his driver's license here. That's Rich Morin all right."

"Why shoot at us, then blow his own head off?" asked Cramer, looking at Jake.

"I don't think he was shooting at us," said Virgil, staring at the mangled corpse and then Jake. "How's Ernie?"

"Bad, but not life-threatening. Yet. We need to get him out of here before he goes into shock, though."

"Well, let's get to it, then."

The three of them lifted Ernie onto Cramer's back, Virgil supporting his wounded leg. When they reached the deadfall pine they eased Ernie across, slipping him into the backseat as gently as possible. Jake got a blanket from the trunk and bandaged the wound with supplies from a first-aid kit while Virgil tried the radio without success. Finally he slammed the mike back into its slot on the dash.

"This damned valley," he muttered.

Cramer gave Jake a questioning look.

"Cell phones and radios don't work well in most of the valley," explained Jake. "There's too many shadow areas, and some people think that iron deposits may cause the magnetic fields to mess with them, as well."

When Virgil put the car into gear the tires spun in the muddy grass. The cruiser didn't budge.

"Damn," muttered Virgil. "That was what I was afraid of. You guys are gonna have to push."

Jake and Cramer climbed out of the car and leaned into it. Sputtering mud and bucking like a bronc, the big car finally slipped past Rich's bumper and started downhill again, and Cramer and Jake slithered back inside. They looked like a pair of mudmen.

"Whoopee," said Cramer.

As they passed by Rich's trailer Jake noticed a face in the window, and he frowned. "Carly must be alone in there."

"I'll send someone out to check on her as soon as I can. First order of business is Ernie," said Virgil.

PAM WAS STANDING ON THE PORCH tapping her feet, arms crossed, as they pulled in. She raced down the path to Virgil's cruiser, and as Jake slid out she shoved herself into the backseat, cradling Ernie's head in her arms. She stared at the tourniquet and bandages on his leg.

"What happened?" she asked, kissing Ernie's forehead and holding his hand.

"Rich shot him," said Jake, leaning into the backseat.

Pam made a face. "Rich?"

Jake shrugged. "It may have been an accident."

"What does Rich have to say for himself?"

Virgil glanced over his shoulder, and when Pam noticed the strained expression on his face her own expression became even more curious.

"Rich is dead," said Jake.

"It was that thing," she whispered. "Wasn't it?"

"We'll sort this all out after we get Ernie to the doctor," said Virgil.

Ernie was conscious but appeared to be in that hibernating state where all he could concentrate on was his own pain.

"He's going to be all right," she insisted.

But Jake couldn't tell if that was a statement or a question.

"What are you going to do now?" she asked all of them.

"After the storm's over I'll get as many men as it takes and search the whole valley if I have to," said Virgil.

"That doesn't sound like quite enough."

"What do you want me to do? Call out the National Guard?"

"Something like that."

"And tell them what, Pam? That we have some kind of unidentified monster running around in Crowley, and would they please come kill it for us?"

"Somebody better kill it."

"We can worry about that later," said Virgil, nodding for Pam to close her door. "And to kill it I suspect you have to see it. None of us saw anything."

"It ain't always what I see that bothers me," Cramer muttered.

"That was one big sucker. Wasn't it, Jake?" muttered Ernie.

Even the pounding rain seemed to settle to silence.

"What?" said Jake.

"That thing on the road. What the heck was that thing?"

Virgil's eyes narrowed, and his forehead creased. "What did you see, Ernie?"

Ernie glanced groggily from face to face. "You guys saw it, too, right?"

"I didn't see anything but the rain and trees," said Jake. "What about you, Cramer?"

Cramer shook his head. "It was too dark."

"I didn't see anything," said Virgil.

"How could you not have seen it?" said Ernie, his head wobbling on Pam's shoulder. "It was as big as my truck!"

"What did it look like?" said Jake, catching Pam's eye.

"Just huge, and black, like a shadow," said Ernie. "But it was there. I swear it was. Moving through the trees up ahead, like a giant bear. Then the shooting started." He shook his head, and his eyes glazed a little. "It was big. Real big."

"Try to hang on," said Jake as he started sliding back into the car next to Pam.

"You two stay here," she said, glancing from Jake to Cramer.

"What?" said Jake. "We're going to the hospital."

Pam shook her head. "Someone needs to be here with Barbara. She's beside herself, convinced that some monster is going to come and get her and Oswald. I gave her another pain pill, and she's out on the sofa. But I don't want to leave her alone."

"Cramer can stay," said Jake.

"Oh, no," said Cramer, sliding out of the car. "You aren't leaving me alone with that crazy old broad."

Jake sighed as Virgil caught his eye in the mirror. "We'll let you know as soon as Doc Burton has seen him."

Jake nodded slowly, squeezing Pam's hand before closing the door and watching the cruiser slide down the drive. Once again someone he loved had been touched by the Crowley curse, and there was nothing he could do about it. Should he have drawn his gun sooner? What good would that have done? And that wasn't the real question that tortured him, anyway.

Had he somehow caused the violence? Was he responsible for Rich's death and Ernie's wound? For the hitchhiker, and Albert, and Dary Murphy? For years he had hidden from his past. He had kept his emotions locked tightly at bay lest some madness escape and an innocent be harmed. Had it gotten out without his knowing?

"You gonna stand out here in the rain all night?" asked Cramer.

He shook his head, following Cramer inside.

THE FRONT TIRE JOLTED through a pothole the size of a basketball hoop, and Jimmy lurched into wakefulness. He glared at Paco, but Paco just shrugged. Jimmy stared out through the slapping wipers at the dark road ahead, wondering what kind of backwoods bullshit he'd gotten himself into. But at least the Maine forest felt more familiar than the rolling farmland of Massachusetts and New Hampshire. He'd spent years in woods a lot thicker and more dangerous than these.

Still, no reason other than family revenge could have brought him to this place or kept him here. But *that* was something that could not be denied. There was never any love lost between himself and José. In fact, they had been bitter rivals from the time they were old enough to crawl, and their old man had seen that the rivalry grew, pitting them against one another whenever he got a chance. Still, the two of them had managed to build the most powerful criminal organization in Houston's history by utilizing their talents—José's for unthinking brutality, and Jimmy's for thoughtful ruthlessness. José had no tact, and few social skills. Jimmy was the essence of savoir faire. He had graduated—if not with honors—from public school, and later, when the empire began to expand, he had taken lessons from a gentleman who claimed to have been educated in France, so that he knew which fork to use on his salad and which knife to use on his enemies. He had also been trained by the United States Army.

In an attempt to escape the barrio and his upbringing, Jimmy had joined the service immediately after graduation. He discovered that he liked the weapons and the thrill of danger so much that he did well, progressing first to Ranger school, then Special Forces. During five years with the elite group, Jimmy had learned to kill in ways he'd never suspected existed. And he had become adept at surviving in all sorts of exotic locales where the average man would have quickly succumbed to the elements.

But his upbringing was deeper rooted than his training. When he was caught selling drugs, a very good military defense attorney was able to get the charges dismissed if Jimmy accepted an immediate dishonorable discharge. Later he had the two soldiers who turned him in murdered.

Every one of their hundreds of "employees" feared José for his sudden deadly temper. But they feared Jimmy more, for his elaborate punishments. Only the month before, a drug dealer named Watson had screwed one of Jimmy's men on a deal. The amount was immaterial in Jimmy's book. The jerk knew the man worked for him.

Jimmy didn't kill him outright or maim him for life the way José would have. Instead, he had another of his men start supplying Watson with even better shit at a better price to gain his trust. During the third deal—a moment after Watson whiffed in a good noseful to test the latest batch—Jimmy walked calmly into the room. The junk Watson had

just snorted was so pure he was barely able to put up any re-
sistance as Jimmy's men tied him to a chair. A week later, the
police discovered Watson's head encased in clear epoxy
resin, resting on the corner of the street in front of his house.

And Watson had only screwed Jimmy's employee out of
money. He hadn't murdered Jimmy's only brother.

"How far are we from Crowley?"

Paco shrugged again. "There's no signs in this fucking
state. I think it can't be that far, though."

"How the fuck could you have gotten us lost again?"

"Boss, I was in here and out of here, and all these backwoods shitholes look the same to me. I'll get us there. If we
don't get washed off the fucking road first."

"See that we don't. And find a place to dump our friend."

"I been looking. But every time I start to pull over a goddamn car comes along. I was gonna drop him down a side
road, but they're all flooded."

"All right," said Jimmy irritably. "He'll have to stay in the
trunk. Just get us there."

As personal as José's killing made things, a tiny voice in
Jimmy's head kept telling him that he should have sent any
one of his remaining enforcers to do this job. He was taking
big chances here, but that went with the territory. It was important that his people knew what he did to anyone who
dared touch a Torrio. One day he was going to have to face
both his father and José again, and he was going to be able to
look them in the eye and tell them that José's killer had died
badly and by his own hand. He crossed himself and spat air
toward the window, a gesture he'd picked up from his father,
who ranted endlessly about the fucking church but sent a
cautious glance skyward whenever he blasphemed.

"Where will we find them?" he asked quietly.

"I don't know," said Paco. "They may be staying in the
old man's house."

Jimmy shook his head. "Not likely. It's a crime scene. Doesn't Jake Crowley have any other family in the valley?"

Paco nodded. "A woman cousin named Pam."

"Why didn't you threaten her the way you were supposed to do the old man?"

"Jesus, boss. After I came to and found the old man dead, I had to get out of town."

That Paco wouldn't hold his eye was no cause for concern, but the sweat on his brow and the slight quiver of his hand on the wheel told Jimmy he was lying. Lying was not something Jimmy accepted from anyone.

"Why?"

"Why what, boss?"

Jimmy's voice was quiet, but he knew Paco would read the proper level of threat into it. "Why did you kill him? You can tell me the truth."

The sweat beaded and trickled into Paco's eyes. He wiped them with the back of his hand and Jimmy enjoyed the show.

"Honest to God, boss, I blanked out. I know how crazy that sounds. But maybe the old man drugged me or something. When I came to he was dead. Blood was everywhere. The old fart looked like he'd been run through a blender. I couldn't have beat him up that bad if I wanted to. I ain't that strong."

That fact was the only thing that had saved Paco's life. Jimmy had seen the police report—he, too, had ways of getting information—and the photographs left little doubt in Jimmy's mind that the work wasn't Paco's. Paco was a knife or pistol man. He was good for a shiv in the back. Not for a beating.

"All right, then. Tell me about the whispering," said Jimmy.

Paco shivered. "I heard it right before I blacked out. It kept getting louder and louder."

"Loud whispering?"

Paco sighed. "Well, hissing maybe. I don't know. But the noise got around the house and it sounded like it was everywhere at once. It was like I was being swallowed up by something, and I was scared. More scared than I've ever been in my life. It felt like . . . it felt like something was trying to get inside of me."

"Inside of you?"

Paco shrugged. "It felt like there was something inside my head—"

"That must have been a new experience for you."

The car rocked again, and Paco struggled to bring it under control. But this time it pulled hard to the right, and the steady thunking noise told Jimmy they had a flat.

"Damn," he said. "Can we get any worse luck?"

"There's a little more shoulder up ahead," said Paco, nursing the car over onto the side.

They sat for a minute staring into the rain, and Jimmy could see Paco gutting up to say something.

"I have to get to the spare," said Paco at last. "I need help moving him around."

Jimmy sighed. A small bloodstain already marred the perfect cotton of his sleeve. He nudged open his door and waited in the deluge while Paco fumbled the key into the trunk. They wedged Smitty farther back into the tight space and dug out the spare and jack then slammed the lid again. Jimmy climbed back into the front seat, turning on the heater to at least warm him if not dry him out, as Paco jacked up the rear of the car. As Jimmy listened to the humming of the fan he stroked the butt of the pistol under his arm.

Because they had bought airline tickets at the last moment, he had known they'd be searched. A drug lord understood the venues through which his booty traveled. So he'd paid a likely-looking kid a thousand dollars to claim that one of Jimmy's bags was his and had not been out of his sight. The kid thought he was smuggling dope, which was fine with him. In fact Jimmy never did drugs or sold them himself anymore. The kid had smuggled pistols for Jimmy and Paco.

So although that part of the trip was a pain in the ass, it was to be expected. But the plane breaking down was not. Neither was the rented car dying on them. Or getting lost too many times to count. And now this. It was as if someone up there didn't want him to get the revenge he needed.

"Screw you," he said, glancing skyward, genuflecting, and spitting toward the floor.

Paco slapped the side window, and Jimmy glanced up to see headlights appearing through the veil of rain ahead. As though to prove that karma really was against them, the car turned out to be a sheriff's department cruiser. Jimmy climbed out to stand beside Paco and act as if he was helping. The last thing he wanted was Paco talking to a cop.

"Got a flat?" the deputy shouted, pulling alongside.

Jimmy wondered if astuteness was on the list of attributes necessary for a cop in these parts. He supposed no more here than anywhere else.

"Yep," he said, shaking rain from his hair and smiling broadly. "We've about got it, though. Thanks."

When the deputy put on his plastic-covered Smokey Bear hat Jimmy cursed under his breath. The cop pulled a U-turn and parked behind them. He climbed out, slipping on a yellow rain slicker, and trotted over to them, leaning around to check the ground.

"Not a great place to put that jack," he said.

"Seems to be holding," said Jimmy. "We didn't want to go too far and ruin the tire."

The cop nodded as Paco slipped the spare on, fumbling

with the lug nuts. Jimmy noticed that Paco couldn't look the deputy in the eye, and he wondered if the cop noticed.

"Where you guys coming from?" asked the cop, glancing at Smitty's out-of-state plate.

"New Jersey," said Jimmy quickly. "We're trying to get to Arcos."

The cop smiled. "How did you get over here? It would have been a lot easier coming up Route Two."

Jimmy smiled back. "We took a wrong turn. We've been lost so long I'm kind of getting used to it."

Paco tightened the lugs and started lowering the jack as the cop watched. Then he picked up the flat tire.

Jimmy jerked open the rear passenger door.

"In here," he told Paco, looking at the frowning cop. "We had to take all our luggage out to get to the spare and now it's soaked enough as it is. Besides, we have to find a garage to get the tire fixed, and I don't want to dig it out again."

The cop nodded, as Paco shoved the tire onto the floor-board. The deputy peered into the backseat as Paco slammed the door.

Jimmy made a face, water trickling off his chin. "Straight up this road?" he said, half into the car already.

The cop nodded, pointing ahead. "About fifteen miles up ahead you come to Route Two. Head east. You'll see the signs for Crowley, but that road could be closed at any time. If it is, you can probably find a place to stay in Arcos. You can get the tire fixed there, too."

Jimmy nodded his thanks. As Paco pulled out onto the road, Jimmy looked in the outside mirror, and he could see the cop memorizing their plate.

The road followed the river, and between swaths of drenching rain the dark stream could be glimpsed swirling and churning and reaching out of its banks with grasping tendrils of water. It reminded Jimmy of Guatemala, and he recalled just how much he'd hated that place, filled with snakes and scorpions, spiders, and every manner of stinging, biting insect. But he'd killed three men there—two with his bare hands—and the experience had left an indelible mark on his mind.

He'd enjoyed it.

Two miles farther along they spotted the taillights of a small coupe ahead of them.

"Weaving," muttered Paco, watching the lights. "Must be drunk."

Jimmy frowned. "Get around him."

Paco nodded, goosing the accelerator. Jimmy felt the rear tires break loose on the wet roadway, but Paco quickly eased off the gas, and they got traction again, pulling past the sedan. Jimmy glanced at the driver—a young man maybe nineteen years old—and decided he wasn't drunk, he was stoned. The kid had the familiar glassy-eyed expression, nodding to the beat of some song on the radio.

Just as Paco gave the car a little gas, Jimmy felt a sickening lurch, then heard the sound of crunching metal as their rear quarter panel connected with the kid's front end. While Paco fought to control the car, Jimmy watched the other sedan rocketing down a steep embankment toward the river.

"Shit!" said Paco, glancing in the rearview mirror.

Jimmy sighed loudly, shaking his head.

"Just fucking keep driving," he said.

VIRGIL SAT IN THE HOSPITAL PARKING LOT, staring at the rain-shimmered pavement. Ernie was going to be all right, according to Doc Burton. But he might limp for the rest of his life.

Like Pierce.

It suddenly dawned on him that the same man might be responsible for both infirmities. But if Rich had hurt the boy all those years ago, he had certainly paid for it tonight. What the hell had caused him to go off his nut like that? If anyone would know, Carly would. He started the car, and pulled out onto the highway.

The story Jake had given him after his mother's death had been so far-fetched that Virgil made sure Jake never told anyone else but him, afraid that the boy would end up in therapy, maybe for life. But now Virgil figured he might have been wrong not to listen. Maybe Jake really *had* seen something impossible back then. And Virgil wasn't all that sure that he and his men, *armed to the teeth,* could kill it the way he'd told Pam. But that was his job. He had to try. Only he hadn't figured out just yet what he was going to tell his deputies. When he neared the intersection with the highway he radioed Rumny, who was on the desk.

"Ernie going to be all right?" asked Rumny.

"Good as can be expected. Pam's worse off than he is. She wouldn't leave his side. Augusta got any more news on that footprint?"

"It's some kind of fancy handmade Italian shoe, Sheriff" came the staticky reply. "They won't be able to give you a run number because it's probably what they call a one-off."

"Made for the person," said Virgil.

"Yeah."

That was good news, but what was a guy wearing handmade shoes doing around Albert's place? What could that possibly have to do with the Crowley curse? Virgil shook his head, too tired to think about it.

"Any more news on the hitchhiker or that hit-and-run?"

"Nothing new on the girl. There's a lot of gray paint on the kid's car, so we can probably trace it to the make, model, and year eventually. If it's not a repaint. But Deputy Grasy just called in and said he thought it might be a couple of suspicious guys he ran into up on Route Five in a Crown Vic with New Jersey plates. I'm running the plate now. Grasy said both guys in the car were Mexican."

Mexican? They didn't see a lot of Latinos in the county.

"You thinking stolen?"

"Maybe."

"Okay. Did you get anyone up to secure the crime scene in the valley yet?"

Slight hesitation. "Not yet. Sorry. We're right out straight. But I'll try to give it priority."

"That's all right. I'm headed back up to talk to Rich Morin's girlfriend. I'll do it."

"You sure you want to try that in the cruiser? The roads

are getting bad fast. Power and phones are going out all over. Hold on. I got another call coming in."

Virgil slowed a mile from the intersection with the valley road, staring at a sheet of water swirling across the highway. It should be safe. But it could be a lot deeper than it looked. Rumny's voice came back on the radio.

"Sheriff, there's a missing persons report out of New Jersey on the guy that owned that Crown Vic."

"Did the kid from the hit-and-run give you a description of the guys that hit him?"

"That just came in, too. Kid said the passenger looked Mexican."

"Okay. Put out an APB on 'em."

"Done."

"I'll call you again from Rich Morin's. Call Pam's place as soon as you get a chance and tell Jake Crowley that Ernie is gonna be okay," said Virgil, snapping the mike back into its holder.

He climbed out of the cruiser just as a bolt of lightning struck somewhere back up the valley. Thunder hammered like a giant fist on top of the car.

He snatched a flashlight out of the trunk and waded into what turned out to be a foot-deep torrent, the current trying to suck his feet out from under him, and he kept going until he was outside the limits of the headlights. The water was a little deeper than when he had come through before, but still fordable.

But once I get in this I won't be able to turn around, and if I try to back out I'll just shove water up the exhaust.

He turned back toward the cruiser, and a sudden sense of foreboding slipped over him. He shone the light through the forest, unsnapping his holster with his free hand.

It's just nerves. Keep walking.

But he couldn't get the images of Albert's and Rich's and

the girl's—and then Jake's mother's—corpses out of his mind. He was almost back within the comforting glow of his headlights when he heard someone whispering, the noise slipping through the rain like a fallen leaf winding through rocks in a stream. He traced the forest with the flashlight again, but saw nothing but trees.

He drew his pistol and kept moving. The car was only twenty yards ahead when he heard the whispering again, close behind him. He spun around so fast the wet flashlight slipped from his hand, flying out into the water. For just an instant he could see it shining beneath the murky flow as it was carried off the road and away into the flood.

Another whisper.

Closer.

"Police! Who's there?" he shouted, backing toward the car.

And then the whispering stopped.

He slogged quickly through the flood and climbed shakily back into the car, slamming the door.

What the hell was out there? It wasn't anything natural. He'd been a hunter all his life, and he'd never heard anything like that sound in the forest before tonight. Instinct warned him to turn around, to head back for town where there were lights, and people. But his sense of duty voted otherwise. No bogeyman was going to keep him from doing a job he'd been doing most of his life. There was something out there that he needed to understand. Something that threatened his citizens, people who had voted for him because they trusted him to protect them. And if anyone had answers it would be Jake. Not Carly.

He stared through the windshield, gauging the water ahead. He could probably make it with no problem if he really gunned the throttle.

He shifted into drive, and the car plowed ahead, Virgil fighting the wheel, listening for the telltale chugging that would signal that the engine had started sucking water. But the big cruiser just kept surging along like an old fishing boat. He knew there was a dip ahead, the one spot that would kill the car if any spot could.

If I'm going too slow when I hit that, she'll never climb back out the other side.

But there was also just a chance that the dip was now so deep that the car would lose its footing there and be washed away downstream, into the wide, deadly maw of the angry Androscoggin. He floored the accelerator, and the big sedan reacted like a steadfast old farm horse, clammering its rubber hooves against the drowned asphalt. Virgil's guts tightened. He felt as though he was on top of a roller coaster as the front end dropped into the mouth of the depression. A wave of green water washed over the hood, and then the car rose up again, chugging and sputtering forward.

If she can get a breath of air she'll make it.

Water splashed alongside his door. The car was climbing, but the engine stuttered, and Virgil heard the rumbling echo of the submerged exhaust beginning to drink.

Come on, baby, dry land must be just ahead.

The car lurched and jerked its way like a drowning swimmer but finally lost the battle, gurgling to a bumping halt in two feet of flood, and he ran the battery dead trying to restart it.

Just then he saw headlights coming up from the rear, and he climbed out to wade into the center of the oncoming lane to warn them off. But the big sedan blasted up out of the dip like a sea monster, rising from the waves. When he could just make out the two dark forms in the front seat he realized that instead of slowing down the car was speeding up, plowing a wall of water before it. Heading right for him. He could hear the engine revving.

He dove into the flood behind the cruiser just as the Crown Victoria surged past. By the time he splashed to his feet and pulled his pistol the headlights were disappearing, and it dawned on him then that the car had been gray, and the right rear quarter panel and bumper were smashed.

He ran back to the cruiser and tried to contact Rumny, but with the battery dead the radio was useless. He threw the mike down and dug his cell phone out of the console. But as soon as he turned it on the no-service light glowed, and he tossed it onto the seat.

Might as well be living in the Old West.

He could head for the nearest house back along the highway and try to call Rumny. But the phone lines were going down fast, and that might well be a waste of time. He could hotfoot it back to town, but there was a good chance the road would already be washed out between here and Arcos.

Or . . . he could hike on ahead and try to get his hands on the crazy pair in the Crown Vic. The highway on the other side of the Crowley intersection was closed. And they couldn't get far in the valley. He knew that going after them without backup was an unprofessional and risky thing to do. But another thought nagged at his mind.

Mexicans. A pair of Mexicans out here crazy enough to run a kid into the river and leave him. Was it remotely possible that *everything* was related? Could it be some of Torrio's men, after Jake?

Virgil *tried* to do things by the book. But sometimes you just had to do things the John Wayne way. He snatched the shotgun from the console and dug extra ammo for it and his pistol out of the trunk along with another flashlight. With any luck the jerks would be sitting in the middle of the washout ahead with a dead car.

raincoat over his shoulders, tugging him out to the car even as he struggled to put his arms into the jacket.

Water puddled all around the little station wagon. Her feet were soaked before she climbed in, and she knew Pierce's were, as well. As she started the car and shifted into reverse, she noticed that the creeping flood she'd seen in the backyard had already reached the side of the house and was flowing around the foundation toward them. Suddenly the car wallowed on slippery mud and slid toward the trees.

Jake paced the kitchen floor. Cramer sat at the table staring at him.

"Why don't you call her?"

Jake stopped, reaching for the phone. His hand hung there for a moment, then dropped.

"What?" said Cramer.

"If she wanted my help, she'd call."

"Jesus," muttered Cramer. "You two really are pieces of work. You're worried shitless and you won't call. She's probably scared shitless, and she won't call, either. Were you two always like this?"

"No," said Jake sadly. "We weren't like this at all."

"What happened?"

"It's a long story."

Cramer glanced into the living room where Barbara dozed on the couch with her mouth wide open. Oswald had his head in her lap. "I have time."

"Some shit happened," said Jake. "I had to leave."

"Something to do with the curse."

Jake shrugged. "Yeah."

"You thought you could take it with you and no one here would get hurt."

Jake nodded.

"But it didn't work," said Cramer. "Your uncle got killed, and then Torrio's men on the beach. That's why you came back. You wanted to prove to yourself that the two weren't related. That Albert's death was a fluke."

Jake glared at him. "I wanted to see if there wasn't some way to end the curse for good. To see if I couldn't stop the horror from starting again."

"Why did you have to do that here?"

Jake shook his head. "I don't know. I just know in my heart that regardless of what happened on the beach, it's all centered here, somehow. In this valley."

"And you think you *can* stop it?"

Jake sighed heavily. "I don't know how. I don't even have any idea what it is."

More lightning flashed and thunder roared. The sound of water pouring off the porch roof grew louder. When the phone rang Jake snatched it out of its cradle.

"Hello."

"This is Deputy Rumny at the county sheriff's office. Sheriff Milche wanted me to call and let you know that Pastor Ernie is gonna be all right. Have you seen Sheriff Milche?"

"Not since he left for the hospital. I thought he was in Arcos."

"No, he was headed back to Crowley. If you see him, please tell him that—"

The house lights went out, and the phone went dead.

"What happened?" asked Cramer. Jake rustled around on the kitchen counter for matches. He found them and lit a candle. Barbara started whimpering, and Cramer called to quiet her.

"The dispatcher wanted to let us know Virgil was on the way back to the valley," said Jake, shaking his head. "Now the phone's out."

"Great."

Jake stared into the storm.

"Get the fuck out of here and go get Mandi and Pierce, for God's sake," said Cramer, rising and shoving Jake toward the door.

Jake didn't argue. "I'll be back as soon as I can. Take care of Barbara."

Cramer frowned. "Don't take all night."

"Back in a flash," said Jake.

Jimmy stood in the middle of the flooded road, staring up into the dark sky, letting the rain pummel his face as though to say *Send it, asshole, you aren't stopping me now.* Lightning flashed ahead, and he crossed himself and spat.

Paco brooded beside him, silent and alert. Jimmy could smell the fear on him, and he smiled because he knew that Paco was still more afraid of *him* than he was of the storm or the flood raging around them. Good. Served him right for stalling out the fucking car. He had a mind to kill the little bastard right here, right now, for all the trouble he'd caused. None of this shit would have happened—including maybe even José dying—if Paco hadn't screwed up royally.

"Come on," he grumbled. "Let's get to a house where we can dry off. Who knows, maybe we'll get lucky for a change and find Jake Crowley in it."

Paco shrugged, trotting along like an obedient guard dog. When they reached the valley road he pointed up it.

"Crowley?" said Jimmy.

Paco nodded.

"First house we come to," said Jimmy, "we find out where Jake Crowley is holed up."

"We'll be pretty noticeable."

"Then we won't leave anyone around to remember," said Jimmy, still leading the way.

He heard an automobile revving in the woods somewhere ahead and quickened his pace. Stationary headlights and the increasing noise of the screaming engine promised easy prey. But just as he and Paco rounded a bend a small station wagon lurched out of a tree-lined drive and slid in the opposite direction, weaving away up the road. Jimmy waved his hands and Paco jumped up and down shouting, but the lights disappeared in the rain.

"Damn!" shouted Jimmy, backhanding Paco.

Paco didn't ask why he'd been punished. He just lumbered along down the empty driveway behind his boss.

Virgil's determination faltered when he reached another dip in the road. He could feel the asphalt dropping away ahead of him like a steepening shore, and the current got stronger the farther up his legs the water climbed. He shone the light out across the flood and could just make out the reflection of taillight lenses on a car in the distance. So the jerks hadn't made it across. But where were they? It occurred to him—not for the first time—that he was over sixty and facing two men who might well be armed and dangerous, and that there weren't only the *men* to worry about. He looked back over his shoulder, but he knew he wasn't turning back. Doris had always said his hardheadedness was going to be his downfall one day. But Virgil knew it had been as much a virtue in his job as a curse. A lawman who let his fear rule his heart was useless. He stumbled forward until the current jerked his legs out from under him, and he began to swim.

He held the shotgun out of the water with one hand and slapped along with the waterproof flashlight in the other.

But he was afraid he was going to be carried away into the river before he could reach shallow water again. He kicked wildly until finally his feet found bottom, and he struggled—wheezing and coughing—up into thigh-deep water again. He stood for a moment gasping for breath.

When he finally spotted the swamped car again he took his time approaching it. The rain whipped the flood's surface into a roiling stew, and the sound of it striking the water and the nearby woods was like being caught inside a rock-crushing machine. He walked slowly around the sedan, sure now that these were the same assholes who'd sent the kid to the hospital.

The keys were in the ignition. Water had already reached the bottom of the dash and was creeping across the gold-colored upholstery. Shining the light on the back of the driver's seat, he saw two reddish brown stains marring the cloth. He scratched at a scabby brown smudge with his fingernail and knew immediately what it was.

He jerked the key out of the ignition and opened the trunk. He hadn't known for certain he'd find a corpse inside. But intuition told him to check, and there it was. The holes in the guy's side told Virgil the pair up ahead *were* armed and dangerous. And he was pretty sure now why they were here. They were heading into Crowley, and Jake had no way of knowing they were coming.

Great.

He slammed the trunk lid and trudged off toward the valley.

Mandi had barely been able to get the little Subaru back out of the ditch and into the driveway again by shifting from drive to reverse and back again. Now, barely a quarter of the way to Pam and Ernie's, she stared into the water ahead and tried to keep her breathing steady. She knew Pierce sensed her fear, but he was quiet, facing straight ahead into the night.

The swirling gray flood seemed to stretch forever through the trees, and she tried to picture the layout of the road hidden beneath. When she peered into the rearview mirror, the washout right behind them—blood-red in the brake lights—continued creeping inexorably toward them. She couldn't believe how fast the water was rising. The rain was sluicing down the mountains faster than the valley could flush it out to the river. If they stopped here now it would just swallow them up.

She took Pierce's hand and signed to him. *We're going through deep water again. I won't let anything happen to you. Don't be afraid.*

He nodded. But his jaw was clenched, and his nostrils flared. She steeled herself for the plunge, praying the little station wagon was up to the challenge. If she went in fast she hoped she could plow through any deep spots. On the other hand, she might also bury the car in the wave of water she built up, splash it right up into the engine and kill it. She elected to compromise. The car didn't hit the water so much as merge with it, like a boat launching off a trailer. She glanced nervously out her window, but the flow barely touched the bottom of the door.

With the water swirling all around it would be easy to wander off the narrow road and into the gully. If the tires slipped over the edge, she and Pierce would be in real trouble fast. The steering wheel gave a jerk, and she whipped it back, praying she hadn't overcompensated, but the trusty little car just kept on huffing through the flood.

Finally she could see the road again, rising gently ahead. But it looked more like a tributary than a dirt lane, and she wondered if the station wagon would be able to get enough of a grip on its slippery surface to climb to safety. She chanced a peek at Pierce, and her heart stopped.

He had his head cocked at an unusual angle, and he was staring out into the night as though he could see. If she hadn't known better she would have sworn he was listening to something.

JIMMY AND PACO trudged slowly down the muddy driveway the car had exited.

"You hear something, boss?" asked Paco meekly.

Jimmy glared at him, wondering again if he wouldn't be
better off just shooting the little bastard right here and stash-
ing the body in the trees. In a wilderness like this the asshole's corpse might never be found.

But he did hear something. And he didn't think it was
something that should be living in any forest. It sounded almost like some kind of crooning.

"That's the noise like what I heard at the old man's
house," muttered Paco, nudging close enough to put his
mouth to Jimmy's ear.

Jimmy backhanded him hard between the eyes, with his
pistol this time, and Paco straightened, holding his head in
both hands.

"Quit fucking freaking out," said Jimmy, shoving Paco
down the driveway. "Move!"

There were no lights on in the house, and Jimmy took

only a moment to discern that there was no other car around before climbing up onto the front stoop, grateful to get out of the deluge at last.

Paco knocked several times. Finally Jimmy nodded toward the door and Paco turned the knob.

"It's open," said Paco.

"Anybody home?" shouted Jimmy, but he was already sure the house was empty. He relaxed his grip on the pistol and entered the house.

"See what's around to eat," he said, flipping the light switch ineffectually. "And look for some candles."

Finding the bathroom by feel, he jerked off his jacket and shirt, then stripped out of his pants and briefs, drying off and tossing the sodden towels onto the floor. It felt wonderful to be dry. He wrapped a fresh towel around his waist and hung another over his shoulder just as Paco showed up with a candle and a plate of sliced cheese and sardines.

Jimmy took the plate into the small living room and plopped into the only chair, resting his pistol on the small table. He wolfed down the sharp cheese and gobbled the salty fish, rubbing his greasy hands onto the towel in his lap.

Paco—still sopping—stood looking at him like a mute, and Jimmy shook his head.

"Go dry off," he said. "You stupid or what?"

"I just wanted to make sure you was okay, boss."

Jimmy belched loudly and set the plate down beside his pistol, studying the room. Whoever lived in the dump was poor. There were a couple of pictures of scenery on the walls, but the frames looked to be plastic, and the artwork could have been bought at Wal-Mart. The carpet was clean but worn. The whole place reminded Jimmy too much of his childhood. He grabbed the candle and started exploring.

There was a small hall closet containing an ancient vacuum and a bunch of cleaning products. The bath where Paco was still drying off. Then there was a small bedroom. The artwork on the walls there was different. Instead of cheap paintings there were framed reliefs that looked as though they'd been done by a kid. But maybe a kid with talent. They were all of the same woman's face. The one above the bed was pretty good. The woman had high cheekbones and a wide smile. Jimmy crossed to the bedside table and lifted one of the large magazines with plain brown covers. Inside he discovered nothing but a series of embossed bumps.

"Braille," he muttered, tossing the magazine back onto the bed. So there was a blind kid living here, and his family had taken him somewhere else to wait out the storm. He glanced across the room at an old metal desk and a wooden worktable.

Atop the desk sat another relief of some sort, and Jimmy studied it. Like the framed sculptures, there was no color and no shading. But it only took Jimmy a moment to decipher that it was a topographic map of the valley. The mountains on both sides had been constructed of modeling clay. Tiny plastic trees were stuck haphazardly into the landscape to denote forest. The highway and the river took up all of one end. Small plastic letters marked each of the little cabins along the one road. The house Jimmy and Paco had discovered read "Morin." He searched up and down the road, finally finding a cabin marked "Pam & Ernie." He knew from what Paco had told him that that had to be Jake Crowley's cousin.

So that was where he'd find Jake.

Climbing the stairs to the loft bedroom, he was struck once again by the feeling of déjà vu. His own parents' bedroom had looked much like this, even to the picture of Jesus over the bed. He crossed himself and spat onto the carpet.

The clothes in the closet told him the woman lived alone with the boy. And she was small, probably well built. Jimmy felt slightly aroused. This was like touching a woman who didn't want to be touched but couldn't do anything about it, and he liked the feeling. He glanced over at the dresser and stopped.

There were two small, gilt-framed photographs side by side. One showed a cute brunette woman standing beside a small boy with dark hair and eyes. But it was the other picture that held Jimmy's attention. He lifted it up to the candle and examined it closely.

The woman was hardly more than a teenager, and the young man who had his arm around her shoulder also had dark hair and eyes. He was a lot younger than the man Jimmy knew. But there was no mistaking the face.

It was Jake Crowley.

"I'll be fucked," he whispered, smiling.

S JAKE STARTED THE CAR and the headlights flashed along the house, his breath caught in his throat. Water ran between the trees in sheets, as though the mountains were becoming one giant sluice.

He gunned the car down the drive, fighting for control in the muck. Just as he turned onto the valley road the rear wheels broke free, and the back end of the car lurched into the narrow drainage ditch and struck a tree. He pounced on the pedal, and the car jerked out of the trough with a grinding screech and a deep rumbling complaint.

As he negotiated sharp curves and washouts, the car swallowed water, and the engine began to chug. He knew he had to slow down, that he was beginning to panic, but he had the sense that something was gaining on him, and the feeling wouldn't go away. The crimson shadows behind the car were as frightening as the flooded road ahead, and he couldn't keep his eyes off the rearview mirror.

He pulled up short in front of yet another wide washout, barely able to make out the other side through the rain. The flood frothed, as though it weren't passing over flat road, but winding around boulders and debris. He thought of the thing out there, somewhere, and against his will images of his mother's death filled his mind.

He was only ten at the time, but he had been allowed to play outside by himself until well after dark. There seemed nothing for a child to fear way up there at the head of the valley, as long as he stayed away from the swimming hole. The cliff over the deepest pool was high enough that even his dad would not leap off it. And the water—though clear and cold—swirled and eddied with secret, dangerous currents that carried the little stream all the way through the valley and into the mighty Androscoggin far below.

That evening his dad had asked him if he wanted to run to Albert's on some errand after dinner. But Jake had chosen to return to constructing a secret fort out of broken branches and boards he'd scrounged from behind the house.

Gradually a strange whispering through the branches had caught his attention. But there was no breeze, and he stood, searching the moonlit forest for the source. Following it back to the clearing behind the house, he had realized that the sound was coming from inside. A shadow had passed across the windows, and the noise increased, until it became a roar, and Jake shivered.

When his mother screamed, he stood frozen for a moment longer, before his legs had started carrying him of their own accord toward the sound of her voice.

Images of his mother—both before and after—blasted his mind. Images of the shadow . . .

Run away, Jake.

As he stared across the roiling water, the hair on the back of his neck began to tickle, and instead of his mother, he pictured Mandi, and his heart stopped. He ached to rush to her and Pierce, to bring them back to safety. But was that what he was doing? Or was he bringing more danger to their doorstep? Would it be better to turn around and leave them to their own chances in the storm rather than have them close to him? A tickling in his gut told him no. Whatever was coming, whatever was loose in the valley—whether he was the cause of it or simply one more victim of the Crowley curse—he could not go back without them. He eased the car out into the water, surprised by the power of the current rocking the vehicle. As he gave the car a little more gas he felt the stream flushing around the sides of the sedan, creating a bow wave like a tramp steamer.

When he reached the other side of the washout he glanced back again. For just an instant he thought he saw something large and dark moving along the road. Then all the shadows flowed together inside the wall of rain, and he drove on.

Mandi slammed her hand against the wheel so hard a sharp pain shot up her arm all the way to her shoulder. Pierce jerked, turning in her direction with a questioning expression.

She took his hand, signing as calmly as she could. *We're going to have to walk.*

Why?

Water in the engine. When I open the door it's going to come inside.

Deep?

She peered out at the water lapping at the bottom of her window. *Yes. But we'll be able to stand up. I won't let you go.*

He shook his head, and she understood why. It would be terrifying enough for her, climbing out into the flood. But at least she could see by the submerged headlights and the occasional lightning flash. How much more terrible would it be for him, feeling the current clutching at him, trying to drag him away into some dark horror that he could hardly imagine?

We have to, she signed.

He signed so fast she could barely decipher it. *Too deep. I'm scared.*

She steadied his hand over hers before signing back. *I'm scared, too. Love me?*

He nodded.

Trust me?

A slower nod.

No choice. We have to go. We'll die if we stay here.

There, she hadn't lied to him.

He took a long breath, letting it out, nodding slowly.

She exhaled in rhythm with him. She couldn't believe the water wasn't already inside. But the little car had good tight doors and windows. She withdrew her hand from Pierce's and studied the flow, trying to decide whether to climb out on his side or her own. She was downstream. Her door should be easier to open, and the car would protect them from some of the current. But either way, if Pierce got out of her grasp he'd be as helpless as a newborn bird in the dark forest. He couldn't even call out for help. The thought of him drifting away from her in that angry flood tore at her heart, and she knew she'd drown before she'd let that happen.

Pierce found her hand and signed again. *How deep?*

She sighed. *Up to your waist. It'll come in when I open the door.*

He clenched his jaw but offered no further comment.

The water was going to be cold. It was already chilling the inside of the car, and she wondered how long the lights would continue to shine beneath the flow before the battery died or something shorted out.

Then the car gave a sickening lurch, and she felt the tires

lose their purchase on the submerged road. The station wagon lurched like a drunk as the stream lifted it and carried them into the trees.

Pierce grabbed her arm, reaching for her hand again, but Mandi was spinning the steering wheel and kicking the brakes as though she still had some kind of control over their destiny.

A MILLION TINY ARTILLERY SHELLS OF RAIN exploded in the flood as Jake stared at the churning water stretching away as far as his headlights shone. The last washout had nearly killed the car, and now the engine huffed and coughed for air. He raced it, the car shaking as the waterlogged cylinders screwed up the firing rhythm.

He tapped the wheel nervously. He knew that if he tried crossing this last overflow the car would stall and probably be washed away into the trees, but he might be able to make it across on foot. Snagging the flashlight from the glove box, he climbed out of the car.

This is not a bright idea. This is definitely not bright.

But he tested the water anyway, letting his foot settle to the bottom. The icy liquid stung his ankles like needles.

Another step, up to his knees, the force of the water surprising him. Off to his left a movement caught his eye, and he swung the flashlight just in time to see a small pine tree come crashing through the woods and across the road in front of him. Its roots had been cleansed of soil and debris by the rain, and they reached raking wooden talons toward him in passing. When the tree was gone he trudged ahead. The stinging became an icy burn as the water reached mid-thigh.

He battled through the current, his arms spread wide for balance as the water reached for his waist, wondering how strong the batteries were in the flashlight.

Mandi struggled to control her rising panic as Pierce clutched the armrest on his door, his face ashen in the glow of the interior light. Miraculously the headlights continued to shine through the swirling water around them like the lights of Nemo's *Nautilus,* illuminating the flooded forest in eerie golden waves. The car bumped from tree to tree as it drifted through the woods, but as the forest thickened there was less and less room for the little station wagon. Finally the water backed up behind the vehicle, surging and shoving until the car was tightly wedged between two bent ever-greens. The flood rushed over the rear window and around the sides of the car.

Mandi took three deep breaths before catching Pierce's hand. *We're all right.*

He turned to her, his lips tight. *Where are we?* he signed.

Caught in the trees.

What now?

That was the same question she'd been asking herself over and over.

We're all right for now. Maybe the water will go down.

Staring into the rain, she knew that was the first lie she'd told him, and she could tell he didn't really believe her. She withdrew her hand from his, and rubbed the sweat on her pants.

*   *   *

Jake climbed wearily out of the water. He was soaked to the skin, and his shoes creaked with every step—reminding him again of his run on the Galveston beach—as he continued down the road, hoping there were no more washouts between him and Mandi's house. But he'd barely made it a hundred yards before he rounded a curve and came upon an even wider flood. He was still winded from his last struggle with the current. If he went back now he was pretty sure he could make it to the car. If he tried to cross here and got carried into the trees he'd drown.

He stomped around for a minute, eyes down, trying to think. Mandi's place was situated on fairly high ground. She and Pierce should be safe there. If they stayed in the house. But what if a flash flood ran down the valley? What if she panicked and tried to get Pierce out? Suddenly he was absolutely certain that Mandi and Pierce *did* need him. He stood with the toes of his shoes in the water staring into the wall of rain. It was almost as far back to the car as it was to Mandi's now, anyway.

"Oh, hell!" he said, starting across.

But this washout was deeper. Before he made it twenty feet the water was up to his waist, and it was all he could do to keep his footing against the current. He clung to the flashlight as though it were a lifeline, holding it tenaciously above the clutching flood. Just when he had decided that he had to turn back after all, a sound louder than the rushing water caused him to jerk to the right, and his feet lifted off the road's surface. He had no choice but to lean back and let the water carry him into the trees. He grabbed the first limb that passed, letting the current lock him into the tree's embrace. In the distance he heard the sound again.

It was a car horn.

* * *

Mandi's hand shook on the wheel. She blasted the horn again, even though she knew that it was a waste of time and that Pierce would feel the vibration, that he would sense her panic. But he sat stoically, gripping the armrest in both hands, his jaw tight.

Water flowed two inches above the bottom of the tightly closed windows. The headlights *still* continued to work, and the thought of them failing, leaving her as blind as Pierce, was terrifying. But water now covered the floorboard, and she could hear it *sss*ing through a million tiny openings.

They had to get outside before the car sank, but she had no idea what they would do once they got there. If she opened a window or a door she was afraid the car would flood and be dragged under the water before she could get Pierce out. Even if they did manage to escape the car she had no idea how she could get Pierce to safety.

In desperation she pounded the horn again, but she knew no one was going to hear.

Jake realized that if he let go of the tree he could drift with the current toward the sound of the honking horn. It would be easy to get lost or knocked unconscious in the trees and submerged bracken. But he thought he saw light in the direction of the noise. It terrified him to think that it might be Mandi and Pierce in the car. But whoever was honking was in big trouble.

Like he was going to save anybody.

He shoved off anyway, still fighting to keep the flashlight above water. Several times the current bumped him against a tree so hard it knocked the wind out of him. He kicked off from a thick spruce and rolled onto his side, doing the crawl.

He was swept between a stand of birch just as he spotted the car ahead and realized it *was* Mandi's station wagon. He kicked in that direction, but the current kept dragging him away into the darkness.

He paddled and kicked as hard as he could, panting like a run-out racehorse by the time his hand slapped the rear window of the car. He scrabbled for purchase on the slippery metal as the current dragged him along the car's body, finally snatching the door handle and spinning himself up onto the hood. The water pressed hard against the little car, threatening to sink it at any minute, and Jake wondered first how he was going to get Mandi and Pierce out, then what they were all going to do once he had.

Mandi chanced rolling her window down just a crack. "How did you get here?" she shouted.

"Took a swim," said Jake. "I thought you might need me."

She tried to smile, but there were tears in her eyes.

"What do we do?" she shouted.

"Will Pierce roll down his own window?" said Jake.

She glanced at the boy and nodded again.

"Set up a signal," Jake shouted, standing on tiptoe to secure the flashlight in the lowest branches of one of the trees. "I want you both to roll them down at the same time. As fast as you can. Then you slide out your side and onto the hood. If you feel yourself slipping grab hold of the tree."

"I don't want to leave Pierce inside."

"Mandi, you have to trust me," said Jake, wondering if she would. "While you're going out your side, I'm going back in the water, and I'm going to grab Pierce and pull him out. Tell him what's happening."

She took Pierce's hand and signed. It was clear from the rapid hand movements that there was a problem.

"What's the matter?" shouted Jake.

"He doesn't want me to leave him."

"You aren't leaving him."

"I'm explaining that concept to him!"

Finally Pierce nodded and put his hand on the window button.

"He knows I'm going to grab him?" said Jake.

Mandi's face was white in the flashlight's glow. "Yes."

"All right. On my mark you both let them down. What's Pierce's signal?"

"I'm going to pat him on the arm."

"Go."

Mandi reached over and tapped Pierce. She waited until his window started down before she pressed her own control. Very quickly, cold gray water started pouring over the top of the glass. By the time the window was all the way down the water rushed in so fast she could barely press herself into the opening. But still she waited, half in, half out, watching Jake across the roof of the car, reaching for Pierce.

"Mandi!" Jake screamed. "Get out! I've got him."

Only then did she pull herself out of the car.

Jake gripped the window frame with one hand, the half-healed bullet wound burning like a brand. With the other he grabbed Pierce and pulled the boy, coughing and gagging, out into the flow.

Pierce was jerked sideways by the current, and Jake twisted with him, hanging onto the window, swinging the boy toward the closest tree. But he could already feel the rear end of the car dipping from the weight of the water, the front end pulling itself out of the wedging trees. He glanced over in time to see Mandi crawling onto the hood, but the current was breaking his grip. He let go of the car and kicked back, allowing the surge to press him against the fender. He slipped along the car to the tree, and when he had a firm grip around its trunk, he pulled Pierce back to him, showing the boy how to wrap his arms around the spruce and let the flood hold him there.

"Mandi!" he shouted. "Over here."

She slid toward them, but suddenly the car rolled away on the current, and she was carried along with it, then dragged under the dark swirling water. Jake kicked off, diving blindly into the flood. He ran his hands over the car grille as it slipped away from him, until his fingernails snagged cloth, and with a firm grip he fought toward the surface. Mandi popped up, gagging and sputtering beside him.

"Pierce!" she gasped, as they spun and bounced through the flood.

"Lock arms!" screamed Jake.

Mandi grabbed his free arm just in time for a tall birch to catch them midgrip. They swung around it, bumping into each other on the far side.

"Pierce is back there!" she shouted.

"I know that," he said, staring toward the meager flashlight glow. He could barely make out the boy's face, fifty feet away through the trees.

"He can't hear or see us!"

Pierce couldn't come to them, and if Jake managed to make it to him he didn't know if he'd have the strength to get back to Mandi with the boy.

"How's your swimming these days?" he said.

"I can get to my son."

"All right. But when we take off there's no stopping. No letting up."

She nodded. "Just let me catch my breath."

When he sensed she was ready he tapped her on the shoulder. "I'll be right beside you. If you need to rest just let me carry you."

"You'll wear out before we get there."

"Let me worry about that."

She surprised him by kicking out into the flood first, stroking hard, her feet making a propeller splash behind her. But headway came dear against the current. Jake watched her for a moment to gauge her strength. She wouldn't give up until the flood killed her. But it might well kill her before she reached Pierce.

He leaped out into the flow, following in her wake.

THE LAST FEW FEET WERE THE WORST. The trees were closer together, and the water rampaged through them. It was all Jake could do to paddle and kick the final inches to the tree, tugging an exhausted Mandi along beside him. Now she and Pierce clung to the first spruce, and Jake was five feet away, wrapped around the other. With the car and the headlights gone, safety and the flashlight were eight feet above their heads. The water was like ice. Jake's entire body felt bee-stung. Hypothermia. The next step would be numbness. Then death.

"We have to climb up in the tree!" he shouted.

"I don't think I can make it," said Mandi.

"You have to."

"What about Pierce?"

Jake took several deep breaths, struggling to get his stamina back. The space between them wasn't much of a jump, but at the moment the distance seemed almost insurmountable.

"I'm coming over!"

Mandi nodded, crowding behind Pierce, wrapping her arms around him and the tree. Jake kicked off upstream, letting the water carry him back to them. He slid his hand between Pierce and the tree and hung on. He glanced up at the flashlight that was now way out of reach.

"Can you explain to him what we need to do?" shouted Jake.

Mandi let go of the tree with one hand and got Pierce to open one palm. She signed rapidly, but Pierce shook his head.

"What did he say?" said Jake.

"He said we need to get out of here."

Jake frowned, spitting water. "Tell him he has a firm grasp of the obvious."

But Pierce continued signing.

"He said he hears the whispers again," said Mandi.

Jake closed his eyes and tried to hear it, but the rushing water and the slapping rain obscured all other sounds. "I don't hear anything."

"He says it's coming this way."

She signed back to Pierce, but before she was finished he began to jerk convulsively in her arms.

"What the hell?" said Jake.

"He's trying to get away!" she said, hugging Pierce against the tree.

Jake glanced up once more at the flashlight, then searched the trees around them for some way out. He tried to spot higher ground through the feeble glow, but everything around them was rushing water. Pierce was about to break away from his mother, and if he did Jake had no idea how he'd get the kid back.

"All right! Tell him we'll get out of here."

"How?"

"Don't ask me how yet! Just tell him!"

Mandi signed to the boy again, and Pierce quieted, but his face was still a mask of terror.

"Here!" said Jake, crowding in closer to Mandi and slipping his hand between her and Pierce. "Have him talk to me."

Pierce bent his elbow nearly double, but managed to spell into Jake's hand.

It's almost here.

Jake shook his head. *I don't hear it.*

It's coming.

Jake wanted to say, So what? It wasn't like the whispers were the only thing they had to worry about. But the look on the boy's face was worth a thousand words, and Jake couldn't get the image of mangled corpses out of his mind. Suddenly drowning didn't seem so bad.

"I'm going to climb up and get the light," he said.

Mandi peered up the slippery tree trunk but said nothing as Jake worked his way around to find a better climbing position. Pierce felt the movement and tried to get Mandi to give him her hand, but she put herself nose to nose with him and shook her head emphatically.

Jake lunged upward, locking his arms and legs around the tree like a boa constrictor, but even as he did gravity pulled him downward. He bumped Mandi's shoulder with the sole of one shoe.

"Sorry."

"I'm all right," said Mandi, twisting her head to see up through the rain.

"There's nothing to get a grip on."

He dug his nails into the bark, vising his knees into the trunk, but the damned tree was slippery as an eel. He tried another leap upward, but he plunged backward into the stream just in time to see the flashlight dropping into the raging flood. He slapped his way to the surface, wrapping his arms around Mandi and Pierce as the flashlight doused itself somewhere in the depths.

Now they were all blind.

"Great," he muttered.

Pierce began to shake again, trying to break free of Mandi's grasp. Jake squeezed his shoulder reassuringly, but it didn't seem to help.

"I can't hold him much longer," Mandi gasped.

"We'll have to keep Pierce between us," said Jake. "Whatever you do don't let go of him, and I won't, either. We can stop at trees for a breather."

"All right!"

He eased around, pressed into her by the force of the water. When he reached the far side of the tree he found Pierce's hand and spelled.

We're going to swim. Just float on your back. Don't let go of our hands.

Pierce squeezed his hand tightly.

"Float with your feet in front of you for protection," Jake shouted at Mandi. "And keep your knees bent! Are you ready?"

"I guess so," she answered uncertainly.

"Okay, then," said Jake. He took Pierce's right hand in his left. As they splashed out into the current, Jake thought he, too, heard the whispering sound.

KEEPING THREE PEOPLE TOGETHER and alive in the swirling black madness of the flood was insanity. Jake's knees ached, and his shoulders were raw from being rubbed against rough bark and broken branches. His mouth was full of foul-tasting, gritty runoff. And each time they were driven into a tree he nearly lost his grip on Pierce. Worst of all, he could hear the whispering clearly now.

It stalked and circled them through the flood like a shark. Pierce struggled frantically between them, and Jake could hear Mandi panting and sputtering on the other side of the boy. When Jake bumped into yet another tree he locked his arm around it, drawing Mandi and Pierce in, even though Pierce continued to kick and splash.

"I've got to rest," Jake shouted at Mandi. "Tell him to give me just a moment."

"He's terrified," she said.

Like I'm not, thought Jake.

Only the occasional lightning bolt revealed any of their surroundings. The entire valley seemed to be under water.

They weren't swimming through tree trunks any longer. They were being propelled through the upper branches. And the sound kept getting closer. To Jake it felt as though the thing was breathing right down the back of his neck.

"Come on," he said, kicking off again just as another lightning bolt flashed.

But the struggle through the current was wearing him to the breaking point. He gave one last hard kick—fearing that his decision had cost them all their lives—and was surprised when his feet touched solid ground.

"Hey!" he said, jerking Pierce to his feet. The water was barely up to Jake's waist. "Keep moving upslope."

They struggled into ever shallower water until they finally huddled, shivering, beneath the spreading branches of a fir, at last out of the flood.

"Do you have any idea where we are?" shouted Mandi.

"No."

"We can't stay here."

"I'm aware of that."

"Well, which way should we go?"

"I can't tell where the damned noise is coming from," said Jake. "One minute it's over here. Then it's over there."

Pierce slapped at Jake's chest, then found his hand again.

It's coming, Pierce spelled.

Jake spelled back, trying to explain to Pierce how dangerous it was to continue stumbling around in the dark, but Pierce took Jake's hand and pointed behind him.

You know where it is? spelled Jake.

Pierce placed Jake's hand on his head and nodded vigorously.

"He says he can tell where the sound is coming from," said Jake.

"Maybe we should just go where Pierce doesn't hear it," said Mandi.

Jake didn't have any better ideas, and the noise was growing again, turning dirgelike and even more threatening than before.

Jake placed Pierce's hand on *his* head and nodded back.

"What if we're moving away from the road, though?" said Mandi, as Pierce dragged them along.

"Right now I'm more interested in moving away from whatever that is," shouted Jake.

They clung to each other, crashing through underbrush, trudging in and out of shallow water, the rain dripping in sheets from the thick canopy overhead. Jake fought his growing panic, knowing that Pierce and Mandi were only controlling theirs because of him.

They wandered for what seemed miles before Jake jerked Pierce and Mandi to a halt. Pierce tugged at his arm, and Jake could feel fear raging through the boy.

"Tell him I need to *think!*" shouted Jake.

She moved close to Jake, wedging Pierce between them. Pierce tugged at their hands, slipping one of his under Mandi's and signing furiously.

"He says he knows the way!" Mandi shouted.

"Mandi, that's crazy."

"Maybe it isn't. He said *being lost is like being broken.*"

"What the hell does that mean?"

"Pierce is good at fixing things."

"We could drown out here, Mandi. If Pierce is in the lead and gets caught in a current he might be pulled away, and we wouldn't see him."

"I know that. But we're running out of time. We have to trust him. He says that thing is coming, right now."

At that instant another bolt of lightning struck somewhere up the mountain, and Jake thought he caught a glimpse of a giant shadow moving at the farthest range of his vision.

"Go on, then," he said, nudging Pierce. Pierce squeezed his hand and pulled them up a muddy slope that seemed intent on impeding their progress. The sound was louder now, nearly drowning out the rain.

CANDLELIGHT FROM A WINDOW drew Virgil's attention to Mandi's house, and a tremor of fear raced through him. He shielded the flashlight with a capped hand and stared through the window at the Latino man sitting in the recliner, clothed only in a towel. The toned arms and tight abs spoke of long hours in a workout room, but the Ranger tattoo and the pistol resting on the table beside him warned Virgil that this was no simple street tough.

The smart thing would be to hike up the road to Pam's house and get Jake and Cramer, then come back here and corral this guy and his partner, who was presumably also in the house. But he was afraid that the road between Mandi's and Pam's might be flooded, too, and getting there and back was problematic. At least Mandi's car was gone. That was good news.

Sometimes you couldn't do the smart thing. Sometimes you had to go with your gut. And at least he had the element of surprise going for him.

Climbing silently up onto the stoop, a patch of mud just

in front of the threshold caught his eye, and he leaned over to get a better look.

"Shit," he whispered, staring at the neat footprint in the wet brown clay. A perfect star was centered on the sole. At least one of the guys inside Mandi's house had been at Albert's the day of the killing. Why? Had Albert died because he wouldn't give out information on Jake?

Virgil flicked the flashlight off and rested it in a corner of the wall. Then he checked to make sure there was a shell in the chamber and the safety was off on the shotgun. But his quivering hand reminded him of his age again and that at least one of the guys inside was mid-thirties, athletic, and trained to kill. God only knew who the other guy was or what kind of training he had. Or where he was. His resolve quavering, Virgil did what came naturally.

He acted.

Gripping the shotgun tightly in one hand, he quietly turned the knob, slamming the door open as he burst into the hallway, pointing the shotgun at the big bastard who was already reaching for his pistol.

"Shove it away!" he shouted, watching the hallway from the corner of his eye.

The guy did as he was told, the pistol clattering to the floor, but not far enough away for Virgil's peace of mind. The bathroom door opened just a crack, and Virgil shouted instinctively.

"Come out with your hands up, or I put a shell right through that door!"

"All right!" said the second crook, swinging the door wide and stepping out, wrapped in a towel.

Virgil swung the shotgun so that he could easily take out either of the two. The second guy was smaller and wirier, and he had a sneaky look in his eye Virgil didn't like.

"If you think you're faster than buckshot," he said, "just try something."

"We weren't causing any trouble, Officer," said the bigger guy. "What do you want with us?"

Virgil laughed. "I thought I'd start with murder, attempted murder, breaking and entering, grand theft auto. I imagine Jake has a few things to add."

At the mention of Jake's name the bravado left the Ranger's face, replaced with a deep-seated rage and curiosity.

"Jake Crowley?"

"So you know him."

The smile that crossed the big guy's face was in no way reassuring, and Virgil found himself tickling the trigger of the shotgun.

"Do you know where he is?" asked the Ranger.

"You must be joking," said Virgil, frowning. "You!" he said, catching the little crook edging back toward the bath. "Get in here with your buddy and spread 'em against the wall. You, too, big fella." He waved the shotgun at the Ranger, who merely shrugged and turned away, placing both hands on either side of the window jamb and spreading his feet. The little guy did the same next to him. Virgil jerked out his handcuffs and poked the big guy in the back with the shotgun barrel. "Give me your left hand."

"Fuck you."

Virgil sighed. This would be hard enough with one perp. With two dangerous criminals it was going to be touchy, to say the least. But if he cuffed the two of them together they should be easier to manage. He stuck the shotgun in the little guy's kidneys, hard enough to knock some of the wind out of him.

"Hand!"

The little guy offered his left hand behind his back and

Virgil snapped a cuff on it and backed away. When the punk glanced over his shoulder, Virgil nodded toward the big guy.

"Hook him up," he said, nodding toward the other man's right hand.

The little guy glanced from Virgil to the Ranger. Clearly he was more afraid of the big guy than he was of Virgil and his shotgun.

"Do it!" said Virgil, taking a threatening step forward.

As the small crook stepped in between Virgil and the Ranger, the big guy kicked the little guy square in the belly, driving him back toward Virgil. Virgil just managed to lift the shotgun so that he took the brunt of the falling weight against the stock as he stumbled out into the hall. He smashed the gun sideways into the little guy's head, knocking him to the floor, trying to get a shot at the bigger guy before he could charge. But the Ranger was already crashing through the window, shattering glass and thin mullions. The candle blew out, and by the time Virgil stumbled to the opening there was nothing to see but broken glass, the hammering rain, and the towel snagged on the sill.

Moaning from behind drew Virgil away from the window, and he hurried over to the smaller crook. Even by the dim light of the candle in the bathroom Virgil could see a welt running up the guy's cheek all the way to the hairline. He was going to have a sizeable headache. And the last thing Virgil wanted once the creep came around was to have to baby-sit him. He glanced around the hallway. Ten feet away, beside the phone table, a heating pipe ran floor to ceiling. Virgil grabbed him by the arm, dragged him unceremoniously across the carpet, and hooked the handcuff to the pipe. The guy lost his towel, but Virgil wasn't too worried about his modesty at the moment.

Now what to do about the other guy?

On one hand the asshole was running around in a valley

he didn't know, buck naked and unarmed. On the other hand Virgil was pretty sure that if he really was an ex-Ranger, the situation might not bother him too much.

Virgil stared at the busted window, and suddenly it occurred to him that the guy might be reentering the house at that moment. Why run away when he could hang around and use his training to kill an old, out-of-shape sheriff? Virgil snatched his flashlight from outside, then locked the door and shoved a chair from Pierce's room under the knob. Then he locked the kitchen door and all the other windows. But there was a broken window in Pierce's bedroom covered with cardboard that wasn't going to stop anyone intent on getting in. And as he passed the handcuffed crook again he saw that the guy's eyes were open, glaring at him.

"You didn't have to hit me like that," said the crook.

"Shut up," said Virgil, crossing the living room to shove the recliner up against the wind-tossed curtains. But of course that left most of the opening still uncovered. The house was a sieve.

He jerked the curtains closed on the other two windows and then got the comforter off Pierce's bed and hooked it over the rod on the busted window in the living room, draping the thick blanket down behind the chair to hold it in place. He wasn't happy with it, but the sills were five feet off the ground outside, so if the bastard did try to slip back in that way he'd have to make some noise. Virgil turned back to the little punk.

"Could I have my towel back?" said the guy, making a face. "It's kind of chilly."

Virgil smirked, kicking the towel across the floor to him. The guy eventually gave up trying to wrap it and simply draped it across his midsection. Virgil picked up the pistol from the floor, stuffed it in his pants, then found another in the bathroom, along with a nasty-looking switchblade. He also found credit cards and ID in the name of Paco Estaban. From Houston. In the other guy's clothes he found ID in the name of James Torrio. Also from Houston.

Jimmy Torrio. The brother of the man Jake had killed on the beach. So he hadn't sent goons to do his dirty work. He was here in person.

On the floor beside the dryer were two sets of shoes. One large. One small.

The smaller set had a star on each sole.

THE EERIE NOISE WAS CLOSE enough behind them that for the first time Jake could tell exactly where it was, and he could have sworn that he heard more than whispers. It sounded like a heavy bass rumble that might have been some kind of out-of-phase motor turning. But whenever a lightning bolt struck there was nothing to see but rain and trees.

Then suddenly Pierce stopped in his tracks, and Mandi and Jake collided. Jake tugged at Pierce's hand, but he quickly understood what Pierce already knew. The whispering had stopped. There were no sounds but the rain and rushing water. Without the whispers and the weird thrumming, even the sound of the rain and the thunder seemed subdued. The three of them stood for long minutes, like shell-shocked soldiers waiting for the next cannon blast. Jake put his free arm around Mandi's shoulders, drawing both her and Pierce into a tight embrace.

"Where is it?" she said.

"Ask Pierce."

She took Pierce's hand, and they communicated silently. "He says he doesn't hear it."

Jake watched her in the flashes, illuminated like a dancer in a strobe show. Her hair was pasted to her head, her clothes were sodden. But she was even more beautiful than he remembered, and his heart ached because of the terror that he felt he had somehow brought down upon them.

When the next bolt struck Jake tried to make sense of their surroundings, but everything around them was just trees and muddy, leaf-lined ground, and the rain lent a sense of continued urgency to their plight. No telling when this area would flood. They could be washed away again at any minute.

And then suddenly Pierce stumbled back against Jake, slapping at Jake's pant leg. A bolt of lightning illuminated a small glade, and Jake saw something large creeping toward them through the rain, something dark as the night itself and almost as shapeless.

"Move!" he shouted, jerking Mandi and Pierce backward. He could just make out the low whispering again, all around them, and Mandi's ragged breaths added a fevered chorus to the weird sounds.

"Did you see it?" she panted, crashing through the under-brush.

"Didn't you?"

"I didn't see anything."

But he could tell by the way she pulled Pierce along between them that she believed him. Jake waved his free hand in front of his face, taking fast steps, kicking out with his toes to test for impediments before placing his foot down. He finally stumbled into a thigh-deep ditch, and two almost simultaneous lightning bolts revealed that they were only paces from his car.

"Made it," he shouted, wondering at just how close to the road Pierce had actually brought them.

"Thank God," said Mandi.

"Don't thank Him yet," said Jake. "I barely got through some of the water back toward Pam's place. We'll be lucky to make it home."

"I just want to be in the car and away from that thing."

"Come on," said Jake, dragging them down the road behind him.

JIMMY DIDN'T WASTE TIME WORRYING about Paco or the cop or how his attorneys might get him out of this one. Things had escalated way beyond that by the time the old sheriff burst into the house. Obviously the cop had already discovered Smitty's body inside the trunk of the car. And he and Paco had left way too many fingerprints and who knew what the fuck else that they hadn't had time to get rid of. And they'd both been seen with the car, anyway.

Jake Crowley had ruined his business and murdered his brother. That was enough to set Jimmy on the killing path. But top that off with a series of events that Jimmy now believed couldn't all be coincidence—the plane, the rental car breaking down, the flood, running into the first cop, hitting the kid on the highway—and Jimmy had begun to understand that the fates were against him. Sometimes you won, sometimes you lost, and there wasn't a goddamned thing you could do about it. But when that happened it was Jimmy's nature to want to take someone else down with him. And he had decided that someone was not only going to be

Jake Crowley but everyone else in this fucking valley that he could get his hands on. Jake had a woman here. Maybe a kid from what Jimmy could tell. He was starting to form a picture inside his head, an image of Jake Crowley watching both of them die. Knowing it was Jimmy doing the killing. Knowing why.

Of course when he was done here, Jimmy Torrio was going to have to die, too. His organization in Houston was finished, and he'd be a wanted man. But he knew that he could resurface with a new identity. Rebuilding his fortune would take time, but it was doable. And eventually he'd probably even bring some of his old staff back on board. Not Paco, though. Paco was far too much of a liability now. Before Jimmy Torrio disappeared, Paco was going to have to disappear, as well.

Jimmy's night vision was better than most. That was one of the reasons he'd made it into the Special Forces. But with the thick storm overhead, the dense falling rain, and the cover of trees all around, it was impossible to see more than dim outlines, and he kept his eyes squinted tightly against the rain and blinding flashes of lightning. The forest was a world of shadow and spectral mist as Jimmy slipped out onto the road, reveling in the feel of slishy gravel beneath his bare feet. In fact he was so immersed in the rain, the forest, the darkness, and the even deeper blackness within that he passed the first driveway before he was aware of it, and he stopped, picturing the kid's map again in his mind, locking the valley into a hard image he could use to his advantage.

This was the driveway to the old man's house. It was a crime scene, and there'd be no one there now. He waffled between wanting to loot the house for weapons or clothes and the desire to remain as he was, a murderous animal freed of human restraint. Finally reason won out, and he padded up the drive, mud *slish*ing between his toes.

He paid no attention to any evidence he might be leaving as he busted the glass with his palm and unlocked the door. He was in a curious state where *everything* he experienced was on a heightened level. It felt just as good to be out of the rain as it did to be in it.

He searched quickly through the trailer, but the old man's clothes were much too small, and there were no guns anywhere. Rage and frustration overwhelmed him, and once again he pictured himself, only this time he was killing Crowley with his bare hands, and the image stirred him so profoundly that he found himself becoming sexually aroused. He glanced at his half-erect penis and laughed out loud.

Too fucking much.

He chose a heavy chef's knife from a kitchen drawer, testing it against his thumb. Not as sharp as he would have liked. But it would do. The knife ruined the image of his fingers around Jake Crowley's throat. But enough of Jimmy's training won through that he was unable to leave the weapon behind.

He strode back out into the rain naked but armed.

YOU ALWAYS WEAR HANDMADE ITALIAN LOAFERS?" asked Virgil, waving one of the shoes at Paco.

Paco gave him a careful look. "How come you know so much about shoes?"

"It's a hobby."

Paco shrugged.

"Pretty unusual pattern on the sole," mused Virgil, pretending to study the star.

"So?"

"Just curious. I found the same imprint at a friend's house just recently."

"What friend?"

"He's dead," said Virgil. "Beaten to death."

"Bullshit," said Paco. "I don't know nothing about no murder."

"Oh, come on, Paco," said Virgil. "I found a corpse in the trunk of that car you and your boss stole. That's one murder. Might as well 'fess up to everything. Make it a clean slate. These are your shoes with the star on the sole. They're too small to fit your boss. So I can place you at the scene of Albert's killing. Why did you murder the old man? You weren't there to rob him. Did Jimmy send you to do it? Was it to get information or to get back at Jake?"

"You're crazy, man. I don't know nothing about no murder or no corpse in a trunk."

"Really? That wasn't you in the car that tried to kill me out on the highway? How did you and Jimmy get here, then?"

"We hitchhiked."

Virgil sighed. "Paco, I'm thinking that you just got sucked into something you didn't want to do. Ain't that right?"

Paco just glared.

"That's usually the way it is," continued Virgil. "The big guy calls the shots, and it's the little guy who has to pay the piper, or spend the rest of his life behind bars, as the case may be. But you're smart enough to know about state's evidence."

"I'm smart enough to know you don't pull that shit on Jimmy Torrio," said Paco.

"Why not?"

Paco laughed. "Because I'd rather spend the rest of my life behind bars than die in this fucked-up place."

"You may die here, anyway," said Virgil.

"What's that supposed to mean?"

Virgil shrugged. "There's talk about the old Crowley curse."

Paco frowned. "Whatcha talking about? There ain't no fucking curse here."

Virgil squinted, leaning close to Paco's face, sensing something new there. A fear neither he nor Jimmy Torrio was responsible for. "You've heard it before, haven't you? You got that look in your eyes. Did you hear it the day you murdered Albert?"

Paco's breathing quickened, and his face colored. "I don't know what you're talking about."

Virgil nodded. "Like a whispering sound . . ."

Paco glared at him.

"It gets louder and louder," said Virgil. "It'll scare the shit out of you."

"Get fucked," said Paco.

Virgil shrugged again. "What are you gonna do when you hear it, Paco? After I'm gone."

"What do you mean, after you're gone?" said Paco nervously. "You ain't goin' nowhere."

"I gotta go find your boss," said Virgil.

Paco shook his head, glancing around the house. "You ain't going out there. You'd have to be crazy. Jimmy's a trained Ranger killer. He's like fucking Rambo. You ain't that stupid."

"You have no idea how stupid I am," said Virgil, rising slowly again. "I sure hope that last candle doesn't blow out, or it's gonna get real dark in here."

"Don't you leave me!" said Paco.

"Then tell me what you know, and don't give me any bullshit."

Paco clammed up again. But his eyes were fluttering with indecision.

"What kind of training does Jimmy have?" asked Virgil, changing the topic.

"He's an army killer. I'm telling you, he's like Rambo."

"How come a Ranger ends up being a crook?"

"Who said we were crooks?"

Virgil laughed. "You wouldn't be crosswise of Jake Crowley if you weren't."

"How come you know so much about Jake Crowley?"

"He's an old friend," said Virgil. "Why are you two here? What's Jimmy planning?"

"Crowley messed in Jimmy's business. Nobody fucks with Torrio business. Then when he killed José, Jimmy went a little crazy."

Virgil nodded. Just as he'd suspected. *That* was probably enough to set off a crazy ex-Ranger.

"What will Jimmy do now?"

Paco hesitated. "Maybe look for Crowley's cousin's place."

Virgil felt his blood go cold.

"How would he know how to get there?"

"Up the road I guess. There's only the highway or the valley. Where the hell else would he go?"

Maybe back out onto the highway to try to get the hell away, if he was as bright as Virgil suspected he was. On the other hand, Jimmy seemed crazy enough to stay and keep hunting for Jake, even naked, unarmed, and lost.

Or he might be just outside the door, waiting for Virgil to come looking for him.

Wind rattled the house, and Virgil glanced at the busted window. On impulse he inspected the windows and doors again by the light of the flashlight. For the first time he noticed the desk in the corner of Pierce's room. Staring down at the stark white topo map, he could see fallen plastic trees where Jimmy's hand must have rested over the plastic letters marking Pam and Ernie's place.

"Shit," he said, hurrying back down the hall to Paco. "Do you know Jake's cousin's name?"

Paco frowned. "Pam."

Rain thrummed on the porch roof so hard the floor vibrated, and the curtain blew inward. Paco and Virgil both stared at it. Then, when neither Jimmy nor some horrible shadow burst through, they each sighed and turned to face one another again.

"You got nothing more to say to me?" asked Virgil.

"About what?" asked Paco, eyeing him nervously.

Virgil shrugged. "About the day you killed Albert? About what you heard or saw?"

Paco swallowed a large lump in his throat.

"I guess I'll be going," said Virgil, starting past him toward the kitchen.

"Don't leave me here!" screamed Paco.

"Then talk."

Sweat trickled down Paco's cheeks. "I don't know nothing about no curse. When I got there, the old man was already dead."

"Don't bullshit me, Paco."

"Okay. Okay. But I didn't kill him. Swear to God. I kind of passed out. When I came to there was blood everywhere. I couldn't beat up a man that bad if I tried."

Virgil stared at the little crook, certain he was telling the truth. Whatever killed the girl had more than likely killed Albert, and probably Rich and those guys on the beach in Galveston, as well.

"But you came here to kill Albert, right?"

Paco shook his head so hard sweat flew. "I didn't. Jimmy didn't want the old man dead. He's really pissed at me about that. He wanted information on Jake Crowley. Any dirt we could dig up. And he wanted Crowley to know that we knew where his family was."

"You left your footprint on a piece of newspaper at the scene of the crime," Virgil reminded him.

"I didn't do it. Honest to God. Maybe I stepped in some blood . . . There was blood all over the fucking place. But I didn't kill him."

Virgil nodded. "I believe you, Paco."

"So what are you gonna do, then?" asked Paco, glaring again. "You ain't gonna leave me here?"

"Got to," said Virgil, not able to put the slightest empathy into his voice.

"You said you wouldn't leave me!" screamed Paco.

Virgil shook his head. "I don't believe I ever really said that."

He hurried quietly through the house. When he reached the back door he hesitated for only an instant, the weight of Paco's and Jimmy's pistols bulging in his pants. He eased open the freezer door and quietly slid them both behind packages of frozen vegetables, closing the door silently.

If Jimmy was watching the house it made sense that he'd be doing so out front, figuring Virgil to exit that way. Instead he slipped through the back door, closing it quickly behind him. He waded across the backyard into the trees where he dropped to his knees, surrounded by bracken, waiting impatiently for his eyes to grow accustomed to the near-total darkness. There was no way he could chance turning the flashlight on, not even for an instant. That would be like sending up a flare for Jimmy.

It took him half an hour to creep from the rear of the house to the road. And all that time he tried to remember everything his father had taught him about hunting more than fifty years before. That was all this was, after all. A hunt. It was just that his prey was an intelligent animal trained in every way there was to kill a man. That thought kept Virgil's heart thumping in his chest, and once again he reminded himself how old and frail he was compared to his quarry.

This is downright stupid, Virgil.

Doris's voice in his head had the self-righteous attitude to it that she took when he *was* doing something particularly bullheaded. But she knew as well as he did that he couldn't allow Jimmy Torrio to sneak up on Jake. His plan—if this fiasco could be called a *plan*—was now more about warning

Jake than trying to catch Jimmy out here in the woods. He knew that he might well get killed attempting even that, but at least he was going to try.

When he reached the road, the forest that had seemed so threatening only moments before turned into a comforting cover that he was reluctant to leave. He tried skirting the lane through the trees, but eventually he realized that he was going to make more noise that way, and take far too long getting to Jake. If Jimmy did know the layout of the valley now—and he wasn't lying in wait back at Mandi's—then he probably wasn't wasting his time prowling through the forest. Virgil crept out onto the slimy gravel lane, wiping rain out of his eyes with the back of his sleeve.

But when he reached the bottom of Albert's driveway he had to make a decision.

Would Jimmy head straight for Pam and Ernie's? Or would he take the first driveway in hope of finding clothes and maybe a weapon? If he was up at Albert's, would Virgil be better off following him—maybe surprising him—or should he hurry on to Pam's place to warn Jake?

Damned if he did and damned if he didn't. Virgil tossed the mental coin even though he already knew how it was going to fall and started up Albert's drive.

THE CAR SPUTTERED AND COUGHED but wouldn't fire. Jake slapped the dash and cursed. He didn't know if the engine was choked with water or whether he'd simply flooded it, but they wouldn't be driving anywhere now.

"Maybe if you pumped the gas," said Mandi. "Sometimes my car—"

"I tried that."

Mandi was wedged into the passenger seat with Pierce, who'd refused to leave her side to ride in the back. Pierce signed into Mandi's hand, and she signed back as Jake tried the starter again. But the battery was wearing down, and before it could die altogether he turned the key off.

"Pierce thinks maybe he can fix it," said Mandi.

"What?"

She shrugged. "I told you. He has this talent for repairing things. Electric motors, televisions. I know it sounds crazy. But he does. He wants to feel the motor."

Jake sighed. The boy *had* led them closer to the car. But

Jake had to figure that was luck. "Mandi, I don't even have any tools—"

"It can't hurt to let him touch the motor."

Jake shook his head, but he found the release lever and popped the hood. Pierce followed the fender around to lean in and slip his hands over the engine. Jake stood in the rain beside Mandi.

"This is crazy."

She frowned. "Just give him a chance. We wouldn't have gotten out of the woods without him."

Jake still wasn't so sure that was true. And, even if it was, fixing a stalled engine with bare hands was something else altogether. He leaned beside Pierce, studying the boy by the light that shone from the car's interior. The kid really did look as though he expected to repair the motor, running quick fingers along the spark plug wires, unplugging and re-plugging them, his face tight with concentration. Finally the boy stood, and when Mandi touched him to let him know she was there he signed to her.

"He says to give it a try."

Jake shrugged, climbing behind the wheel. He twisted the key, and the car coughed but started.

"I'll be damned," he muttered. Mandi slammed the hood, and she and Pierce climbed back into the car.

But Jake noticed the boy still seemed to be staring out into the woods. Mandi took the boy's hand and signed. Pierce signed back, and Mandi frowned.

"What'd he say?" asked Jake.

"He said he can *almost* understand what the whispers are saying."

Jake managed to get the big sedan turned around without depositing them in the ditch, and they chugged their way back through all the washouts, finally plowing up Pam's driveway. Jake rocked back and forth for encouragement, patting the dash.

"Come on, old girl. Just a few more yards."

When they rounded the last corner to the house they could see candles in the windows.

Cramer stepped out onto the porch and waved them up. "I was about to call the Coast Guard to come get you guys," he said as the three of them splashed up the steps. "You people look like something the cat dragged to the dump."

"It's a long story," said Jake, shivering. "I'll tell you all about it as soon as we get into some dry clothes."

"Everybody okay?"

"Yeah," said Jake, eyeing first Mandi, then Pierce. "We're all gonna make it. Hope you've been keeping Barbara entertained."

"I was about to kill her. But then she passed out again."

The old woman was sitting bolt upright on the sofa in front of the fireplace, snoring loudly.

"Seems to like the heat," said Cramer. "I been thinking about setting her on fire."

Jake showed Mandi and Pierce to the downstairs bath, leaving them with a candle. "The water's out with the pump off. But there's towels, and I'm sure I can find you something to wear."

"Don't bother," said Mandi. "I'll do it. You need to get dried off yourself."

Jake grabbed a couple of towels and headed upstairs to his bedroom. But he couldn't seem to get dry or warm. It was as though the rain had found cracks and crevices in his body that even the towels couldn't discover. He finally put on clothes again and wandered downstairs in his socked feet.

Standing in front of the roaring fireplace, he let the flames bake the chill and exhaustion out of his joints.

"Mandi and Pierce still in the bathroom?" he asked Cramer.

Cramer nodded. "What happened to you guys?"

Jake gave him the whole story.

"How did Pierce know which way to go?" asked Cramer.

Jake shrugged. "At first it was because he said he could *hear* that thing. After that he still led us in the right direction. But fixing the car was the weirdest thing."

"That could have been a coincidence, too."

Jake shrugged, backing closer to the fire.

"Barbara told me the whole Crowley family was famous for being nuts," said Cramer.

Jake frowned. "That's the way she put it?"

"Pretty much. She said every male Crowley since the first Jacob Crowley has gone crazy. She said every one of them lived in the same house, up at the head of the valley. Right up to you and your father."

"My great-grandfather and my grandfather both ended up institutionalized."

"What happened to your dad after the killing?"

Jake stared hard into the fire for a long time. "He disappeared."

"Disappeared?"

Jake nodded. "I think he drowned . . . I hope for his sake he did."

"Now you're last in the Crowley line."

"Looks like it."

"Ever feel yourself getting a little strange?"

"Just when I'm around you."

"Seriously."

Jake hesitated. "There have been times . . . when I thought maybe I was crazy."

"What were your grandfather and great-grandfather locked up for?"

"For seeing things, I think."

"The shadows."

Jake shook his head. "I never heard the whole story. But I wonder if that wasn't the case."

"Which would make them maybe *not* so crazy."

"Maybe."

Just then Mandi and Pierce returned, both wrapped in blankets.

"We were discussing Jake's nutty family," said Cramer.

Mandi aimed Pierce at a seat beside Barbara on the couch. The boy managed to slide into place without waking the old woman. "Does that thing out there have anything to do with the secret you and Pam have kept all these years?" she asked Jake.

Jake flushed.

"You never told me what happened the night your mother was killed. But ever since your mother's death I've known that you and Pam shared something about that night. Something more than just her murder. Virgil knew it, too. If it has something to do with what's going on, then we have a right to know."

"What really happened to your father?" asked Cramer.

Barbara stirred but didn't wake. The old woman's shallow breathing sounded as loud as a thunderclap in the room's sudden silence.

Jake frowned. "That was when I heard the whispers for the first time."

The lights of the old house had been burning brightly on that moonlit night. He crept out of the woods in a trance, following the weird sounds and his mother's screams. As he passed the little stone chapel in the backyard, he noticed that the door was open. He'd never seen it unlocked before, never actually been allowed inside. But that night his mother's screams were far more compelling than a small boy's curiosity.

"Mother?" he called quietly as he climbed the back stoop.

He slipped through the creaking screen door and into the kitchen. The table was overturned, and broken dishes lay scattered across the floor and the counter. The refrigerator door stood ajar, and Jake closed it quietly.

"Mother?" he called again.

The eerie whispering hissed all around him like a leaking gas line.

He stumbled from room to room, stepping carefully around broken shards of pottery and splintered glass from picture frames littering the hardwood floor. Taking catlike steps up the long staircase, he found his mother sprawled across an old throw rug in the hall. Her head rested against an antique end table, blood swathing her face, head, and bare shoulders. He ran to her, dropping onto the floor, raising her head gently into his lap, terrified that she would be cold, dead, already gone. But she was still alive.

Barely.

She clutched his wrist with a feeble hand and shook her head. "Run away, Jake," she whispered.

"So she was alive when you found her?" asked Cramer.

Jake nodded.

"And that's all she said? *'Run away, Jake'*?"

"Yes."

"What happened then?"

"Just after she died in my arms, my father showed up. He went crazy. Crying, pulling his hair out. He kept asking her what she'd done, like it was her fault somehow that she was dead."

A sudden spark of memory tingled, and he frowned.

"What?" said Cramer.

Jake shook his head. "I seem to remember him taking something out of her hand."

"What was it?"

"I don't remember if I even got a look at it. Maybe I'm just imagining. It was only moments later that we heard the whispers again, and my father lifted me to my feet and shoved me toward the stairs. And he shouted the same thing my mother had said."

"'Run away, Jake,' " whispered Mandi.

Jake nodded. "I didn't want to go. I was terrified. But he dragged me down the stairs as the noise got louder. He pushed me through the front door and down the front steps, pointing to the trees. Screaming at me all the time."

"And you ran," said Cramer.

"Into the forest. And when I heard someone crashing after me, and heard the whispers, I really ran. I lost my direction, and I ended up running right off the cliff into the swimming hole. I thought I was going to drown. When I bobbed to the surface I saw someone falling toward me, and I backpedaled. But it was my father. He swam to me, shoving me toward the rapids. And all the time I was trying to cling to him. But then something dark dropped over both of us, and I was pushed underwater. I really was drowning then. I think maybe I passed out. When I came to I was alone, on my back in the dark, floating downstream. And I was already past the rapids. I dragged myself to shore, and I huddled in the dark, scared shitless, until dawn. Then I followed the stream back to a small trail I knew and crept back to the house.

"There were cop cars everywhere, and when Virgil spotted me, he dragged me aside, bundled me in a blanket, and took me into a bedroom to talk. But after listening to my story three or four times, he told me to just say that I'd heard screams and hid in the woods. He told me to *never* tell anyone else what I'd told him. Later I confided the truth to Pam, and ever since I wished I hadn't."

"And your dad?"

"Never found."

"Know what a good shrink would say about that story?" said Cramer, shaking his head.

"That's why I don't talk to many shrinks," said Jake. "What do *you* think of it?"

"Up to a day or two ago I would have agreed with the shrinks."

"And now?"

Cramer shrugged. "So everyone thought your father went crazy and killed your mother. The Crowley curse again. But what started all the killing? What set that *thing* off? What do you know about your great-great-grandfather?"

"Jacob Crowley fought at Gettysburg, with distinction if you can believe the stories. He moved into the valley because it was about as remote as he could get and still stay in the States. He ended up marrying an Indian woman. Jacob and his family started out living at the mouth of the valley on a small farm, but it was washed out by a flood, and when their kids were mostly grown he and Weasel—that was his wife's Indian name—moved up to the head of the valley where Jacob and the kids built a large house for the family. He was killed along with Weasel and two of the kids still living at home."

"*After* they moved into the house up the valley," mused Cramer. "How was he killed?"

"According to the story there was another terrible flood, and during it Jacob murdered Weasel and one of the kids. Then for some unknown reason he tried to save one of the surviving children that had been sucked into the water, and he got swept away himself, and was never found."

"Floods seem to be a bad habit around here. Didn't your mother's death ever make you wonder about that story?"

Jake frowned. "Yeah. About that and other stories. But after a few years it seemed more likely that I really was crazy. That I had been seeing things and imagining them, covering up for a murder my father really did commit. That had me pretty conflicted."

"Your baggage," said Cramer, nodding. "Where did the old man get the money to build a big house away up here in the mountains?"

"Logging, mostly. Later he sold land. But the majority of the valley is still owned by the family."

"By you," said Mandi.

Cramer stared at Jake. "You own this valley?"

Jake shrugged. "A few thousand acres."

"Holy shit. I was just kidding about you being the King of Crowley."

"It isn't that big a deal. The taxes eat up whatever I make in logging leases. It's more of a pain in the ass than anything."

"So you've been worried all this time that maybe you had hallucinated the death of your mother, that your father really did it. And you were afraid of going crazy like your dad?"

"Something like that," said Jake. That was all the story Cramer needed.

"And then the Torrios' men got killed on the beach, and the same thing happened to Albert."

"Yeah."

"There really is something in this valley killing people. And by my book it pretty much has to be what killed those guys on the beach. You aren't crazy, Jake. You never have been."

Pierce stirred in his blanket on the couch, and the three of them turned toward him, but he instantly settled down, almost as though he could feel their eyes on him.

"Is he all right?" said Cramer.

"I think so," said Mandi, taking Pierce's hand but not

signing. "But what I want to know is *why* that thing kills people. And what we can do to stop it."

"My memere say, 'Spooks is hard to figger. And de bad ones is hard to get rid of,' " said Cramer, tossing another log onto the fire.

"Your memere?" said Mandi.

Jake frowned. "Cramer's grandmother is a Voudou queen."

"She's a *Houngon*," said Cramer. "A priestess. And times like this maybe she knows better than you and me. Memere told me once that the spirits can't always be understood. But they can usually be . . . the English would be *appeased*, I think."

"And how do we do that?" asked Mandi.

Cramer shrugged. "I guess that's what we have to find out."

"I wish we'd find out pretty soon."

Cramer nodded, reaching out to rest one giant hand on her arm. "You may not have heard of Ogou. But he's a good spirit to know. And he doesn't take kindly to those that threaten women . . . or children." He glanced meaningfully at Pierce, and Mandi smiled.

JUST AS VIRGIL NEARED THE HEAD of Albert's drive he heard the sound of splashing footsteps, and he moved silently, slowly placing one foot behind the other, back toward the woods. Suddenly the figure of a man—huge, muscular, and nude—appeared right beside him. Virgil swung the shotgun, but just as his finger jerked the trigger, a dull stinging sensation burnt his left bicep and his own gun blast blinded him. He staggered backward, pumping another round into the chamber, searching for a target, wiping rain out of his face with his sleeve.

Where was the sonofabitch?

Feeling along his left arm, he discovered a gash running from shoulder to elbow, stinging as cold rain hit the open wound. He had no idea if the blade had clipped an artery, but he didn't have any time to worry about it.

He backed down the drive, keeping low, his eyes peeled, the shotgun gripped tightly, his finger on the trigger.

Had he wounded Jimmy with that shot? If he had he'd heard no gasp, no cry of pain. More than likely the guy had moved so fast the attack had ruined his aim, if a snap shot like that could be called aiming.

When he reached the road he hurried across, staggering through the waist-deep runoff and up into the trees on the far side. He knelt beneath a large oak and rested the shotgun beside him, ripping off his shirt sleeve and using it to make a tourniquet around his upper arm. That was the best he could do for now. He hefted the shotgun again and tried to get his mind to work.

He no longer had the luxury of even thinking about himself as the hunter. He was the hunted for sure. And it was a mile or better of deep woods or flooded, open road from where he was to Pam's. To top things off, he thought he heard whispering. But it seemed to be disappearing up the road. Whatever else the sound might be, it was definitely a harbinger of doom. Dary had heard it and ended up dead. Barbara had heard it and nearly died. And they had all heard it before Rich was killed. Virgil was glad to hear it moving away, though it seemed to be headed toward Pam and Ernie's place, and he didn't want to think what that meant. But at the moment he had a bigger problem than the Crowley curse on his hands.

Jimmy tasted the blood on his blade and smiled. The feel of cold steel biting through flesh excited him. He knew that he hadn't dealt the old sheriff a killing blow, any more than the man had seriously wounded him. Only one ball of the buckshot had hit, and it had merely grazed his left thigh. It would sting worse with time, but the bleeding would stop fairly quickly, especially with cold rainwater cleansing the wound.

He closed his eyes and tried to make out his prey's movements by sound. But the constant patter of rain everywhere blocked that avenue of pursuit, and even with his better-than-average night vision he could see only a few feet in any direction. The trouble was that if the sheriff spotted him first, *he* had the shotgun, while Jimmy had only the knife. That made things considerably more dangerous. But chances were the sheriff would make enough noise sooner or later so that Jimmy could stalk him and strike. And this time he wasn't going to miss.

When he heard the whispering again he angled his head to catch the exact direction of the sound.

But then it was gone.

Virgil peered through the misty shadows, wondering when he'd feel the sharp blade slip around his throat or hear a gut-wrenching cry as Jimmy dropped onto him from one of the trees. He slipped slowly out of the forest and as quietly as possible back through the runoff and up onto the road.

He stroked the trigger of the shotgun, and more than any-thing at that moment he wanted to see Jimmy in his sights so he could finish this. The longer he stood in the center of the road the more convinced he became that he was too late, that Torrio had used the attack as a ruse, that he was already heading toward Pam's.

Fuck it.

Either way, he was playing Jimmy's game. He turned toward Pam's and began to trot. But he hadn't splashed through the ankle-deep water more than a hundred yards when he had to stop for a breather.

Doris was right as usual. This was definitely a damn fool place to be and a damn fool thing to be doing for a man his age. But there were people in danger who deserved his pro-tection, and he knew that he'd rather die at Jimmy's hands than wake up tomorrow in a nice warm bed and realize that he hadn't tried hard enough to save them.

He started off again, walking this time, fast as his heart would allow.

A flash of lightning lit the road like gunfire, and Virgil whirled, trying to see behind him in the afterglow. He had to hope that Jimmy hadn't been staring right at him when the flash occurred. A peal of thunder followed fast on the lightning's heels, and when his ears adjusted to the soft sounds of the rain again he noticed the whispering had returned. It kept coming and going like someone playing with the dial on a radio. And over the whispering he could hear Doris.

You're gonna do what you're gonna do. So go on, then, hon. Don't pay no attention to that thing. It's that criminal out there you got to worry about right now.

Even in the middle of the storm, surrounded by danger, Virgil smiled. When the day came that he found out whether or not that *was* Doris talking, he was going to be terribly disappointed if it wasn't. He waded through yet another waist-deep runoff, leaning into the flood, hoping he didn't get carried away into the woods. By the time he struggled out onto the far side of the washout he was chilled to the bone. His arm was beginning to really hurt, a dull throb running from shoulder to elbow. He loosened the tourniquet for a moment, cringing at the fiery sting of the blood rushing back in.

As the noise slowly fell away behind him, the terror that had tried to break free inside began to ease, the images to blur, and he took strength from that, ignoring his burning lungs and his aching legs. By the time he stumbled across Pam's drive he was so exhausted he had to make the climb one agonizing step at a time, but instinct told him that Jimmy had fallen behind. And he wondered if the thing was going back for him. He hoped so. If anyone deserved to be pummeled or frightened to death it had to be Jimmy Torrio. Then he thought of Paco, alone and afraid of the dark, handcuffed and naked, and although he knew in his heart that he was probably just as much a cold-blooded killer as his boss, Virgil felt a tiny twinge of pity for the little bastard.

When he finally made it to the porch and saw lanterns and candles inside and more than one shadow moving, he breathed a sigh of relief. Jake opened the door, and the shock and concern on his face was priceless as he jerked Virgil into the house.

WHAT HAPPENED TO YOU?" asked Jake, shoving Virgil into a chair in the kitchen. Mandi ran to get the first-aid kit and more towels from Pam's linen closet.

Virgil told them the story while Mandi daubed antiseptic into the wound and bandaged it. She gasped when she realized how close she and Pierce must have come to being in the house when Jimmy and Paco arrived, and Jake frowned. At least Ernie and Pam were safe in town.

"I would have thought Jimmy was smarter than that," said Jake. "If anything I'd expect him to send more of his hit men after me."

"Smart's got nothing to do with it," said Cramer. "Jimmy's from the barrio. You killed his brother. It's personal."

"I heard that whispering noise out there on the road," said Virgil. "With any luck maybe that thing and Jimmy Torrio will do each other in."

"That *would* be nice, but I wouldn't count on it," said Cramer. "Jimmy's meaner than a whipped pit bull. The good news is he's naked as a jaybird and armed with only a knife."

"For now," said Jake. "There are other houses in this valley. Other people. And we have no way of warning them now
that the road's flooded and the phone lines are down."

Cramer frowned. "I was just trying to look on the bright
side."

"Cheery you," said Jake, staring through the door at
Pierce, who was resting on the couch. Suddenly the darkness of the window behind the boy seemed ominous, and
Jake crossed quickly to it, jerking the heavy curtain closed.
As he moved the lantern from the coffee table to the smaller
table beside the sofa so as not to silhouette anyone in the
room, Pierce reached out and caught his arm, and Jake
waited as the boy spelled each letter into his palm.

What's the matter?

Just closing the drapes.

Pierce nodded, but his brow was furrowed, and he seemed
to learn as much from the feel of Jake's hand as he did from
Jake's slow finger spelling.

You're scared of something besides that thing.

Jake was shaken once again by the boy's perception.

Everything's gonna be fine.

*That's what Mom says when it's not. What are you afraid
of? You're making me more scared.*

Jake nodded to himself, knowing he had to tell the boy.
*There's a man out there who wants to hurt me. But it's just
me he's after.*

Why does he want to hurt you?

Jake smelled Mandi's perfume as she slipped beside him.
Pierce noticed, as well, turning his head in her direction but
refusing to release Jake's hand.

I killed his brother.

Why?

He was a bad man trying to kill me.

Pierce nibbled his lip, nodding.

Jake stared at the boy, wondering what went on in that thirteen-year-old head.

"What are you two talking about?" whispered Mandi, glancing at Barbara, still out like a light on the other end of the couch.

"Just letting him know everything was all right."

Jake patted the boy on the shoulder and gently extricated his hand. But Mandi seemed stiff and unsure of herself.

"How bad is this guy, Jake?" she asked.

Jake frowned. "Bad. Both he and his brother disposed of a lot of people getting to the top. Jimmy was always the brains of the operation. But right now he's probably hightailing it out of the valley."

But, of course, he knew that was a lie. Jimmy Torrio had never run from a fight or a killing in his life.

Sunday

ANDI WAS AWAKENED JUST AFTER MIDNIGHT by a strange drumming that seemed to be coming from downstairs. She glanced at Pierce in the low orange light of the candle on the dresser, but he didn't stir as she climbed slowly out of bed and followed the rhythmic noise down the hall. As she neared Jake's door he slipped through it, pulling on a robe and preceding her down the stairs. Virgil stood in the living room, staring into the kitchen. When he saw the two of them, he gave Jake a questioning look.

The kitchen was lit by candles on the table, counter, and stove, and Cramer stood in the center of the floor, bare to the waist, his back to the living room door. On one arm a blood-red strip of cloth draped to his elbow, and beneath his other arm he held a large stew pot which he thumped lightly as he chanted in something that sounded like gutter French. On the floor a strange, angular design had been created with yellow powder, and Mandi noticed an old box of cornmeal on the table. Near the design Cramer had balanced a tall, round piece of cordwood on end, and beside it another candle glowed next to a bottle of what looked like cooking sherry. Beside that lay a leather bag stuffed with feathers. As Cramer turned slowly in her direction, Mandi was shocked to see that there was no sign of recognition in his eyes. It was then that she noticed he was drumming with the handle of a giant carving knife. She stepped backward, butting into Jake.

"It's all right," he whispered, wrapping her in his arms to still her shivers.

"What's he doing?" she whispered back, staring at the knife.

"Talking to the spirits," said Jake. "It's a Voudou ceremony."

Virgil stared at Jake uncertainly. "What's with the knife?"

"The knife should really be a machete, and it's just a symbol, the embodiment of Ogou. He's kind of like Cramer's patron saint."

"The cornmeal?" said Mandi, gesturing toward the design on the floor.

"A *vévé*. That one's a symbol for Ogou, too. The wine is an offering, but it's supposed to be rum." Jake smiled ruefully. "I don't know how Ogou is taking the sherry or the cooking pot drum, either."

"You think this is funny?"

Jake frowned. "I used to. But then I realized that Cramer didn't, so I learned to just accept it."

Mandi shook her head. "He acts like he doesn't even know we're here."

"When he's like this he's out of it completely. He's possessed by Ogou."

"That's crazy."

"So's eating the blood and body of your God," muttered

Jake. "I've learned from Cramer not to judge other people's beliefs. He doesn't hurt anyone. And he doesn't try to convert people, much. He's just trying in his own strange way to help."

"You understand what he's saying?" asked Virgil.

"It's Cajun French. I think he's asking Ogou for guidance."

"No dead chickens?"

"You've been watching too many old movies. But actually I'm surprised at how quiet he's being. I think he's still in control enough to realize he doesn't want to disturb us. Normally these things can get pretty rowdy."

"You've been to more than one?" asked Mandi.

"Cramer's memere really is a *Houngon,* a Voudou priestess. I've had to attend several ceremonies over the years that I couldn't beg out of. There's a lot of howling and chanting, people possessed, falling on the floor, crying, laughing."

"What does the Houston police department think about this?" asked Virgil.

"If Cramer would denounce his religion or treat it as a joke, he'd probably be head of the department by now. He won't. Oddly enough, that's one of the things I respect most about him."

Cramer rested the "drum" on the table and replaced it with a jar full of dried beans that he rattled as he waved the knife high overhead and danced around the *vévé.* His eyes were glazed, and his voice sounded raspy and distant, and Mandi noticed that although he never actually looked at the floor, he meticulously avoided stepping on the strange angular design. Finally he dropped to his knees and began to whisper, as though speaking to someone directly in front of his face.

"It won't last much longer," said Jake. "Either he'll get

the answer he's looking for, or he won't. I'll help him clean up. He'll be pretty exhausted."

Without warning she turned in his arms and hugged him tightly.

"We'll be okay," he promised, hugging back.

Speaking quietly in the same patois he had used before, Cramer gently brushed the *veve* with the palm of his hand until the symbol was nothing but scattered grains. He carefully placed the *paket kongo* on the table, set the wine back under the sink, and blew out the candle on the floor. When he saw Jake and Virgil, he smiled, rising slowly to his feet, wiping perspiration from his gleaming forehead with a cloth from the counter.

"How's Ogou?" asked Jake, finding a broom and sweeping the grains into a neat pile.

"He say to you, be careful. You done stirred up a passel of bad medicine around here."

Jake nodded. "Glad to hear from him. Wish he could tell me something I didn't already know."

"What's this Ogou look like?" asked Virgil.

Jake couldn't tell if he was smiling with his eyes or not. But he really didn't believe that Virgil would insult Cramer.

"Big," said Cramer. "Big and black with a machete this long." He held his arms half spread.

"Sounds mean."

Cramer shrugged. "Only if you piss him off."

"How did Ogou feel about the tin drum and the cooking sherry?" asked Jake.

"I didn't have a real *poto mitan* or *ason,* either. The sacred post and the rattle are very important. But at times like this Ogou is not so particular."

"Evidently not."

"He is disturbed by this valley."

"Everyone is disturbed by this valley right now," muttered Jake.

"What else are you worried about?" asked Mandi.

Cramer frowned, staring at her. "You a mind reader?"

She shook her head. "I can see it in your eyes. You're not just worried about Jimmy Torrio or even that thing out there."

"Memere tole me I was too open to the spirits. Too easy for 'em sometimes."

"What did she mean by that?"

Cramer shrugged. "You got to be careful with Iwas or other spirits. They can get into you."

"Possess you."

"Something like that. And one thing's for sure. There's a bad spirit here. It isn't one of the Voudou. Not something Ogou can help us with. He say the only thing protecting us from the spirit . . . is Jake's blood."

"My *blood*?" said Jake, frowning.

Cramer nodded. "I never felt Ogou so worked up before. He kept showing me your *blood*. Whatever the mystery is, it's something about your blood."

"You're freaking me out, Cramer."

Cramer shrugged. "Sometimes Ogou don't know shit."

PIERCE HAD LAIN PERFECTLY STILL when his mother climbed out of bed, waiting to see if she'd just gone to the bathroom. But when she didn't return immediately he arose stealthily, craning his head like an antenna, trying to locate the strange sensation that had been keeping him awake, tugging at him like gravity. He couldn't get the idea out of his head that there was something in the house that he needed to find. But he had no idea what it might be.

Even if his mother hadn't told him, he would have known they were sleeping in Pam and Ernie's bed. The clean sheets couldn't disguise the smell of Ernie's aftershave or the peculiar odor his body gave off, and the aroma of Pam's favorite perfume was equally evident to the boy's hypersensitive nose.

He placed his hand very lightly against the wall, exploring the dry powdery feel of the old wallpaper. When his fingers glided across the cool glass of a windowpane he jerked them back, afraid to sense something on the other side, looking in.

Shaking off his fear, he began again to search for the cause of the sensation that would not let him rest. He made it out the door and into the hallway, instinctively turning left, bumping into a side table. He didn't know how much noise he might have made, but he could feel something on the table doing a pirouette. He gently slid his fingers across the lace-covered top and caught a large porcelain lamp. He slipped his hand up toward the space where the lightbulb should be, but the glass there was cool. When he brought his hand back he smelled kerosene. An unlit oil lamp.

After that he was more cautious, waving his left hand slowly back and forth, testing with his toes, running the fingers of his other hand along the flaking surface of the old wallpaper. His hand slipped across the panels of a door, finding the knob. He sniffed his fingers, smelling Barbara's eau de cologne, and he stood for a moment, waiting for the tugging to give him direction again. Then he moved on. When he reached the next doorway he touched the knob, and a jolt shot through him.

It was in there.

Ever so slowly he pressed his shoulder against the door, feeling for the telltale shiver in the wood that would give him away to anyone who could hear. But he was sure he wasn't making a sound now. He figured he could be the world's first blind cat burglar.

When the door was open just wide enough for him to enter, he slipped inside and began easing along the wall again. He just missed bumping into a bureau that was lower than his outstretched hand, and he slid his fingers along the drawers of the low chest, sidling around to discover the size of the piece. Gently he began to explore the top. A perfume bottle. He'd never smelled the scent before. Maybe it had belonged to Pam's mother. He knew she had lived in the house before Pam and Ernie.

Suddenly strong hands dropped onto his shoulders, and he twisted instinctively. His back hit the sharp edge of the bureau top, and he winced, thinking of the deep, dark emptiness, the long fall down the stairs. The dresser quivered, but nothing crashed. He sniffed the air, catching a whiff of soap and shampoo, and he relaxed.

It was his mother.

She took his hand and signed rapidly. *What are you doing here?*

Looking for something.

For what? This is Jake's room.

Where's Jake?

Downstairs.

He nodded to himself as he caught the faintest whiff of Jake's deodorant and the peculiar musky scent of Cramer's aftershave. He slid his free hand across the bureau top again. His fingers rested on a faceted object—a jewel, maybe—the size of a small radio dial. On one end of the jewel a chain had been attached. But Pierce knew instinctively that this was not one of Pam's necklaces. The chain was heavy and bold, like something a man might wear. And the jewel tingled in his hand.

Mandi spelled to him. *Put that back.*

But he didn't want to let it go. The stone felt as though it were glued to his palm, and it had a peculiar feeling, almost as if it were some kind of electronic machine. But the internal workings were a mystery to him, and he felt his consciousness sinking down into the gem, searching.

JAKE STOOD IN THE DOORWAY, staring at Mandi and Pierce's backs.

"Mandi?" he whispered.

"I'm sorry," she said, turning. "Pierce woke up and wandered in here, and now I can't get him to leave. He won't give up this necklace."

Jake struck a match, lighting the oil lamp on the bureau and peering at the jewel. "How'd he find that?"

Mandi shrugged. "He says he *had* to come in here and get it. He's not making any sense. It doesn't look like something Pam would wear."

Jake shook his head. "It isn't. I took it off Jimmy Torrio's brother, José, in Galveston. I don't really know why I kept it."

He stroked Pierce's face, and Pierce sniffed his hand and reached for it.

Jake finger-spelled, *What's up?*

Pierce reluctantly set the necklace down on the bureau but kept his body close to it.

This, spelled Pierce, tapping the stone.

Jake frowned. *How did you know the necklace would be here?*

I wasn't looking for a necklace.

What then?

Pierce shook his head. *I don't know.*

The boy's frustration at not being able to explain himself was apparent. His eyes watered, and his hands fisted and then unclenched. He reached for the jewel again, but Mandi caught his hand.

"Let him take it, if he wants," said Jake.

She shook her head. "It isn't his. And now that you've told me where it came from, I don't think I want him to have it."

"He looks pretty upset. Will he be all right if you insist?" asked Jake, shrugging.

Mandi signed forcefully into Pierce's palm, and eventually he nodded. But it was clear he still wanted the gem. He kept angling his head almost as though he was *listening* for it.

"I can get him back to bed, I think," she said, nudging a very reluctant Pierce back into the hall.

Jake watched them until Mandi closed the door behind them. He held the necklace in his hand, feeling the same strange tingling he had the day José was killed. What power did the amulet have? Where had José gotten it? What drew Pierce to it?

He lifted the blood-red jewel up to the lantern light, staring into the facets, but there was nothing to be seen but fractured images of his own reflection. He laid the bauble back down on the dresser and blew out the lantern. Then he tramped over to the bed and lay down atop the sheets.

Picturing Mandi, walking away down the hall in Pam's short robe, he felt a stirring, and he let it warm him, remembering what it was like making love to her. He could still feel the heat of her body against his, hear her panting, remember the clean, hot smell of her sweat. It had always seemed so right being with her, and he'd known from the beginning that they were going to be together forever. Only it hadn't turned out that way. And every time he'd thought of her over the past fourteen years he was carried back to that final night in the old house. But he could never quite get that last twenty-four hours with her back into focus. It was all a wash of fear, rage, frustration, sorrow, and pain.

He rubbed his fingertips across his palm, still feeling Pierce's touch. A question that had been playing at the back of his mind finally sounded like a knell, as he mentally ticked off the years. It was possible. Pierce didn't look anything like Rich. He didn't have the beady eyes or the curly brown hair. He was dark-eyed and dark-complected, like a Crowley. And he was too intelligent to be Rich's kid.

The whole night was itching at Jake. The thing was on his mind; so were Pierce, Mandi, and now the oddness of the boy's *having* to find the necklace. He tiptoed down the hallway to Mandi's room, raised his knuckles to knock, and stopped. The house was deadly silent.

He dropped his hand to his side and stared at the door, picturing Pierce. But what was he going to say if she denied it?

All the Crowley men go crazy.

Was that why Mandi had never told anyone that Pierce was his child? Because in her heart she still believed the old stories, regardless of what she said?

It might be. Mandi knew the history of the Crowleys as well as anyone. But he couldn't rid himself of the overwhelming urge to find out if Pierce was his, and if he was, to tell the boy the truth. Pierce was tough enough to deal with it. But was Mandi? What would she think about him bursting in right now like a klutz? He started slowly back to his room, then whirled back to the door again.

To hell with that. If he's my son then let's get it out in the open right now.

He raised his hand to knock on the door, and stopped again.

Calm down. Think about what you're going to say.

Hi, Mandi, I was just wondering if Pierce is my kid.

Smooth.

I've been noticing that Pierce looks a lot like me.

Better. But it still sucks. You were right the first time. Why not just try the straight skinny?

Mandi, is Pierce my son?

Oh, shit. Yes, that's good. And when she gives you the look that says you really have gone crazy, how do you back out of that one?

The way she looked at him, the way she'd felt in his arms tonight . . . he was sure she still cared, and maybe she would be willing to try to work things out. He knew in his heart that if he knocked on her door and simply opened his arms, more than likely things would progress from there. But that was a different issue. Being together again was more than he had ever hoped for when he'd climbed on the plane in Houston. But now there was Pierce. Was he or wasn't he? The question was going to have to be asked and answered, and soon.

But did it have to be this minute?

When the door jerked open and Mandi stood there staring at him, Jake found himself tongue-tied.

She nodded, gazing into his eyes. "I keep catching you looking at me like you want to ask something, Jake. What is it?"

At that moment he wanted to hold her, not talk to her. But she was waiting. Was he going to make a fool of himself? Would she think he was a jerk for asking such a stupid question? He knew if he didn't say something quick he was going to start babbling.

"Tell me what you remember about that night," he said. "Our last night up at the old house."

"That's what you came down here to ask me?"

"Please tell me," he repeated quietly.

She shook her head. "You must remember as well as I do."

"I recall sneaking to the old house when everyone thought we were at the dance. I remember going inside, lighting candles. I remember the furniture covered with sheets and all the dust. Whenever I've smelled dust for the past fourteen years I've thought of that night."

"It was dusty, all right."

"I remember wishing we hadn't gone there."

She frowned. "Is that what happened to you? Did you hear that thing? I always wondered why you acted so crazy the next morning."

Jake steeled himself for something else he had to say. "Mandi . . . I tried to kill you."

"What?" she said, stunned.

"I went crazy. Just like I was always afraid I would. Just like all the Crowleys do, sooner or later—"

"That never happened, Jake. You never hurt me. Ever. I promise you that."

He shook his head. "A lot of that night is a haze to me. But I remember that all too clearly. How can you *not* remember it?"

"Because it never happened, Jake."

"Then tell me what *you* remember. Give me details."

"You want details?"

He frowned. "Not those kind of details. Tell me what we did. What we talked about. Before."

"You started reminiscing about your mother. It made you sad. I kissed you, and we didn't really talk much after that. Jake, we were very young, and we had a whole house to ourselves for the night."

"It doesn't make sense that what I remember feels so real."

"Then tell me what else you think you remember."

"I remember thinking that the inside of the house had always looked bigger to me before."

"But you hadn't been back in years."

"I seem to recall starting a fire in the fireplace."

Mandi slipped into the hall and drew the door almost closed behind her. "We carried a mattress from the downstairs bedroom to lay in front of the fire."

Jake nodded. "And then we lay down on the mattress . . ."

Mandi smiled again. "You forgot that we took our clothes off first."

"I remember lying there with you, and the next thing I knew I heard the whispering, and I was terrified, because I recognized it. I remembered it. I turned to you, and all of a sudden it was like there was someone else inside my head, controlling me. I had my fingers around your throat. I could feel your pulse slowing, then stopping. I could see the terror and the . . . surprise . . . and hurt in your eyes, and there was nothing I could do about it. Then I guess I blacked out. I woke up in the morning, and you were alive, sleeping there beside me. I couldn't understand . . . It had been so real. Too real to be a dream. And I knew then what had happened to my mother. Or at least I thought I did."

"That's why you left," she whispered. "All this time . . . If I'd just known . . . If you'd just told me . . . But none of that happened. We made love. Right there in front of the fire. And then I went to sleep in your arms. I've never forgotten it."

The way she said it left no doubt that he should definitely feel guilty that *he* had. And he did. He'd much rather have remembered *that*.

"And later?" he asked.

"When I woke up early the next morning you were already dressed, and acting real strange. Now I understand why."

"Strange how?"

"Just weird. Like you didn't know where you were. You kept pacing around, shaking your head, mumbling to yourself. You scared me a little then. But I wasn't so much afraid of you as I was *for* you. I thought you might be sick or something. That's when you told me you were leaving. I didn't believe you. But I guess I should have."

"I remember you crying."

"Of course I was crying. I thought we were always going to be together. I'd just spent my first whole night sleeping in your arms. And then I wake up, and you tell me you're leaving forever. That *thing* drove us apart, Jake. You shouldn't have let it. You should have trusted yourself, and me, more than that. You aren't crazy. You never were."

She was right. Running away had been the worst decision he'd ever made, and it had solved nothing. It had only cost them fourteen years of happiness that they could never get back. He was through running, though. Whatever it was that had tortured him and his family was going to end, one way or the other, before this storm was over. He was tired of hiding, tired of being alone.

She surprised him by slipping into his arms and resting her head against his chest. He could barely breathe. The smell of her, the feel of her, the warmth of her was overpowering.

"Are you back for good?" she whispered.

"If you want me to be," he said with a sigh.

She pressed harder against him, and he kissed her on the lips, and for an instant it was as though the intervening years had never been. He wanted her so badly he felt as though he were on fire. But at the same time the memory kept hammering, and he feared his own hands as they gently stroked her back through the thin cotton gown.

A cough from the end of the hallway shocked him, and Jake turned to see Cramer, holding up both hands.

"Sorry," said Cramer, looking sheepish. "You two should really get a room."

Mandi chuckled, pushing herself out of Jake's arms and backing into her bedroom.

"We'll talk later, Jake," she promised.

He nodded, staring into her eyes until the door closed.

THINGS WORKING OUT BETTER THAN YOU THOUGHT?" said Cramer, blocking Jake's way into the bedroom.

Jake smiled. "I guess they might."

"Might not, too," said Cramer, frowning.

"What's that supposed to mean?"

"There's more in this valley to worry about than some old curse. Jimmy sounds like he's gone crazy. I don't really believe he's likely to go away. Do you?"

Jake sighed. "Probably not."

"So where's your gun?"

"What?"

Cramer reached behind him and slipped his pistol out of his pants.

"You wore that downstairs, with Virgil on guard there?"

"What if Virgil was dead? Should I run back upstairs and get it?"

"If you're worried about Jimmy creeping in while we're asleep, why aren't you down there?"

Cramer shook his head. "I seem to make Virgil a little

nervous. And I don't think he'd take it kindly, me acting like he *needed* backup. But that's not my point, and you know it."

"I wasn't thinking. Okay?"

"You'd better start thinking. Because if Jimmy really did stay in the valley, then sooner or later he's gonna make his move. And there isn't gonna be time for you to figure out what you want to do."

He knew Cramer was right. Bad enough he had spent the past fourteen years always on the edge of getting himself or his partner killed because he was afraid of what he might do, how he might act. Now that same indecision could get Mandi or Pierce killed, as well. He stared past Cramer at his pistol holster, hanging on the headboard, and made a mental note not to leave it behind again.

Suddenly the house shuddered, as though the very boards and beams were being rent asunder. Jake stumbled, catching himself against the door frame until the structure slowly settled again, and the old building seemed to hold its breath.

He started toward Mandi's room, but she stuck her head out to tell him that she and Pierce were okay and that she would take care of Barb. Jake raced down the stairs with Cramer right on his heels. Virgil was shining a flashlight around the living room.

"What the hell was that?" muttered Cramer, as he and Jake followed the sheriff into the kitchen, where a section of ceiling had collapsed onto the counter.

"Better take a look outside," said Virgil, hefting his shotgun from its resting place beside the recliner.

The flood was level with the decking, and the top of the foundation was no longer visible.

"It felt like a tank hit this place," said Cramer, as Virgil shone his flashlight around the front yard.

Jake stepped down into the water, fighting the current to the corner of the house.

"Here," he said, waving Virgil and Cramer over.

"Mother of God," muttered Virgil as he shone the light along the side of the building.

A maple tree that must have been standing tall before the house was even built had lost its grip on the forest floor and fallen across the yard. The upper branches had crashed down on the roof over the kitchen, and now that section of the house looked as if it had folded in on itself.

"Jimmy?" asked Cramer, studying the woods, then glancing pointedly at Jake's empty hands.

Jake shook his head, frowning. "Jimmy didn't knock that thing down. Not without a chain saw. And we'd have heard that."

"Whatever. That was close," said Virgil, shining the light up the wall. "If that tree had hit a few feet north it would have taken out Mandi and Pierce's bedroom."

Jake had been worried about a flash flood or the slopes washing out and carrying a mudslide down into the house. He hadn't considered a tree simply smashing them flat. And there were plenty more where this one had come from.

"We can't stay here now," said Virgil, shining the light on the knee-deep water encroaching on the house. "If the slopes here are washing out, anything could happen. The old house is the only real high ground left in the valley."

"I guess you're right," Jake reluctantly admitted, following him back into the house.

"What caused that?" asked Mandi, leading Pierce and Barbara into the living room.

Jake told her, watching Barbara blanch. Mandi signed to Pierce. The boy looked shaken, but he just nodded and gritted his teeth.

From inside the kitchen a nasty creaking sound could be

heard over the wind and rain that was now working its way into the house. Jake glanced at Virgil, and Virgil shrugged.

"Right," said Jake, turning to Mandi again. "We're going to have to make our way up to the old house. Get Pierce ready. Cramer, look in the closets. I'm sure Ernie and Pam have a pack or two. We'll carry all the supplies we can."

"Jake," said Mandi. "Are you absolutely sure?"

"Yeah," he said, not wanting to risk the storm again any more than she did. "We really can't chance staying here any longer."

"Okay," she said weakly.

She signed to Pierce, and Jake could tell he didn't like the idea any better than she did. But he was pleased to see that the kid swallowed his fear and went along with Mandi with dry eyes. Whether or not the boy was his son, he was a son to be proud of.

By the time they had loaded up canned goods, matches, candles, the first-aid kit, and a couple of blankets, Mandi, Pierce, and Barbara were standing beside the door. Virgil wore some of Ernie's clothes and carried his shotgun under his good arm. Cramer shouldered one of the packs and Jake took the other, his wounded shoulder aching beneath the strap. Mandi had dressed Pierce in what Jake guessed were a pair of Pam's jeans, which poked out of his rain suit.

The instant Jake had agreed to evacuate to the old house the jewel had flashed into his mind and he had grabbed *it* even before strapping on his holster and pistol. As he led them all out onto the porch he could feel the necklace in his pants pocket.

What power did the gemstone hold? Why was he drawn to it? Why was Pierce drawn to it?

It's in your blood. Something about your blood.

The only thing he knew for certain about the jewel was

that he could no more have left it on his bureau upstairs than he could have left Mandi or Pierce.

"All right," said Mandi, nodding across the miasma of rain-churned lawn. "Which way?"

"There's the old trail to the swimming hole through there," said Jake, pointing toward the trees on the side of the house.

Barbara shook her head, staring into the dark brush. "I can't hike through that."

Cramer frowned. "You don't have any choice unless you want to stay here."

"What about Oswald?" argued the old lady. The dog sat on the porch at Cramer's feet, lolling its tongue and studying the two feet of water in front of it.

"He'll probably do better than us," said Virgil. "But we'll carry him as far as the trees."

"Come on, Barbara," said Mandi, picking up the little dog and handing him to Cramer. "We can't stay here. We'll all help you."

Jake climbed down the steps, catching himself on the newel post at the bottom as his feet threatened to slip out from under him. The water was barely above his knees, but the weight of the pack screwed up his balance. The thought of walking two or three miles through the woods carrying that load, and trying to take care of the group at the same time, was daunting, but it had to be done. He reminded himself that Jimmy was probably out there, as well, and he shifted, feeling his pistol scrunched under his arm.

But if Jimmy leaped out in front of them, would he use it in time? Or would he hesitate, more afraid of himself than of Jimmy? He couldn't allow himself to do that. He couldn't allow something to happen to Pierce or Mandi because of fourteen years of self-inflicted fear.

When Pierce's foot hit the water he tried to back up, but

Mandi shook his hand sternly, and he trudged reluctantly beside her into the flood. Jake could see that between leading Pierce and helping Barb they were going to be hard-pressed to make a few hundred yards an hour, but they couldn't carry the pair on their backs up and down the slippery slopes.

"Shine the light over there," he said, pointing around the corner.

"Oh, my God," said Mandi, catching sight of the giant maple crushing down on the house. "It looks even worse out here than it did inside."

"We have to cut into the trail through the woods," said Jake, pointing along the length of the tree's trunk toward the forest.

As they trudged toward the trees, the sound of the rain striking the leaves and pine needles reasserted itself, but at least the canopy appeared to offer some shelter. Cramer set Oswald down as they slipped through the brush alongside the fallen tree, and Jake kicked bracken out of their way, muscling through small saplings. When they reached the upturned roots Jake stopped, shining the light around to inspect the crater left by the tree's demise. The hole was already filling with water.

Cramer and Barbara eased up beside them.

"That thing went deep," said Cramer, his eyes following Jake's flashlight down into the hole.

Jake nodded, pointing the light at the base of the tree, then back down into the crater.

"We can make it around the hole easy enough," said Mandi, staring deeper into the woods.

But Jake was still studying the wide taproot that seemed to have snapped in half like a twig.

"What's the matter?" asked Cramer.

"Nothing," said Jake, working his way around the hole.

Virgil stopped for a moment, shining his light into the dark forest.

"Anything?" asked Cramer, looking back over his shoulder.

Virgil just shook his head and closed the gap between them.

THE RAINDROPS SLAPPING PIERCE'S PLASTIC JACKET were only slight distractions from the rest of the night-world bombarding him with new sensations. As he inhaled the rich smell of wet humus, pine sap, and the mixed, acrid odors of damp weeds and bracken, he could feel every twig twisted into the slurry through the rubber soles of his sodden sneakers.

His mother jerked him along, and he tucked himself in tight behind her to avoid the branches that kept slapping at him. Now and then the old woman bumped into his back or the dog slipped between his legs.

They finally stopped, and his mother signed to him that Jake had gone on ahead to look for the trail. Pierce nodded.

When his mother let him go for a moment, he knelt, holding both hands out in front of him, the rain tickling his fingers. After a second he felt the dog's rough, warm tongue lapping his palm, and he ruffled the fur on the back of its head. Oswald tried to lick that palm, as well, but Pierce caught him by the collar and pulled him close, petting him gently. He settled against Pierce's calf, and the boy sheltered him from the rain with his body. The rich, earthy odor of wet fur was so thick around him he couldn't smell anything else. He ran his fingers down the animal's sides to its belly, and Oswald rolled over on the soggy pine needles to let himself be rubbed, pedaling both rear legs like he was riding a bicycle. Pierce smiled, continuing the massage.

Suddenly the dog rolled over and away, and Pierce's mother jerked him back to his feet.

What's the matter? he signed.

Oswald heard something, she signed back.

She stiffened, and he questioned her with rushing fingers, but she gripped both hands in her own, signaling him to wait. When she did answer her own hands were shaking.

Barbara ran off after Oswald.

Into the woods?

It'll be all right, his mother signed. *Virgil will find her.*

Pierce felt his guts tighten. *Virgil went into the woods?*

Yes.

Suddenly he was certain that neither the old woman nor Virgil was coming back.

Are you okay? signed his mother.

We need to find Jake and go.

We have to wait for Virgil and Barbara.

There was no sense arguing. Cramer and his mother weren't going to run away and leave Virgil or the old lady, no matter what he said. But he could feel the presence, beginning to slip around them again like a mist, and he could almost read it, the way he read a bad circuit. It seemed to be trying to tell him something—or maybe *ask* him something—but he just couldn't quite get it.

Feeling his mother's hands, tense on his own, he knew to the bottom of his heart that she would die before she let anything happen to him. But he also knew that at this moment *he* was probably better suited to protect *her*. He just hadn't discovered how. But he had to find a way. Because the presence wasn't going to give up. It was going to keep coming back until it got whatever it was it wanted.

His mother squeezed his hand again, and he shrugged a question.

Virgil's calling for Barbara. I guess he hasn't found her yet, she signed.

He shook his head. Maybe Virgil would make it back. He said a silent prayer for both the sheriff and the old lady. Then he added a heartfelt plea for the rest of them.

"Oswald!"

Barbara's voice cut through the rain, and when Jake heard the dog yapping away through the forest he realized the woman had run off after the mutt.

Great.

"Barbara!" That was Virgil.

What the hell was Cramer doing letting the group get broken up like that? He could have done a better job herding cats. But it dawned on Jake that it was just as much his own fault for keeping the old woman in the dark about Jimmy. By the sound the dog was moving fast. Jake shone his flashlight in the direction of the barks, but all he could see was the sheen of the light on rain-soaked foliage.

Hurrying back down the trail, he lost his footing and hit the ground hard on his back. He crashed down the slimy slope like a wild bull, tucking the flashlight tight against his chest and balling up to protect his vitals. He was bounced from tree to tree through the slick mud, finally splashing to a stop in three feet of water.

He slapped his way to his feet and surveyed his surroundings.

It looked like he was in the Murphys' backyard. What was left of a screen house was pressed up against the porch by the current, and the handle of a mower was just visible above the surface in the middle of the lawn. A lone candle shone in one window. Jake had figured that the Murphy place would have flooded already, but the water was only up to the floor line.

He could barely hear Barbara's screams over the rain and rushing water. She was still calling Oswald's name, and he thought he heard Mandi shouting, too. But he knew Cramer would never leave Mandi and Pierce alone.

He climbed the back stoop and knocked, and when no one answered he tried the door, but it was locked. So he knocked again. The echo of his knuckles against the wood seemed to hang in the yard. He shone the flashlight around, hoping Bert and Karen had evacuated already and weren't stuck in the valley like they were.

But then surely they wouldn't have left a candle burning. The sense of wrongness tightened his stomach.

He leaned over the porch rail trying to see inside the kitchen, but the window was too far away. So he kicked the door. It rattled in its frame but held. He kicked it again, harder, nearer the knob. The jamb burst beside the striker, and the door flew open, extinguishing the candle on the counter. But more flickering light created wavy shadows down the hall. Reluctantly he unholstered his pistol.

"Hello?" he called, realizing immediately that might have been a stupid thing to do.

The probability kept nagging at him that the reason the candles were burning was that the Murphys hadn't *left*. They just weren't in any shape to answer the door.

The silence sent a prickling sensation up the back of his neck as he slipped quickly through the kitchen, peeking both ways down the corridor before entering it. An open window gusted air through the curtains in the bedroom, but the room was empty. He turned back toward the living room, where all the candlelight seemed to be coming from. But the rest of the house was so dark behind him that he kept peeking back over his shoulder.

Numerous candles burned around the room, lending it a funereal feel. The smell of tobacco smoke hung in the air, and Jake stared at the package of cigarettes and lighter on the end table beside the sofa. A tiny grating noise caught his attention, and he spun, tracing the sound to the front door. More than likely debris from the storm, blowing around the porch. Finally he eased the door open.

A gallon jar clattered onto its side on the threshold and rolled toward the steps. Jake caught it, shining the flashlight across the glass.

At first his mind refused to wrap around what he was seeing. He stood slowly, his stomach heaving, shining the light across the flooded front yard and surrounding trees. But no one was there. He lowered the light once more, and found himself staring into Bert's unseeing eyes. His friend's face was crushed into the tight confines of the jar, his nose broken against the glass, creating a wide-eyed mask of horror and fear. Jake gently lowered the jar to the porch floor and backed quickly into the house, slamming the door behind him.

He rushed down the hall and through the kitchen, bursting out into the water in the backyard. Tree limbs and bramble bobbed along on the swift current. Suddenly a man's laughter cut through the rain and water noise, and Jake spun just in time to flash the light in Jimmy's face.

He was stark naked with a butcher knife in one hand and a rifle in the other, and his eyes were bulging with madness. Jake aimed his pistol at Jimmy's chest. At that range he could hardly miss, and the thought crossed his mind that he should pull the trigger. But just as suddenly the old fear returned, and he knew he couldn't let the monster out. Not now. Not here. What if he killed Jimmy but couldn't get the thing out of his head? What would happen to Mandi, and Pierce, and the others?

"Drop the weapons and step into the clearing!" he shouted.

Jimmy laughed louder, staring down his nose at Jake and raising the rifle.

"Put down the weapon!" screamed Jake, his finger tightening on the trigger.

As Jimmy's rifle leveled with Jake's face, Jake leaped aside, the flash of the gun blinding him at the same instant he ripped off two quick shots of his own. Then the forest went dark again, and when he roved the light across it, Jimmy was gone.

Jake crouched in the waist-deep water, creeping slowly toward the last spot he'd seen Jimmy. When he got there he spotted tracks in the mud and pine needles. He also found the rifle, but no sign of blood.

But he must have hit the bastard, or he'd never have left the weapon.

The thought of shooting yet another human being—even Jimmy—sickened him. But what choice had he had? He snatched up the rifle and backed carefully down into the water again. When he reached the spot where he had crashed into the backyard he scrabbled up the slope through the surrounding brush.

"Mandi," he screamed, finally stumbling out onto the path. "Cramer!"

"Yo!" Cramer called back.

Jake was staggering toward the sound of his partner's voice when a light flashed in his eyes. He plunged, exhausted, into the small clearing where the group had gathered.

"Jimmy's out there," he told Cramer, just as Virgil

appeared out of the woods. "But I think I winged him, or he wouldn't have dropped *this*."

"Couldn't find Barbara," said Virgil miserably. "You say you saw Jimmy?"

Jake nodded. He could see Virgil gearing up to go crashing into the forest again. He grabbed the older man by the arm—leading him and Cramer away from the others—and gave them a brief account of what he had seen at the Murphys'.

"A jar?" said Virgil, grimacing.

"Yeah," said Jake.

"He's crazy," said Cramer. "He likes playing with his victims and with people's minds. And this is Jimmy's turf now. He's better trained for the woods than we are."

Jake nodded. "I hate to say this, but we can't save Barbara by getting everyone else killed. We need to get to the old house."

"Because we may have more to worry about out here than Jimmy?" asked Cramer.

Jake shrugged.

Virgil shook his head. "Barbara isn't either of your responsibilities. She lives in my jurisdiction. And I'm sworn to protect her."

"And Mandi and Pierce," Jake reminded him.

"You two can get them to the Crowley house."

"And if we don't? If Jimmy's waiting ahead in ambush while you're running around like a loose cannon?"

Virgil shook his head obstinately, stepping to the tree line. "Barb! Can you hear me? Answer for God's sake!"

"Virg," said Jake, "if Jimmy doesn't know she's out there, you're gonna tell him."

Jake could see the reasoning slowly sinking in. Virgil didn't like it. But Barbara would have to be written off, at least for the moment. Jake didn't like it, either. But there it was. If Virgil insisted on going out searching for her now, he'd just be playing into Jimmy's hands.

"Damn," muttered Virg, hanging his head.

"Come on," said Jake, wrapping an arm around the old man's shoulders and nudging him back to the group.

Mandi didn't care much for the idea, either. But when Jake explained about Jimmy, and that staying where they were was endangering Pierce, as well, she reluctantly acquiesced.

But Virgil kept glaring out into the trees as they hiked, and Jake had the feeling that Jimmy made a far worse enemy in this backwoods valley than he'd ever managed to in Houston.

THE SUN MUST HAVE RISEN, but the only light flashed irregularly from the storm still thundering overhead. To their right the mountain sloped upward into the gloom. To their left it dropped away precipitously into equal darkness. The rain-laden wind gusted and swirled.

They hadn't heard the dog barking for a couple of miles. And Jake was afraid that the gutsy animal and its master had run afoul of a homicidal maniac. Whenever he glanced over his shoulder he saw Cramer and Virgil scanning the trees uphill and down.

Most of this trail ran high up along the mountainside away from any landmarks, and it was surrounded by forest and overgrown from years of disuse. If it hadn't been for deer and the occasional hunter it probably would have disappeared altogether. Jake tried to estimate how much farther it was to the old house, but the twists and turns and fourteen years away from the valley conspired with the storm to disorient him.

They stopped under a maple tree for a breather, and Jake nudged close to Cramer. Virgil eased up alongside.

"Shouldn't be too much farther," said Jake.

"Meaning you don't know," Cramer replied.

"What do you think about lynx now?"

"I wish I was one."

Glancing around, Jake wondered if this wasn't the worst place they could have chosen to rest. They were on the inside elbow of a sharp turn that reminded him of the spot on the burnout trail where Ernie had been shot. He had to peer in either direction around the bulk of the trees to make out the way they had come and the way they were going. And the forest was denser here, lined with bracken and brush. A distant sound caught his attention, and he stiffened, holding out his hand to Cramer for silence, but he could barely make the noise out over the slapping of the rain on the foliage. Then it was gone.

"Did you hear it?" Jake asked.

Cramer frowned, checking out the terrain. "Hear what?"

"The whispering."

"Great. Which way was it coming from?"

"I couldn't tell. Maybe it was just my imagination. I'm jumpy."

"Ain't we all?" muttered Virgil.

"Pierce heard it," said Jake.

The boy seemed to be searching the storm with his blind eyes as Mandi tried to communicate with him.

"How the hell could he do that?" asked Virgil.

"I don't know," said Jake, shaking his head. "How the hell did he fix my car?"

"How good a look did you get at Jimmy?" asked Cramer.

"Maybe thirty feet away. He's still naked. He had the knife and the rifle."

"Thirty feet?"

Jake frowned. "Yeah."

"And you missed?" said Virgil.

"Damn, boy," muttered Cramer.

"I shouted for him to drop his weapons," said Jake.

"And when he aimed the gun in your direction you did what?" said Cramer. "Try to shoot it out of his hand like Roy Rogers?"

"It happened fast," said Jake.

But he knew it was his fault now if Barbara was dead. And he wondered which was worse, maybe letting the demon out, or keeping it hidden and allowing someone else to do the killing. Pierce started flailing in Mandi's arms, and the three of them edged back toward the boy, watching as Mandi tried to break through. But Pierce continued to ignore her.

"He wants you," Mandi told Jake, holding out Pierce's hands.

Did you hear it? Pierce spelled quickly into Jake's palm.

Jake glanced at Mandi, and sighed before spelling back. *Yeah. I think I heard it again just now.*

Pierce nodded. *It knows you.*

Jake frowned. *What do you mean?*

I think it knows both of us.

Jake stared at the boy for a long moment, ignoring the rest of the group who watched in silence. He turned slowly to Mandi with the question on his lips, but when he faced all of them in the gray cavern of rain he couldn't voice it. This definitely wasn't the time or the place.

When we get inside again we'll talk, spelled Jake, extricating his hand and making sure that Mandi had a firm hold on Pierce again before starting down the trail.

They moved at an even slower pace than before, eyeing every shadow, but as they rounded yet another bend in the path a large, jagged boulder jutted out of the mountainside,

and Jake smiled, pointing it out to Mandi. She nodded in re-
sponse.

"What's that?" asked Cramer.

"Indian Rock!" Jake shouted back to Virgil. "We're close
to the swimming hole."

Mandi's shoulders sagged from exhaustion, and Jake
stroked wet hair out of her eyes.

"Put Pierce between us. It gets steeper here."

The path began to slope downward along the mountainside. The trail was as slippery as wet ice, but the sodden
grass and pine needles alongside were no better. Several
times Pierce bumped into Jake's back, causing him to lose
his balance.

"Everybody watch your step," he shouted.

When Pierce stumbled and caught himself against Jake's
hip, Jake felt the gem in his pocket pressed into his side. He
glanced at the boy and saw realization in Pierce's face. Even
through the wet cloth, the boy knew what he'd felt. Why was
it so important to him?

He steadied the boy and led on.

THE OLD HOUSE SOARED over the landscape like an albino vulture, with wide overhanging eaves for wings and dark window eyes blinking at each bolt of lightning. Grass grew as high as the porch floor, and an apple tree that had been shattered by some long-ago storm stood rotting in the front yard. One shutter slapped wildly in the wind. But it was Albert's bulldozer resting beside the porch that held Jake's attention.

"What's that doing here?" he asked.

Virgil shook his head. "Bert Murphy said he heard Albert drive it up here a couple of days before he was killed. Got no idea what he was planning to do with it."

"We have to get inside," said Mandi, feeling for the key over the door. "Pierce is freezing."

As Jake's hand rested on the doorknob he stared at his reflection in the darkened glass, but saw instead a boy of ten, eyes wide with terror, jaw clasped shut. He stared into those eyes for what seemed an eternity, wondering if this house really was the cause of all the horror somehow.

Mandi's hand slipped over his, and he let her twist the knob, listening to the creaking of the old lock. They pushed the door open together, and when he turned to look at her she nodded.

"There's nothing in there to be afraid of," she whispered, too low for the others to hear. "Just old memories."

But Jake knew better. The ghosts of his past were hidden beneath the sheets covering chairs and tables, concealed in every nook and cranny.

Pierce sneezed as they entered, then coughed and cleared his throat. Mandi signed to him, and he nodded.

"What did you tell him?" asked Jake, dumping his pack onto the floor.

"I told him where we were and what the smell was. Pierce has never been around this much dust."

"Reminds me of home," said Cramer.

Jake noticed Virgil standing in the doorway staring out into the storm, and he slipped beside the sheriff.

"There was nothing you could do to save her," insisted Jake, knowing that Barbara's disappearance would eat at the older man until he found her—alive or dead.

Virgil sighed. "I think maybe this valley really is cursed."

Jake nudged him gently aside and closed the door.

Mandi was trying to get a shivering Pierce out of his dripping rain gear, and Jake could see by the tears in her eyes that pent-up fear had finally taken its toll. He went to her and wrapped his arms around both of them.

"It's over," he whispered into her ear. "We're safe now."

She shook her head. "No, we're not. That killer is still out there. That *thing* is still out there. And now maybe Barbara's dead, too."

Seeking refuge in the old house did seem like jumping from the frying pan into the fire. But what else could they have done? Events seemed to have conspired inevitably to this conclusion, from the killings on the beach, to the storm, to Jimmy. Jake felt as though he had been herded here against his will, but he could find no way to reason them all out of the dilemma.

"Who's got the candles?" asked Cramer, waving his flashlight.

"There used to be kerosene lamps and matches stored in that closet," said Jake, reluctantly releasing Mandi and pointing at a door.

"All fueled up and ready to go," said Cramer, digging out a lantern and shaking it.

"That's funny," said Jake, unscrewing one of the caps and swishing lantern fuel around. "I would have thought the fuel would have evaporated by now."

Cramer shrugged, lighting lantern after lantern until warm, golden light flooded the hallway. "Shall we?" He waved toward the parlor, and the others followed him inside. "Here we have the sitting room, complete with Victorian decor. The floor is done in old-world dust, and the windows are frosted with same."

Mandi chuckled. "It does need a woman's touch."

"It needs the Women's Army Corps," said Cramer.

Mandi started pulling sheets off of furniture. She shook one out and wrapped it around Pierce, who was still shivering.

"There may still be wood out back," said Jake, heading into the hall again.

"Jake!" said Mandi, freezing everyone in place.

He turned.

"Be careful," she said at last.

He smiled reassuringly. "It's okay. Just getting some firewood. I'll be right back."

"Need me?" whispered Cramer.

Jake kept his own voice low. "Jimmy's wounded, at the

very least, and all he's got now is the knife, anyway. If I get into trouble, I'll yell."

"With your reflexes a knife might be all he needs," said Cramer, frowning.

"I'll be all right," growled Jake.

"I'll stay with the housekeeping staff, then," said Cramer, wadding up a sheet and tossing it into a corner.

S JAKE PASSED THROUGH THE KITCHEN he was struck by haunting memories.

He recalled surprising his parents at the sink. His father had Jake's mother wrapped in his arms, nuzzling her neck while she giggled and shifted flirtatiously against him. That was a good memory and one that hadn't surfaced in a long time. He tried to hold onto it, but the scene faded, replaced by the night he and Mandi had snuck up here together. He could remember the *beginning* of that night, picture the house, smell the dust and Mandi's perfume. Regardless of what he'd told her, he did recall making out furiously just before he began to sense the presence in the house.

What in the world had he been thinking, letting her talk him into coming here? Even a horny twenty-two-year-old should have been smarter than that. But by that time he'd pretty much convinced himself that Virgil and Pam were right, that there was no such thing as the Crowley curse, that what he remembered of his mother's death was the imagining of a terribly traumatized child's mind.

Only it wasn't.

As much as he wanted to, he still couldn't recall making love that night. He remembered lying on the mattress in front of the fire, his arms around Mandi, the feel of her, the smell of her hair. He recalled wanting her and her wanting him, her eyes closed in anticipation and desire, her breath like a hot breeze against his throat.

Then the memories became disjointed and surreal. But what he did remember most vividly was the sound of the whisper, creeping through the old house, the sudden sense of something *inside* his head. Most horrifying of all, he witnessed his own hands as they slipped slowly around Mandi's throat and began to tighten, her eyes confused, then angry, then panicked, then paralyzed. He had no control of those hands, as though he were outside his body, screaming at himself to let go, watching helplessly as *he* committed the murder of his beloved.

When he came to the next day he was afraid to open his eyes. But Mandi was sleeping soundly, curled in his arms. She was shocked when he awakened her and told her to get dressed. He had no idea what had happened in the night. But he feared that something similar might have happened to his own father on the night his mother was killed. And he knew that this had been his only warning. He couldn't allow anyone close to him again.

For fourteen years he had believed that his decision had been the right one. For fourteen years he had watched himself constantly for signs that the monster was taking over again. But it hadn't happened. Until the fight on the beach he had never hurt anyone. But *he* hadn't killed all those men, either. So, had his father gone crazy? Or had there really been a monster that had killed his mother? Could it have been some combination of the two? There was definitely *something* that seemed to exist outside his head. Other people had heard the whispers. Hell, even *Pierce* heard them.

Whatever it was that plagued his family—whether madness or monster or both—some part of it had finally followed him to Houston. It had killed outside the valley. But it had to end here. Now, where it began. Because he wanted Mandi back. He needed her back. And he would not allow it to have either her or Pierce.

A bolt of lightning zigzagged through the trees behind the house. Silhouetted by the flash, the branches waved a thousand tiny hands in warding gestures against some approaching menace, and the outline of the old Crowley family chapel flared, pointing an accusing finger skyward as a peal of thunder rocked the house. The storm center was right over their heads and gaining in fury.

Pellets of rain battered Jake as he stepped out into the wind. A stack of cordwood—rotten and ingrown with fungus and weeds—rested against the house beneath a narrow shed roof. Jake tossed the pulpiest pieces off the top, searching for drier, firmer wood beneath. He gathered as much as he could carry and hurried back up the porch steps. Before he could cross the threshold, though, a singsong whisper wove through the rain and wind, setting the hair on the back of his neck on end. A shadow deeper than the surrounding darkness meandered through the trees as the sound competed with the furor of the storm.

Jake shone the flashlight across the tall grass as he backed into the house, kicking the door closed behind him.

When he dumped the wood on the hearth in the living room Cramer knelt beside him, giving him an appraising look. "Wood's half rotten. Gonna need a lot more."

"We'll go get it together, then," said Jake, refusing to look him in the eye.

He felt a tap on his shoulder and turned to see Pierce

standing over him. When Jake glanced at Mandi she shook her head.

"He got up off the sofa . . . He went right to you."

Jake took Pierce's hand. *What's up?*

Can I have it?

Jake knew instantly what the boy wanted. Hesitantly he reached into his pocket and handed the jewel to Pierce.

The boy held it in one open palm, the chain dangling, fingering the facets with his other hand. He nibbled his lip thoughtfully. Finally, he nodded his thanks and dropped back onto the couch.

"Jake . . ." said Mandi, staring uncertainly at the necklace.

Jake shrugged. "I don't think a piece of jewelry is gonna hurt him."

PIERCE HUDDLED ON THE SOFA, soaking up the warmth of the fire. He had yet to figure out what drew him to the necklace. But there was a definite attraction, and he knew the jewel wasn't just a jewel. It buzzed in his hand like some kind of machine. Only it was broken, somehow. It still had power. But the power seemed to be leaking or switching the wrong circuits.

Vibrations tickled the floor, and when he turned he sensed three vague figures. But not through the vibrations. Through his *eyes* . . . It felt similar to the sensation he'd had for just an instant on the day Dary Murphy had been killed. He waved his hands slowly in front of his face, following their silhouette, trying to understand how this new phenomenon—comprised of familiar darkness and what had to be *light*—worked, but when he aimed his fingers back in the direction of the figures the talent suddenly disappeared, and he felt a terrible sinking sense of loss.

He squeezed the jewel tighter, feeling a higher-pitched vibration tingle through it. Then the odd sensation shocked

him again. Light and dark. Movement and stillness. That's
what it had to be.

He was seeing.

Mandi watched Jake and Cramer heading down the hall
toward the kitchen as she busied herself with making beds
for all of them on the floor. She'd enlisted Virgil's help to
drag mattresses down from the rooms upstairs, and they had
scattered four of them around the fireplace. Now they were
covering them with musty-smelling old blankets. Once that
was done she intended to dig out the canned goods from the
packs and see about rationing out a first meal. She also
needed to put pots and pans out front to collect water.

It felt good to have something to keep her thoughts off of
Jimmy Torrio or the whispering terror that lived out in the
storm. But her mind kept wanting to go back to that moment
when Barbara had disappeared into the trees. In her mind's
eye Mandi saw not the old lady trying to save a dog, but herself, running through the darkness after Pierce. What if *he*
had gotten away from them instead of Oswald? Would she
and Pierce have been sacrificed for the good of the group?
She imagined Jake's arms around her and knew that it would
never have happened. He had forged his way through the
flood to save them. He would never forsake them again.
Never.

Pierce sat on one of the mattresses, facing the fire. His
brow was furrowed, and he was squinting into the fireplace.
He had one hand cupped over an ear as though trying to hear
the crackling flames. Mandi knelt slowly beside him.

Pierce's eyes always moved along with his head. It was
one of the traits that gave his blindness away to people. But
now they followed the jittering flames as she watched him
twist his head, cupping one hand over his ear.

Dear God. Don't let me be imagining this.

"Pierce," she said, in a voice firmer than she felt. "Pierce, can you hear me?"

To her amazement, he turned toward her voice, his eyes roving her face. He ran his fingers lightly along her cheeks. And she saw curiosity, and love, in his eyes, for the first time since his birth. Her chest ached, and her throat constricted.

"Pierce?"

He took her hand and signed to her. *I don't understand what you're saying.*

Of course not. He'd never heard *anything* in his entire life. He wouldn't be able to recognize his own name or any other words she spoke. Her heart hammered in her chest. She was so shaken she could barely will her fingers to sign back. *Can you really see me?*

He nodded vigorously, never taking his eyes from hers. She pulled him toward her, crushing him in her arms, stroking his hair, kissing the top of his head. When she held him out to arm's length his eyes found hers immediately again. Tears welled in her own eyes.

Dear God, she thought. *Dear sweet Jesus. Thank you. Thank you.*

Since the boy was born she'd felt guilty about his infirmities, no matter how much the doctors reassured her that neither his blindness nor his lack of hearing was her fault. Then, when he was crippled and she wasn't home to protect him, her guilt had multiplied. Seeing him cured like this was like the lifting of a vast weight that she had been certain she would have to carry for the rest of her life.

"What's going on?" asked Virgil, leaning around her to look at Pierce.

"He can see," she gasped. "He can hear."

"Are you serious?"

Pierce glanced over Mandi's shoulder at Virgil and made a face, trying to place the smell with the sound and the face.

"He doesn't understand or recognize you," said Mandi, the tears flowing freely down her cheeks. "He's never heard speech or seen anyone's face before."

Pierce's eyes went back to roaming the room, but when either she or Virgil spoke he turned to them instantly.

Virgil shook his head, smiling. "What could have caused it? It's some kind of miracle."

"It is a miracle," she whispered, clutching Pierce tightly again and kissing his cheek.

But Pierce slipped out of her grasp and climbed to his feet. She thought for a moment he was going to reach into the fire, and she rushed to stop him. But he sensed the heat, and drew back. Instead he wandered around the room like a toddler, touching the windowsill, sniffing the dust on the curtains, leaning to pick up one of the cans of vegetables from Jake's pack, sniffing it, squinting at the picture on the label. Mandi watched him, barely able to breathe. He was halfway around the room, making his way back to the mattress, when she gasped again.

"What's the matter?" asked Virgil.

Mandi nodded toward Pierce who was now fingering the old brocade upholstery on the sofa.

"He's not limping," she whispered.

"What's he saying?" asked Jake, as Cramer moved in beside them, dropping his own armload of wood beside the hearth. Both men watched the boy.

Pierce kept signing to his mother, his fingers racing through the symbols like a piano player doing warmup exercises.

Mandi frowned. "He says the jewel is broken, but it's

doing things to him. I guess he believes the necklace is responsible for his sight and hearing."

Pierce looked right at Jake. The boy's eyes followed his every move. Jake took one of Pierce's hands to spell into it. But when they touched, Pierce jerked away, and Jake knew instantly what had frightened him.

I won't take it back, I promise, spelled Jake, but the boy still pulled away, huddling against his mother.

"Tell him he can keep it," Jake told Mandi.

"But what else is it doing to him?" asked Virgil, frowning at Pierce's closed fist.

Jake shook his head. "It doesn't seem to be hurting him."

"But it's connected to all this, to the Crowley curse, isn't it?" said Cramer.

Jake shrugged. "I don't know how it could be. I took it from José Torrio in Galveston."

"Baggage," muttered Cramer.

"What?" said Mandi.

Cramer shook his head.

"Tell Pierce I just want to look at the jewel again," said Jake. "Not take it."

Mandi signed to Pierce, and he answered back with his free hand. Jake sat down on the floor beside him, resting his own hands in his lap in what he hoped looked to Pierce like a nonthreatening gesture. Finally the boy seemed relaxed, but all he would offer was for Jake to touch the jewel while he continued to press it to his own chest.

Can you see me now? asked Jake.

Pierce nodded slowly, his eyes following Jake's other hand uncertainly.

How many fingers? spelled Jake.

Three, signed Pierce, frowning.

Right.

Jake gently rested his fingertips on the jewel. At first it felt exceptionally cold. But then the feeling abruptly changed, and he was afraid it was about to burn his skin. He jerked his fingers away, and Pierce closed his fist again. But a memory had been rekindled in the back of Jake's mind. An image of his mother on the night she was killed. He was sitting on the floor just like he was now, staring at the form of her broken body, when his father had dropped beside him. There were tears in his dad's eyes as he reached beneath Jake's mother's hand and slipped something into his own. Something gleaming and red. Jake stared at the chain dangling from Pierce's hand, and in that instant he recalled his father's words.

Oh, Sylvia, what in the world did you do? Why?

Had his mother found this same jewel? Had his father known that *it* had somehow caused her death? But then how in the world had it ended up around José Torrio's neck? What unbelievable concatenation of events had led it back to him? Albert had been up to the house. Torrio's man killed Albert, or he was there when Albert was killed.

Things began to click into place.

}DIDN'T HEAR ANYTHING OUT THERE THIS TIME," said Jake. He and Cramer were carrying yet more wood into the kitchen.

"It's there," said Cramer, shaking off the rain. "A spirit like that don't cause this much trouble, then just run off. Memere says the only way to stop a spirit is to either figure out what it wants and *appease* it, or find its power and cut the heart out of it."

"Pleasant old thing, Memere."

"Very knowledgeable," said Cramer with a toothy grin.

"And what else would Memere say?"

Cramer's grin hardened into a frown. "That maybe that necklace is like a juju for the spirits. Maybe they're following it around. Maybe they want it back."

Jake considered it, but shook his head. "That just doesn't ring true. If the spirits were here all along they'd have known where the jewel was before Albert found it. I think it was meant to come to me, for some reason. That's how it ended up in Houston to begin with."

"And what are you supposed to do with it?"

"I wish I knew."

Cramer shrugged. "You gave it to the boy. Maybe that's what you were supposed to do."

Jake shook his head. "Pierce was already here. Why send the jewel on a four-thousand-mile round trip just to get it to him?"

Mandi sat in front of the fire hugging Pierce, both of them wrapped in a blanket. Since Pierce's astounding recovery she seemed reluctant to be more than arm's length from the boy, as though by her proximity she might stop the miracle from fading.

Although her eyes were sliding closed, Jake noticed that Pierce was still staring into the fire. He knelt quietly beside the boy and took his hand, receiving a shy grin in reply this time.

Who are you? Pierce spelled.

Jake was shaken, suddenly wondering if they'd made a mistake, if the gem that appeared to have repaired Pierce's vision and hearing, and his leg, had somehow damaged his mind. He spelled back, slowly, *Jake.*

Pierce shook his head. *Why do I know you?*

Jake sighed. *I'm not sure,* he signed.

But it was clear from Pierce's steady expression that he didn't buy that. The boy had the same instincts that he did. Only he didn't have the information that Jake had in order to reason from them.

Cramer tossed another log onto the fire and slipped silently over to the front windows beside Virgil. When Jake turned back toward Pierce he noticed Mandi was wide awake and watching him, and he saw just an edge of distrust in her eyes.

He shook his head. "I didn't ask him for the jewel."

"What were you two talking about?" she whispered, eyeing Pierce's hand in Jake's.

Jake glanced over her shoulder, but Cramer was on guard, and Virgil seemed to have nodded off. "I don't really know how to ask this."

"What's so hard?"

He stared at Pierce first, reassuring himself that although the boy could hear him, he still wouldn't understand what was being said. To Jake his own whisper sounded shallow and weak. "Was Rich really Pierce's father?"

"No," said Mandi simply.

Jake's shoulders sagged, and his breath caught in his throat. The crackling fire sounded like gunshots.

"It's all right," she said softly. "I never expected anything from you."

"I guess no one did."

"It was a long time ago," she whispered, placing her hand over his and Pierce's. "And you did what you thought you had to do."

"I would never have left if I'd known."

Her answer seemed to come a heartbeat too slow. "You were already gone before *I* knew. We just have to get by all that now. You thought you were doing the right thing."

He wanted to accept her forgiveness, but another part of himself needed punishment before absolution. Regardless of *why* he had run, of *what* he had known or not known, he had abandoned the woman he loved, and his own son.

Pierce questioned Jake with his fingers, but Jake just shook his head. "He wants to know what we're talking about, and why I seem so familiar to him. I don't know what to tell him."

Mandi frowned. "I guess that's up to you."

"But what do *you* think?"

"Pierce has never had a real father, and he's always wanted one. The question is, what do *you* intend to do about it?"

Her voice told him she was ready to accept whatever he decided. Jake felt as though new possibilities were opening wide before him just when the whole world might still come crashing down around them. But he knew that he already loved Pierce more than he had ever loved anyone except Mandi, and come what might, he could never leave either of them again.

Hesitantly he began to spell, watching the boy closely. *I'm your father.*

Pierce's head jerked. He slipped his hand from Jake's and offered it to Mandi, signing rapidly. When she signed back the boy swallowed visibly before offering his hand to Jake again.

Why did you leave?

I didn't know about you, signed Jake. *I didn't know you were going to be born, or I never would have left. I'm sorry.*

But why?

Jake had had a hard enough time trying to explain to Mandi. How was he going to tell Pierce in the cumbersome finger spelling? *I thought if I left, your mother would be safe.*

Because of the thing outside?

Yes.

Why did you think that?

Jake hesitated, as Pierce stared up into his eyes. *Because I didn't know if it was real. I thought I might be crazy. That I might be dangerous. I didn't want to hurt your mother.*

Pierce signaled with his shoulders that he'd accept that answer. But the boy's expression added *for now.*

Do you love my mom?

Yes.

I think she's missed you a lot.

What about Rich?

Pierce's face told Jake he didn't understand the question.

Was he hard on you?

Pierce frowned. *I got by.*

Jake smiled, seeing in the boy the man he would become and feeling a sense of pride he had never experienced before. *I'll bet you did.*

I used to mess with the TV so he'd leave.

The TV?

Pierce beamed. *It was easy to break. Rich couldn't live without TV.*

Jake chuckled, and Mandi asked him what Pierce had said.

"I think he was way ahead of you about Rich," said Jake. "Did you know he sabotaged the television so Rich would leave the house?"

Mandi stared at the boy as he opened his palm again, showing Jake the gemstone and signing.

Where did you get this? Pierce spelled into Jake's palm.

Jake explained briefly about the night on the beach, and Pierce frowned, shaking his head.

It belongs here.

How do you know that? spelled Jake.

I can feel it. It's broken, but it's stronger now than it was before, at Pam's. That thing outside is connected to it. On the road . . . I almost understood what it wants.

Jake frowned. *That jewel was here the night my mother was murdered, and I think that thing out there killed my father, too.* Jake hesitated before continuing. *I think maybe it tried to make me kill your mother a long time ago.*

Pierce's eyebrows rose. *What stopped it?*

I don't know.

Pierce nodded. *Maybe you did.*

How?

But Pierce shook his head, looking down at the gem in his open palm. *It pulls me to it.*

Me, too.

Pierce held the jewel out to Jake, signing. *Touch it again.*

Jake discovered that now he was reluctant to make contact with the gem even though he'd been carrying it around for days. But the boy was insistent, nodding at him. Finally Jake rested his hand over Pierce's open palm.

The electricity that surged through him was much stronger than even the heat and cold he'd experienced moments before. When he felt as though his consciousness was being drawn down into the gem he jerked his hand away, and glanced at his palm, once again expecting to see the skin blistered, but there seemed to be no damage.

What just happened? he spelled.

Pierce shook his head. *It's broken. But when both of us touched it for a minute it felt better.*

But what's it supposed to do?

Pierce frowned, shaking his head in exasperation. *I can't figure it out yet. And if I don't know what it does, I can't fix it.*

You really think you could do that?

Jake wasn't sure that was a good idea, anyway. If the jewel really was broken like Pierce thought, it had already been responsible for uncounted deaths. What the hell would happen if the boy repaired it?

Is it doing anything to you now? signed Jake, studying Pierce's face.

The boy cocked his head, thinking. *Sometimes I can see inside it. And I feel it, inside me.*

A part of Jake wanted to jerk the jewel out of Pierce's hand and throw it into the fire, regardless of his promise to the boy. But he knew that the answer to their dilemma couldn't possibly be that simple or his father would have destroyed the gemstone decades ago. And if it really was the cause of all the terror, then why did it seem to be making Pierce better?

We're gonna figure this out, he spelled.

Pierce nodded, but there was fear in his eyes again. *It's getting stronger.*

The jewel? signed Jake, frowning.

Pierce shook his head. *The thing outside.*

Jake took the boy by the shoulders and pulled him into a tight embrace. He noticed tears in Mandi's eyes again. There were tears in Jake's eyes, as well.

We'll figure it out, Jake promised, spelling into the boy's hand.

JULES WATCHED THE CRAZY OLD WOMAN stirring another pot on the stove. She'd offered him a bowl of gumbo, but he didn't trust her. Instead he ate the cold canned chili he'd found in the cupboard.

Although it seemed impossible, he was sure she'd been drugging him somehow. There was just no other way to explain some of the crazy shit that had been going on. He wished that Jimmy had just offed the freaky old bitch and been done with it. But now he was beginning to wonder if even thinking something like that was a bad idea.

On the day that Jimmy and Paco had left, Jules would have sworn that voodoo or magic or whatever the fuck you wanted to call it was all just hocus-pocus bullshit. Now he wasn't so sure. He stared at the back of Memere's gray head and wondered if she could hear everything he thought.

"I don' be needin' to read you mind," she said, laughing.

Jules started, dropping the spoon onto the counter and splattering chili into his lap. He genuflected instinctively, but Memere never even turned around to look at him.

"You 'fraid you don' know anymore what real and what not. You 'fraid maybe since you cain't hear nuttin' from you boss that he dead. He ain't dead."

"How do you know that, old woman?"

Memere cackled again, then took a healthy taste of the gumbo and smacked her lips loudly. " 'Cause the snake ain't killed him yet! I tole you! I set a ole snake against you boss, and that snake ain't done wit him yet. They gonna slither round each other for a while longer."

Jules glanced into the far room at the aquarium where the old woman kept the big rattlesnake. He couldn't figure out how he'd missed the thing before. It was as though the snake and the aquarium had just *appeared*. But when he did find it, he'd covered it with an overturned end table, just to be sure. This morning he'd awakened to hear the snake snapping again and again at the glass. He was shaken to see that it had cracked the aquarium, and he wondered if it had been trying to get at *him*. When Memere lifted it out he noticed that the snake had cut itself. A long gash ran from the back of its head halfway down to its rattles. Memere had bandaged it as she might have a human and then put it away again.

Jules had an idea that the snake in the apartment and the one the old woman claimed to have set against the boss were somehow connected, but he couldn't see how. It was all just too fucking far out for him. He wanted desperately to be sitting in a bar sipping rum and Coke and shooting the shit with pretty secretaries playing hooky from work, not stuck here baby-sitting this nutcase.

And it wasn't just the snake.

He'd slid the armchair in the living room over to give him a clear view of the old woman when she went into her bedroom. He could see the small window over her bed from there so he knew she couldn't signal to anyone outside. But so far she hadn't seemed interested in escaping or trying to

draw attention. Instead she just went on with what he assumed were her daily rituals. Cooking her meals. Placing
food and rum in front of each of the weird little altars . . .

That was one of the things that had begun to really
bother him.

So far, he'd seen her put fruits and breads and even bite-
size pieces of cooked meat in front of each of the alcoves in
the other room. Then she'd fill a shot glass at each station
with dark Jamaican rum. And he had yet to see her remove
any of the offerings. But each time he went into the room,
the offerings were gone. The second time it happened he'd
stayed by the door for almost three hours, watching her
while she was in there, watching the altars out of the corner
of his eye when she was elsewhere. When she went into the
bathroom he followed her to the door. When he returned to
the altar room all the food and booze had vanished. He
searched the whole place while the old woman was still on
the toilet. The offerings were nowhere to be found. He stared
at the idols and wondered again just what the hell he'd gotten himself into. It was getting to the point where not only
was sleep impossible, he was almost too nervous to blink.

"You gonna sleep all you want pretty soon," said
Memere, laughing into the gumbo pot.

Jules jumped, jerking his pistol out of its shoulder holster
and aiming it at the old woman's back.

"Stop doing that!" he screamed.

She turned to look at him, and he could have sworn that
her eyes were glowing. She pointed a long, sharp nail at his
face and glared back. "You won' be a-hurtin' me none. You
boss punish you some awful bad you do dat widdout he say."

"I don't give a shit what he says. You keep fucking with
my mind, and I'm gonna blow your head off."

She nodded slowly. "All gonna come done soon. My serpent he hurt now. Some dat hurt you boss's doin'. Some dat

hurt Jake Crowley's doin'. But all same, my serpent he follow you boss to his dyin' day."

"One more day and night, old woman," said Jules, clicking the safety back on. "That's what you got. If I don't hear
from Jimmy by then I'm gonna do you anyway."

Memere shrugged. "Maybe so you will. Maybe so you
won'. But I tinkin', we gonna be all done soon, anyhow-
somever."

She laughed again, and turned back to taste the gumbo.

IRGIL'S SNORE STARTLED JAKE INTO WAKEFULNESS. His watch said it was late afternoon, but his exhaustion argued for the middle of the night. When he heard someone walking through the house, he left Mandi and Pierce by the fire to investigate. At the foot of the stairs he stopped, glancing up at the dancing shadows. Cramer poked his head around the corner of the landing, his lantern blinding Jake.

"What are you doing?" Jake called quietly.

"I couldn't sleep. So I'm checking the place out. Seems like we should have done that *before*. Come on up."

Jake shook his head. "You go ahead."

"Fine backup you are," said Cramer, disappearing.

Jake sighed. He really didn't want to climb those stairs. In fact, he hated the thought of *anyone* being up there. The second floor was a place of both horror and sacred memory, the last spot on earth he had seen his mother alive, and the scene of her bloody death. With agonizing slowness he climbed to the top of the landing, gripping the railing so tightly his fingers ached. Once again he wondered how in the world Mandi had ever convinced him to return to the old place at all that night. Had the jewel been drawing him to it even then?

The original Jacob Crowley's portrait hung at the end of the long hallway staring disdainfully at all who entered, but it was the worn cherry side table that held his attention. He stumbled to it in a daze, kneeling beside it, his hand sliding gently down the knurled leg. The wallpaper was still stained with dark, dry splotches. His free hand slipped along the dusty surface of the floor where his mother had lain, and he was shocked to recall even more vivid images of that terrible night, accepting the horror as a penance for the things a ten-year-old could not do.

Cramer's voice jarred him. "Are you okay?"

As Jake rose shakily to his feet, still staring at the floor, he felt Cramer's giant hand on his shoulder.

"That where it happened?" asked Cramer softly.

Jake nodded, and they stood there in silence for a moment until Cramer cleared his throat.

"You should have stayed downstairs, after all. I'm sorry. That was stupid of me."

Jake struggled to look him in the eye. "No. I'm here now. Find anything interesting?"

"More old house full of sheet-covered furniture."

Jake nodded.

"Looks like an older version of you," said Cramer, point-ing toward the dour portrait on the wall.

"I've been told that."

"Must have been a wealthy man to afford a portrait like that."

"Before he died, I guess he had quite a bit of money. Af-ter all, he owned the whole valley, and I've seen pictures of trains of wagons hauling lumber out."

"What happened to the business?"

"The big interests beat him out. Jacob owned a valley. The big timber companies ended up owning most of Maine."

"But he kept the land."

"The Crowleys have managed to eke out a living in timber since then. But we never built any more houses like this one."

Jake followed Cramer down the hall, glad to be moving away from the side table and its memories. Cramer opened the last door and led the way into what had been Jake's parents' bedroom. Jake was stunned that he could still smell his mother's perfume, and the sense of her presence made his knees weak.

"How many brothers and sisters did your father have?"

"One. A sister."

"What happened to her?"

"She married a salesman and moved away to New York. I don't think anyone in the family ever heard from her again."

"Nobody else but Crowleys ever lived here?"

"My grandfather had a live-in maid at one time. A housekeeper, I guess you'd call her. My mother spoke of her a couple of times. She was killed by a falling tree."

"You're kidding."

"Why would I be kidding?"

"What was she doing under a tree that was falling?"

"Stories like that aren't so unusual in timber country. My grandfather and my father had been logging the day before, and they left a tree half-felled. They found her the next day, crushed."

Cramer said nothing.

"What?" said Jake finally.

"Oh, come on. You're a cop, for God's sake."

"I guess it does sound strange. But she'd been dead for twenty years by the time I was born. I asked my father about it once, but he wouldn't talk about family history. The Crowleys don't *reminisce*."

"I can see why. So the housekeeper went out into the woods and just happened to be standing underneath a tree that your father and grandfather had *half-felled* the day before. Were they in the habit of leaving trees like that in the forest? Seems pretty dangerous."

"I doubt it. But I don't really know what their work habits were. You think that thing killed her?"

Cramer shrugged. "What do you think? Do housekeepers around here do a lot of hiking?"

"To tell the truth I've spent the last fourteen years trying to convince myself that the things I saw, the things I knew, the things I'd heard weren't real. That they were just hallucinations, figments of my imagination."

"You don't believe that anymore, though."

"It's getting kind of hard to hold onto that now."

Cramer nodded. "What was the final straw? Why did you really leave?"

Jake told him everything. The whole story of that night in the house with Mandi, what he remembered, and what she did. Cramer's bushy eyebrows had knitted together long before the tale was finished.

"Did your father kill your mother or not?"

"I don't know. When I was little I wanted to believe that thing killed her, and then he just found us. But after what happened to me here that night, I began to think maybe he did murder her just like I . . . like I *thought* I almost murdered Mandi. Now I just don't know. Pierce thinks the necklace and the thing outside are connected, but that they aren't the same thing. He thinks the gem is broken, and maybe that's why that thing is killing people."

"Pierce is yours, isn't he?"

Jake stared at him, stunned. But he knew he should have

expected Cramer to find out. Jake told him about his conversation with the boy.

"Man," said Cramer. "This has turned into a hell of vacation, eh?"

"Better than I ever expected," said Jake. "If we live."

"You planning on dying on me?"

"Not planning on it."

"Good. Then snap out of it, and help me finish searching this house."

Jake frowned. "You want to tell me what we're looking for?"

"What are we always looking for? Evidence."

"Of what?"

"Of what your family has to do with this curse. Jacob Crowley lived in this valley for a long time without dying. Then something set the damned thing off. I want to know what it was. I think your grandfather and your father knew. So why didn't your father tell you?"

"Maybe I wasn't old enough before he died."

"So the knowledge died with him. But there must be something."

"I know it sounds crazy, but I'd swear my mother had that jewel on her the night she died. I'm wondering now if Jimmy's man didn't take it from Albert. Maybe Albert came up here, found it . . . I don't know. Both Pierce and I feel drawn to that thing somehow."

Cramer nodded thoughtfully. "You had the jewel when the killings happened on the beach. Then you brought it back here and the girl died, Dary Murphy died, and Rich was killed. How come you never mentioned this before?"

Jake shook his head. "The whole idea just seemed so crazy."

"Maybe it's not so crazy. Memere says that things can have an attachment for people just like people get attached to things."

"Maybe Memere's not as crazy as I thought."

Cramer chuckled. "She's crazy like a snake."

"What did she tell you about me?"

Cramer frowned. "What do you mean?"

"You wouldn't have come here without going to see her, without telling her what you were doing. What did she say?"

"She said your baggage might get both of us killed."

"And you believed her?"

"I always believe her."

"But you came anyway."

"What would you expect? You think I'm gonna sit on my ass in Houston while you're up here getting your white ass kilt?"

Jake smiled. "No . . . I wouldn't expect that at all."

Cramer tossed old clothes out of the closet onto the floor. Jake recognized his mother's winter coat and winced. The gray wool reeked of mothballs, but he could picture her in it as though the recollection were an old sepia print.

"What?" said Jake, noticing Cramer staring.

"The pockets," said Cramer, nodding toward the pile of clothes.

The thought of touching the old familiar garment was too much like holding her in his arms. Jake just couldn't do it.

"I'll search the drawers," he said, turning away to open the old Victorian dresser.

The smell of mothballs was even stronger there, and Jake was surprised to find that *nothing* in the room seemed to have been touched over the years. A neat stack of his mother's nylon underwear lay alongside cotton camisoles and socks. He closed the drawer quickly, rifling through the others haphazardly, feeling like a Peeping Tom.

"We're not going to find anything here," he mumbled.

"What do these go to?" asked Cramer, jangling a set of keys.

"They may be my father's spare car keys."

"What happened to the car?"

"I seem to remember it being sold after the . . . murder."

"Thought you said no one locked their doors around here?" said Cramer, flipping several keys on the chain. "These look like they open doors."

Jake nodded. "One of them's probably for the cellar. My father always kept it locked."

"How come?"

"I have no idea."

"Let's have a look," said Cramer, grinning mischievously and leading Jake back out into the hall.

"What were you guys doing up there?" asked Mandi, yawning at the foot of the stairs.

"Searching the place," said Cramer.

"What did you find?"

"Nothing but some old clothes," said Cramer. "Where's the cellar door?"

"Under the stairs," said Jake.

Cramer unlocked the door, tugging it open when it dragged on the floor. The odor of raw earth circulated around them as Cramer waved the lantern inside.

"Well," he said, shrugging. "Let's have a peek."

Jake gave Mandi a long-suffering look. "When Cramer gets his teeth into something, you can't get them out."

"That's not necessarily a bad thing," said Mandi.

She frowned as they heard footsteps, and turned to find Virgil and Pierce standing behind them.

HE FIVE OF THEM STOOD in the center of the dirt-floored cellar, with its low-beamed ceiling and million cobwebs. Three steamer trunks with corroded metal banding rested against one wall. To Jake's right a long workbench held numerous dusty woodworking tools and rusty cans of paint. Cramer opened each of the trunks in turn, but all of them were empty. He toyed with an old wood plane on the workbench, peering thoughtfully around.

"This is an old house with a lot of skeletons in the closet. But we can't find the closet," he said. "What's in there?"

Jake glanced toward the corner where a dark panel door blended with the shadows of the granite foundation. To his surprise, Pierce was already standing in front of it, jerking at the knob. Jake just shook his head.

Cramer hurried over, trying keys until he found the one that turned the creaking lock. He shoved the door inward, waving a lantern around in the small space. The ceiling was even lower inside, and he had to lean forward to enter. There was barely space enough for the five of them to stand. And the room itself was totally empty. Cramer frowned.

"Why lock an empty room?" asked Cramer, reaching up to feel inside the pockets where the joists rested on the stone foundation.

Nothing there.

They wandered back into the main cellar where Cramer made the same inspection of the dusty spaces between the floorboards. Nothing there, either.

But when they turned to go they noticed that Pierce was down on his knees in the shadowy, empty room, clawing at the hard earth with his bare fingers. When they all slipped back inside, Jake spotted a small exposed area of what looked like old concrete, and he dropped alongside Pierce to help scrape the clay away, leaning past the boy to read the inscription they had uncovered.

" 'Set herein by Jacob Elias Crowley, August 10, 1886.' " Jake looked at Cramer. "I guess he placed it here when they built the house."

"Lift it up," said Cramer, retrieving a crowbar from the workbench and returning to bury its chisel point in the clay beside the marker.

The concrete was small and easily moved by the heavy tool. Beneath the lid lay a rusting metal box containing a leather-bound book. Jake lifted it gently and blew off a thick coating of dust.

"I'll be damned," he said, flipping the first page. " '*The Personal and Private Journal of Jacob Elias Crowley.*' "

"The original Jacob?" asked Cramer.

"My great-great-grandfather," said Jake, nodding, and flipping another page.

But Cramer squinted around the dark room.

"Not down here," he said, shaking his head.

* * *

Jake sat on the sofa in the study, the journal in his lap. The pages were thin and fragile, and the flowing script took practice to read. He flipped quickly through the beginning, mostly dedicated to the war years, finally slowing about halfway through the book.

" *'I cannot face the killing any longer. The valor of my men is not in question. Unfortunately neither is the valor of the enemy. Death lies before and behind in a vast sea of gore where the cries of the dying seem to ever dwell in the air. I feel as though I shall never smell a breeze untainted by powder smoke or blood again, that I shall never know the peace within my heart that once dwelt there. I witnessed the charge of Pickett's soldiers as my men cut them down like wheat before a scythe, and their faces were no different from ours in life or in death. I am told that we won this engagement because of the courage of a stouthearted group of Maine men under Chamberlain. I have met Chamberlain, and I have seen the same dismal distance in his eyes that I know is now in mine. He told me he longed for the faraway green valleys of Maine where death was less than a memory.*

" *'Though I have never seen them, I long for them, also.' "*

Jake flipped a couple of pages.

"Does it say anything about the gem?" asked Cramer.

" *'I feel drawn to a place always before me, ever northward into the dark dank woods, where I can find peace and solace at last,'"* Jake continued. " *'It seems to me that the natives, these Passamaquoddy, who are so kind and not at all like the hostiles one hears so much about out West, know how to live at one with the earth. I have spent the winter with these kind people, and they have taken me in like one of their own. In fact I have taken to wife a woman known in their tongue as Weasel. She bears no resemblance that I can see to that animal. In fact she is comely and pleasing to me. But her people do not want me to venture into the next valley where I genuinely long to go. The little that I have come to understand of their language tells me that they believe it to be a place of death. But I do not sense such. And I find that—just as I was drawn here—I am drawn there even more.*

" 'It is a valley filled with vension and rabbit and good timber. I mean to build a house at the mouth and to get by farming and living off the land. Weasel will come with me, even though she seems to hold the same unreasoning fear as her people.' "

"So even the Indians were afraid of this valley," muttered Cramer.

" 'We have built a good home, and I have begun cutting logs and have purchased a saw to be powered by the creek that runs through here. I intend to sell finished lumber as there are growing communities on both sides of the valley, and I have staked a claim to all lands that I can lay a hand to, as the locals seem as frightened of this place as the natives. That is their loss, and I mean to make the most of it. Weasel is with child.' "

Jake skipped ahead again. "This one is dated 1880. They must have been in the valley quite a few years by then.

" 'The boys are a wonder when they work and they bring great credit to their mother and me. I love them so, and the business goes well. Men are building farms in the valleys all around and all require lumber. I have managed to put enough money aside that we are now constructing a fine home on a site I discovered near the head of the stream at the far end of the valley. There is good water there. The boys have taken to a beautiful swimming hole that lies not far from the foundation of the new house.

" 'I have told no one about what I discovered there. I will

write it here and then never speak of it again. For I believe I have found the root of the heathen myths and legends that have long kept man from this place. While excavating a boulder for the foundation of the house, I discovered a giant gem that I believe is an amethyst. When I first recognized its gleaming pink light I have to admit that I was taken with greed, and I quickly uncovered the gemstone only to find that someone or something had been there long before me, for the stone had been carved to hold a much smaller, polished jewel.

" 'I realized immediately that this was a place of demon worship, for touching the smaller stone I could feel its power. I ripped it from the place of worship and I have hidden it away for all time. Never again will demons be worshiped or hold sway in this valley. And I know now that the Lord will hold them bound. This must be why I was drawn to this valley, as I have sensed a purpose to my coming here since the very first. But I fear that there is much more to this story than I am given to understand. Sometimes I feel as though the jewel were worming its way into my innermost thoughts, just as I sometimes feel as though I am being sucked into it like smoke through a pipe. I fear that I am losing my mind.' "

Jake turned the final page and frowned. "That looks like blood," he said, flipping the book so they all could see the stain blurring the neat script.

"Crowley blood," said Cramer, staring at Jake.

"Read it," said Mandi.

" 'I have tried in every way that a man might to rid myself of this cursed jewel. I have thrown it in the river, only to have my sons bring it to me as a gift when they discovered it during a swim. I have placed it upon the hearth and roasted it so hotly that steel itself would have melted away, and yet it remained cool to the touch. I have hammered at it and it

breaks not. Finally, in desperation I thought of replacing it, into the stone where I had found it. But that only served to call forth something I fear even to describe herein. I removed the small jewel immediately, and I have hidden it away once more.

"'I have done all that I can do. I have called on the God of my fathers and have preached His word in the low and dark places, and nothing avails. Anyone who comes into this valley does so at the risk of their necks now. As God is my witness I do not know if the dark beast of the woods took Weasel or whether it was an accident. My sons still search the riverbank for her body, but I know in my heart that they will never find her. My life ebbs with every moment, and I place this journal beneath the dirt in the fervent hope that none might ever find it or need to. With the last of my strength I intend to set this house ablaze and then be done with this vale of tears. But should all else fail, I have informed my eldest son of the true nature of the jewel. And should I perish, then he must see that no other ever finds it. For I fear it may do great evil in the wrong hands.'

"That's all," whispered Jake, closing the book. "The legend was that he drowned or disappeared, just like my father. In any case, he never set this house on fire."

Cramer shook his head. "I don't think that thing would let him. He probably did disappear, *just like your father.*"

"Then the jewel must have been passed from eldest son to eldest son," said Virgil.

"And your mother found it," said Cramer.

"That doesn't explain why it killed her," said Jake.

"Maybe she wasn't supposed to have it," said Cramer. "Albert took it, and he's dead. José got a hold of it, and he's dead. It was looking for you."

"Maybe," mused Jake, staring at Pierce.

Virgil shook his head. "If José got hold of it, Paco must have taken it to him. Last I saw *he* was still alive."

"Maybe," muttered Cramer. "Or maybe it was just using Paco to get itself to Jake. José being killed might have just been a coincidence."

Jake sighed. "That's one way of putting it."

AS IT JACOB WHO BUILT THE CHAPEL OUT BACK?"
asked Cramer, rubbing his head.

"Yeah," said Jake. "I guess he really got religion."

"Then I think we need to search that next."

"Looking for what?" asked Virgil.

"I don't know," admitted Cramer. "The place Jacob found the jewel, maybe. That stone he took it from?"

Virgil screwed up his face. "And you're thinking maybe he built the chapel over it?"

"Why suddenly get religion and build a church out back?" asked Cramer.

Jake noticed that Pierce had moved over to the fire and was shaking his head.

When Mandi signed to the boy he made a cutting gesture with both hands that Jake understood immediately as a no.

"He knows what you're talking about," said Mandi. "And he doesn't like it."

"I thought you said he couldn't understand what we said," said Virgil.

"You go," said Mandi, to Jake and the others. "Pierce and I will stay."

But the boy seemed to understand that, as well.

"Naaugh!" he shouted, stamping his foot. There was fear in his eyes, and he glanced at Jake pleadingly.

Jake took his hand and spelled. *What is it?*

Bad place.

The chapel?

Pierce frowned. It was clear no one had told him what the little building out back was, but he obviously knew something was there.

The building in the backyard? spelled Jake.

Pierce nodded.

Why?

It's where the thing lives.

Jake suppressed a shudder, squeezing the boy's shoulder. *Stay here with your mother.*

Pierce grabbed Jake's hands and clasped them tightly, but Jake slowly pulled away and shook his head to let the boy know that this was something he and Cramer had to do. Finally Pierce sagged and nodded, signaling that he was coming, too.

I think you should stay here, spelled Jake.

I'm the only one who can fix it.

If there *was* a way to fix the thing—which Jake doubted—Pierce really might be the only one capable of doing so. After all, the jewel had apparently "fixed" him. But it still didn't make Jake feel any better that the boy was now going to accompany him to a place Pierce seemed terrified of. In the hallway they all slipped on their rain jackets, and Jake followed Cramer out the back door. Pierce came next with Mandi and Virgil holding up the rear. Cramer swung a lantern in one hand, the key ring in the other, and as they strode out toward the lonely building they all glanced nervously at the woods.

But no bushes rustled, they could hear no whispering sounds, and Pierce gave no hint that he sensed the dark thing nearby.

The tiny covered landing was barely large enough for Jake and Cramer, so Jake held the lantern while Cramer tried the keys until he finally found the one that opened the heavy lock. The ornate door swung wide, and they hurried into the small church to allow the others to get in out of the rain. The walls were of heavy river stone, and the windows—at chest height and so narrow that a man's head would barely fit through their frames—were built strictly for light and ornamentation, not egress or ventilation.

"Seems more like a fort than a church," mused Cramer.

Jake shrugged. "Who knows what was going on in Jacob's mind when he built this place."

Cramer rested the lantern on the lectern and glanced around at the three short pews on either side of the aisle. "Not much room for a congregation."

"The stories I heard said Jacob preached mostly to his own family," said Jake. "Then one of his sons became the first faith healer in this part of the country. He performed baptisms in what we call the swimming hole, and he preached to his patients here."

"Your father ever preach?"

"Not that I remember," said Jake, turning to Virgil.

"Not that I know of," said Virgil.

"Well, there's no place here to hide anything," said Cramer, shaking his head as he glanced around the tiny chapel. "I figured there'd be a cellar, closets, something."

"What you see is what you get, I guess," said Jake.

Pierce slipped out of Mandi's grasp and strode up to the lectern, lifting the lantern and setting it gently on the floor. Jake and Cramer exchanged a glance, but both stood still, waiting. Mandi rushed up beside the boy, but Pierce ignored her. He placed both hands on the old worn oak pulpit and rocked it as though it were a stubborn fence post that needed to be replaced. Jake noticed that the lectern moved easier toward the front of the building. So did Pierce. As the boy stepped back and pulled, Jake and Cramer hurried to help him lower the heavy piece of furniture into the aisle.

"Hinged," said Cramer, staring down into the hole in the floor.

"You were looking for a hiding place," said Jake, turning to Mandi. "Ask Pierce how he knew it was here."

But he was afraid he already knew.

"He says he could feel it pulling him," said Mandi, frowning.

Cramer lifted the lantern and lowered it into the hole, peering inside. "Is that what I think it is?"

Jake leaned into the hole and discovered that rather than a cellar the opening revealed little more than a tiny crawl space. In the center of the floor a half-buried stone the size of a washtub lay exposed.

"It's amethyst," whispered Jake, staring at the twinkling pink crystal.

"So Jacob's story was true," said Cramer. "Isn't that thing worth a fortune?"

Jake shrugged. "It's a semiprecious stone. There's a lot of it in the mountains. But I never heard of a piece anywhere near this large before."

"There's an empty hole for your jewel, just like Jacob wrote," said Cramer.

Pierce gripped the edge of the floor and slipped past both of them into the hole. The boy's fingers roved gently over the empty cup, his eyes delving deep into the semiopaque stone. Jake took the lantern and shone the light around the enclosed space to assure himself once more that there was nothing down there to hurt Pierce.

Thunder pealed outside and lightning lit the little chapel

for a split second. They all listened for the ominous whispering sound, but the steady rain on the roof was the only noise.

"Maybe we should try putting the jewel back, anyway," whispered Cramer, too low for Mandi to hear.

"Pierce isn't gonna like that idea," said Virgil, kneeling beside them.

Jake glanced at Mandi, realizing that she *had* heard. Her eyes were full of hurt and desperation.

"He can see, Jake," she whispered. "He can hear, and walk."

Her words were like daggers, and the look in her eyes was worse. *You left us before. You betrayed us. Are you going to do it again?* How could he do that to her, to his own son? How could he ask the boy to give up the jewel if it had really given him everything he lacked? He couldn't. He shook his head.

Cramer sighed. "We should at least just try it. Maybe his sight and hearing are permanent now."

"You don't know that," argued Mandi.

"Mandi," said Virgil slowly. "We ought to at least try putting it back. Pierce's vision won't help him if we all get ourselves killed."

"No," said Jake firmly, staring both the men down. "Jacob tried it, and all he accomplished was to draw that thing out into the open again."

Mandi nudged between the men to the opening. "Get him out of there. I don't like him being down there alone."

"I'll get him," said Jake.

He signaled to get the boy's attention before sliding down into the tight space beside him. Pierce eyed him nervously, but offered one hand.

What can you tell me now? signed Jake.

Pierce shook his head, signing back. *This is where the jewel came from.*

Jake nodded. *Do you think it belongs here?*

Yes, signed Pierce hesitantly.

Should we put it back?

Pierce shook his head vehemently this time.

Why not? asked Jake.

Pierce's eyes told him all he needed to know, and Jake nodded. How could he ask the boy to do that even if it *had* been a good idea? How could anyone ask him to?

Jake reached out to pat Pierce on the shoulder, and he was hurt when the boy cringed. He lowered his hand back to Pierce's.

I'll never ask you to do that, he signed, shaking his head. *Never.*

The boy relaxed and Jake gently lifted him out of the hole. Then he and Virgil slammed the lectern shut over the stone once more.

Cramer gave Jake a questioning look.

"There's got to be another way," said Jake, turning to Mandi.

Her eyes told him all he needed to know. They were going to face this all together. As a family.

"*You* got any other ideas?" Jake asked Cramer as the group gathered at the door and prepared to run through the storm back to the house.

Cramer shrugged, staring at Pierce. "I'd say *he's* gonna have to be the one to come up with answers. If anyone does."

Jake nodded, hurrying out after Mandi and Pierce.

Virgil followed.

But when they reached the porch he stood alone in the rain, staring into the dark woods.

"You see something?" asked Jake, trying to follow his gaze.

Virgil stared a moment longer into the trees, then shook his head and followed Jake down the hall.

RAIN CONTINUED TO BATTER THE WINDOWS like flying gravel, and wind screeched through the trees. Deeper darkness was gathering again as the sun went down somewhere behind the clouds. Cramer stared out through the windows into the storm as Jake joined him.

"Albert taught you to drive that thing, right?" said Cramer, nodding toward the bulldozer.

Jake frowned. "If the keys are in it. I'm sure Virgil could probably run it, too. But we've got nowhere else to go until the storm blows over. Don't get me wrong; I hate this place, and if there's any chance that it or the chapel really is connected to this curse I won't lose a minute's sleep over knocking either of them down board by board or stone by stone. But right now I kind of like the roof over my head."

Cramer nodded. "Just checking."

"That thing hasn't bothered us as long as we've been inside the house," said Jake, knowing that was a feeble excuse. Something *had* happened to him within the confines of this building on that night alone with Mandi. Something *had* happened inside the night his mother was killed.

"Yet," said Cramer sullenly.

"You think something's changed?"

"I think we're on its ground now. That's all I really *do* know for sure. According to the journal, Jacob Crowley thought he *got into the jewel* and that it somehow *got into him.* That sounds to me a little too much like the story you told about your night alone here with Mandi."

Virgil strode over and leaned against the wall.

Jake shuddered. "I'm afraid it did get into me that night. You two just keep an eye on me. Okay?"

"I've *been* watching you," said Virgil quietly.

Cramer chuckled. "So far you don't seem any crazier than usual."

"At least I'm not praying to Ogou."

"Go ahead, make jokes," said Cramer. "When push comes to shove, see what Ogou do."

"Why doesn't Ogou get off his ass and take out that thing?"

Cramer frowned. "Ogou don't work that way. He just help us."

"Why do you talk that way sometimes?"

Cramer shook his head. "Memere starts to come out in situations like this."

"Keep watching."

Cramer slapped him on the back. "Nothing to watch. You're stronger than any bad spirits. You proved that the night you were here with Mandi."

But Jake could tell by Cramer's eyes that he wasn't *that* sure.

Jake glanced over his shoulder as Mandi approached. Pierce appeared to doze in front of the fire. Suddenly he re-membered Pierce's words.

It's not bad. I think it's broken. I can feel something wrong in it, like a bad circuit.

There was a bad circuit in the thing, all right. A circuit that drove men to murder their families, that drove strangers to kill each other and sometimes themselves. The more Jake thought about it, the more he concluded that their best bet would be to survive the storm and then return to the head of the valley with a whole box of dynamite to blow the jewel, the amethyst, the chapel above them, and even this old house to hell and gone.

"I'll make us something to eat," said Mandi, brushing by them.

Cramer eyed Jake and nodded toward the kitchen.

PIERCE'S MIND DRIFTED. He could feel the satisfying warmth from the fire as he lay on the mattress with his eyes closed. But with his hand clenched around the jewel he kept being drawn down into it. And the more he gave himself up to the sensation, the more he almost understood the workings of the *machine* within.

The gem seemed like some kind of *transformer*. It was meant to take one kind of power and amp it up and then give it back. And some of the power that it stored had given him his senses of sight and hearing, and healed his limp. But he also sensed that in doing so the bauble had used up almost all of the last of its power.

So what did it have to do with the monster that lived in the woods, the whispering darkness that had been living in the valley? It was almost as though the two were connected in the same way that radio waves are "connected" to a transmitter. But because the gem was broken in some way, its *message,* the whispering thing, had been created or become flawed, as well.

He was pretty sure that if he could fix the jewel, the whispers would just fade away, the way a radio signal did. But he was afraid. More afraid that he'd ever been in his life, because down in the hole with Jake he had begun to get just an inkling of what might be involved in repairing the jewel, of what the cost might be.

Jake leaned over Mandi to take down a pot she couldn't reach. When he handed it to her their hands met. They both sighed at the same time, and finally she returned his smile.

"I'm sorry for everything, Mandi," he said at last, hoping that she knew that by "everything," he meant things in the distant past and in the past few hours, as well.

She shrugged. "We'll work it out."

Jake shook his head. "You have no idea how bad it hurts that I had a son all these years, and I wasn't there for him. That I wasn't there for you."

"You didn't know."

"I won't ask him for the jewel again. No matter what, I won't ask that."

Setting the pot aside, she moved into his arms, and he held her close. "What if that's the only way?"

"There's got to be another answer. There has to be."

He wanted desperately to believe that as much as she did. He could feel the soft lift and fall of her breathing beneath his hands, her warmth against him. She raised her lips to his. The kiss was soft and gentle, and yet Jake's entire body tensed. Finally she pressed her hands against his chest and eased a couple of inches between them.

"This old house brings back a *lot* of memories," she whispered huskily.

Jake nodded, but even as he reveled in the feel of her against him once more he had the sense of viewing his surroundings through two different sets of eyes. He felt his hands slipping slowly up her back, pressing her more tightly against him, worming their way up toward her throat, and an unspeakable horror overcame him as he realized that he had no more control over himself than he had had on that long-ago night. He struggled, willing his hands to relax . . .

"Mandi," he managed to gasp.

She looked up at him with those bright, trusting, loving eyes, and her expression turned questioning just as Jake began to hear the whispers echoing inside his head.

"Are you all right?" she asked, concern in her face.

Jake's fingers seemed to slow but not stop, and he searched frantically within himself for control. He could feel his hands beginning to clench, testing, the fingers worming their way up to her collarbone as she twisted in his grasp.

"You're hurting me," she gasped, trying to shake loose.

"Run," he sputtered, somehow managing to break his grip but not shove her away.

She staggered backward, confused, unsure.

"Run," he gasped again, staggering toward her, watching her turn and race away down the hall.

Jake sat at the table, barely able to return Cramer's stare. "You've got to lock me up."

"What?" said Mandi.

"Do it," said Jake. "It's the only way. If that thing gets inside me again none of you are safe."

"We'll watch you closer," said Cramer, shaking his head.

"The only way you'd be able to stop me is by shooting me. I'd rather you didn't do that."

"What if it happens to one of us instead of you?" asked Virgil.

"So far it hasn't affected any of you."

"That jewel did something to Pierce," said Virgil.

Jake sighed again. "It didn't do anything *bad* to him. And besides, Pierce isn't big enough to hurt you or Cramer. This is the only way. I barely had enough control just now to stop myself from . . . It's the same thing that happened that night Mandi and I came here together. I don't know why or how I controlled it either time. But we just can't chance it happening again."

"He's right," said Virgil reluctantly, glancing at Cramer who frowned but nodded.

Mandi was still shaking her head. "No. You're not locking him up."

"It's for everybody's good," said Jake. "When this storm blows over we'll burn this old house and the chapel to the ground, bulldoze them to powder and bury them, then turn this end of the valley into a no-man's-land. If we have to, you and I and Pierce will move far away from here. But for now we have to make sure I don't hurt any of you. We have to."

"Please, Jake."

Jake closed his eyes, shaking his head. When he opened them again the tears in her eyes stung him.

"All right," he said, nodding at her. "You can keep the keys. How's that?"

"Please don't do this—"

"Mandi."

"How long?" she asked. "How long are you gonna stay locked up?"

Jake considered. "Just until the storm blows over. Once we can get out of here, we'll tear the place down or burn it and get the hell away."

She just stood there with her arms crossed, shaking her head.

"So where?" asked Cramer.

Jake frowned. "I'd rather not be locked down cellar. And I guess the pantry is the next most secure place in the house."

So, in the end Cramer dragged one of the mattresses in from the living room and managed to fit it snuggly in the pantry. When they had Jake situated as comfortably as possible, Virgil, Cramer, Pierce, and Mandi stood at the door. There were more tears in Mandi's eyes, and Cramer still seemed uncertain, as well.

"You sure about this?" he asked Jake.

Jake just nodded toward the door.

"Sorry, partner," said Cramer.

The clicking of the tumblers in the lock grated on Jake's nerves, and the room seemed half its size with the door closed and the lamp hissing. The mattress reached from wall to wall, and the old chamber pot from upstairs had had to be placed on a lower shelf. He didn't want to think about using it in the confines of the closet, but the odds were heavy that he'd need to before he got out.

Mandi had given him a plate and utensils and plenty of fresh canned goods and an opener, along with a large jug of water. He wasn't going to starve, but he might well die of boredom. He sank to the floor against the far wall, staring at the door and then at his watch. He couldn't hear the rain anymore, but he knew one of the others would tell him if it stopped. He could hear them muttering through the door, but couldn't make out what they were saying.

He was afraid it was going to be a long wait.

JIMMY SPOTTED THE LIGHTS of the house through the trees ahead and knew he'd found his quarry again at last. Tracking the group through the darkness and the storm, getting lost and staggering through water and mud up to his armpits—only to finally find the trail again by luck as much as training—the cold and exertion had driven him to the limits of his endurance. And he was fast running out of anything resembling patience.

He stropped the knife against his bare leg, massaging a bloody scratch that ran up his thigh and across his swollen scrotum. The bullet wound through his left arm was painful but clean, and he'd bandaged it with a scrap of cloth he'd ripped from the old woman's blouse. He wished now that he hadn't killed her outright. But he'd been in such a rage when he caught her that there was no controlling himself. And besides, he'd have probably killed her dragging her here through the woods, anyway. But none of his prey here could know she was dead for sure. That would work to his advantage.

He was hungrier than he'd been in years, and he wished he'd managed to snuff the little dog, too. But he'd gotten one near miss with the blade and a glancing kick at the fucking mutt, and it had cringed away into the night. Too bad. It would have made a good meal. But the fuckers inside the house had to be eating something. Soon he'd have whatever they had.

He cleared his throat, spitting into the mud between his bare feet. Then he gave a low guttural howl, not loud enough to be heard in the house, just stretching his vocal cords. Finally he let out a high-pitched, feminine shriek. But to his ear there was still just a little too much masculine feeling to it, so he tried again. Higher, louder.

Like a woman terrified or in pain.

Mandi had taken Pierce back into the study. Cramer and Virgil shared the kitchen table. Outside, the sparse light was dying so fast it looked as though the clouds had finally drowned the sun.

"It *may* be the right thing to do. But I still don't like locking him up like that," whispered Virgil.

Cramer glared at him. "Do you think I like it any more than you do? He said the same thing happened to him before in this house, and he was convinced for years that he nearly killed Mandi. What choice do we have?"

Virgil shrugged. "None, I suppose."

Cramer shielded one ear. "Did you hear something?"

Virgil shook his head. "A whisper?"

"No. I thought I heard—"

A shriek outside caused both men to race to the back door. By the time they reached the stoop another scream rent the air, like a woman scared out of her wits.

"Barbara," said Virgil.

Cramer shook his head. "We're a long way from where we left her."

Another shriek, this one closer. Then silence.

"Damn, I can't take that," murmured Virgil, his fingers tickling his pistol. "Whoever it is, she's getting killed."

"But by what?" muttered Cramer, glancing around as Mandi and Pierce appeared at the back door. "Or who?"

Yet another scream cut Virgil to the heart. He had to do *something*.

Suddenly a masculine shout echoed around the clearing. "You fuckers got no *cojónes*!"

"Jimmy," spat Cramer, staring into the woods.

Virgil disappeared back into the house, returning gripping the shotgun in both hands.

"No, Virgil," said Mandi, following him outside. "You can't go out there."

Cramer kept his eyes glued to the dark woods. "It's a trap, a setup."

"I know that. But Jake said Jimmy was left with just a butcher knife last time he saw him."

"Jimmy with a knife in those woods is nothing to sneer at."

"I know that too," said Virgil, with a heavy finality.

Cramer nodded. "All right," he said, waving Mandi back into the house. "You're right. We can't just leave her to him. I got your back, then."

But Virgil shook his head. "You have to stay here with Mandi and Pierce. They have no one else with Jake locked up."

"You and Jimmy *mano a mano* is bad juju, and it's what he wants. He's taunting us, using her like a staked goat."

"It doesn't matter," said Virgil as another scream slashed the air. "I can't just let him kill her."

Jimmy's voice wailed through the trees. "You fuckers gonna let me butcher this bitch?"

Virgil stepped down into the rain, Cramer still with him, shaking his head.

"Think!" said Virgil. "If we both go, Jimmy can lose us in the woods, and Mandi and Pierce will be unprotected in the house."

Cramer grunted, but Virgil could see he'd won the argument, even though the last thing in the world he wanted was to have to face Jimmy Torrio alone again. But he knew it was the only thing to do. It was his job. Luckily Doris wasn't badgering him at the moment.

"Watch your back," said Cramer reluctantly, slapping him on the shoulder. "And I'll ask Ogou to watch it, too."

Virgil smiled. "I'd much appreciate Ogou doing that."

But even before he'd made it across the lawn to the nearest trees, the screams had stopped. He stood for just a moment, glancing back at Cramer, who regarded him with a baleful expression. Then a low keening moan came from the forest to his left, and Virgil hunched his shoulders, slipped his finger onto the trigger of the shotgun, and crunched through the bracken into the woods.

ANDI LEFT CRAMER standing on the back porch, staring into the forest and the storm. She stood over Pierce in front of the fire, trying to gather its warmth, but an inner chill would not leave her. She couldn't get an image of Virgil—old and haggard and alone in the dark woods—out of her mind. As much as she felt sorry for Barbara, and guilty for leaving the old woman, she wished Virgil hadn't gone after her, because she feared he wasn't coming back.

When she turned, she noticed that Pierce was awake and had that faraway look on his face that he got when he claimed to hear the thing whispering. But try as she might, she couldn't make out anything but the steady patter outside the window. When his eyes cleared suddenly the terror she saw there caught her breath in her throat.

He clambered to his feet, snatched her hand, and jerked her frantically toward the hallway, but she grabbed his arm and whirled him around.

What are you doing? she signed.

Although he was shaking with fear he managed to signal back.

It's here.

Inside the house?

He shrugged, quivering with fear. *It's here!*

But she still could not hear the eerie whispers, and other than the incessant patter of rain the house was deadly silent. She snagged one of the lanterns, and her knees shook as she let Pierce creep ahead of her to the parlor door. The lantern light sent darting shadows everywhere, turning the old mansion into a haunted house.

But there still seemed nothing to worry about inside. It was outside now where the danger lay, and at the moment that danger was Jimmy. Even with Pierce tugging at her arm she couldn't get Virgil—out there in the storm with *that* monster—out of her head. He was an old man, wounded, frail. He was no match for a trained killer. They should have let Jake out of the closet and then Cramer could have gone with Virgil. She stared into Pierce's terrified face, and suddenly she knew what it was that he sensed.

Is that thing inside Jake? she signed.

Pierce shook his head slowly, staring into her eyes, and suddenly she *knew*. There was no reason to be afraid of Jake even if the thing did manage to possess him. Jake was locked safely away.

Cramer.

The image of the giant black man, naked to the waist, flashed across her mind, and she saw her own recognition mirrored in her son's eyes.

Memere tole me I was too open to the spirits. Too easy for 'em sometimes.

It couldn't be. Surely they hadn't locked up Jake, only to have Cramer possessed by the whispering horror. But once again his words echoed in her mind like a threat.

You got to be careful with Iwas or other spirits. They can get into you.

They both glanced toward the kitchen, and then Mandi nudged Pierce toward the front door. On the porch, rain pummeled both of them, and the lantern bobbed and swung in her hands as she closed the door behind them. Pierce signaled for her to follow him. But she couldn't.

Go to the chapel, she signed.

Pierce frowned at her, shaking his head.

I have to see if Jake is okay, she signed, pushing him toward the steps.

I'll wait here.

She knew she wasn't going to get him to go by himself, and there was no time now to argue. She rested her lantern on the porch and slipped quietly back through the door. She padded down the hall, hating that the water dripping from her pant cuffs sounded like hammer blows against the hardwood floor. The light through the kitchen door spotlighted her as she approached, and every creak of the old house shattered her nerves. She rested her fingers tentatively on the door frame as she leaned slowly around to glance into the kitchen.

Cramer sat with his back to her, staring at the lantern in the middle of the table, and for just a moment Mandi was tempted to believe that Pierce had made a mistake, that nothing was amiss. But the longer she stared at the man's giant shoulders, the more certain she became that Pierce *was* right. She noticed Jake's pistol under Cramer's big paw, and there was something strangely different, something weird about the way he sat, the way he held himself.

"Ogou," he gasped. "You gotta help this here boy. I got things trying to get in. Bad things . . ."

He shivered as though suddenly struck by frigid wind, and she saw his fingers tighten on the pistol. His head twitched, and she had the terrifying notion that he knew she was watching as he slowly turned in her direction.

Before his eyes could find her, she drew back around the corner and pressed herself against the wall. But she couldn't seem to get her feet to work. When she had to breathe again or burst her lungs, she drew in slow painful breaths through slitted lips, and she noticed over the almost silent hissing through her teeth the sibilant sound of Cramer humming. When it began to sound more like muttering she leaned closer to the door again until she could just begin to make out what he was saying. But it reminded her somehow of the whispers . . .

She shuddered, fingering the keys in her pocket, slipping silently down the hall. Even if the thing was in control of Cramer, it shouldn't be able to get to Jake without the keys. That meant she and Pierce were in more danger than he was, and there was nothing she could do for Jake right now, anyway. Her first duty was to protect Pierce. Just as she reached the front door Cramer's weird whispering noises froze her like a deer in a car's headlights.

She glanced over her shoulder just as his massive bulk blocked the light from the kitchen, and she ripped the door open. Cramer wailed, and Mandi ducked as his lantern crashed against the wall beside her. She staggered out into the storm, snatching her own lantern and grabbing Pierce's hand, dragging him along with her, racing around the house toward the chapel, the only place she could think of that might be safe. On the tiny stoop she fumbled for the key, finally finding it, the heavy door swinging open from its own weight. She shoved it closed and locked it behind them. Then she huddled with Pierce in the corner behind the fallen lecturn and began to pray.

J AKE THOUGHT HE HEARD SOMETHING STRANGE from the kitchen. But the door was so thick and tightly built it was hard to tell whether the sound had been real or merely his imagination. He pressed his ear against the wood trying to make out the noise, but it stopped as suddenly as it started, and when it didn't return he went back to inventory-ing the pantry shelves.

There were twenty-four dusty cans of soup, twelve cans of green beans, twelve of peas, twelve of lima beans, and twelve of potatoes. Everything was in counts of twenty-four or twelve, except the pickles, of which there were three quarts. He was glad they hadn't come in gallons.

There were stacks of soda cases and a box of toothpicks. Jake read the label of a can of mushroom soup again trying to figure out if they were serious about the chicken recipe. It didn't seem all that appetizing to him. He set it back on the shelf and stared at the door, leaning his head against the wall, struggling to quit feeling sorry for himself.

The door was a heavy pine-paneled number, and—like

all the other doors in the house—the frame was thick and reinforced at the lock with a big brass plate. If he started trying to rip it down the others would hear him, and Cramer would know what to do. Neither Cramer nor Virgil would want to kill him, but Jake knew they would if they had to in order to protect Mandi and Pierce.

The noise sounded again, just a little louder, but Jake still couldn't make out what it was.

"Hey, Cramer!" he shouted.

His voice echoing in the confined space made him feel even more bottled up, as though the air suddenly tightened around him. And he noticed for the first time how stuffy the room had already become. He knelt in front of the door and pulled the mattress back a little to let in some air.

"Cramer!" he shouted again.

A shadow fell across the bottom of the door, but no one answered. Jake waited a second, playing the game, but then his nerves began to twitch. "Is that you, Cramer?"

"Yeah."

There was the familiar Cajun lilt to the voice, but it was throaty and strange, and Jake tensed.

"How you doing out there?" he asked conversationally, his skin crawling.

The shadow seemed glued to the floor. Out of the corner of his eye Jake could see the second hand of his watch.

Dear God, don't let me be right.

"You okay, Cramer?"

"Yeah."

"Where's Mandi?"

The second hand kept turning. It seemed like forever before Cramer replied, and when he did his answer made no sense.

"Gone."

"Shit," muttered Jake, his throat constricting at the same time a cold sweat broke out on his palms.

The second hand went around two times.

Then the shadow moved away, and Jake began to scream.

JAKE JERKED WILDLY AT THE DOOR, but all he accomplished was knocking the pickles off the shelf and sending spikes of pain through his wounded shoulder. He continued screaming at Cramer even though he got no further replies.

"Goddamn it, Cramer, come back here!"

Anything to distract him from Mandi and Pierce. And where was Virgil? They *had* to be alive. Sweet Jesus, what had he done? Why hadn't he realized the thing might not just take him or Pierce? He didn't have the jewel anymore. And even when he had had it, it had still driven José's men crazy. It had still managed to get Rich killed somehow. How had he made such a stupid mistake? It was just that he'd had the idea beaten into his head for so long that *Crowley* men went crazy . . .

He kicked the door again and then again, mindless of the pain in his ankle, trying to break through one of the panels. The ancient pine cracked but didn't show any sign of snapping. He kept kicking until finally he thought he saw a little light through a paper-thin crease in the wood. But even if he could knock out the whole panel, he couldn't reach through and open the door without the key.

He stared at the ball knobs at the top and bottom of the top hinge. If he had a hammer he might be able to get them apart. He worried at the bottom-most ball with his finger-nails, splitting the paint at the joint, finally unscrewing the balls from all three hinges. Then he glanced around for some kind of tool, snatching a couple of soup cans, putting the edge of one under the top ball of the upper hinge and using the other can as a hammer. But he only scratched the paint on the hinge and bent the cans into useless masses of folded, leaking tin.

He dropped the soup and kicked at the door even harder. The hinges rattled, and a long crack appeared down one panel, but it still didn't look ready to give, and he knew he didn't have the strength to break through that way. When he saw Cramer's shadow cross the door frame again he stopped, holding his breath.

It seemed like hours that Cramer stood silently on the other side of the door, and Jake wondered if the thing had a hard time controlling him or whether it was simply deciding what to do next.

"Fight it, Cramer!" he screamed. "Memere would want you to fight it!"

When he heard the unmistakable sound of the slide on an automatic pistol ratcheting into place his heart stopped, but his mind raced. He climbed the shelves like a monkey, pray-ing they'd hold. But they weren't wide enough to support him so he reached across and pulled his feet up on the op-posing shelves, supporting himself above the door frame, pressing his back tightly against the metal ceiling, just as Cramer began to blast the closet, blowing cans and jars to hell. The smell of vinegar and something long gone bad seeped through the air.

One of the bullets managed to douse the lantern, miraculously without causing a fire, and Jake was thankful for that. In the silence that ensued he stared below him into the near-total darkness. He flexed the muscles of his arms, pressing his hands harder into the rough old plaster near the ceiling, trying to will a cramp out of his lower back. Cramer's whisper sounded like a leaky gas main in a sleeping house.

"Jake . . . ?"

Jake practiced being a piece of ceiling trim while Cramer called for him three more times. Finally there was continued silence, and Jake risked climbing down to explore the tortured door. A million splinters cratered inward from the bullet holes, through which he could make out a small area of the darkened kitchen.

He ran his fingers along the lock, praying that the shots might have damaged it enough for him to twist it open, but no dice. The old brass-plated contraption, though pitted and bent, held just as it had been intended to. His fingers explored the wide, paint-encrusted hinges again, and he noticed that he could slip a fingernail between the pin cap and the hinge on the top one. Finally, in desperation, he removed his belt, but the buckle was too thick to use as a lever, so he tried the buckle point. The hinge pin gave just enough to slip the blade of the heavy buckle between the cap and the hinge. A tiny creaking noise told him the pin was moving, and he pressed upward with all his strength, knowing that if the damned thing froze again he'd have to hammer on it to get it moving, and that wasn't an option. Finally the rusty pin dropped onto the mattress, and Jake heaved a sigh of relief.

He ran his fingers along the door frame to the middle hinge, but try as he might he could not get the pin to budge. He stood again and, tugging, managed to slip his fingernails between the door and the frame near the top. The upper hinge creaked as the unpinned halves rubbed against each other, and Jake slipped one hand down to it, wedging his fingers there, jerking hard at the door. That shift loosened the middle pin, and he jerked it out. Now the door gave enough to get his hand *outside,* and he pulled harder, with steady motion, listening for Cramer.

It had already occurred to him that if Cramer had had the key he would have opened the door. That gave Jake hope that at least Mandi and Pierce had escaped. He was clinging to any straws he could find.

When he spotted flickering light through the cracks in the door and smelled smoke, he realized that Cramer must have set the old house ablaze. He worked feverishly at the door, gashing his fingers on the hinges. Finally he felt the lock bolt slipping out of the receiver, and he reached across to catch the door, but it was heavier than he had expected, and he fell back a step onto the soft mattress, struggling for balance. Thick smoke wafted into the pantry, and he dropped the door and leaped over it, catching himself against the wall in the kitchen as a deep roar sounded from outside and the floor rocked beneath his feet. He didn't know whether the old house had simply shifted on its foundation from the rise in the water table, or a flash flood had reached the high ground. But whatever had happened, Cramer had to be just as shaken as he was. He spotted his pistol on the floor and snatched it up, checking the clip. One shot left and one in the chamber. Stumbling through the kitchen, he shoved aside the overturned table, oblivious to any noise he might be making in the storm of vibration and sound all around.

But as the house settled he glanced out the back window and discovered that the rumbling noise he'd been hearing was coming from Albert's dozer. It must have rammed the house in passing; Cramer had left a muddy trail across the back lawn with the machine and now seemed intent on knocking down the chapel. Jake could only assume that the others had taken refuge inside. It looked as though Cramer was still having some trouble figuring out how to run the big beast, but when he crashed it into the corner of the chapel again the roof shook, and Jake knew that pretty soon the structure was going to come crashing down.

Pierce cowered with his mother in the corner of the chapel farthest from the lights of the dozer that flashed through a million cracks in the stone walls. Two heavy beams had collapsed from the roof onto the floor, and rain poured through a huge hole over their heads.

Fix it.

That thought struck him like a blow, reinforcing what he had already guessed. The jewel was broken. It was like a transformer, storing up power and turning it into some kind of other power. And the original power had to come from the big stone in the floor beneath the lectern. But he sensed that just replacing the jewel would not repair it or reload it with the power it needed to recall the thing that had taken over Cramer. Not until the stone was fixed, as well.

He clenched the gem, trying desperately to read its strange alien "circuits." Circuits almost dead now. Slowly a pattern began to emerge. The giant stone drew power from an unknown source from the very ground beneath it. The jewel was made to receive that force from the stone and convert it to power to be used by someone, a person. A person who could read and understand it. A person just like him.

And the jewel knew it was broken.

Its circuits had always contained a program to contact a living, breathing person. A person who would understand and know how to repair it. Somehow it sensed that *he* had that understanding. Or it had known that his family did. That was why it had been searching for the right Crowley all that time. And over the years, as the jewel failed, the search circuit had become more and more corrupt. Sometimes it killed people. Sometimes—in its never-ending search for a repairman—it got into people's heads and caused them to go crazy, to murder or commit suicide.

Words filled his head again, a deep resonant voice.

Do what you do. I must not end.

How can I fix you? he asked soundlessly.

Fixing me is in your blood. You are the fixer.

After a moment, when silence reigned, Pierce sensed that he would get no more answers, and he turned toward the hole in the floor just as he heard his mother scream.

Another huge beam crashed to the floor beside them, and Pierce swallowed a thick lump in his throat as his mother tried to drag him back to her.

Giant tongues of flame shot out of melting windows, whipping in the wind, licking the sheets of rain that did nothing to extinguish the roaring fire inside the old house. Glimmering light sparkled through the droplets, turning the surrounding forest into a bejeweled wonderland. Heavy air forced the smoke downward where it curled around the old house and drifted out across the lawn toward the chapel.

Jake raced for the dozer, mindful of the fact that Cramer was not only obsessed but still probably packing his own pistol. But before he could reach the machine it swung in his direction, and he was blinded by the headlights as Cramer tried to run him down.

The dozer moved slower than Jake could run, but the tall grass was wet and slippery, and he stumbled to his knees, clambering quickly to his feet, backing toward the trees.

"Help!"

Mandi's voice cut through the storm and the roar of the machine, and Jake hesitated. A glancing blow from the blade clipped his hip, throwing him down onto the lawn, and he caught a glimpse of Cramer's face. His lips were pulled back in a wide, cruel grin, and his eyes seemed to glow with their own inner fire. Jake dragged himself aside as Cramer jerked the control lever and tried to spin the blade into him, the metal edge crunching deep into the muck.

"Cramer!" Jake screamed, rolling onto his back and aiming his pistol at his partner's chest. "It's me! Jake! Fight! Call Ogou!"

For just an instant he thought he saw something resembling the old Cramer behind the fiery eyes, but it was gone so fast he couldn't be sure. He staggered to his feet and broke for the chapel. Cramer misjudged, swinging the big machine in the wrong direction, snapping his head around as Jake whirled past, then jerking the other lever, spinning the dozer back around. Jake was halfway to the little stone building when another of Mandi's shrieks shattered the night.

Jake careened up onto the tiny stoop to pound on the locked door.

Cramer throttled up the dozer, heading right for him. Jake leaned against the heavy wood panel, squinting through the headlights to take aim again. But the thought of killing Cramer shook him to the core. If he couldn't shoot Jimmy, how the hell could he bust a cap on his partner? But he knew in that instant that it was the only thing to do, that the monster he had been afraid of all these years wasn't something inside him. It was something that had been *outside* him all along, wanting in. Now it was inside Cramer, and the only way to stop him was to kill him.

Slowly Jake's finger tightened on the trigger.

*　*　*

Virgil knelt on the mucky forest floor—resting the shotgun against a gnarly pine—and untied and removed his shoes, leaving the soaking socks on his feet. He didn't think Jimmy could hear the tiny squishing sound the shoes made, but he wasn't taking any chances, and his traction on the slippery ground could only get better without them. When he stood and hefted the gun again, he took a deep breath of air that was thick as water.

It felt as though his entire life had been building to this one moment, this one place. Virgil knew that the odds of killing Jimmy were about nil. Jimmy really *was* a stalking beast. But he also knew that he could not leave another person to her fate without at least trying to stop the bastard. He could not wait peacefully while Jimmy came at leisure to do as he would with Jake and the others. This might have been the stupidest stunt he'd ever pulled, but it felt right, and Virgil wondered if maybe Ogou wasn't really with him after all.

He hadn't heard a peep out of Jimmy in the past five minutes, but he expected at any moment for a crazed Jimmy to leap out at him, or to come stumbling across Barbara's mangled corpse. If it was the former he had no intention of trying to take him alive. If he got half a chance he was going to blow the sonofabitch to hell and gone. And he wasn't going to lose a minute's sleep over the killing.

Virgil was creeping along, peering nervously into the darkness, when a powerful fist latched onto the barrel of the shotgun, ripping it from his hands. He reached for his pistol, but the butt of the gun swung up under his chin, lifting him off the ground and breaking his jaw with a nasty crunching sound. He hit the ground hard, still fumbling for his pistol, but he had no target as he jerked the gun from the holster. Jimmy had faded away into the pitch-black woods again.

Shit. Now the bastard was armed with a shotgun, and all *he* had was a pistol.

Virgil rose shakily to his feet, quickly scanning three hundred and sixty degrees, ready to shoot anything that moved. To pull the trigger and keep firing until there were no bullets left in the gun. Either he or Jimmy was going to die out here, but he was afraid it wasn't going to be Jimmy. Still, Virgil was protecting home turf and family, and he thought that gave him just a little more heart than even a crazed killer out for revenge.

Of course he could be wrong.

Jimmy gripped the shotgun tightly in one hand, still packing the butcher knife in the other. He had cuts over every square inch of his body from burrs and brambles, and he was nearly hypothermic from exposure, and *that* had caused his lack of focus. He'd lost sight of the old man when he first slipped into the woods. But when he'd stumbled suddenly onto the sheriff—just as surprised as the bastard was to see him—he'd reacted instantly. Now he had the gun *and* the knife, and the old cop had a pistol. This was going to be fun. He'd kill the sucker slow, get his hands on some clothes that would fit him at last, find a place to dry off, and then plan on how to take out the rest of the group, leaving Jake Crowley till last.

He listened for movement, tried to catch a whiff of the cop's aftershave or now-familiar body odor, but the rain covered everything and exhaustion was dulling his senses. When a twig snapped he froze, smiling, then edged in that direction in a half-crouch, playing the waiting game.

You move. I move. You move. I move.

A rustling sound told him the cop had just brushed closer, and he caught a glimpse of shifting shadow through the branches. He stood stock-still, mimicking the trees around him, his finger on the shotgun trigger.

Virgil thought he heard something to his left. He spun in that direction, silently sweeping the forest with the pistol. But nothing moved. No new sound followed, and he breathed in again.

He waited, listening, hoping to hear anything that would give the fucker away. But he knew Jimmy wasn't likely to do that. He was a pro. There was only one way to beat him. Surprise. Do something unexpected. Maybe something stupid.

Tired of the game, using his rage and frustration like a scourge, Virgil stood full height and strode out through the woods as though it were broad daylight, and he was on a sightseeing excursion. The sound of crashing brush and slapping branches echoed through the trees.

Pierce struggled to get away from his mother, but she gripped him tightly, refusing to let him go. Her hand shook violently in his. Finally he slipped his hand into her other palm and made her look at him.

He signed feverishly.

You have to get Jake to come here. Now!

She shook her head, signing back shakily, almost as though she'd never used the symbols before. *We can't open the door. That thing will get in.*

But she knew as well as he did that no door was going to stop what was happening. The jewel and the stone were broken nearly beyond fixing. And Pierce was afraid that when the power ran out of both of them, the thing that they had sent out in search of a *fixer* would still live on its own, with nothing at all to control it. But he had finally realized that it was going to take both him and Jake to repair the jewel and stone.

They were of the same blood.

The thing the jewel had sent out searching for a repair-man had tested everyone it came across and found them wanting. And when it did, it killed most of them. But not him or Jake. Because he and Jake had something within them that the jewel and the stone recognized. Just maybe, between the two of them, enough to fix both.

He jerked his hands away and slipped past his mother before she could stop him, throwing himself toward the access hole, finding the edge with his fingers and tumbling down inside.

The blinding darkness in the crawl space was nothing new to him, but the icy feeling that hit him like a wall was a shock. It was as though his blood had suddenly turned to glacier water, and an overwhelming fear surged through him. As the last of the power continued draining from the stone, a deep emptiness seemed to surround it that reminded Pierce far too much of the feeling he'd had on that long-ago day when Rich had thrown him down the stairs. Suddenly he wanted to claw his way back out of the dark, run to his mother, and bury his face in her side. He wanted to be away, anywhere away, but he knew there was nowhere left to run.

His fingers followed the contours of the dirt floor like a braille map. Knowing that their only salvation lay in some-how *fixing* what was broken in the gem and the stone was one thing. But this wasn't some old television where he could feel the circuits and sense his way to a solution, where a twist of a wire, or a tightened connection, could repair the damage. There was a *magic* to the stone and the jewel that still defied his comprehension.

Fix me. You are the fixer.

But he was afraid right down to his bones that he didn't

have enough power alone. Jake was outside, and his mother wouldn't get him.

The icy, empty darkness seemed to crush against him the same way the water had pressed against him in the flood, pushing him down, until his face was nearly flat against the floor, and he tasted damp soil on his tongue. He was exhausted from the struggle with his mother, and from fighting to understand the stone and the jewel. But he took a long deep breath, willing away the aching in the muscles of his arms and legs, clawed his way back to his knees, and gripped the jewel tightly in his fists.

Virgil shoved aside a sapling birch, releasing it as he passed. A muffled grunt spun him around, and he jerked the pistol trigger while he was still turning. The first bullet struck the tree beside Jimmy's head just as he fired off a round from the shotgun. Pellets stung Virgil's already wounded left arm and twisted him sideways, but he squeezed the trigger again and again. When Jimmy disappeared again he stopped, trying to remember how many shots he'd fired. The trigger was still tight and the slide was forward, so there was at least one more shot in the pistol.

Instinct prompted him to step aside just as the shotgun flashed again less than ten feet away. He fired at the blast, charging through the trees, crashing into Jimmy and driving him back into a tight spot in the brush where he couldn't bring the shotgun to bear. Virgil shoved the pistol against his torso and pulled the trigger. One shot fired and the slide locked back. Jimmy's fist slammed against the side of Virgil's head, and Virgil dropped the empty pistol, fighting for the shotgun.

Virgil tasted blood and smelled it in the air as they rolled through the mud, slithering and gasping. Finally his fingers found the barrel of the shotgun, but at that moment Jimmy rolled on top of him, knocking the wind from his lungs.

Virgil slugged at the spot where he thought he'd wounded the bastard. Jimmy grunted, and Virgil punched again, and this time Jimmy gasped, cursing, and Virgil was able to shove him aside and roll out from under him. But the shadow of the shotgun caught his eye, aimed at his head.

Suddenly teeth flashed, sinking into the soft flesh of Jimmy's face. A high-pitched growling noise accompanied the sound of Jimmy cursing as the fat little dog nipped viciously at his exposed throat. Virgil jerked himself to his feet and kicked Jimmy hard, and then again, driving his heel into Jimmy's chest so hard that bone and cartilage snapped. As Jimmy rolled over onto his back Virgil leaned to rip the gun out of his hands, and turned it on him, keeping a growling Oswald at bay with his foot.

"Where's Barbara?" he managed to mumble through his aching jaw.

"The old bitch?" gasped Jimmy, clutching both hands over the spreading blood at his belly. "Where do you think?"

Virgil shook his head. "The screams—"

Jimmy laughed. Then he let out a soprano wail. A woman's shriek of terror and agony. "Fuck you," he said, rolling to his knees, reaching for the barrel.

Virgil pulled the trigger, blowing the bastard back into the brush. He trudged up alongside the spasming legs, stared down at the body, pumped in another shell, and blew Jimmy's head off.

Oswald ambled over to sniff the corpse, then kicked up a leg and peed on Jimmy's arm. The wind stirred the trees as another lightning bolt struck and Virgil jumped, raising the shotgun at what had appeared to be a man, standing amid the trees. When his eyes readjusted he saw that Oswald was staring in the same direction, sniffing the breeze.

But after a few moments, when nothing moved and the specter didn't reappear, Virgil's heart slowed, and he shook off the image.

Just imagination. There was no one else out here now that Jimmy was dead.

Certainly not a giant black man with a machete.

"Come on, Oswald," he said, nudging the dog.

He searched the trees, trying to get his bearings, but it was impossible to spot anything familiar in the darkness and rain. When a gust of breeze brought the smell of wood-smoke and he saw faint rippling firelight ahead, he trudged in that direction.

Pierce's body rested against the huge stone as he clasped the jewel tightly in his fists. Icy knives seemed to search for his heart. His skin prickled as though a million needles were being pressed against it everywhere, and his breath came in gulping gasps.

You are the fixer.

Why me?

It is in your blood.

What are you?

I am the source.

The source of what?

Power.

Just as he'd thought.

What kind of power?

You would call it magic.

Why my blood? What's special about me?

Your blood has always been open to the source. Your blood was lost to me for time beyond telling. But now you are here.

But Pierce shook his head.

I don't know what to do.

But just like inside the stone and the jewel, there were circuits twisted inside Pierce's head that were starting to make sense to him. He felt as though he could see every synapse in his brain, every bad connection. And he could see the ones where the jewel had jumped them, causing him to begin to hear, to begin to see. But fixing him had made the stone and the jewel worse. It was as though the jewel had passed its good circuits on to him so that he could understand. So that he could fix it. But he understood something else, as well. Something he had feared all along.

I'll be blind and deaf again. Won't I?

There seemed to be a hesitation before the whisper replied. *For now.*

Was that a promise? How long was *now*? Or was it just a trick to get him to fix the gem and the stone?

But he knew he had no choice. As he listened to the rush of wind overhead, the sound of rain pattering through the broken ceiling onto the floor, he knew he had to fix the jewel and the stone or his mother and Jake and everyone else was going to die.

He heard scrabbling noises on the floor above, like jagged nails being dragged across the old boards. A hand appeared, and then his mother's fear-filled face, the darkness hanging above her like a shroud. She dropped into the hole and huddled beside him.

He nodded to her as he slammed the jewel into the slot in the stone and closed his eyes.

He had the strangest sensation of being stuck between opposite poles of a battery. A charge surged up his arms and exploded somewhere near his heart. Suddenly not only could he see and hear everything around him, he could see Cramer and Jake outside. He could see into the heart of the storm itself, and he could tell for sure that it was no normal storm. The power that rushed through his body controlled the wind and the clouds, as well.

He reached up and signed to his mother.

You have to bring Jake here now. I can't do this alone.

Just then there was the sound of a shot outside. He stared at his mother, and she stared back.

But slowly her eyes began to change.

Jake watched the thin trickle of blood above Cramer's heart. The big man sat on the idling dozer like a mannequin, his eyes boring straight ahead into the forest beyond the chapel, and Jake was afraid that *this* time his aim had *not* been faulty, that the shot had been fatal. But when Pierce let out a guttural scream, he knew that he didn't have time to waste finding out.

He shoved his pistol into his pants and kicked at the chapel door until he burst it open.

"Mandi!" he shouted. "Where are you?"

Pierce called again. But this time it was a garbled half-scream, cut off abruptly.

Jake instantly realized that the thing had abandoned Cramer and possessed Mandi. The image of *her* hands around her own son's throat, around *his* son's throat, threatened to paralyze him. Cramer's voice echoed in his head.

It's your blood.

It *was* his blood. And this was *his* valley, and *his* family. No spirit or shadow was going to destroy them. He wasn't going to allow it. He clambered through the debris, throwing himself blindly into the hole, falling against Mandi. He was shocked when she lifted him like a toy and slammed him against the stone wall. But he heard Pierce gasping for air. The boy was alive. He shoved himself forward, and Mandi fell on him, wrapping tight fingers around his throat, crushing her thumbs into his Adam's apple. He tried to break her grip, but her hands were like vises, and he could feel the deadly pressure increasing on his carotid. He kicked and shoved and tried to roll out from under her, but she forced him back down.

I won't die here. I won't let them die here.

In desperation he drew his pistol again and shoved it against her belly. He'd shot Cramer. But Cramer wasn't Mandi. If surviving cost her life, could he live with that? The answer should have been no. But he knew that if the thing inside her forced her to kill him, Pierce would be next. Jake couldn't even imagine what it would be like to try to explain to the boy that he had had to kill his mother. But there didn't seem to be any other way. His finger slid onto the trigger.

But Mandi was faster. *Her* finger slipped behind the trigger and jerked forward. Jake felt a crushing pain as the trigger actually snapped off. Her strength was incredible.

He tried to strike her with the gun, but she slapped it away into the darkness. He reached out, searching for another weapon. Anything. But there was nothing but stone wall and dirt floor. As she wrapped both hands around his throat again, and he felt consciousness slipping away, Pierce's hand slipped into his own, and the boy squeezed. Jake noticed that a febrile light was now shining in the chapel above them, and he wondered if it was the light at the end of the tunnel he'd heard about.

Suddenly a huge black hand reached out of the light and wrapped around Mandi's hair. She clawed at Jake as she was dragged up out of the hole, kicking and screaming.

Cramer leaned down with a pain-wracked expression and actually smiled at Jake and Pierce.

"You're alive," gasped Jake. "Thank God."

"You're as lousy a shot as ever," said Cramer, grimacing.

"Now whatever you two are doing, I suggest you get it done."

Just then Mandi landed on his back, and the two of them disappeared in a rumbling commotion.

Jake turned back to Pierce, and when his hands fell on the boy's shoulders Pierce acknowledged him with a one-armed hug, drawing him closer. The boy spelled into his hand so fast Jake had to struggle to understand.

You have to put your hands over mine on the jewel.

What are we doing?

Fixing it. I can't do it alone.

But Jake sensed a terrible sadness in the boy, and guessed the cause immediately.

Will you still see?

There was a moment before Pierce answered.

No.

Jake didn't have to ask about his hearing or his walk. That was all part of the deal.

If we don't do this, Pierce signed, *we'll all die.*

That was part of the deal, too. And Jake knew the boy was right. What kind of kid was this to make such a decision? What kind of world was it to force him to make it? Jake was proud and saddened beyond belief. He squeezed the boy even tighter, tears streaming down his cheeks. Over their heads Mandi shrieked like a banshee, and Cramer shouted back in Voudou patois. Grunts of pain followed from both.

We have to, signed Pierce. *Before they kill each other. Put your hands over mine.*

Jake did as he was told, instantly experiencing almost the same feeling he had when he had one of his hunches. Only now, instead of wandering through his own subconscious he was wandering through the stone's depths, sensing the broken synapses that matched synapses he began to sense inside his own head. He realized then how Pierce fixed things, how he knew what was wrong with them without seeing. He could sense Pierce's mind inside the stone with him, working together. With a twist here and a tweak here, they began to *repair* the giant stone and the jewel that rested upon it. And with each tiny repair Jake knew a little of Pierce's vision and hearing was slipping away, until it was done, until the giant stone and the jewel were as they were intended to be.

Until his son was deaf and blind and crippled once more.

And after a moment he felt Pierce's hands slip out from under his and wrap around him, and he drew the boy into his embrace.

Jake peeked cautiously out of the hole into the glare of the dozer headlights through the front door. Mandi was straddling Cramer, who lay on his back. Their hands were locked, but they both appeared dazed. Jake clambered out, reaching to lift Pierce behind him. Jake helped Mandi up off of Cramer, but when he offered, the big man shook off his hand and struggled to his feet, one hand covering the wound in his bloody shoulder. The four of them stumbled wearily out of the ruins of the chapel just as Virgil staggered out of the woods. The old man shook his head and waved, and just then Jake noticed Oswald, tagging along at the sheriff's feet.

"You okay?" Jake shouted.

"Mm-hm!" Virgil called, holding his jaw.

One last peal of thunder rolled, and for the first time Jake noticed that the rain seemed to be subsiding. A crack in the clouds allowed one slender moonbeam to snake across the sodden lawn and then creep into the trees behind Virgil, and Jake heard Mandi gasp. For just an instant, he was certain he saw something impossible just inside the cover of trees. A giant naked black man, waving a huge machete. Then, like a will-o'-the-wisp, the image was gone, and the clouds covered the moon again.

AS THE MOON STRUGGLED to break through the thinning clouds again Jake, Mandi, Virgil, and Cramer shielded themselves from the heat of the flaming house behind the bulldozer.

"Where the heck are we gonna go?" asked Cramer.

"The dozer will get us through water a lot deeper than any car," said Jake. "And even if we have to hole up in what's left of one of the houses, we're not staying here."

Cramer glared at the raging fire, his hand over the rude bandage Mandi had fashioned from his shirt. "I'll second that," he muttered.

"You sure you don't want us to make you a pallet on top of the hood?"

Cramer chuckled. "I've been shot by better men than you."

Jake shook his head, boosting Mandi up onto the dozer, and then turned to help Pierce. Mandi watched the boy as Pierce tested the muddy track with his fingers.

"There was nothing else we could do," Jake whispered, ashamed and guilt-stricken.

After a moment she rested one hand on his shoulder and squeezed, nodding sadly. But Jake knew the hurt of having seen Pierce whole and then broken again would be with both of them for the rest of their lives. Their son had saved all of them and given up the most precious of gifts to do so. Jake was proud of the boy, despondent, and confused.

As Pierce settled into the seat Jake noticed that the rain had completely stopped, as though even nature itself would have nothing to do with saving the old mansion. Finally he helped Virgil up beside Cramer on the engine cowling, just ahead of the driver's seat. The machine would carry all of them, but not comfortably. Oswald woofed at Jake's feet and he lifted the little dog up into Cramer's arms.

He clambered aboard, easing into the wide seat beside Pierce, Mandi sitting on the thick armrest. As he started to shove the machine into gear, Pierce took his hand, spelling.

Are we going home?

Jake spelled back. *Yes.*

Are you going to stay now?

I'll never leave you again.

Pierce smiled, and Jake sighed, but the boy seemed to sense his discomfort.

It's all right, Pierce spelled. *They're fixed now. They won't hurt anyone ever again.*

Are you sure of that?

Yes.

But you can't see or hear.

Pierce squeezed his hand before spelling. *It was a fair trade.*

Then he wrapped his arms around Jake's neck and squeezed even harder.

JULES ROSE WEARILY TO HIS FEET. The first rays of dawn creeping through the windows had wakened him from a fitful half-sleep.

The phone had not rung all night, and he'd made up his mind. This was the day. Now was the time. He wrapped his fingers tightly around the walnut grips of his pistol to keep his hands from shaking. He planned to place the barrel of the gun directly against the old woman's temple and pull the trigger before she could move. The closeness of her skin would deaden the noise of the shot. Nothing to it.

But he was afraid.

He glanced toward the doorway into the altar room, and he could have sworn he heard whispers coming from that direction. Muffled voices. Threatening sounds. But the old woman was in the bedroom. He could hear her snoring.

"There's no voice," he muttered to himself, continuing the chant until the whispers disappeared.

He grasped the pistol tighter, wanting nothing more than to be done with this job, to kill the old bitch and get the hell out of this apartment, out of this crazy neighborhood. The long thin rays of the sun through the living room drapes caused the shadows inside the bedroom to be deeper and darker, and as he entered the room he was momentarily blinded.

As his eyes began to readjust, he was shocked to see that the old woman's bed was empty. He spun, ready to blow the bitch to hell and gone, but she was nowhere to be seen. It was impossible for her to get out of the bed so fast. But she had. She was always doing things like that, driving him crazy.

She had to be in the bathroom. The door was half open, the night-light still on. He slipped over against the wall, listening, waiting for her to come out. He could hear water running, and when he glanced through the door he saw steam rising from beneath the shower curtain, and the mirror was fogged. He edged into the room, careful not to slip on the wet floor or to get between the light and the curtain and throw a shadow.

He couldn't understand how the old woman had gotten to him. He'd killed dozens of men in his life and a couple of women. He'd been in situations where the slightest misstep or misspoken word could have cost him his life, and he'd never broken a sweat. But ever since Jimmy had left, he'd been living in fear of a woman so ancient her teeth had rotted out of her head. And now he was going to end it. He tightened his grip on the pistol and reached out to grab the slick shower curtain.

But suddenly an image of a corpse flashed before his eyes. An emaciated, rotten thing, with bones showing through the decaying flesh but living eyes and a gummy grin, tufts of gray hair still clinging to its skull. And the corpse was standing on the other side of the curtain, showering just like a living, breathing person. It was all he could do to not run screaming from the room.

It's all in my head. She's doing it to me, somehow. She's trying to stop me from killing her by driving me crazy.

He forced himself to jerk the curtain aside, almost filling the empty shower with lead before he realized that there was no one there. No wrinkled old woman with her blue hair pasted to her head. No laughing corpse. The shower was running, but no one was home. He whirled, aiming the pistol back into the bedroom, his heart pounding against his ribs. He leaped back out into the room, expecting the old woman to be making a break for the door, but there was no one in the room. No one in the living room, or the kitchen, either, when he checked to see if she was hiding behind the counter. That left only the room full of idols. The room where he'd just heard the whispered voices.

He crossed the carpet slowly, glancing through the door to make sure the snake was still coiled up in the aquarium and the top was held down tight. He didn't want the old bitch pulling some shit and throwing the snake on him or something. Once again he leaned against the wall, listening. And again he was sure he could hear voices whispering. But there was no way there was anyone in there but the old woman.

Shit.

He couldn't even figure out how *she* had managed to slip by him and get into the room, much less anyone else. She had to have a recording or something. Trying to freak him out. Well, this was going to be over in a heartbeat. He strode into the room, ready for a quick couple of shots. Then he was out of here.

The room was darker than he'd expected. All the altar candles were out. Not even a trickle of light seemed able to make its way into the place, and the whispered voices were louder inside, closer. He couldn't understand what they were saying, but it sounded like the Voudou Cajun crap the old woman was always jabbering. Only the voices weren't hers. They didn't even sound human. It was more like the noise a grinder might make chewing up broken glass. When something hard struck his gun hand his finger tickled the trigger, and a shot burst through the back wall.

Jules spun toward his attacker, but suddenly hands seemed to be all over him, grabbing, choking, punching, pinching, chopping. The wind was knocked from his lungs, the gun dropped to the floor, and he struggled to make it back through the door into the living room, but it looked as though it were a million miles away and he *ran* toward it, as though it were receding. When he was finally able to reach the jamb and jerk himself back into the living room he staggered on to the front door, fumbling open the locks with trembling fingers, whipping open the door, blinded by the direct morning sun. He stumbled out onto the landing but was caught by more powerful hands and forced hard against the side of the building.

"Whoa, partner!" said a heavy male voice in his ear.

He felt cuffs being clicked onto his wrists, but he didn't care. He was outside. In the sunlight. Away from the crazy old bitch. Away from whatever the hell she'd unleashed inside.

"You okay, Memere?" said another male voice.

"Oui," said the old woman, as Jules's eyes began to adjust again.

She was standing in the doorway, smiling a toothless grin at him and stroking her snake.

"I am so glad you caught dis man," she said, nodding at Jules. "He has held me the—how you say—kidnapped."

"Jesus, Memere," said the first officer. "Are you okay? Cramer just called and asked us to check on you."

"I am the plenty okay now," she said, smiling and nodding at Jules again. "Dis one here and his boss, dey is not so okay. But me and my snake, we be fine, t'ank you. It good to be out of de shadows and see de sunlight again, dough."

"What's a big, nasty fella like you doing picking on a nice old lady like this?" said one of the cops, jerking Jules away from the wall.

Memere laughed. "I tink dis one he gots what you calls *de baggage.*"

ABOUT THE AUTHOR

Chandler McGrew lives in Bethel, Maine, and has four women in his life—Rene, Keni, Mandi, and Charli—all of whom wish it to be known that he is either their husband or father. He is the author of the suspense novels *Cold Heart, Night Terror,* and *The Darkening.* Chandler can be reached at www.chandlermcgrew.com.